I0675481

THE

FIFTH

OPTION

A NOVEL

Jac Jacobsen

BITTERROOT PUBLISHING, LLC

This book is a work of fiction. Names, characters, places, and incidents are products of the author's imagination or are used fictitiously. Any resemblance to actual events or persons, living or dead, is entirely coincidental.

Copyright © 2013 by Jac Jacobsen

All rights reserved. Except as permitted under the U.S. Copyright Act of 1976, no part of this publication may be reproduced, distributed, or transmitted in any form or by any means, or stored in a database or retrieval system, without prior written permission of the author. Inquiries regarding this book should be directed to the author at: JacJacobsen@The-Fifth-Option.com.

ISBN-10: 0989178005
ISBN-13: 978-0-9891780-0-6

PRINTED IN THE UNITED STATES OF AMERICA

ACKNOWLEDGMENTS

A good many friends and family helped me to complete this novel, but are in no way responsible for the excesses of my writing. I would particularly like to thank Anita Roman who encouraged me to begin the book. An author in her own right, severely debilitated by arthritis, she typed her books one finger at a time. But write them she did. Anita was, and always will be, an inspiration. I would also like to thank Rick and Nancy Jacobsen, John Lorenz, Joanne Schroeder, Bill Erambert, John Konogeris, Rene Lehman, Jim Hughes, Bob Parkinson, and Marge Solé. It was they who voiced encouragement when needed, offered constructive criticism where warranted, bucked me up when I was ready to throw in the towel, and took the time to endlessly read and reread the manuscript. Whatever errors remain are solely my own.

"If you are just, then don't fear the warrior who walks among you. If you are not just and inflict pain and suffering on the innocent, then fear the law and the warrior that brings it."

Anonymous

"Let your plans be dark and as impenetrable as night, and when you move, fall like a thunderbolt."

Sun Tzu, The Art of War, C. 500 BCE

THE
FIFTH
OPTION

Chapter 1

THREE DAYS PRIOR
TAKUR GHAR MOUNTAINS
PAKTIA PROVINCE, AFGHANISTAN

WHAT A SHITHOLE this place turned out to be, Lieutenant Commander Jake Stoneman thought as he looked out over a broad, sun-baked plain bathed in the light of midmorning, a desolate landscape crisscrossed by ancient arroyos and dried-up gullies that stretched far-off into the distance. He'd also come to realize that he was probably getting too old for this line of work, having humped over twenty klicks of godforsaken mountains with a seventy pound rucksack and one damned heavy rifle strapped to his back.

Jake Stoneman and Petty Officer Third Class Steve Martinez had been dropped off by chopper four nights ago and had taken two days to thread their way through the foothills of the Takur Ghar Mountains, foothills riddled with militant jihādist fighters from the Chumara Valley floor up to their present position. And prior to their insert they had spent hours poring over satellite photos to map out their best means of ingress and egress, with close attention paid to their best means of egress. They both knew it didn't pay to get in without having a damned good way of getting out.

They had been in position now for two days, blistered by the high-country sun during the day and freezing their asses off at night, their attention focused on a narrow tunnel entrance that rested on the Shahi Kowt valley floor one thousand meters to their front and three hundred meters below their hide. All had been quiet up to now, but today was supposed to be the big day as far as their intel was concerned.

Jake, a former troop commander of SEAL Team Three and now the commanding officer of the CIA's Hearthstone team, knew their targets were to be picked up between 1100 and 1200 hours to attend a council of war in Gardiz—the capital of Paktia province—thirty kilometers to the north. Their targets identified as two senior al-Qaeda operatives and one Pakistan Taliban warlord. The warlord, they had been told, purported to be the youngest brother of Qudos Mehsud who headed up the entire Pakistan Tehrik-e-taliban. Early or late though it made no never mind to Jake, just as long as they showed up. He looked forward to killing a few more of these jihādist assholes and was confident in their intel, the CIA's information having always been pretty much dead-on. As far as he was concerned, patience was a virtue and he was good at what he did, the best that SEAL Team Three and now the CIA's Special Operations Group had.

"Range . . . one thousand, one hundred, thirty-two meters. Left cross wind two knots. No thermals, Boss," Martinez softly called out, spread-eagled on the dirt to Jake's right with his eye pressed to a Leupold sixty-power spotting scope, focused on the movement of telltales he'd mapped out yesterday. "We also got a nice clean sight line down to the tunnel, and all that haze shit from yesterday has cleared out."

"Good," Jake said, glad to have Steve along.

Jake knew that Steve was the best damned spotter he'd ever seen, who had an uncanny ability to accurately determine the velocity and angles of wind downrange. Winds that, if not adjusted for, would severely impact the flight of a round toward its target, particularly given the range they would be using today. And Steve, just by watching puffs of sand off distant ridgelines, or broken twigs and other items that skittered across the valley floor, or bushes that rustled in the slightest breeze, could tell the nuances of the wind as if he'd read them in a book.

At twenty-four years of age Steve was ten years younger than his boss with skin burned dark by the sun, and stood no more than five-foot-seven with a stocky build inherited from his mother's side of the family. Built low to the ground like a fireplug. And his jet-black hair—way too long by military standards—was pulled back into a tight ponytail that hung well below his shoulders; his ponytail kept neatly in place by a black bandana that he wore for good luck. Jake had always thought that Steve looked more like an irascible Apache scout, one that endlessly roamed the barren wastelands of southern Arizona keeping a wary eye out for the Cavalry.

With Steve's take on conditions, Jake rolled onto his side and pulled out his dope book, flipping it open to page eight. It had taken him over a year to put this book together, with countless hours spent on rifle ranges to come up with the matrix of click adjustments needed to put his rounds on target first time, every time. Noting the clicks needed for today's shooting conditions, he grunted and folded up the dog-eared book, and then absently stuffed it into the top pocket of his soiled, brown-camouflaged BDUs.

Turning back to his Barrett Mark-107 .50-caliber sniper rifle, he unscrewed the protective covers for the elevation and windage turrets of the weapon's variable-power scope and dialed in the clicks. Once done, he blew into the covers sharply to make sure that no sand or dirt was lodged in their threads, and then screwed the covers back in place.

With his muscular frame once more settled behind the large rifle, Jake grasped the 107's charging handle and pulled it to the rear. When the bolt-carrier reached the end of its stop, an M33 armor-piercing round was disengaged from the weapon's ten round magazine and seated into the upper receiver assembly. With a quick look to make sure the round was properly seated, he let the bolt move slowly forward to load the cartridge into the firing chamber.

Since he didn't know if his targets would be wearing body armor, he'd opted for this particular round that could pierce up to four millimeters of steel at this distance, a round that weighed forty-five grams and had a muzzle velocity of 887 meters per second. He knew it would take less than a couple of seconds for the round to reach the tunnel entrance below, well before the sound of the weapon's firing, giving him more than enough time to line up on the other two targets slated to be neutralized. The bad guys would never know what hit them.

"Boss?" Martinez suddenly said, "I've got movement out in the valley. Dust trails. Looks to be four small trucks making their way to the tunnel. Maybe eight, nine miles out."

Jake squinted into the distance where he could just make out four plumes of dust that billowed straight up into a cloudless blue sky.

"Betcha that's the greeting party," he replied matter-of-factly, then lowered his head to scope out the tunnel's entrance. "Well, and speak of the devil, say hello to our guests of honor."

Jake watched as three insurgents exited the tunnel and stood abreast from one another with cigarettes in hand, one dressed in camouflage while the other two wore more traditional Afghani garb, the vehicles now approaching most likely to provide transportation for these three.

"Okay, Steve, time to get down to business. We need to take these guys out before those trucks get here."

"You got it, Boss!"

Still focused on his targets, Jake scrunched his body firmly into the dirt—ignoring a sharp rock that poked painfully into his hip—then used a trick he'd learned years ago to relax his body for the shoot. With his eyes closed, he visualized an isolated sandy beach set on some shimmering South Pacific tropical isle. He could also imagine a scent-laden breeze that caressed his cheek as he dug his toes into warm sugar-white sand. As he looked out at the clear turquoise-blue water of the nonexistent cove his body began to unwind, the blood pumping through his veins reduced to no more than a trickle.

"We'll take 'em out from left to right," he announced.

Steve shifted his scope to the left and thumbed the laser range finder one last time to reconfirm distance.

"Range is now one thousand, one hundred, twenty-eight meters. Estimated left cross wind is still two knots."

"Close enough for government work," Jake said, grateful he didn't have to fuck around with any click adjustments to the scope.

Now settled back with the rifle pulled hard into his shoulder, he snapped off the weapon's safety—his index finger lightly caressing the trigger—then took a deep breath, let it partially out, and held it steady, squeezing the trigger with the crosshairs centered on the top portion of the first target's chest. Just a tad below his neck on the broadest portion of the body.

With no warning the rifle fired, exploding as if a minihowitzer had gone off beside them, slamming the buttstock of the weapon hard into his shoulder. Shards of white-hot blowby gasses, erupting five inches horizontally from each side of the weapon's muzzle brake, kicked up small clouds of dust in their wake. As the crackling thunderclap of the rifle's firing rumbled throughout the canyons of the mountain, the Mark-107 recycled and chambered a new round.

Jake shifted the crosshairs slightly to the right, lined up on target two, and gently squeezed off his second shot.

"Target one!" Martinez barked, indicating the first round had found its mark.

Jake nudged the rifle further to the right, lined up on target three, and fired. In total, three rounds having been fired downrange in just under five seconds.

"Target two!" Martinez shouted as he continued to stare through his scope.

Then a couple of seconds later, "Target three!"

Jake maintained his rigid firing position, scanning for any signs of life—his subconscious mind noting the bloody carnage and body parts splattered about the tunnel's entrance—then he couldn't help but smile when Steve muttered, "Oh, dude!"

Steve continued to peer through his scope, but he too couldn't see any further signs of life.

"All targets are down, Boss! Just bits and pieces left from what I can see. Sure hope those fuckers in the trucks brought a couple of big goddamned rakes. They're sure gonna need it to scrape up that mess!"

Steve pulled away from his scope, his weathered features split by a quick, derisive grin.

"Boss? That was some damned good shooting!"

"Thanks, Steve," Jake said as he hunched on both knees and grabbed the rifle's carrying handle, then jerked the twenty-eight pound weapon off the ground as if it were no more than a featherweight.

"Time to get the hell out of Dodge, don't ya think?"

"You got that right!"

Three hours later and more than five kilometers distant and two thousand feet below their hide, Jake and Steve—both sweating like overworked racehorses—lounged beneath an outcropping of stone, patiently waiting for their ride home. After thirty minutes or so, finally rewarded with the low-level drumbeat of distant rotors that thumped through thin air, their rhythmic sounds muffled off canyon walls no more than ten to fifteen minutes out. Both were happy campers knowing their ride was on the way, courtesy of the Nightstalkers, otherwise known as the 160th Special Operations Aviation Regiment.

With his head laid wearily back, Jake was shaken from his reverie by a furtive scuttling motion he caught out of the corner of his eye.

Turning toward the movement, he was surprised to see the biggest goddamned camel spider he'd ever seen in his life, hunkered down on the dirt less than four feet from where he sat. *And this guy's gotta be the granddaddy of all camel spiders!*

Light beige in color, with its legs splayed out to its sides, it looked to measure over eight inches in length. It also sported two large, wicked looking mandibles from which drooped a lizard just a little smaller than itself; the lizard writhing from side to side in its death throes as it tried to break itself free from the spider's grip. The spider, as it continued to rest undisturbed on the rocky soil, just stared at him as if asking, "Who the hell are you?"

Jake had seen many of these guys during his frequent tours in the Middle East, and thought they had to be one of god's ugliest little creatures he'd ever seen. After a few seconds of motionlessness, the spider finally made up its mind that he wasn't a threat and pulled the still living lizard up to its jaws to feed.

Well, little buddy, good for you! At least somebody's having breakfast this morning!

As he watched the life and death struggle play out before him, he remembered these guys also had an unnerving habit of producing a high-pitched screeching sound whenever they ran, loud enough to scare the shit out of anyone. He tapped Steve on the shoulder and pointed out their new guest.

"Remind you of anything?"

Steve looked over and smiled, chuckling as he shook his head.

"Yep. Sure does, Boss. You thinkin' of Squealer?"

This particular spider brought back a memory they hadn't thought of for at least a year, an event to be remembered for all time. One of their team members, Petty Officer First Class George Tolman—a large black Navy SEAL who stood six-foot-five in his bare stockings and weighed-in at two hundred and fifty pounds of pure muscle—had laid claim to a rare small patch of shade just outside Kandahar. It had been late in the afternoon and they'd just come off a particularly tense mission.

Jake could still picture George as he'd laid out his massive frame in the dirt, his legs stretched out full with his boots crossed at the ankles, thinking to catch a quick nap with his soft-cover pulled low over his eyes. But before you knew it one of these guys—almost the same size as this son-of-a-bitch—had sprinted across the trail screaming its head off, determined to share the same patch of shade occupied by George.

The spider must have thought that George was just another ob-stacle because it had jumped up about a foot and landed smack-dab on his ankle, then scrambled like hell up his trousers toward his chest. But the sound, weight, and movement of the spider had caused George to jerk awake. With eyes as large as saucers, he'd looked down in horror as the hairy creature raced up his leg.

Scared to death, George had jumped up in a flurry of dust—squealing like a little girl—and frantically slapped at his trousers while jumping up and down in an effort to dislodge his new found friend. The team members had never seen George move so fast in his life. As he continued to slap at his body, the spider finally got pissed and clamped itself onto George's groin. It must have stung like hell.

With a scream stifled deep within his throat, and the spider hang-ing on for dear life, George had shifted into high gear as he torqued up his frenzy of twirling, dancing antics, shouting at the top of his lungs, "Jesus! . . . Jesus! . . . Jesus!"

Finally, having summoned the courage to reach down with a shaky hand, he had grabbed the huge thing by its neck, jerked it off his body, and threw it across the road with all his might—losing his balance in the process and crashing backwards onto the dirt. It had not been one of George's finer moments as a Navy SEAL.

But Hearthstone had thought it was one of the funniest damned things they'd ever seen, and almost died laughing as they'd watched him trying to get rid of that big damned spider. To this day George was known as Squealer.

Jake watched the spider chow down for a couple of more seconds, but then dismissed it from any further thought, his attention now fo-cused on the distant sound of the approaching choppers. *You know?* he suddenly thought. *I think my buddy over there had the right idea. Maybe it's time to have a little something to eat.*

"Steve? Got any of that pepper jerky left? Got kinda hungry just lyin' here and waiting."

"Yeah, think so, Boss," Martinez said, laying his weapon aside and rummaging around in his cammies' cargo pockets. When he fi-nally found a thick wad of dried beef, he pulled it out and frowned at it for a second. He could see that it was all covered with dirt and shit. So he blew on it hard a couple of times to try and clean it up, then used a grimy fingernail to pick off some of the larger bits of crud. Satisfied it was as clean as it was going to get, he handed it to Jake.

"Thanks, Steve."

Jake took the lump of beef and bit off a large chunk, trying to conjure up enough saliva to soften the rock-hard jerky. Then, with nothing further to do, he laid back and waited for their ride home.

A highly modified MH-60K Blackhawk suddenly burst over the ridgeline, coming in hot and fast as it as it swiveled around a hundred and eighty degrees in midflight just prior to landing. Jake also spotted an AH-6M Little Bird riding shotgun off in the distance.

Much smaller than the Blackhawk, the Little Bird was perfect for suppressing enemy fire with its six-barreled M134 miniguns. Guns that spun around their axis in a blur that spit out over four thousand rounds of 7.62mm per minute, or sixty-seven rounds per second. Jake knew they made life very nasty for the bad guys and, needless to say, the jihādist assholes hated the small choppers with a passion.

When the Blackhawk thumped hard onto the landing zone, Jake and Steve ran out from under their covered position, both with a hand pressed hard against their heads to keep their soft-covers in place. Once they'd jumped into the chopper's side-entry door, the crew chief hurriedly buckled them into canvas seats while the pilot pulled full collective and left the ground in a flurry of dust pointed northwest, the Blackhawk straining to gain altitude in the thin mountain air as the Little Bird circled to the right and took station less than a quarter of a mile to their front.

After Jake strapped the Mark-107 to the chopper's deck, the crew chief handed him a battered flight helmet and mimed for him to plug it into the intercom. Pulling the helmet onto his head, he plugged into the Blackhawk's communication system.

"Commander Stoneman?" he heard over the thumping racket of rotor blades.

"Yes, sir!" Jake shouted over the roar of hurricane winds that blew straight through the troop compartment.

"As soon as we reach firebase Tripoli, you're to contact CIA headquarters in Kabul. They want a sitrep on how your mission went down."

"I heard that, Colonel. And thanks."

With nothing further to do but enjoy the ride home, Jake relaxed into the canvas seat, leaning back against the insulated bulkhead that separated the cockpit from the troop compartment. With his long legs stretched out before him, he took a moment and glanced outside the side-entry door as the Blackhawk thundered home over a sea of rolling, brownish-colored Afghan hills.

Now able to relax for the first time in four days, he turned from the door, smiled at Steve, and tucked his chin into his chest. Not two minutes later he was asleep, still chewing on the now softened jerky.

Chapter 2

DAY ONE, 0530 HOURS
MUSHAF AIR FORCE BASE
PUNJAB PROVINCE
SARGODHA, PAKISTAN

HAVING COMPLETED HIS final morning Raka'ah to Allah, the one true God, Squadron Commander Zalmay MahMund of the Pakistan Air Force pushed his body upright and leaned back into a sitting position, his lips pursed in silent condemnation as he looked around the sparse, empty room. *So many,* he thought, *so many believers had strayed from the light of the one true faith, only to find themselves cloaked in the darkness of the unfaithful, as once had I.*

Zalmay, who had just turned thirty-seven years old, was a small-ish man with medium-length dark hair and close-set intelligent eyes, dressed in a faded khaki flight suit and wearing a pair of well-worn, but highly-polished black flying boots as he contemplated his last day in the Air Force. A day he had dedicated to Allah and all true believers.

He had been upset for some time as to what had been happening within his country—the political cronyism, corruption at the highest levels of government, and even within the military itself. As a young officer he had also felt it his due to take what he wanted, when he wanted, thinking he deserved a life much better than that of the average Pakistani. But in pursuit of what he had once considered success, he had lost his way from Islam and Allah's grace, interested only in advancement along with the material possessions and pleasures of the flesh that it could buy. Paying only lip service to what he considered to be the outdated teachings of the Qur'an.

But his views had changed. Not only had he watched the Pakistan people become poorer each year, but he was angered by the way his government kowtowed to the Americans. Zalmay knew full well that his political and military leaders kept their own secret bank accounts in Switzerland and other places where they could hide the fruits of their graft, along with a percentage of every dollar provided by the Americans' foreign aid, all due to the Americans trying to buy influence within his country. But the final straw had occurred when his parents were killed by an errant missile strike intended for Taliban militants, an American Hellfire missile fired from one of their Predator drones.

It had been Allah's way, he was sure, of punishing him for his past misdeeds; for having forsaken the path of the one true faith. With his allegiance now changed, he had secretly sworn allegiance to Qudos Mehsud—a fellow Pashtu from the Shabikhel sub-tribe of the Mehsud clan, the undisputed military commander of the Tehrik-e-taliban—and, prior to takeoff, would call the number Qudos' intermediary had given him to embrace the jihād in all its glory.

Zalmay slowly stood up from the cold concrete floor—rooted to the spot for several seconds in silent meditation while he chewed on his rather long, well-kept mustache—then rolled up the frayed prayer rug and gently placed it among the others stacked haphazardly against the wall. Exiting the prayer room, with his boots smacking rhythmically down the long, polished linoleum hallway, he made his way down to the flight ready room. He didn't notice the walls were bedecked with the framed photos of Pakistani aircraft and previous Pakistani commanders; his mind was focused elsewhere.

Turning to his left, he entered the ready room and retrieved his battered headset, an aluminum kneeboard that held today's frequencies and instrument approach procedures, and lastly, his Air Force issued POF PK-9 semiautomatic 9mm pistol snuggled deep within a supple, dark-brown leather shoulder holster, a holster he had splurged on just over a year ago.

Placing the items on a battered metal folding table, he picked up the matte-black-finished pistol and pulled it from its holster—staring at it for a second, knowing it to be his means of joining the jihād—then flipped it on its side and thumbed the magazine release button. Satisfied it was loaded with its complement of thirteen copper-jacketed rounds, he reinserted the clip and pushed it home with a distinctive, metallic snap.

With the pistol gripped in his right hand, he pulled back the operating slide with his left and let it slam home, stripping off the first round in the magazine and loading it into the firing chamber. Now in the cocked and locked position, he lowered the pistol's hammer by slowly letting it down with his thumb while depressing the trigger with his forefinger. When the hammer was down, he flicked on the safety and returned the pistol to its holster, then slipped into the whole apparatus with its leather retaining strap fastened firmly across his chest, the pistol now snuggled securely beneath his left armpit.

Minutes later he found himself on the flight-line, his hands resting on narrow hips while he gazed at the C-130E Hercules four-engine transport parked fifty meters to his front. When he looked at the aircraft he couldn't help but feel a deep sense of remorse, as if saying goodbye to a very dear friend. He knew that after today the odds of him ever flying again would be remote, and he would miss flying such a magnificent machine. Although not a fighter such as the F-16 he had hoped to fly, he had learned to appreciate the Hercules' staunch character: it was sturdy as a rock, faithful as a mule, and had been a very good friend to him.

The C-130E was a large aircraft that measured twenty-nine meters in length by twelve meters in height, and had a wingspan of close to forty meters. Made by Lockheed Martin in the United States, it was powered by four Allison T56-A-7 turboprops each of which generated forty-two hundred shaft horsepower; the aircraft fully capable of hauling a twenty-one ton payload over one thousand nautical miles at a cruise speed of three hundred knots. But what he liked most about the Hercules was its ability to operate from primitive, rough-dirt airstrips—or no airstrip at all—thanks to the C-130E's fully reversible-pitched props and barnyard-door-sized flaps that reduced its landing roll to less than seven hundred meters. All he needed to plant the giant aircraft on the ground was a level patch of hard-packed earth free of large rocks and of sufficient length to stop.

Zalmay paused and breathed in the pungent odors of JP-4 jet fuel mixed with diesel smoke, scents carried to him by the slight whispers of desert breeze that came from the southwest. Smells he would always remember. The smells of flying and the flight line.

With a glance towards the east, he saw the first streaks of dawn as they made their way down the distant Hanuman Tibba Mountains. Normally an early riser, he loved the mornings with their occasional fiery displays of color, and could tell that today's sunrise was just such a morning. It was as if Allah had painted a blank canvas across the eastern horizon with vivid brush strokes of yellow, red, and orange, all splashed on a background of dark ultramarine-blue. Mornings such as these, he knew, were Allah's gift to the faithful.

Hearing a commotion to his front, he turned back to the aircraft and allowed himself a brief smile at the hectic activity that was taking place. The Hercules' loading ramp was down and locked with two large military six-by-six trucks—each painted in olive-drab and brown camouflage—parked adjacent to its ramp. Their drivers seemingly bored as they languished against the truck's fenders where they smoked and talked.

A squat orange forklift, belching grayish-black diesel smoke high into the morning air, had just off-loaded from one of the trucks a rather large, rectangular, olive-drab metal container that measured three meters in length, by one meter in height, and one meter in width. But what had made him smile was his loadmaster, Chief Technician Mohammad Khosa, who was waving his arms frantically about while shouting instructions at the forklift driver, trying to direct the forklift as it bumped its way over the lip of the aircraft's loading ramp and disappeared into the dark confines of its fuselage.

Zalmay also noted the platoon of Air Force Special Services Wing soldiers—called the SSW for short in the Pakistan military—that surrounded the transport. Battle-hardened veterans with bloody clashes under their belts with the local Taliban militants, all dressed in their chocolate-chip-camouflaged BDUs, black side-zippered combat boots, and web-belt harnesses festooned with spare magazine pouches; the flight line secured by their presence with their Belgian made FN F2000 5.56mm assault rifles carried at the ready.

He frowned when he observed the SSW. He knew these troops were to accompany them on their flight, but that could not be helped. *Hopefully,* he prayed, *they will be sent to be judged by Allah and will not endanger today's mission.*

Zalmay looked down at his expensive, stainless-steel Breitling chronometer he had purchased in another lifetime. It was close to 0545 hours and they were scheduled to take off no later than 0700 hours for Samungli Air Force Base, an Air Force base located five hundred and eighty kilometers due south in the Baluchistan province.

Chapter 3

**DAY ONE, 0610 HOURS
MUSHAF AIR FORCE BASE
SARGODHA, PAKISTAN**

ABDUL FAROOQI, A thirty-one-year-old senior nuclear technician on contract with the Pakistan Air Force, was a short thin man with a scraggly black beard and widely spaced eyes, eyes magnified by a pair of thick, black-framed eyeglasses that gave him the startled, pinch-faced look of a starving ferret. He turned one last time to the second container lashed to the aircraft's cargo deck and pulled hard on one of its nylon securing straps.

"Jamel," he said, standing back up, "try the one across from me."

Jamel Syed, Abdul's junior assistant, double-checked the opposite strap by tugging on it with all his might.

"It's tight, Abdul."

"Good! That should do it then," he concluded, wiping his hands on an already soiled rag. "I'll tell Captain Ramay and Commander MahMund that everything is ready for the flight. And Chief," he said to the aircraft's ubiquitous loadmaster, Mohammad Khosa, "thanks for your help."

Chief Khosa just nodded his head.

"No problem, sir," he said as he lumbered his way forward to the bulkhead to return a large, steel, cinching lever to the aircraft's tool compartment.

Abdul looked once again at the containers, each of which contained a one-hundred-kiloton nuclear warhead configured for delivery by Pakistani F-16 fighters, the first of twenty to be repositioned to the recently completed nuclear weapons storage site located at Samungli Air Force Base; the military high command in full agreement that their current storage facilities at Mushaf Air Force Base outside Sargodha, and Minhas Air Force Base outside Kamra, were too close to the Taliban strongholds in the Northern Territories and FATA—Federally Administered Tribal Areas—that adjoined Afghanistan. But most importantly, their movement was to allay the fears of the United States government that Taliban militants could attack one of these sites and make off with one of the warheads. The military higher-ups knew that the probability of this happening was nonexistent, but it was better to be safe than sorry. It was a small price to pay to placate the paranoid Americans to ensure their continued flow of military aid.

"Jamel?" Abdul asked again. "Double-check the testing equipment, make sure it's tied down, then meet me outside, okay?"

"Okay," Jamel said.

While Jamel tended to his task, Abdul threw the soiled rag onto one of the containers and walked down the cargo bay loading ramp, careful not to trip over the numerous steel, ring-like stanchions used to tie down equipment. When he approached the end of the ramp, the six-by-six's parked next to the aircraft started their engines—each truck shooting plumes of black diesel smoke high into the air every time their overzealous drivers pressed their accelerators to the floor—and drove off into the distance.

Not concerned with the trucks, Abdul stepped off the ramp and looked to his right. He could see Captain Shadi Ramay, the SSW company commander, and First Lieutenant Kamil Chadhar, the SSW platoon commander, standing next to the aircraft where they smoked and talked.

Captain Ramay, when he saw the senior tech heading their way, took one last drag of his cigarette and dropped it to the tarmac.

"Well, Mr. Farooqi? How do things look? Are we all set to go?"

"Yes, sir! We're all set," Abdul said, pointing back at the cargo bay. "Jamel and I have both checked the load. Everything's ready to go, sir."

"Good! Very good! Well, Kamil? It looks like you'll get off on time today."

"Yes, sir," his lieutenant said. "It sure does. But with your permission, I need to speak with Sergeant Abbasi to make sure the men are ready to board."

"Go ahead, Lieutenant," Ramay said.

When Captain Ramay turned back to the tech, he glanced over

his shoulder and saw Squadron Commander Zalmay MahMund, the aircraft's pilot, and Pilot Officer Tamir Kolhi, the aircraft's copilot, as they exited the C-130E's left-side crew door, the pilots having just completed the Hercules' preflight.

Captain Ramay came to attention and snapped off a crisp salute.

"When would you like the men to board, Commander?"

"Now's as good a time as any, Captain," Zalmay replied easily. "We've got less than thirty minutes before our scheduled takeoff."

Chapter 4

DAY ONE, 0645 HOURS
MUSHAF AIR FORCE BASE
SARGODHA, PAKISTAN

SQUADRON COMMANDER ZALMAY MahMund grunted as he slid the pilot's seat forward to make sure he had full access to the rudder pedals, then wiggled his butt around to get as comfortable as he could. Once settled, he slid open the left-side cockpit window and looked outside to confirm that the auxiliary power unit was attached to the aircraft's power input receptacle. With a shout at the airman who manned the APU, he twirled his finger in the air to indicate that he wanted the unit powered up. As the APU sputtered to life, then settled into a throaty roar, he flicked on the Master Battery Buss switch. When the instrument panel came to life, he pushed the small red intercom button on his control yoke.

"Kolhi? How do you read?"

"Five-by-five, sir," his copilot replied.

"Loadmaster? How do you read?"

"Loud and clear, sir," Chief Khosa answered from the cargo hold.

"Everyone strapped in back there?"

"Yes, sir! Everyone's strapped in and secure!" Then Khosa took a quick look around to confirm what he had just told his commander.

The platoon of SSW troops, their platoon sergeant, and platoon commander were seated in red, fold-down nylon seats on opposite sides of the cargo bay; their backs to the fuselage with both rows of men separated by the two large, metal containers lashed to the deck lengthwise end-to-end. And due to the height of the containers, the soldiers could barely see their counterparts across the cargo bay, the men feeling as if they had been crammed into an oversized aluminum sardine can with their knees less than a meter from the warheads.

"Okay, Lieutenant, let's go ahead and wind her up," Zalmay said.

When the turboprops were spooled up and running normally, with all of the instrument gauges in the green, they adjusted the aircraft's flaps to fifty percent for takeoff; set the rudder, elevator, and aileron trim tabs; checked the flight controls for free and easy movement; confirmed the readout on the radar altimeter matched the base's elevation; and then listened to Mushaf's automated terminal information system—the ATIS' sole purpose to announce the base's current winds, temperature, density altitude, altimeter setting, and runway in use.

Pilot Officer Kolhi, being the copilot, copied down all the pertinent information on his kneeboard. Once the aircraft was ready to go, Zalmay keyed the radio.

"Mushaf Ground, Mega Zero-Three on the tarmac in front of base operations with the numbers. Request taxi to runway Three-Two direct to Samungli Air Force Base. Altitude ten thousand feet."

As in the majority of countries worldwide Pakistan used the metric system for measurements, but in aviation, airspeed and height above mean-sea-level was always measured in knots and feet.

"Mega Zero-Three, you are cleared to runway Three-Two via taxiway Bravo. Wind is from three-zero-zero degrees at eight knots. Altimeter is two-niner-niner-seven. Ceiling is clear and unlimited. Squawk three-two-eight-nine. Please contact the tower on one-two-seven point three when ready for takeoff."

"Understand cleared to runway Three-Two via Bravo, squawk three-two-eight-nine, contact the tower on one-two-seven point three," Zalmay repeated.

"Read back is correct, Mega Zero-three."

"Thank you, Mushaf Ground."

When Pilot Officer Kolhi heard the squawk code issued by ground control, he punched the unique, four-digit identification code into the aircraft's Mode C transponder—Mode C capability that allowed the aircraft's transponder to be interrogated by ground radar. The aircraft's blip on the ground controller's radar screen now identified by the four-digit code along with the aircraft's heading, height above mean-sea-level, and true groundspeed.

With a quick glance at Kolhi, Zalmay grasped the throttles in the center console and edged them gradually forward to apply power to the turboprops. Ten minutes later, the aircraft lumbered to the threshold of runway Three-Two and came to a smooth stop just short of the runway hold-line.

"Mushaf Tower, Mega Zero-Three at the threshold of Three-Two. Ready for takeoff."

"Mega Zero-Three, you are cleared for takeoff, and have a good day, sir," the tower operator said.

"Thank you, Mushaf. Mega Zero-Three's rolling."

Zalmay pulled the aircraft onto the runway and aligned its nose with the centerline, then pushed all four throttles forward to the stops. As the C-130E surged forward, rapidly gaining airspeed down the runway, he reached down and pressed the speed dial button of his cell phone.

Chapter 5

DAY ONE, 0710 HOURS
TWO KILOMETERS FROM AFGHANISTAN BORDER
BALUCHISTAN PROVINCE, PAKISTAN

THERE WAS THE slightest breeze from the west. Even at this hour of the morning the air was dry and unforgiving, devoid of moisture as was the rocky, sun-bleached ground spread before him. Already he could see the shimmer of mirages that danced above the ground in the distance, mirages that undulated and distorted the landscape as if seen through a warped piece of glass.

For three days now they had awaited the Pakistanis' arrival and had used that time wisely—preparing, consolidating, and camouflaging their firing positions with care to erase all signs that anyone occupied both sides of the dry, parched intersection of river beds. They knew too well the capabilities of the American and Pakistan surveillance drones that crisscrossed the brilliant blue skies of the desert.

Mahmood Tahqi—a sub-commander of the Tehrik-e-taliban and a direct subordinate to Qudos Mehsud—squatted on his thin haunches in a dust-filled firing position, his bony knees tucked under his chin while he studied the ridgelines of the Taharai Ghar Mountains to the west. Then he turned into the glare of the morning sun, his eyes crinkled into two dark slits as he stared at the Sānde Ghar Mountains to the east—both mountains flanking a small valley that was two kilometers wide at this point, but then narrowed to a point as one traveled northwest into Afghanistan.

Qudos could not have chosen a better site, he thought as he eyed their position with care. It was screened, well-hidden, and located at the junction of two ancient riverbeds, the largest of which ran north to south with a smaller one that spilled from the foothills to the east.

The intersection of the two riverbeds looked not unlike the capital letter V, and from the point of the V to its broad tail there was a small raised plateau that stood no more than two meters in height. He and his fighters, after preparing their fighting positions, had scoured the surface of the plateau for more than a kilometer south to remove any large rocks they could find on its broad expanse.

Mahmood picked up a small pebble and popped it into his mouth, hoping to savor what little moisture it could develop, then he turned and focused on his men. He had eighty fighters, himself included, positioned on both sides of the plateau; most of the men armed with AK-47s, but he also had four RPG-7 launchers and one American M60 machine gun that could spit out up to five hundred and fifty rounds of 7.62mm per minute. This gun he had placed at the pointy-end of the plateau so that it could fire directly south. In addition to the RPG-7s and M60, he had four Stinger-B antiaircraft missiles recently stolen from an army ammunition depot, the missiles intended for any aircraft that may appear. He just hoped, with Allah's grace, that the damned things would work if needed.

Mahmood continued to think these thoughts when the satellite phone given him by Qudos rang noisily by his side, vibrating on the dirt lip of his fighting hole. Jarred back to the present, he was surprised the damned thing worked at all. Qudos had told him it would, but he was surprised nonetheless. He knew that being in such a valley flanked by tall mountains meant that radios could not work here, much less cell phones. That was why he had been given one of their satellite phones to receive the incoming signal. As he stared at the phone's display, his face broke into a broad smile when he recognized the incoming phone number. *Allah provides. The Pakistanis should be here in roughly thirty minutes.*

Chapter 6

DAY ONE, 0742 HOURS
FOUR MILES EAST OF THE HISĀRI MOUNTAINS
BALUCHISTAN PROVINCE, PAKISTAN

THE C-130E CONTINUED its uneventful journey south at an altitude of ten thousand feet with an indicated groundspeed of two hundred and seventy-five knots, bucking a fifteen knot headwind on a heading of 185 degrees. The sky crystal clear and smooth as silk with just a slight haze of crystalline cirrus clouds far above their flight level.

Squadron Commander Zalmay MahMund checked the GPS every now and then to confirm their position, making occasional adjustments to the throttles and trim to keep them on course and altitude. He had spurned the use of the autopilot, opting instead to hand-fly the aircraft to savor every moment of what he considered to be his last flight.

Pilot Officer Kolhi occupied himself by keeping track of their flight path with occasional updates to an aeronautical sectional chart he kept on his lap, every few seconds—like clockwork—lifting his head to glance outside the cockpit to search for identifying landmarks. When he noted the Obasta Tsukai Mountains that rose to well over fifteen thousand feet off their starboard wing, he lowered his eyes and made a deliberate tick mark on their planned course line.

Forty-two minutes into their flight, Zalmay saw they were less than ninety nautical miles due east of his intended landing site.

"Kolhi!" he shouted. "Check out engine three! I think we have an oil pump failure! Take a look and tell me what you see!"

Startled, Kolhi abruptly looked up from his chart.

"Yes, sir!"

With his head craned up and to the right, Kolhi stared at engine three and its surrounding nacelle. After ten or fifteen seconds, though, he couldn't see anything wrong. No signs of smoke, oil leakage, or anything else that seemed to be out of the ordinary.

"Sir?" he questioned as he continued to stare at the turning turboprop. "The engine seems to be operating normally. Everything looks fine."

When he turned back to his commander, he froze like a deer caught in the headlights of an on-rushing truck—his eyes wide with fright, unable to breathe—fixated on the deadly round bore of a matte-black-finished POF PK-9 semiautomatic pistol pointed just centimeters from his head. But before he could utter a word, a 9mm round punched a hole through his forehead and blew off the back section of his skull, splattering the right side of the cockpit with a heavy spray of bright-crimson blood and brain matter.

Kolhi's head, slammed backwards by the initial impact, rolled forward and lolled chin downwards on his chest, his body and shoulders restrained only by his safety harness. A thick, metallic, coppery smell also began to permeate the dry air of the cockpit, the smell caused by the large stringers of blood that fell from his shattered head onto the sectional chart still clutched in his lifeless hands. No one in the cargo bay, however, had heard a thing; the roar of the engines, Kevlar helmets, and headsets having muffled the sound of the pistol's firing.

With sweaty hands, Zalmay decocked the pistol that had cycled another round into the firing chamber, then clicked on its safety and returned the still smoking weapon to its shoulder holster.

"May Allah have mercy on your soul," he mumbled as he activated the intercom. "Loadmaster! Are you there? We've got a problem!"

Loadmaster Khosa, strapped into his seat with his arms crossed over his ample stomach, had been almost asleep when the commander's strident voice crashed through his headset. Jarred instantly awake, he keyed the intercom wondering what in the Prophet's name was going on. He had heard the panic in his commander's voice and it scared the hell out of him.

"Yes, sir! I'm here!"

"We've lost oil pressure in engines two and three, and one and four are marginal and overheating!" Zalmay lied. "I'm shutting down two and three now! We can't make it to Samungli on just two engines and we're too far to go back to Mushaf! Prepare everyone for an emergency landing!"

"Yes, sir!" Khosa shouted as he looked frantically at the seated troops—energized by the shots of adrenaline that exploded throughout his system—and then jerked his seat belt free, disconnected the intercom from his helmet, and stood up.

With his arm pressed against the fuselage to steady his bulk, Khosa stumbled his way down the cargo bay, muttering curses when he got caught up in the tangle of soldiers' legs. He had to get to the SSW lieutenant as quickly as possible to let him know about the emergency landing.

Back on the flight deck, Zalmay knew he needed to get under Approach Control's radar and to point the nose of the transport opposite from his intended destination, to throw off the many search parties that would be sent to scour the countryside. With that thought in mind, he grasped the throttles for engines two and three—the two opposite inboard engines—and pulled them all the way back; the huge aircraft instantly decelerating as if it had been a car trying to plow its way through a flooded intersection.

Turning to his left, he looked outside the cockpit as the aircraft continued to slow, then yanked the Hercules into a steep, forty-five degree bank to port—the transport's right wingtip raised toward the sky. Not three seconds later, he slammed full forward on the control yoke, abruptly nosing the Hercules over with negative g's and pointing it almost straight down toward the mountainous ridgelines below. Zalmay knew he had no choice, he needed to lose altitude as fast as possible to get down to five thousand feet—the elevation of the terrain below him—to get lost in the ground clutter and drop off Approach Control's radar.

Zalmay kept the aircraft pointed down in its steep, descending, left-hand bank until the directional gyro steadied up on an indicated southeasterly heading of 120 degrees, opposite from his intended landing site.

Now on his new heading, he leveled the transport's wings, but kept the Hercules pitched down in its sickening descent. When the aircraft approached five thousand feet he pulled back hard on the yoke—grunting from the pull of g's—his eyeballs feeling as if they were being sucked from their sockets as he raised the nose of the Hercules, and then jammed the throttles for engines two and three forward to the stops to apply power to the idle turboprops.

With the Hercules now level, he adjusted the trim and once again looked outside the cockpit. He could see they were just meters above the terrain as the aircraft skimmed the rocky ridgelines below. Confident he was now below any radar coverage, he looked out the right side of the cockpit—past the body of his dead copilot—and cranked the transport into a violent, fifty degree bank to starboard.

With the Hercules standing almost upright on its right wingtip, he again pulled back hard on the yoke—stressing the aircraft with additional g's—to keep it from plowing into the rock-strewn mountains just meters below the aircraft. Finally, he brought the wings back level and steadied up on his new course of 295 degrees. With the C-130E now on its new heading, he called up the GPS route display and quickly punched in the waypoint of his new landing site, the GPS telling him he was no more than ten minutes out.

Suddenly his headset crackled to life.

"Mega Zero-Three! Mega Zero-Three! This is Samungli Approach Control! Come in, please! You have diverted from your approved flight plan! Come in, please!" a distraught voice asked.

Zalmay did not respond.

Not three seconds later his headset again crackled to life.

"Mega Zero-Three! Mega Zero-Three! This is Samungli Approach! Come in please, over! You have diverted from your flight plan! Please advise!" the strident voice demanded, a voice now edged with the stark panic of alarm.

At the end of the second transmission, Zalmay swore at the offending voice and switched off the radio.

Inside the cargo bay bedlam and confusion reigned supreme when the aircraft had abruptly nosed over into a gut-wrenching, roller-coaster-like descent, the soldiers' involuntary moans and screams filling the void as their stomachs lurched into their throats. Several of the SSW troops, thrown violently against their seat belts by the chaotic gyrations of the aircraft, had lost their grip on weapons that now rattled back and forth along the aluminum deck.

Not understanding what was going on, and hanging onto their seats for dear life, more than half of the soldiers became airsick, emptying their stomachs with abandon—the aircraft's cargo deck quickly becoming slick and sticky with their morning's breakfast, not to mention the sour smell of vomit that enveloped the confines of their metal prison. The putrid smell of feces also filled the air as several of the soldiers voided their bowels in fear, smells that caused the remaining soldiers to spill the contents of their own stomachs to mix with the growing pile on the floor.

Chapter 7

DAY ONE, 0750 HOURS
ELEVATION 7,200 FEET MSL
AIRSPEED 275 KNOTS

THE HERCULES BURST over the Sānde Ghar Mountains with just meters to spare, kicking up dust clouds in its wake while Squadron Commander Zalmay MahMund furiously craned his neck to look for his landing site. In what seemed like an eternity, but was only a few brief seconds, he spotted the small plateau no more than five kilometers to his front.

As the Taharai Ghar Mountains fast approached filling his windscreen, he knew there was no room left for a standard-rate turn. With his decision made, he wracked the aircraft into a forty degree bank to port, retarded the throttles on all four engines, dumped in fifty degrees of flaps, hit the electric trim button to lower the nose to counteract the lift of the flaps, and then slapped down the gear, all in an effort to slow the Hercules down and put it into a manageable descent.

Once leveled off, he traced a path parallel to the mountains whose summits soared far above his altitude. At one hundred and fifty knots indicated, he flew down the valley as he eyed their landing zone coming up on his left. He could see the apex formed by the intersection of the two riverbeds. Then he glanced at the radar altimeter. *Fifteen hundred feet off the deck.* When he drew abreast of what he considered to be the runway threshold, he trimmed the aircraft up for a five-hundred-foot-per-minute descent rate and started a gentle fifteen degree bank to port.

Now on his base leg and perpendicular to the landing site, Zalmay slowed the aircraft up even more, steadied up now at one hundred and thirty knots by having dumped in full flaps and lowering the nose with a couple of more down hits to the elevator trim. Once they were opposite the landing threshold, he made another gentle left turn to final, leveled the aircraft's wings, double-checked to make sure he had three wheels down and locked with the props set to full increase, and raised the aircraft's nose a few degrees to reduce its airspeed to one hundred and fifteen knots.

When the C-130E flashed over the approach end of his makeshift runway, he retarded the throttles on all four engines and pulled back gently on the control yoke to keep the Hercules' nose level with the horizon. Now stabilized in the landing configuration, the transport continued its inexorable descent toward the rough sand- and rock-strewn field below him and then, seconds later, thunked gratefully onto the unforgiving terrain.

Once he felt they were planted firmly on the field, Zalmay slammed the nose wheel to the ground, reversed pitch on all four props, applied full power to the turboprops to slow the aircraft down, and lastly—through instinct and training—hit the flaps retract switch and stood on the brakes.

The C-130E shook and rumbled its way down the plateau toward the junction of the two riverbeds, closely followed by an avalanche of dust that streamed to its rear and sides. The aircraft, slowed by the turboprops' reverse thrust, dipped and bobbed wildly from side to side on its nose wheel. As the swirling clouds of dirt engulfed its fuselage like a dirty-brown snowstorm, the Hercules finally came to rest just meters from the end of the plateau.

With the aircraft now stationary, Zalmay once again reversed pitch on all four props, stomped hard on the left rudder pedal, and applied full power to engines three and four on the starboard wing. With its engines roaring in protest, the aircraft abruptly pivoted 180 degrees to the left—its landing gear digging rough trench lines into the soft soil of his makeshift landing strip—and then lurched to a stop facing due south.

With his flight suit now drenched in sweat, he pulled back the throttles to shut down the turboprops, the rear of the aircraft no more than thirty meters from where the two riverbeds met. As the props slowly spooled down, a deathly silence enveloped the Hercules as grainy shrouds of dust settled to the plateau floor.

Wrestling himself back to the present, Zalmay tore off his headset and threw it to the flight deck; the only thing he could now hear being the clings and clangs of red-hot metal as the engines slowly cooled. With a silent, grateful prayer to Allah for his guiding hand, he remembered his duty and frantically groped for the cargo bay ramp switch in the center console. Once toggled in the open position, he was rewarded with a thump and a whining noise as the ramp began to lower.

Slumped exhaustedly in his pilot's seat, and wrung out with his body shaking from the adrenaline that still coursed throughout his veins, he could faintly make out the shouted orders and confusion that was erupting from the cargo bay.

Zalmay, however, did not move. He just stared outside the windscreen stiff as a statue. He had been told to wait and not to exit the aircraft. They would come for him.

Chapter 8

DAY ONE, 0756 HOURS
31° 35′ 01.55″ NORTH LONGITUDE
68° 53′ 23.09″ EAST LATITUDE
BALUCHISTAN PROVINCE, PAKISTAN

PLATOON COMMANDER LIEUTENANT Kamil Chadhar sat stunned, unable to comprehend what the hell had just happened. He remembered that Loadmaster Khosa had just made it to his seat to say something about an in-flight emergency when the plane had violently nosed over and lurched drunkenly from side to side, as if a dog had grabbed it and shaken it like a rag doll.

When the bottom dropped out the aircraft, he watched in disbelief as the bewildered chief actually floated off the floor as if in the weightlessness of space, desperately trying to grab a handhold as he bounced off the cargo bay's overhead. When the plane abruptly pulled out of its dive, Khosa—as if shot by a slingshot—had crashed back downwards to the deck, his body slammed hard onto one of the metal containers strapped to the center of the bay. Chadhar vaguely remembered having to grab one of the nylon straps bolted to the bulkhead just to keep from being thrown out of his seat.

With his safety belt unbuckled, he stood up on wobbly knees and looked frantically around the cargo bay. He could see that his platoon was sick and disoriented from their chaotic ride, many of the men pale with their uniforms splattered with vomit. A few he could tell were injured, moaning where they lay on the deck when they had been thrown from improperly fastened seat belts and tossed about the cargo bay like so much flotsam.

Suddenly, he felt a jolt when an electric motor kicked in, accompanied by a high-pitched whining sound. Quickly looking for its source, he saw the noise was coming from the top of the cargo ramp where it met the rear fuselage. At that moment a thin wedge of welcome sunlight appeared, quickly becoming larger as it pierced the gloom of the rank cargo bay. The ramp was being lowered.

"Platoon Sergeant!" he shouted hoarsely, surprised that he could even speak.

"Yes, sir!" Sergeant Abbasi bellowed, trying to stand after unbuckling his own seat belt.

"The ramp's going down! Get the men up and outside! We need to set up a security perimeter!" he ordered, pulling his pistol from its holster.

"All right, everybody!" the platoon sergeant shouted. "Listen up! Lock and load! First Squad to the right, Second Squad to the left, Third Squad straight out back! Spread out and cover your sectors!"

The platoon sergeant then paused when he saw several of the men lying injured on the deck.

"Medic!"

"Yes, Platoon Sergeant!"

"Take care of the injured!"

"Yes, Platoon Sergeant!"

The men frantically began to unbuckle their seat belts, only to stand up on jellied knees like a bunch of old men, hanging onto the red nylon strapping for balance as they loaded magazines into their rifles. Those who had dropped their rifles during the wild flight groped frantically in the filth of the cargo deck in an effort to locate them.

When the ramp was fully down and locked in place, Lieutenant Chadhar ran toward the rear of the aircraft followed closely by his radio operator and several of the men. With his eyes squinted almost shut from the outside glare, his feet suddenly slid out from beneath him, his face smacking hard onto the deck. Quickly scrambling to his feet, he saw he had slipped on a large pool of blood.

Confused, he saw the loadmaster's body spread-eagled on the cargo deck, his head bent oddly back at a ninety degree angle. But what had caused the pool of blood was a large, splintered white bone that protruded grotesquely from Khosa's thigh, the wound pumping out a thick torrent of bright-red blood. *Must have cut the femoral artery,* he glumly thought as he continued his way out of the aircraft.

Chapter 9

DAY ONE, 0758 HOURS
31° 35′ 01.55″ NORTH LONGITUDE
68° 53′ 23.09″ EAST LATITUDE
BALUCHISTAN PROVINCE, PAKISTAN

MAHMOOD TAHQI LAY quietly in his fighting hole, peering over its lip next to the M60 machine gunner, his left hand resting lightly on the gunner's shoulder as he whispered cautiously, "Steady, Ashraf, steady"; the rear of the large aircraft just thirty meters to his front engulfed in a quickly dissipating cloak of dust.

The gunner—lying prone on the dirt behind the M60—just gently stroked the trigger, sighted-in on the ramp of the aircraft with his left hand clamped firmly over the top of the gun's feed cover; the machine gun's deadly links of belted, copper-jacketed 7.62mm rounds held off the ground by his assistant gunner.

Mahmood, with his head tilted inquisitively to the side, listened closely, his eyes bright with expectation as he slowly licked his dirt-encrusted lips. He could hear the muffled shouts that came from within the transport, but nothing he could understand. The only other sounds that disturbed the morning's stillness being the crackling expansion and contraction noises of the aircraft's engines as they slowly cooled.

Tearing his gaze from the transport, he watched as his men silently removed the camouflage covers from their firing positions and cast them aside, the muzzles of their AK-47s aimed at the ramp and both sides of the aircraft.

When he heard a muted whining noise, he quickly looked back to his front and saw the ramp was being lowered, with dust and dirt cascading in sheets off its upper lip. As the ramp continued down, shouts within the transport became more understandable. He could now hear orders being hoarsely shouted at the soldiers.

"Steady, steady," he again cautioned his machine gunner.

When the ramp was fully lowered, he could see directly into the aircraft. With a grim smile, he saw the confusion that surrounded the hated SSW soldiers, most of them busy trying to load magazines into their rifles while others fumbled about the cargo deck as if searching for something they had lost.

At that moment a young officer began to run out of the aircraft, but suddenly slipped and fell down hard at the beginning of the loading ramp. Staggering back to his feet, the officer looked frantically around, then shouted something into the cargo bay and once again ran down the ramp, followed closely by troops who boiled out of the cargo bay as if an anthill had been kicked over.

Two groups of soldiers quickly split to the right and left with their weapons at the ready, their web gear clinking madly against their sides. A third group, led by the young officer, ran straight toward his position. Mahmood knew this was what he had been waiting for. He squeezed the gunner's shoulder and shouted, "Now!"

The gunner depressed the M60's trigger, the machine gun's recoil pounding into his shoulder over and over again in a staccato-like rhythm; the rounds initially stitching the ground in front of the soldiers, but then lifted when he raised the muzzle of his gun. The initial burst of gunfire smashed into the young officer first, throwing him backwards as if hit head-on by a Mack truck—his stomach decorated with a medley of bright-crimson blossoms as the thudding impact of bullets raised small puffs of dust on his tunic.

Lieutenant Chadhar, now flat on his back with his knees bent and slowly moving from side to side, still clutched his unfired pistol, his mouth filled with a stifled gurgling sound while his sightless eyes stared skyward. The young lieutenant could also feel a burning sensation in his midsection as if someone had drawn a red-hot branding iron across his stomach. Not understanding what had happened, he commanded his left hand to move slowly down his body where it encountered a warm, wet mass—his last thoughts confused as he stiffened in death; his hand immersed in a steaming pile of ropy, pinkish-white intestines that spilled from his bullet-riddled stomach.

At the sound of the M60's firing, seventy-nine other AK-47s immediately opened up, catching the soldiers in a withering crossfire that knocked them back as if a giant scythe had cut them off at the knees. Those soldiers not initially hit stopped in panicked confusion, frantically looking about for signs of their attackers. Others, as they watched their comrades being cut to pieces, threw themselves to the ground.

The fusillade continued unabated, kicking up a hurricane of ricocheting dust and rocks. The bullets, as if they had a mind of their own, relentlessly probed the ground like a searchlight in the dead of night, seeking out the hapless soldiers as their screams joined the cracks of rifle and machine gun fire that echoed off the nearby mountain cliffs.

With no commands being given, and their platoon commander and platoon sergeant killed outright, the few uninjured soldiers called out wretchedly at the top of their lungs for mercy, their weapons tossed aside as they buried their faces deep within the sunscorched soil. But the firing continued until every soldier had been killed or seriously wounded.

"Cease fire, cease fire!" Mahmood finally shouted as he raised himself off the ground, cradling his still smoking AK-47 in his arms.

The firing continued for several more seconds, but then it slowly tapered off and stopped altogether; the only sounds now heard being the groans and screams of the wounded intermingled with the noxious smell of cordite that drifted over the killing field.

Mahmood hastily scrambled up the soft sand of the berm and shouted, "Qasim!"

Qasim Wassan, a short, wiry man of indeterminate age, stood up from his firing hole, his rifle pointed at the wounded soldiers to his front.

"Yes, Mahmood!"

"Have all of the weapons and equipment collected and put over there!" he ordered, pointing his rifle muzzle at a small ravine to the left of the aircraft.

"It will be done!" Qasim answered obediently.

"And kill the wounded!" Mahmood added, spitting the forgotten pebble from his mouth.

Qasim, with the death-pit look of a viper, nodded in silent acknowledgment.

"But don't use rifles," Mahmood commanded. "We don't want to waste the ammunition. Use knives, and have them all beheaded.

Those were Qudos' final instructions, and make sure that Hafiz uses the video camera to film it all. Qudos wants it on tape to give to al-Jazeera, to show the Pakistanis what we think of their stinking soldiers and how we deal with those who sleep with America."

Qasim looked at the wounded soldiers scattered about the ground, grinning when several of them tried to claw their way to safety on their bellies like snails; their paths marked by slick, sticky trails of blood.

"It will be done, Mahmood."

The rest of his fighters, now up and out of their fighting holes, laughed and slapped one another on the back with the victor's bravado while several fired their weapons on full automatic into the sky. Others gleefully ran over to the wounded soldiers and entertained themselves by poking their razor-sharp knives into the bullet wounds of some of the less injured, most thinking it great fun to see how loud they could make the soldiers scream.

Mahmood quickly made a slashing gesture with his arm, his eyes glaring from beneath dark brows.

"Stop it! We do not have the time to act as children! The Pakistani helicopters may already be on their way!"

The rejoicing ended as soon as it had begun.

"You men, there! Help Qasim with the weapons and wounded," he ordered, pointing at a group of twenty fighters. Then he spoke to a fighter who stood by his side.

"Zahid, get the mules. We don't have any time to waste. We need to begin the loading as soon as possible."

"Yes, Mahmood!" Zahid said, motioning for several of the men to follow.

"You, there!" Mahmood said sharply to five fighters standing around stupidly doing nothing. "Come with me."

But before he headed toward the aircraft, Mahmood watched as his men strode with grisly purpose among the Pakistani soldiers, the fighters still joking and laughing as they pushed one another about in order to lay claim to the wounded. They knew it was much more fun to behead the living with their screams and anguished appeals for mercy, rather than having to settle for those who could not feel the blade of their knives.

Mahmood watched dispassionately as his men selected their victims and dropped down hard onto their bodies, their knees planted firmly in the backs of the soldiers as they ripped off their Kevlar helmets and grabbed the fallen men by their hair—jerking their heads up and back to expose the soft, fleshy under parts of their necks.

The dead, of course, were mute, but the wounded cried out in stark terror, bleating like young sheep going to slaughter when they saw the large, razor-sharp knives being drawn from the fighters' sheaths. With deft swipes, his fighters slit the throats of the living and dead from ear to ear, trying their best not to get splattered by the dark fountains of blood that spurted across the ground. Once the blood flow had lessened, they hacked away with wild abandon through exposed throats, muscles, and vertebrae, then lifted up their prizes in triumph.

The remaining fighters rounded up the Belgian FN F2000 rifles, web-belt harnesses, ammunition belts and other equipment, while others stripped the dead and wounded of their uniforms, underwear, and boots; the soldiers' stark, naked bodies left to the tender mercies of the Pakistan sun.

Mahmood turned from the carnage and made his way toward the aircraft. With five of his men following, he stepped lightly onto the loading ramp and walked into the dim stink of the cargo bay. After just one or two steps, however, a bullet suddenly snap-cracked past his head, followed instantly by the explosive sound of a rifle's firing. Instinctively, he lurched to the side as another shot rang out, the round hitting one of his men who grunted and fell heavily from the ramp. But he had seen the shooter, a soldier who wore a helmet with the green crescent of Islam on its side. *A medic!* he thought.

The medic, desperate when he heard the firing outside the aircraft, had barricaded himself behind the metal container lashed closest to the flight deck, not knowing what else to do but pray for deliverance while he loaded his rifle and waited for the attackers to enter the cargo bay.

Mahmood calmly leveled his rifle and got a good sight picture, patiently waiting for the soldier to once again peek over the container. When the medic slowly lifted his head he fired, hitting his target in the left cheek just below the eye, smashing the medic backwards in a tangle of arms and legs against the flight deck stairs.

Mahmood moved quickly and stood astride his victim in mere seconds. With a quick look down, he kicked aside the soldier's weapon and pressed his rifle firmly into the medic's forehead, staring into his pleading eyes with satisfaction. But then he changed his mind and grinned. Laying his rifle on one of the metal containers, and in full view of the soldier's gaze, he slowly drew his knife and flipped it from side to side, the medic's eyes tracing every movement of the blade. *His men could not have all the fun,* he thought, relishing the fear that now transformed the soldier's face into a stark mask of horror.

Mahmood straightened up from the bloody corpse and cleaned his knife on the medic's tunic. After he sheathed his blade, he called sharply to the fighters who had followed him into the cargo bay.

"You men, clean out this trash," he said, pointing at the injured SSW troops the medic had been attending.

His men charged into the upper reaches of the cargo bay and roughly collared the wounded men, oblivious to their screams as they were dragged by their legs or the scruff of their necks into the daylight of death.

Seeing everything he had ordered was being done, Mahmood glanced at his cheap soviet watch and saw it had only been thirty minutes since the airplane had landed. *Maybe another hour to finish everything up*, he thought as he mounted the flight deck stairs that led up to the cockpit. Suddenly, he heard a noise and spun quickly to his left.

Two men dressed as civilians, cowering like feeble old women, were wedged against the corner bulkhead, both obviously scared shitless. *Ah! These must be the ones we need. The ones Qudos told me to make sure we took alive.*

"Who are you? Why are you here?" he asked in a sharply demanding tone, pointing his rifle from one to the other.

The man closest to him fearfully pointed at himself and managed to croak, "Sir, my name is Abdul Farooqi. And this is my assistant, Jamel Syed. We are both nuclear technicians."

Abdul knew he was a dead man. He had just watched this militant slit the throat of the medic as if he were no more than a sacrificial goat.

Mahmood moved to the side and gestured roughly at two of his fighters.

"Kaseem, Sarkis, take these two outside. Make sure they are treated as our honored guests and that no harm comes to them."

Kaseem and Sarkis moved carefully forward to escort the now two hopeful men outside. As they passed by Mahmood, he mockingly bowed his head. When his men and the technicians stepped onto the loading ramp, he turned back to the flight deck. *Now, time to collect our final guest.*

Chapter 10

DAY ONE, 0945 HOURS
NATIONAL SECURITY MEETING
THE PRESIDENTIAL PALACE
ISLAMABAD, PAKISTAN

"WHAT IN THE name of hell happened?" President Assif Chutto demanded, slamming his clenched fist so hard on the conference table that pens and pencils jumped into the air, glaring in turn at each attendee of the National Security Meeting.

President Chutto, a tall, well-set-up man in his late forties with prominent cheekbones, dark short hair, and full expressive mouth—characteristics of his Sindhi Tribal ancestry—was not a happy man. He was furious and pissed.

"I mean, what stupidity is this? How could something like this happen?" he shouted, almost spitting as he thrust his purpled face over the table. Then, in a softer voice laced with menace, he continued, "I want answers, and I want them now! How this happened and what we are doing to get the warheads back!"

The twelve members of the Security Council glanced awkwardly at one another, as children would have looked when scolded by their father. None wanting to speak. None wanting President Chutto's anger directed at themselves. Finally, after several moments of silence, Air Chief Marshal Anwar Khattack, the chairman of the Joint Chiefs of Staff, loudly cleared his throat.

"Sir," Marshal Khattack said in a low, scratchy voice abused by too many cigarettes, "as you know, it was decided last year to disperse our nuclear weapons due to the increased Taliban activity around our two main nuclear weapons storage depots. At Mushaf and Minhas Air Force—"

"Yes! Yes! I know that!" President Chutto shouted as he made a slashing motion with his arm, cutting the Marshal off in midsentence. "I was told the new facility at Samungli was much more secure! But what the hell happened this morning? How could we let the militants get their hands on two of our warheads?"

"Sir," Marshal Khattack calmly replied, taking a short, deep breath, "those two warheads were the first of twenty being repositioned to Samungli. We also felt that transporting the warheads by road would have been too dangerous given the terrain and distance. Too susceptible to ambush. So we decided to transport them by a C-130 aircraft which should have been less than a two hour flight, and reduced our exposure accordingly."

The marshal paused to gather his thoughts.

"Sir, it was also decided to have as low a profile as possible, with only one aircraft and a security detail of SSW soldiers onboard."

"But why were there no escorts? That makes absolutely no sense!"

"Sir, the transport cruises at around three hundred knots, much too slow for a jet fighter escort and too fast for helicopters. We therefore decided to send the aircraft unescorted, with contingency plans in place should there have been any problems. They could have diverted to Zhob about halfway between Mushaf and Samungli. And, as you know, sir, Zhob is the headquarters for the 29th Infantry Brigade. They could have provided more than ample security. Also, given the relatively short distance between Mushaf and Samungli, we could have had support troops and helicopters over any emergency landing site in less than ten minutes. We also had two Mi-171s on strip alert at Samungli, with a platoon of troops on standby, just for this eventuality."

Marshal Khattack briefly looked around the table, but no other member of the Security Council would meet his eyes, their heads downcast as they studied the surface of the table with rapt attention. The marshal sighed.

"Sir, I'm not trying to make any excuses. I take full responsibility for what happened."

"So . . . what happened?" President Chutto asked frankly.

"Sir, that we are still trying to figure out. The aircraft diverted from its flight plan and started to head southeast, but then it abruptly lost altitude and was lost from radar in the clutter of the mountains. The two helicopters on strip alert at Samungli were immediately dispatched to search east of the aircraft's last known heading, and were later joined by four more Mi-171s. The 29th Infantry Brigade at Zhob was also mobilized. We finally located the transport more than a hundred kilometers due west from where we thought it had gone down. In a very isolated, hard-to-find dry riverbed with steep mountains on both sides. Directly opposite from its last known heading and only two kilometers from the Afghan border. From what we can tell, sir, it landed under its own power and was then ambushed by Taliban militants, with all of its troops onboard killed. And, sir, what we didn't want to get out was that the soldiers, over thirty of them, had been beheaded."

"Beheaded?" President Chutto asked, shaken by the marshal's revelation. "This is the first I've heard of that! Why in Allah's name would they behead them?

"To make a point, sir," Marshal Khattack said firmly. "To let us know they will not give, nor receive, any quarter."

"But what of the warheads?"

"Sir, our preliminary findings show that the pilot, Squadron Commander MahMund, had to be in on the ambush. We had considered every contingency, but not that the mission commander would be on the side of the militants. The copilot was found dead, still strapped in his seat with a bullet in his head. MahMund must have killed him shortly after takeoff, and the commander's body was not found at the landing site. Neither were the two nuclear technicians who accompanied the warheads. From the tracks we found, it looks like a group of seventy to ninety militants was involved. Sir, that platoon didn't stand a chance. They were cut down as soon as they exited the aircraft. We could also tell the militants had mules to transport the weapons. I must tell you, they picked one of the best spots to have an ambush, and had probably crossed into Afghanistan well before our search parties even found the aircraft."

"General Pasha?" the president suddenly asked, his attention directed at a small, prim man with narrow features, pencil-thin mustache, and dark lifeless eyes. "What's the ISI been able to find out?"

Director General Umar Pasha, a lieutenant general in the Pakistan Army, was the current head of the Inter-Service Intelligence Bureau, the largest and most ruthless intelligence service in Pakistan. If anyone knew what was going on, the ISI would.

"Sir," Director General Pasha said softly, barely in a whisper, "we concur with the marshal's analysis. The weapons are now probably in Afghanistan under Taliban control. Most likely Qudos Mehsud. We also concur that the aircraft commander, Squadron Commander MahMund, was most probably a sleeper agent of the militants. Our preliminary findings show that MahMund lost his parents to an American Predator strike just a few months ago. It was all a ghastly mistake; the militants had already left the town. But given his parents were killed by an American missile, that would have been more than enough motive for him to join the Taliban."

"Mr. President," Marshal Khattack said, once again taking the floor. "There is some small consolation here. Even though they have the warheads, they are useless to them. Except for maybe as dirty bombs."

"And why is that?" President Chutto asked, hopeful but confused with what Khattack had just said.

"The reason, sir, is that each of those weapons requires a PAL code in order to be armed. A PAL code, which stands for Permissible Action Link, sir, is a security device that has been incorporated into all of our newer weapons of this type. Its purpose to prevent any unauthorized arming of the warheads. A PAL code is an eight-digit alphanumeric code that has to be electronically downloaded into each weapon. Think of it as a combination lock, sir, needed to activate the weapon's internal systems, and without the PAL codes the weapons cannot be armed. And if the wrong code is entered, safety locks within the warhead automatically shut down the bomb's arming devices, making them useless until the arming links can be reactivated. And the only person authorized to release those codes is yourself."

President Chutto thought for a moment.

"So . . . what you're telling me is, there is no way these weapons can be armed without their PAL codes? Is that correct?"

"Yes, sir, that is correct. But that would not keep the militants from trying to use the warheads as dirty bombs. For example, rigging them with explosives to try and breach their outer shell casings. To spread radioactivity within a population center," the marshal hastily added.

"Given the alternative," Chutto said visibly relieved, a smile cracking his face the first time that morning, "that's much better than having armed nuclear weapons in the hands of the Taliban. Now, what are we doing to get them back?"

"Sir," Director General Pasha interjected, "that is going to be very difficult, I'm afraid to say. Number one, we cannot go to the Afghan government; their government is filled with Taliban sympathizers, as is ours, as you well know. Anything said to the Afghans would most certainly be conveyed to those who stole the weapons. Probably within a day or so. Number two, we have to assume the militants will try to hide the weapons in their tribal areas where they are strongest. Once they are lost in those mountains, our chances of recovering the weapons will be very low."

"Then what are we doing to get them back?"

President Chutto didn't want to hear that the weapons may not be recovered.

"Sir, I think Marshal Khattack can better answer that question," the director said with a nod at the chairman.

"Well?" President Chutto pointedly asked, his eyes locked on those of the chairman of the Joint Chiefs of Staff.

"Mr. President, if you would please bear with me a moment."

The marshal reached down and pulled out a thick wad of papers from his briefcase. With the documents placed on the table, he donned a pair of wire-rimmed reading glasses and rustled through the thick sheaf of papers. When he finally found what he wanted he grunted.

"Sir, right now we have two squadrons of Mi-171s totaling twenty-four aircraft patrolling the most likely escape routes of the militants. Onboard each helicopter is one squad of SSW troops fully combat-loaded. The 29th Infantry Brigade has also been mobilized from their base at Zhob and, as we speak, are being airlifted to cover the most likely entry points into the tribal areas. We have also launched our own drone surveillance aircraft and will keep them up twenty-four hours a day. Currently, we have thirteen drones airborne and will rotate them as needed."

The marshal turned to Director General Pasha.

"Director? Do you have anything you want to add?"

The director general looked at President Chutto.

"Mr. President, we are now activating our intelligence resources within the Taliban. Although I can't go into the specifics here, we do have deep-cover agents within the ranks of the militants. The one problem we do have is communications. It is not as if we can get on a radio or a phone to call them. Most of our agents are in the mountains where radio and cellular communications is almost impossible. Sir, we will receive intelligence on the militants, but it will take time. Normally, communications take place when various units of the Taliban are rotated into more populated areas. Once that happens, we will get more information, sir."

Director General Pasha closed his reference materials.

"Mr. President, we will get a possible location on the weapons, but for now we need to be patient."

"All right, then. Please keep me advised. And when the weapons are located, I want to know immediately! Regardless of the time! Is that understood?" President Chutto ordered.

"Yes, sir," they both said.

Chapter 11

DAY ONE, 0845 HOURS
THE OVAL OFFICE
WASHINGTON, D.C.

PRESIDENT GARRETT TAYLOR, the former governor of Colorado and third youngest president of the United States at the age of forty-four—only Theodore Roosevelt and John F. Kennedy having been younger—sat slumped in his high-backed, well-broken-in black leather judges chair, his back to the desk with his brown ostrich-skinned cowboy boots resting comfortably on the windowsill. Taylor stared absently outside the Oval Office window while he patiently waited for Steven Clarke, his Director of National Security; General Marion Gray, United State Marine Corps and the current chairman of the Joint Chiefs of Staff; and Allen Jefferson, the director of the CIA, to arrive.

An early riser, two hours previously he had been in the White House gym thirty minutes into his daily workout, a workout that normally consisted of twenty minutes on the treadmill and forty minutes on the various weight machines. But in the middle of his workout, Jason Tanner—the head of his Secret Service security detail and who willingly doubled as his weight-lifting spotter—handed him the handset of a flashing red phone affixed to the south wall of the gym.

President Taylor had just completed his first set of ten reps on the bench press when he inwardly flinched at the obnoxious buzzing tone of the phone, thinking more than a few unkind thoughts of the person who had forwarded the call, his staff well aware that he hated to be disturbed during his morning workouts. They knew he considered his time in the gym as sacrosanct, his own personal time away from the grind of his White House duties. He had also made it quite clear that he was only to be disturbed in the event that Chinese or Russian tanks were on their way down Pennsylvania Avenue with the intention of assaulting the White House. A former captain in the United States Marine Corps and infantry company commander in his more youthful days, he had seen more than his fair share of combat in Iraq and was a firm believer in physical conditioning.

It's funny, he often thought, *how one's life took different turns.* He had never planned on being the president of the United States, not like most of the other politicians in Washington whose sole ambition was to claw their way to the top of the heap. It had just happened. But during his second term as governor, and in a surprise move by his party during a tumultuous, brokered convention, he had been nominated to head his party's presidential ticket.

A dark horse candidate from the get-go, he had never expected to win, his campaign focused on national security with a hard-core view toward Islamic terrorism. Initially far behind the polls to the incumbent who, as in his previous election, had promised everything to everyone and had the full support of the unions, his sober view and no-nonsense approach to the Islamic threat had crashed to the forefront of the campaign just two months prior to the election. Islamic militants, having smuggled chemical weapons into the United States, had perpetrated simultaneous terrorist attacks on the citizens of Los Angeles and Atlanta.

Disturbingly reminiscent of 9/11, over four hundred American citizens had lost their lives, and the major news networks—as usual—had been more than willing to provide 24/7 Blitz Krieg coverage that showcased their horrific deaths. If the media had known what they were doing, they wouldn't have provided the nonstop coverage that they did. But they had, and he had won in a landslide.

The phone call had been from Director Allen Jefferson who had told him in no uncertain terms that the Pakistan Taliban had managed to hijack two, one-hundred-kiloton nuclear warheads from the Pakistan Air Force.

Not thirty seconds later he had received a second call with the same information from Steven Clarke. His response to both individuals was uncharacteristically blunt—telling them to meet him in the Oval Office at 0900 hours. He had also directed Steven Clarke to contact General Marion Gray to have him also attend.

After the calls, President Taylor hoisted himself out from under the bench-press machine and gestured resignedly at Jason that their session was at an end. As he looked about the gym, he had unconsciously wrapped his workout towel around his broad muscled shoulders—the ends of the towel grasped in calloused hands—then exhaled a slow, inaudible breath as he made his way down to the second floor residential apartments to take a shower and dress for the day. He had a feeling that today was going to be a shitty day.

Four feet to his rear, Jason Tanner bent his head toward his lapel and announced, "Shooter's on his way to the second floor."

Chapter 12

DAY ONE, 0859 HOURS
THE OVAL OFFICE

"MR. PRESIDENT?" KAREN Dodds said over the intercom. "General Gray, Director Jefferson, and Steven Clarke are here for their nine o'clock appointment."

Karen Dodds, a stout, formidable woman of seventy-two years with grayed frizzy hair pulled back into a tight bun, had been with the president ever since he'd first run for the Colorado state legislature. Standing all of five-foot-two on a good day, she considered herself the "Keeper of the Portal" and was ferociously loyal to her president.

"Thanks, Karen. Please send them in."

President Garrett Taylor quickly unfolded his legs from the window ledge and stood up, buttoning his suit coat as he made his way around the desk toward the Oval Office door, but before he got there it opened and General Gray, Allen Jefferson, and Steven Clarke grimly filed into the room.

"Good morning, Mr. President," they said almost in unison.

"Good morning," President Taylor responded.

Taylor smiled and walked up to General Gray, his hand extended.

"General, it's good to see you. I'm glad you were around for today's meeting."

"Thank you, sir," General Gray said in his typical baritone voice, shaking the president's hand.

Gray, when you thought of a Marine Corps General, was exactly what you would have imagined, his ramrod posture looking as if he were on the parade deck at the original Marine Corps barracks located at 8th & I Streets in Washington, D.C. Obviously fit and hard as a rock, he was of medium height with a barreled chest and short-cropped gray hair shorn so close to his head you could see the freckles on his deeply tanned scalp. And his broad face, with just a hint of jowls, was lined like the arroyos of the Grand Canyon; a living testament to the many life and death decisions he had been forced to make over his thirty-odd-year military career. The president was well aware that General Gray was one individual you definitely wanted in your corner when the going got tough.

President Taylor turned to his director of the CIA, Allen Jefferson, and shook his hand. In stark contrast to General Gray, Director Jefferson was tall, about six-foot-three, and had a thin whipcord body with skin blacker than the ace of spades; his head topped off with short, black, wiry hair shot through with wisps of gray. The sixty-four-year-old director, with sleepy brown eyes and a detached contemplative manner, looked more like the proverbial absentminded professor of some small, southern, rural college, rather than the head of the world's largest and most professional intelligence organization.

Today the director was dressed, as usual, in a nondescript baggy dark suit he'd probably bought off the rack at Sears, a white shirt with frayed collars, and a paisley bow tie that was forever out of fashion. He also spoke slowly and deliberately with the thick southern accent characteristic of his home state of Alabama. When he said the word "sir" it came out as "suh", and he consciously had to make the effort never to say the word "ya'll".

The majority of people when they first met the director thought he was a tad slow mentally—mostly due to his deliberative nature when he answered questions and his slow, methodical speech patterns— and erroneously dismissed him as someone whose success had been based on race or affirmative action, and was therefore not a person to be taken seriously. Those people—more often than not—paid an enormous price later on down the road for their mistaken belief, unaware that Director Jefferson concealed a highly-trained, critically objective mind that had been well-polished at Dartmouth University during his undergraduate years, and then sharpened to a razor's edge when he had completed his doctoral studies in International Affairs at Georgetown University. In addition, in his younger days, the director had been awarded the CIA's Intelligence Star—the CIA's second highest award for valor—which confirmed that warriors came in all sorts of different packages. Taylor knew that Allen Jefferson, just like General Gray, was a good man to have on your team.

President Taylor nodded at Steven Clarke, his longtime friend and confidant from Colorado, who was dressed in his usual Brooks Brothers suit of dark navy wool accented with muted gray stripes, crisp white linen shirt with French cuffs, and Princeton school tie. Fair-skinned at thirty-eight years of age, with a lithely muscular frame and sharp angular features to his face, Steven had always provoked the interest on the part of the fairer sex, but given his duties at the White House, he rarely had the time to reciprocate.

President Taylor motioned for everyone to take a seat on the plush couches centered in the middle of the Oval Office, then selected for himself one of two, blue- and white-striped wingback chairs set at the ends of the couches, their backs placed toward the fireplace.

As everyone got situated and pulled notebooks from their briefcases, Taylor pointed at a sterling silver coffee service that sat on the coffee table.

"Gentlemen, if you'd like some coffee, please help yourselves."

"Thank you, sir," Clarke said, pouring himself a cup, then he glanced at Jefferson and Gray.

"Yes, thank you, Steven. Don't mind if I do," Director Jefferson said, accepting a cup from the security director.

"Not for me, Steven," General Gray said with a firm shake of his head. "I've been drinking that stuff since 0500 this morning. I'm wired enough as it is, but thanks just the same."

After the coffee had been served, Taylor turned to Director Jefferson.

"Okay, Allen. Take it from the top and tell us what's going on."

President Taylor leaned back and crossed his legs to get comfortable, then rested his elbows on the chair's armrests with his fingers steepled in front of his chin, totally focused on what the director had to say.

"Well, suh," Jefferson began, taking a sip of coffee while looking down at his notes, "around three this mornin' we received a communiqué from John Bradsen, our chief of station in Islamabad. Must've been around one in the afternoon his time given the ten hour time difference. Anyways, suh, the Pakistanis were repositionin' two of their nuclear warheads to a new storage facility located at Samungli Air Force Base. That's one of their larger Air Force bases located in the southern part of their country, down in their Baluchistan province. And, just to let you know, suh, we already knew they was goin' to do this. The two warheads were being transported by a C-130 aircraft out of their other Air Force Base near . . ."

The director paused to consult his notes to make sure of the city he was going to name.

"Mushaf, about two hundred kilometers south of Islamabad. Mushaf bein' one of their main nuclear weapons storage depots. In any event, suh, from what Bradsen could tell us, it seems the aircraft diverted to a landin' site very close to the Afghan border where it was ambushed by Taliban militants and the warheads taken."

President Taylor still found it hard to believe that the Taliban had managed to hijack two nuclear warheads and could now be considered a nuclear power. He knew the Pakistan military had to be shitting their pants right about now.

"Okay, Allen. You said two weapons were taken, is that correct?"

"Yes, suh, that's correct," Director Jefferson stated flatly. "Two, one-hundred-kiloton nuclear warheads. These weapons, again accordin' to Bradsen, are of the type used by their F-16s for aerial delivery."

"Excuse me, Allen," Taylor interrupted, clearly upset with the situation. "General? What are we looking at here? Just how powerful are these warheads?"

"Well, sir," General Gray responded firmly, "I took the time to bone up on that before coming over here, thinking you would ask. So, just to put things in perspective, a one-hundred-kiloton warhead is roughly ten times the size of the bombs we dropped on Hiroshima and Nagasaki. Although not considered large by today's standards, given we still have warheads in the multi-megaton range, they're powerful enough if detonated in an urban center."

"Okay, General," President Taylor said with an impatient come-on gesture. He needed to know the facts. "Give me the bad news. What would be the effect on a city if detonated?"

"Well, sir, it really depends on the climate conditions at the time. Wind speed, humidity, things like that. And whether the device was detonated as an air or a ground burst. But seeing as the Taliban doesn't have an air force, let's assume a ground burst. So, in general terms, the fireball would completely vaporize anything within roughly two miles from ground zero. In addition, the over pressure, or shock wave from the blast, would destroy almost any type of building within approximately five miles of its detonation. But of more concern," Gray continued, "is the radiation and fallout. People within fifty square miles of the detonation site would most likely receive a fatal dose of over five hundred rems of radiation, killing them all off in a week. And within forty-eight hours, depending on the winds, this area could expand to over one hundred square miles.

"Thermal radiation, or heat from the blast, could initially reach out to approximately eight miles. And when I talk about thermal radiation, sir, I mean anything flammable within eight miles would most likely be incinerated. Basically, that's what we could look forward to if they managed to detonate only *one* of those nukes, not two," he concluded gravely.

"Thank you, General," Taylor said, completely taken aback by Gray's explanation. From his own military experience in the Marine Corps, he had known in general terms the effects of a nuclear explosion, but not the specifics as laid out by General Gray. He nodded at Director Jefferson to continue.

"Thank you, suh. The best intel we have, accordin' to our sources in the Pakistan military, is that the weapons are now makin' their way north into their tribal areas. They also feel pretty damned sure they were taken by the followers of Qudos Mehsud, the warlord of the Pakistan Tehrik-e-taliban. And, Mr. President, this Qudos character is the same sumbitch that's sworn revenge on our country. Now more so since we snuffed out his old buddy Osama bin Laden. He's stated numerous times that his greatest goal in life is to attack the United States, and now, with these nukes, he's got the means to do just that."

"Well, shit!" President Taylor muttered under his breath. "This is all we need. What are the Pakistanis doing about it?"

"Again," Director Jefferson calmly continued, "from what our sources tell us, the Pakistanis, excuse my French, suh, are shittin' a brick as we speak, and have a full-court press laid on. They're busy pourin' troops into those mountains, tryin' to shut off the various routes into their northern tribal areas. But that's gonna be tough. This is where the Taliban are strongest and, just last year, after the Pakistan Army got their asses kicked big time by the Taliban militants, they basically gave 'em these areas. But, excuse my French again, suh, I think the Pakistanis are just pissin' in the wind. Walkin' around with their dicks in their hands. There's just no way they can plug up all those routes into their tribal areas. It's just way too mountainous with way too many secret trails. The Pakistanis would have to be extremely lucky to locate the warheads, much less recover 'em."

Director Jefferson sighed and removed his reading glasses.

"The other problem they have, as you well know, is their own government is riddled like a termite mound with Taliban sympathizers, with a lot of their own folks on the side of the militants. That's one of the reasons it was so hard for us to take out bin Laden. Every time we tried to put together a joint operation to try and kill that sumbitch, bin Laden's supporters in the Pakistan government and military, and sympathizers within the Afghan government for that matter, tipped him off."

"Speaking of Afghanistan, Allen, how do we know the weapons just won't stay there?" President Taylor asked hopefully. "I mean, how sure are we it was the Taliban that took the weapons?"

"Suh, our sources are pretty damned reliable. On a scale of one to ten, we're talkin' about a fifteen heah. From what we've heard, the pilot of the aircraft transportin' the warheads had to be in on the hijackin'. Bradsen found out that he was a Squadron Commander, name of MahMund, and highly thought of in their Air Force. But the fact that it looks like he was in on it, and given the evidence at the ambush site, it couldn't have been anyone other than the Taliban and Qudos Mehsud. We're more than sure of that."

"Mr. President," Steven Clarke cut in, "whether Pakistan or Afghanistan, we've got to figure out a way to either destroy those weapons or mount an operation to get them back. I have zero confidence in the Pakistanis. And if they end up being smuggled into the States, which we all know they'll try to do, we've got a real big problem on our hands. We also can't rule out the possibility that they'll try to use them on one of our Afghan bases."

President Taylor looked thoughtfully at his security director, and then back at General Gray.

"General, give me your thoughts, please."

"Well, sir," General Gray began, his shoulders hunched forward on the couch, "I agree with Steven. I think we need to rely on our own resources to try and neutralize those warheads. And just to let you know, I thought about this pretty damned hard on the way over here. What I do know is that we're going to have the same problems we have now. That is, if we do try to mount an operation to get them back, we've got to keep it to ourselves if there's going to be any chance of success. Same thing as what happened with bin Laden. What I mean by that is, we gotta keep the Pakistanis in the dark, just like the director said."

With a nod at Jefferson, the general continued.

"Once the Pakistanis know what we're gonna do, the Taliban will know. Now, even assuming we can locate the warheads—and that's a big assumption, sir—we'd most likely need to mount any operation from one of our Afghan bases. The only problem is, it would be almost impossible to keep that kind of an operation secret."

General Gray, his left knee beginning to ache from an old shrapnel wound from Beirut, shifted his body to the right to try and relieve the pressure on it.

"We also have to assume the Taliban are going to have a large force protecting those nukes. Sir, as far as I see it, we've got four options, none of them very good. Number one," he said, holding up his index finger, "is that we do nothing and rely on the Pakistanis to recover their own warheads."

At that statement, President Taylor's steel-blue eyes narrowed and took on a flat, flinty look as he quickly shook his head in the negative.

"That isn't an option, General. We will not sit here and wait for those nukes to show up on our own shores, or be used in an attack on one of our Afghan bases. And we absolutely can't rely on the Pakistanis to get them back. Allen? What do you think?"

"Suh, I agree. That's not an option," Director Jefferson said slowly.

"Mr. President," General Gray interrupted, his hands thrown up as if in surrender, "you're preaching to the choir, sir. I know that isn't a viable option, but it had to be put on the table. I want you to know I fully agree that we can't rely on the Pakistanis to get those nukes back. So . . . let's deep six that one and go on to option two."

The general held up a second finger.

"Option two is that we insert a large force into the area. Not only to assault the Taliban positions, but to try and cut off any escape routes they may use. And, by a large force, sir, I'm talking divisional strength, if not larger, given the amount of ground that needs to be covered. The only problem with that scenario is the assault force would need to go in by chopper. No other way for them to do it given the terrain. That area would be like trying to insert a combat force into the foothills of the Rocky Mountains, and most likely there wouldn't be any landing zones (LZs) close enough to the gomers' positions. So the choppers would need to land some distance away, forcing our troops to march in on foot. Sir, I just don't see that happening. What we'd be requiring them to do is to conduct an uphill assault into mountains that the Taliban know like the backs of their hands. The casualties on our part could be enormous, and that would just give the gomers more time to take off with the nukes. In addition, how could we be sure that all of their escape routes were closed down? There must be a thousand ways out of there for those guys. This would require another large force to try and isolate the battle area. What we're talking about, sir, is a very large area to try and cordon off, and we still wouldn't know if all of the escape routes were covered.

"And this option, you know as well as I do, wouldn't set well with the Pakistan military, much less their government. I can almost guarantee they would intervene militarily. Most likely they would shoot first and ask questions later. You know, protecting their sacred sovereignty or some such excuse, particularly since we accidentally took out twenty-four of their border guards last year with one of our Predators. You know as well as I do that our relations with the Pakistanis are tense. So, to avoid that situation, we'd have to let 'em know we're coming. Maybe not until the last minute, but they'd need to know."

"General, I'm afraid you're right," President Taylor said with a quick nod of agreement. "That would definitely cause a problem with the Pakistanis. And to avoid the possibility of getting into a shooting situation with their military, they would have to know what the hell we're doing. So . . . we're back to square one. Please continue," he said, becoming more than a little frustrated.

"Thank you, sir. Option three," General Gray continued, holding up a third finger, "would be to insert a Special Forces A team, Navy SEAL, or a Delta team, or teams for that matter, into the area once we have a better handle on where the nukes are hidden. Now, in this case, we could probably do that without letting the Pakistanis know what we're up to. But again, their insert would need to be by chopper. There's no way they could do a high altitude jump into that kind of terrain. And, once again, their LZ would most likely be quite some ways from where they needed to go, forcing them to march in on foot. I can almost guarantee the gomers would sure as hell know that choppers had come in, and that means they would know we had troops on the ground. They would turn over every goddamned rock in those mountains trying to find 'em. So, *if* their infiltration was successful, and *if* they avoided detection, and *if* they were able to find the nukes, and *if* they could destroy them in place—that's four big *if*'s Mr. President—how do we get 'em back out? In thinking this scenario through, this option looks more and more like a suicide mission to me. The odds of them making it out on foot would be almost nil, and they most likely couldn't be extracted by chopper. The risk to the choppers would be too great. We all know the gomers have Russian and American handheld antiaircraft missiles, in addition to Russian Quad 23mm antiaircraft guns. Their only option would be to try and exfiltrate out of the area with a whole bunch of pissed-off ragheads chasing them back to their extraction point."

"Now, now, General," President Taylor said, a smile on his face for the first time that morning. "Hasn't anyone told you that *raghead* is a politically incorrect thing to say?"

General Gray smiled and chuckled, then shook his head.

"Yes, sir. Now that you mention it, I guess I have heard it's politically incorrect to call a raghead a raghead."

Once the brief levity had passed, the general continued.

"But seriously, sir, getting back to the option of inserting smaller teams into the area, there's just too many *if*'s for that kind of an operation."

With that last statement General Gray began to massage his knee. The damned thing was really beginning to hurt.

"So, Mr. President, that leaves us with option four."

"And that is?" Taylor softly asked. He already had a pretty good idea where the general was going with this.

"Well, sir, you're not gonna like this," General Gray cautioned as he inhaled audibly. He already knew the reaction he was about to receive. "Once we have a pretty good idea where the nukes are located, the fourth option would be to deliver a low-yield, tactical nuclear weapon into the area. Preferably by cruise missile or a B-2, sir."

Everyone, the president included, sat silent for many moments, not wanting to look at one another. Not wanting to contemplate the political repercussions of what the general had just proposed.

President Taylor gathered himself as if he were about to consider what the general had just said, but then he exploded, uncharacteristically losing his cool.

"Well, hell! All we've managed to do here is paint ourselves into a goddamned corner! What appears to be the only viable option is to nuke a country, a supposed ally no less, and poison a few hundred square miles of their country! And then kill off who knows how many civilians along with the militants, just hoping the warheads are destroyed! Then try to justify our actions to the rest of the world!"

President Taylor fumed as he tried to think through the various scenarios as laid out by General Gray. Not seeing a way out, he broke through his maze of thoughts. "Allen?"

"Mr. President," Director Jefferson said as forcefully as he could. "As outlined by General Gray, either we do nothin' and hope the Pakistanis recover the weapons—which we all know is probably wishful thinkin'—or we invade an ally with thousands of troops and incur god only knows how many unknown number of casualties. All without any guarantees, of course, of recoverin' or even destroyin' the weapons. Or we send in smaller teams in what amounts to be suicide missions, again without any guarantees of success. Or, god forbid, we attack a supposed ally's territory with a nuclear weapon and incinerate the bastards, earnin' the wrath and scorn of the rest of the world."

Jefferson sighed and pulled a handkerchief from his suit pocket, then began to polish his reading glasses. He knew it was a no-win proposition at this point.

"And I can almost guarantee," the director continued, speaking down at his glasses rather than looking at President Taylor, "if we nuke the Pakistanis, the opposition party will sharpen their knives and introduce a bill for your immediate impeachment. Same thing if we send in a whole bunch of troops."

President Taylor leaned back and contemplated Allen's statement. He could tell that his director was upset. Jefferson, for the most part, was extremely good at concealing his innermost feelings, and had one of the best "Poker Faces" he'd ever seen. But he had picked up on one unconscious mannerism of the director. Whenever he was unsure or doubtful in a high-risk situation—which didn't occur very often—he had a habit of taking off his glasses, pulling out a handkerchief, and then polishing the hell out of them. He had been amused at first when he'd discovered this idiosyncrasy on the part of his director, but he was not amused now. He took very seriously what Allen had to say.

"Mr. President," Steven Clarke said suddenly, setting down his coffee.

Taylor, not having heard Steven, was still thinking through their various options. *If they did nothing they would run the risk—a high risk—of having the Taliban possibly smuggling one, or both of those warheads into the United States. Or attack one of their bases in Afghanistan.* He knew they couldn't implement the nuclear option, that was unthinkable. They would either have to rely on the Pakistanis and lose all control, or invade with thousands of troops, or send in smaller teams and hope for the best. Given his experience in the Marine Corps, he knew the probability of a FUBAR occurring was greater than the sun rising in the east—FUBAR being a well-used military acronym that meant "Fucked-Up Beyond All Recognition". *But what other options do we have?* Their best option, as far as he could see it, was to sacrifice as many smaller teams that it took. To send them in one after another until, hopefully, they found the nukes.

"Mr. President," Clarke said again, more forcefully this time, "I just had another thought. It may sound a little crazy and way out there in left field, but from what the general just said, the main problem seems to be getting someone on-site without being detected."

Steven Clarke looked at General Gray.

"Is that a correct statement, General?"

"Yes, sir, that's the problem," General Gray said. "Once the weapons are located, we have to have folks on the ground to verify the warheads are actually where we think they are, even if we had intel as to their location and tried to use cruise missiles or B-2s to take 'em out. But there's a couple of problems with that: number one, we wouldn't know if the warheads were destroyed or had been moved; and number two, missiles or bombs may not be able to get at their location. I would think the gomers would have them buried pretty goddamned deep in some cave or something just for that eventuality. They're not stupid, gentlemen. I doubt if they would keep 'em above ground where we could get at 'em."

"But just for the sake of argument," Clarke pressed, "what if we could get a team on-site, let's say, undetected, with their function being more of spotters. And assuming they can pinpoint the nukes, they could call in either laser-guided bombs or missiles onto the site. At that point I would think our chances of getting the warheads goes up. Would that be a correct statement, General?"

"Steven, I would say our chances would be extremely good at that point in being able to take out the warheads," General Gray agreed, wondering where the hell this conversation was going. *Hadn't he already pointed out the problems of trying to get a team in there? Much less getting them out?*

"And, once again," Clarke continued, "a spotter team could verify the weapons were actually there, I mean prior to any attack."

Clarke turned from General Gray and caught his commander in chief's eye.

"Sir, I think there's a fifth option we haven't considered. One that could actually put one or more of our people on the ground without detection. And, better yet, have the means of getting them out without their having to exfiltrate the area. Like I said, it's a long shot, Mr. President, way out there in left field, but one I think we should take a very close look at."

"And what option's that, Steven?"

President Taylor didn't have the foggiest idea of what Steven was driving at, but he did see the confidence in his security director's face.

"Sir, even though experimental at this stage, do you remember the briefing we had a few months ago from Dr. Samantha Johnson? Regarding Project Gabriel?"

Taylor searched his memory banks for a couple of seconds, and then he remembered. He saw exactly where Steven was going. *Damn it, he's right! There could be a fifth option! It would be a long shot, and probably not doable, but an option nonetheless. An option that did away with all of the problems outlined by General Gray. Much better than sending in Special Ops teams to be served up as sacrificial lambs to the Taliban.*

"Mr. President," Director Jefferson said, putting away his handkerchief and donning his glasses, "I see exactly where Steven's goin' and I agree with him. Although experimental, it sure would solve a lot of the issues regardin' takin' out those warheads. Maybe it's time we brought the general up-to-date, so to speak."

Allen Jefferson had also been present at Dr. Johnson's briefing.

General Gray—totally confused—glanced at the director, and then back at Steven. He had no idea in hell what they were talking about. With a quick look back at the president, he could tell that Taylor was seriously thinking through whatever they were talking about.

"Mr. President," he said, knowing he was way out of the loop on this one. "I have absolutely no idea what Director Jefferson and Mr. Clarke are talking about. What briefing? And how could it get around the problems of trying to take out the nukes?"

Before answering, President Taylor continued to think through Steven's scenario, liking the idea better and better. Besides, it was the only viable option they had at this point.

"Steven, I think you're right. That's a hell of an option, and one I think we should take a very close look at. And I agree with Allen; I think it's about time we brought the general up-to-date on Project Gabriel."

President Taylor caught General Gray's eye.

"General, what you're about to hear is classified 'Top Secret Presidential–Gabriel'. There are very few of us here in Washington or, for that matter, anyone else in the United States who knows any of the particulars. But I think now's the time to bring you onboard with a few select members of your staff that you designate."

Taylor felt more optimistic than he had all day.

"Steven, why don't you go ahead and tell the general what our mad scientists have been up to."

"Yes, sir," Clarke answered with a smile. He knew if they utilized Project Gabriel, General Gray would have had to be made privy anyway, even if from a logistical standpoint. Steven began to brief the general on one of the United States' most closely guarded secrets.

Ten minutes later, after having asked numerous questions, General Gray sat there speechless, fervently wanting to believe what he'd just been told. Finally, when the ramifications hit him full-bore, the only thing he could bellow was, "Well, I'll be goddamned!"

"Well, General?" President Taylor said, smiling as he unknowingly slapped General Gray smack-dab on his throbbing knee. "That seems to be the understatement of the century!"

As far as Taylor was concerned he was all in. Totally convinced that Gabriel was the only way to go.

"Okay, Steven. If we're going to do this, what do we need to do now?"

Clarke thought for a moment.

"Well, sir, just shooting from the hip; we need to get an update on Gabriel, identify the team members to go on-site, conduct training, and also get a handle on where those nukes are stashed. Allen? Got any ideas who the team members ought to be?"

"Yes, suh, as a matter-of-fact I do," Director Jefferson stated flatly. "Our best Special Ops team is now in Afghanistan. They've been there for the last several months searchin' for bin Laden's replacement, and in their spare time takin' out the upper echelons of the al-Qaeda and Taliban leadership whenever we find 'em. These boys I'm talkin about know the culture, know the terrain, speak several dialects of the local languages, and got a real hard-on for the militants. I gotta admit, they've sure made a reputation for themselves over there."

"Allen?" General Gray interrupted, now fully onboard with this fifth option and Project Gabriel. "I think I know this team. You're not talking about Hearthstone, are you?"

"Yes, suh, I surely am."

"Well, shit! Then god help those Islamic ragheads!" General Gray said with a gleam in his eye. He could tell that President Taylor wasn't familiar with the name Hearthstone.

"You see, sir, we provide logistical support to Hearthstone. These guys are major players and a terrorist's worst nightmare. Hell, they even scare the crap out of our guys that have to work with them. These guys are ruthless, dedicated, and I don't know of any mission they haven't completed successfully once they've accepted the assignment. To put it bluntly, sir, just picture a pack of pissed-off Pitbulls with their dicks all tied to a leash. Once you point 'em at the bad guys and let go of the leash, there's just no stopping them."

President Taylor sat back and savored what the general had just said. He couldn't help but chuckle at his colorful description. All he could now envision was walking a pack of pissed-off Pitbulls down a dirt road with their dicks all tied to a leash, jerking him along as they strained with all their might to get loose.

"Allen?" Taylor asked, still smiling. "These sound like the guys we need. Any problem getting them back Stateside?"

"No, suh, no problem a'tall. I do know they're out in the field, but we can get 'em back here pretty damned quick. May take a couple of days or so, but no problem, suh."

"All right, then! Allen? I want you to spearhead this operation. Coordinate with General Gray in getting Hearthstone back Stateside as soon as you can. See if they'll take on this assignment. And I want both of you working full-time on trying to locate those warheads."

"Yes, sir," General Gray said.

"Yes, suh," Director Jefferson replied.

"And, Steven?"

"Yes, sir?"

"I want you to work with Allen to make sure that Gabriel's up-to-speed."

"Yes, sir," Clarke said.

"Allen? Any problem with Steven coordinating the training of Hearthstone with Gabriel?"

"No, suh, not a'tall. Glad to have 'em onboard, Mr. President."

Chapter 13

DAY FOUR, 2118 HOURS
ANDREWS AIR FORCE BASE
WASHINGTON, D.C.

LIGHTENING FLICKERED CRAZILY in the distance, splitting the turbulent sky with jagged streaks of brilliance while thunder rumbled over the base. Low-slung black clouds, whipped and churned as if in a sea of empty space, blew past the field at no more than pattern altitude. With the brief but violent downpour almost over, a thick sheen of wetness blanketed the tarmac with its passing, the reflections of runway lights glistening starkly in the evening.

The mammoth C-17 Globemaster slowly emerged from the dark as if an apparition from Jurassic Park, then pulled off the active runway One-Nine Right onto taxiway Charlie and stopped in place. After close to seven thousand miles flying distance, three en route midair refuelings, and twelve hours total flight time, both aircrews who manned the aircraft were exhausted, not to mention their having to fight the turbulence and winds for the past three hours prior to landing.

The pilot tiredly keyed his radio.

"Andrews Ground, Astra Zero-Seven clear of the active. Request taxi to Hangar Six."

"Astra Zero-Seven, Andrews Ground," the tower responded immediately. "Taxi to Hangar Six via Charlie and Whiskey."

"Roger that, Ground. Taxi to Hangar Six via Charlie and Whiskey."

"Read back is correct, Astra Zero-Seven," the ground controller acknowledged.

The pilot nudged all four throttles forward, but the giant aircraft—as if too tired to continue its journey—just shuddered in place, refusing to budge as huge sheets of rainwater kicked up by its massive engines screamed with hurricane force toward its rear. Then finally, slowly and reluctantly, the behemoth began to move as it made its way down the pitch-black taxiway.

At no more than a fast walk, the Globemaster proceeded the short distance down taxiway Charlie to where it intersected taxiway Whiskey. At the junction, the pilot made a shallow turn onto Whiskey and made his way directly toward Hangar Six no more than three hundred yards to their front. As he peered through the cockpit's rain-splotched windscreen, the pilot saw several black Chevrolet Suburbans and a large cargo van parked adjacent to the hangar's open door.

"Commander Stoneman?" the pilot called over the intercom.

After several seconds of silence, Lieutenant Commander Jake Stoneman responded from the cargo bay.

"Yes, Major?"

"Just thought you'd like to know. Looks like your greeting party's already here. I can see a couple of Suburbans and a cargo van parked next to the hangar."

"Thanks for the heads-up, Major."

Jake turned to his team and shouted over the din of engine noise.

"Okay, everyone! Listen up! Looks like our greeting party's already here. Don't know who it is, but make sure you got all your gear together. Once we stop I'll find out what's going on. Brett?" he said, motioning for his second in command, Lieutenant (j.g.) Brett Thompson, to join him. "Go ahead and start unlashing the gear, but keep everyone onboard until I find out what's what. Once I know I'll fill everybody in. Okay?"

"You got it, Skipper," Lieutenant Thompson said.

When the aircraft lumbered to a stop in front of Hangar Six, the pilots pulled back the throttles to begin their shutdown procedures. While the engines slowly spooled down, the crew chief unlatched the left-side crew door and lowered it to the ground, its built-in steps extended to the tarmac. Once in place, he stood aside as Jake nimbly made his way out of the aircraft.

Standing briefly on the rain-soaked parking ramp, with his field coat pulled tight around his midsection while the wind whipped across the field, Jake looked toward his front. He could see the Suburbans parked to the right of the hangar not sixty feet from the aircraft. He was also surprised to see Allen Jefferson, the Head Honcho of the CIA himself, planted firmly in front of the lead vehicle; the director wearing a long black raincoat while he waited patiently in the blustery weather.

With his chin tucked into his neck, Jake jogged across the rain-swept field with a large grin on his face, greeting the director with his hand outstretched.

"Good evening, sir! Good to see ya again! Didn't know you'd be the one meeting us tonight! So tell me, what's so goddamned important to drag us back from the sandpile in such a hurry? And for you to meet us in this god-awful weather?" he shouted over the roar of the storm.

Allen Jefferson shook Jake's hand and smiled at the Hearthstone team commander.

"Jake, you're lookin' good," he said softly, pausing as he looked skywards, briefly watching as the clouds boiled past overhead. "And yes, suh, the weather could be a mite better," he continued, lowering his eyes. "But first things first. Let's get you and your boys and your gear all loaded into the vehicles. I'll brief you in after we reach the Farm."

The Farm, Jake knew, was a large complex of turn-of-the-century homes and outbuildings that had been purchased by the Office of Strategic Services—the predecessor to the Central Intelligence Agency—during World War II. The Farm, well off the beaten path and surrounded by an ancient stone wall that dated back to the revolutionary war, was situated on over four hundred acres of rural countryside adjacent to the sprawling Marine Corps base located outside Quantico, Virginia. The Farm, and what the CIA did there, still cloaked in secrecy and one of the Company's most guarded installations.

"Okay, sir. Let me get the men rounded up and our equipment loaded."

Chapter 14

DAY FOUR, 2246 HOURS
THE FARM
OUTSIDE QUANTICO, VIRGINIA

"JAKE! JAKE, MY boy! Get out of that damned wet coat and take a seat over here by the fire!" Director Allen Jefferson warmly said, gesturing with a drink dark with Maker's Mark whiskey at a chair next to his own.

"Yes, sir! Thank you, sir!"

Lieutenant Commander Jake Stoneman looked curiously around the expansive living room while he wiped his muddy boots on the entry mat. All he could think was *"Very Nice"* as he made his way to the chair indicated by the director. He had never been invited to the main residence before, and it more than reminded him of a Montana hunting lodge, one that wouldn't have been out of place snuggled up to the foothills of the Bitterroot Mountains.

The living room, large and spacious, had rough-hewn beamed ceilings fifteen feet in height and an enormous split-granite fireplace that dominated its western wall. The fireplace hearth—well over six feet in width and four feet in height—all ablaze with massive logs. The room also had large Native American rugs dyed in geodesic patterns of red and green and black strewn randomly about its scuffed, wood-planked floor. And scattered about the various side tables were antique oil-burning lamps—long ago converted to electricity—that cast muted, golden shadows into the room's darkened recesses. Jake could also smell the aroma of expensive cigars that lingered in the room.

"Can I get you somethin' to drink?" Jefferson asked as he made his way to a built-in bar. "Sorry to have you come over so late, but I needed to talk to you tonight rather than tomorrow mornin'. So just set yourself down and get comfortable. I know you gotta be bushed after that god-awful flight."

The director pointed at the bottles arrayed along the bar.

"I think we might have anythin' you'd like."

"Yes, sir. Thank you, sir," Jake said, setting himself down in the chair indicated by the director. "I'll just have what you're having, if that's all right."

"A man after my own heart," Jefferson said with a chuckle. "One Maker's Mark comin' up."

After mixing the drink, the director handed Jake a Waterford cut-crystal tumbler that brimmed with whiskey and water as dark as his own.

As he settled comfortably into the leather chair, Jake watched as Jefferson made his way to the fireplace and placed his drink on the split-log mantle, then slid aside the grate from the fireplace's massive opening. With a large black-iron poker in hand, the director proceeded to push the logs around until their burning-red underbellies faced upwards, his efforts accompanied by an avalanche of sparks that crackled and sputtered in protest as they made their way up the chimney's flue.

Satisfied, Director Jefferson grunted, then laid aside the poker and slid the grate back across the opening. After pausing to savor the heat for a couple of moments, he plucked his drink from the mantle and made his way back to the chairs.

"Always did like stokin' a fire," he said absently as he sat himself down. "Don't know why, but I always found it kinda soothin'."

With his legs crossed and the whiskey glass perched on his thigh, Jefferson leaned back and stared into the flames.

Jake, with nothing to say, relaxed into the thickly cushioned chair and took a healthy swallow of his drink, lost in thought as he too stared into the flames.

"Are all your men bedded down and taken care of?" Director Jefferson suddenly asked out of the blue.

"Yes, sir. No problems, sir," Jake answered.

"Good, good," Jefferson said softly as he continued to stare into the bright-red coals. "Sorry I couldn't fill you in on the trip over from Andrews, Jake. I know you must be wonderin' why we had you and your boys hauled back so sudden to the States."

"Yes, sir, I am," Jake said as he took another long pull of his drink, patiently waiting for the director to continue.

Jefferson sighed and turned towards Jake.

"Well, Jake, I'm gonna tell you why. Four days ago to be exact, we found out the Pakistanis had two of their nuclear warheads hijacked by the Taliban. They were transportin' the weapons to a new storage depot located at one of their southern bases by a C-130. Anyways, the warheads never made it. Seems the pilot was in cahoots with the Taliban and diverted the aircraft to an ambush site. And, just to let you know, we're pretty damned sure it was Qudos Mehsud's outfit that did the hijackin'."

Jake stared at the director in disbelief, his drink all but forgotten, taken totally by surprise by what he'd just heard.

"You've gotta be shittin' me, sir!"

Qudos Mehsud, Jake knew, was the head Taliban asshole in Pakistan and Hearthstone knew all about this guy. He was one ruthless son-of-a-bitch, more ruthless than Osama bin Laden had ever been, and was numero uno on their termination list.

"Yep, none other than our old friend Qudos. And nope, I'm not shittin' you at all, Jake," Director Jefferson said gloomily. "Wished I was. So that brings us back to your team. To Hearthstone. Why we had you boys come back so quick. You know as well as I do that Qudos could use those weapons against our troops in Afghanistan or, god forbid, smuggle them into the States. No need to paint a picture worse than that. So, with that in mind, President Taylor's made a Presidential Finding—that the threat posed by these nukes requires extreme measures."

The director took another swallow of his drink and leaned back in his chair, once again staring into the flames, trying to figure out the best way to bring Jake and his Hearthstone team onboard with Project Gabriel. Then he uncrossed his legs and placed his glass on the coffee table.

"Jake, what we're gonna do, assumin' you and your boys agree, is chop you from the Special Operations Group. Your chain of command will now be President Taylor, myself, the president's Director of National Security, Steven Clarke, and General Marion Gray. In that order."

Jefferson searched Jake's face for any questions, but only saw him sit silent like a sphinx, his thoughts masked.

"Okay," he continued, picking up his drink and taking another healthy swallow. "Logistical support will be through General Gray, the chairman of the Joint Chiefs."

At this point, the director dug a handkerchief from his coat pocket and began to polish his glasses.

"Sir? I'm confused. Just what are you asking us to do?" Jake asked. He had no idea where Jefferson was going with this. "Please, excuse me, but why do we need a new chain of command? And will no longer report to the Special Operations Group?"

"Well, Jake, those are all good questions. So I guess I oughta stop beatin' around the bush, as they say. I've been tryin' to come up with a way to tell you what we've got in mind, so I guess the best way to do it is just throw'er out there on the table and see what you gotta say."

Jefferson stuffed the handkerchief back into his suit pocket and donned his glasses.

"Now, what I'm about to tell you is gonna sound pretty goddamned farfetched. Even has a little booga booga in it, and it's classified 'Top Secret Presidential–Gabriel'."

"Okay, sir," Jake said, his curiosity more than aroused, "I'm all ears."

"Now . . . don't worry. I'm not gonna have you sign any secrecy papers or anythin' like that. You and your boys have signed enough of those damned things. You know as well as I do that Presidential Findings are rare. But the research project I'm gonna tell you about, Project Gabriel, has been goin' on for close to twenty-five years. And, if you and your team agree, we're pretty damned sure we can utilize it in an operational way. Now, what I'm gonna tell you hasn't been done before. This is real twenty-third century stuff, Jake, and I would be remiss if I didn't tell you there could be a great deal of personal risk to both yourself and your team if it doesn't work. But we've been assured by the scientists workin' on the project that it does work, that it's worked in their experiments."

Director Jefferson then launched into a brief dissertation that outlined the objectives of Project Gabriel, and the reasons why President Taylor had concluded it was the best means to destroy the warheads. At the end of his talk, with the pros and cons of Gabriel laid out, he took a healthy slug of his Maker's Mark.

"Well? What do you think? Reckon you and your boys might want to have a go at it?"

Jake took a stiff pull of his drink, and then another. As the whiskey glowed within his midsection, he settled back in the plush leather chair and thought over what the director had just said. If he hadn't heard it from the mouth of Allen Jefferson himself, he never would have believed what he'd just heard. He would have told anyone else they were nuts and ought to reserve the next padded room at Bellevue. It sounded almost like Star Trek. He also understood that something like this could be very dangerous. But he knew if what the director had just told him was true, then this could be the best means of killing a whole shitload of those radical Islamic terrorists that infested the earth. He also had to agree that Project Gabriel, if it worked, was probably the only way to destroy those nukes and save who knew how many innocent lives.

"Sir," Jake said, coming to a quick decision, "if what you just told me is true, and works, you can count me in. And assuming everything pans out the way you just told me, I'm pretty damned sure the rest of Hearthstone will join in."

Director Jefferson exhaled a breath he hadn't known he had been holding and slapped Jake's thigh.

"Good boy, Jake! I can't tell you how glad I am to hear that! And so will the president."

"So, what do we do now?"

"First of all, speak to your team. Time is of the essence here, Jake. Do that first thing in the mornin'. But just give 'em a broad outline of what we're intendin' to do; don't go into any of the details I just told you about."

"Can I tell them about the Presidential Finding and the nukes?"

Jake knew he had to come up with a way to break this new mission to his team—and Project Gabriel.

"Yes, of course you can. Also tell 'em why we think we're out of options. Now, assumin' they're willin' to listen, the next step will be to introduce y'all to the details of the program, the nitty-gritty as they say. I've already arranged that for the day after tomorrow, for you and your team to meet the senior scientist, a Dr. Samantha Johnson, who heads up the project. We'll have the meetin' right here in the lower level conference room. Steven Clarke and General Gray will also be attendin'. Now, if the meetin' goes okay, and if you and your boys buy into the project, we're gonna ship you all out to Los Alamos for in-depth orientation and trainin'. That's where the project's located."

Jake nodded and stood up, then placed his drink on the coffee table.

"Sounds good to me, sir. I'll speak to the team first thing in the morning. And thanks for recommending Hearthstone."

"Jake, the choice was easy. We needed our best men for this mission."

Chapter 15

DAY SIX, 1130 HOURS
THE FARM
QUANTICO, VIRGINIA

THE DIRECTOR OF National Security, Steven Clarke, walked down a long hallway lined with cheap fluorescent lights as he made his way toward Conference Room B, a conference room located in the lower-level basement of the Farm facility referred to by most of the worker bees as the "Dungeon". *And with good reason,* he thought. He'd been here a couple of times before and thoroughly detested the place.

When he neared the entrance, he lifted up his red, diagonal-striped identification badge to show the plainclothes CIA guard who flanked its door, the coveted red stripes granting him "Any Access, Any Floor" within the sprawling complex.

"Good morning, sir," the guard said, taking the ID.

"Good morning," Clarke answered as the thought crossed his mind that this guy could have been a defensive linebacker for the Dallas Cowboys.

The guard was tall, probably six-foot-two or -three, and looked to weigh around two hundred and ten pounds without an ounce of fat, and had a neck as big around as his own thigh. He could also tell by the bulge under his suit coat that he was armed. *That's a little unusual,* he thought, *being armed within the facility.* But given the subject matter of today's meeting, he guessed that it made sense.

The guard scrutinized the ID for at least five seconds, comparing Clarke's face to the photo on the card, and then handed it back.

"Thank you, sir," the guard said.

"Have Director Jefferson, General Gray, Dr. Johnson, and Lieutenant Commander Stoneman and his men arrived?"

"Yes, sir. They're all inside. The director escorted them down just a couple of minutes ago."

"Okay, thanks again," Clarke said with a brief smile as the guard opened the door, stepped aside, and allowed him to enter.

Steven Clarke loathed this room, always had. It was about as depressing as any conference room could get. There weren't any windows and the walls were painted in that obligatory mist-green-shit color so prevalent in government buildings. He'd always thought that some government worker must have fucked up really bad and bought a trainload of the stuff, and now the government felt obliged to use it up. The room's only redeeming feature, as far as he was concerned, was an oval-shaped walnut conference table, polished to a mirror-like sheen, that dominated the center of the room.

The table could seat a total of sixteen people, eight per side, and had a lectern with a built-in, touch screen computer terminal to operate the visual displays recessed in the conference room's walls. He also saw that carafes of water and coffee, in addition to writing pads and pencils, had been placed along both sides its length.

Clarke looked around and saw that everyone was present. Director Jefferson stood casually to the left speaking with General Gray, and what he assumed to be the Hearthstone team was grouped together on the far side of the table, standing almost at parade rest behind their chairs. Dr. Samantha Johnson, who was to give the bulk of the briefing, was seated near the head of the table busy with her meeting notes.

"Good morning, Allen," he said, stepping over to the director. "Sorry I'm late, but the president's intel brief took a lot longer than I thought. It seems we're still having a problem getting a line on those Pakistani nukes, and President Taylor's very unhappy about that."

"That's okay, Steven. No problem," Jefferson said in a muted tone, knowing better than most the problems they were having in trying to locate the whereabouts of the nukes. Then he gestured at the other attendees who stood about the room. "We just arrived ourselves."

Clarke nodded at General Marion Gray, United States Marine Corps and the chairman of the Joint Chiefs of Staff, who stood to the right of Jefferson.

"Good to see you again, General. Glad you could make it," he said, grasping the general's outstretched hand.

"Good to be here, sir," General Gray answered in his typically blunt way.

With a pat to the general's arm, Clarke turned back to Allen, but before he could say anything further the director had stepped over to the Hearthstone team leader and brought him from around the table.

"Steven? I'd like you to meet Lieutenant Commander Jake Stoneman, the Hearthstone Team Commander. Jake? This is Steven Clarke, President Taylor's Director of National Security."

Jake shook Clarke's hand.

"It's a pleasure to meet you, sir."

"Jake, it's good to have you and your men onboard. And please, call me Steven. I also wanted to convey the president's heartfelt appreciation to you and your men for considering this assignment."

"Thank you, sir," Jake said, signaling for his men to join him. "Sir, if you don't mind, I'd like to introduce the rest of the team. As you know, we've all been chopped over to the CIA's Special Operations Group for the past three years, and all of my team members are volunteers from SEAL Team Three. The best of the best."

Clarke smiled and nodded as Stoneman continued.

"The short, hairy Mexican guy with the non-regulation ponytail is Petty Officer Third Class Steve Martinez."

"Good to meet you, sir," Martinez said, shaking the security director's hand.

"Next in line is Petty Officer First Class George Tolman, better known as Squealer."

"Nice to meet you, Squealer," Clarke said, wondering how in god's name this guy had got stuck with a nickname like Squealer. He had to bend his head way back just to meet Tolman's eyes. *This guy's gotta be at least six-foot-five and weigh-in at around two hundred and fifty, two hundred and sixty pounds! And I bet he spends most of his time in the gym given the size of his neck and arms. He makes that guard standing outside look like a goddamned cheerleader.*

"Glad to meet you, sir," Tolman said in his deep, southern, baritone drawl.

"And, Steven, this is Petty Officer First Class Jung-su Pak. Petty Officer Pak doubles as our medic, and he's also our martial arts expert," Jake added.

Clarke looked down as Jung-su stepped forward. What he saw was a small, thin, wiry man who looked more like a piece of old tanned leather with a clean-shaven skull burnt dark by the sun. He also guessed Jung-su's height to be around five-foot-four or -five, and probably tipped the scales at no more than a hundred and thirty pounds dripping wet. But when he shook Jung-su's hand, it was like trying to shake a thick band of steel covered with knobby calluses. His hand actually ached after he retrieved it.

"Nice to meet you, Jung-su," Clarke said, flexing his hand to try and get some feeling back into it.

"Same here, sir," Jung-su replied, stepping to the side.

Next in line was Lieutenant (j.g.) Brett Thompson.

"Sir, this is Lieutenant Brett Thompson. Brett's our Assistant Team Leader and responsible for planning and logistics. He's been with Hearthstone from the start."

"Pleased to meet you, Brett," Clarke said, thinking Thompson reminded him of your typical southern California surfer, given his tanned face framed by an easy-go-lucky smile, slim build, and unruly shock of sun-bleached, light-brown hair.

"It's a pleasure, sir," Lieutenant Thompson responded.

"And, last but not least, is Chief Petty Officer Walter Moczarny."

Jake had to smile as the chief marched forward with military precision and thrust out his large, beefy hand.

"Walt is the one that really runs this ragtag outfit," Jake added, amused by the chief's stiff demeanor.

"It's a pleasure, Walt."

Chief Moczarny said nothing, just bobbed his head in silent acknowledgement and headed back towards the table.

With the introductions concluded, the team members filed back to their chairs and unconsciously came to the position of parade rest.

Clarke couldn't help but like what he saw. They were young—obviously well fit—and had a reserved, professional air to themselves. He could also tell they were more than a little nervous not knowing what was going to be asked of them. Even though Allen had told him earlier that Stoneman had briefed his men on the broad brush strokes of their mission, he could tell that they were reticent. *Well, that's the reason for this briefing. To bring them onboard to form them into the best twenty-first century combat team against terrorism.*

He was also impressed with Lieutenant Commander Stoneman, and had an uncanny ability to size up individuals within seconds of meeting them. What he saw in Stoneman he liked. He was a man not much younger than himself and, like his men, was fit and muscular with broad shoulders. His darkly tanned face and arms also proved that he had spent more than his fair share of days out in the field. But the most striking feature about Stoneman was his piercing blue eyes that stared out from beneath a head of closely-cropped blonde hair almost bleached white by the sun. Eyes that seemed to miss nothing. Just like a hawk's.

He could also sense a deep intelligence that emanated from the commander, but there was something else about Stoneman—and his whole team for that matter—that was hard to put his finger on. Something rare and never seen in the power halls of Washington, D.C.

With a flash of comprehension he realized what it was. Stoneman and his men were predators, pure and simple. Warriors in the true sense of the word. Warriors who unflinchingly placed themselves in the path of a ton of folks who hated the United States. Their sole purpose to kill for the United States of America with no questions asked. Their country, right or wrong. He could also tell by the way they carried themselves that they were supremely confident in their abilities.

Clarke could tell that he too was being sized up by the Hearthstone team leader, as to whether he could be trusted. Like a wolf would do when it met something unknown in a forest, assessing his strengths and weaknesses. *Well, well*, he thought again. *I think Jake and his team will do just fine!*

Prior to the briefing, Jake had done his own research on the president's Director of National Security. He'd always made it a habit to find out all he could of both friend and foe alike—knowledge that had saved his own ass in more ways than one—and since not only his own life, but those of his team would be placed into the hands of Mr. Clarke, he felt it had behooved himself to find out as much as he could about the man.

What he had found out through his Capitol Hill and military sources was that Steven Clarke had a reputation for being one mean, ruthless son-of-a-bitch, and never got flustered. Some of his sources who had seen Clarke in action told him the security director was quick, decisive, and deadly in taking out the political competition. They had also told him that Clarke was no pussy. When President

Taylor occasionally removed his leash, he'd been told that Clarke would strike, and strike hard with his opponents rarely seeing him come until the final moment. He respected that and felt he could work well with the president's Director of National Security. He too liked what he saw. *At least he doesn't come off as one of those limp-dicked, weak-kneed, bureaucratic pantywaists. One of those guys who would pee all over himself and wring his hands in indecision when the going got tough.*

"Allen?" Clarke asked. "Have Jake and his team been introduced to General Gray?"

"Yes, suh, they have. We got the pleasantries out of the way just before you arrived. Didn't have a chance to introduce Dr. Johnson, though."

"That's okay, I'm sure Dr. Johnson will take care of that when the briefing starts."

Clarke stepped up to the conference table, but before he sat down he looked to his right. He couldn't help but admire Dr. Samantha Johnson who sat by herself toward the head of the table. He knew she wasn't being aloof, but just focused on today's presentation; her head bent down while she unwittingly chewed her full red lips; her luxuriant blonde hair cascading forward in disarray toward the table; her brow furrowed by a look of deep concentration as she reviewed her briefing notes.

He sighed inwardly thinking of what could have been. Being President Taylor's Director of National Security certainly had its perks, but it kept him so damned busy that he never had the time for any type of ongoing relationship. But if he had, he would have made a play for Sam. She was smart, probably one of the smartest people he'd ever met, and had a direct approach that intimidated most men.

He also knew that she was absolutely sure of her own abilities and, when she spoke in that very sexy, husky voice of hers, one had to be careful not to drown in her deep-set turquoise eyes that reminded him of the Caribbean Ocean. The other thing about Sam was that she was beautiful. Not just good looking, but jaw-dropping beautiful. Tall at five-foot-eleven, she had the slender grace and well-endowed figure of any top model one would find in a Victoria's Secret lingerie catalogue, and for today's briefing she was dressed in a muted, navy-blue Nanette Lapore skirt that stopped fashionably about four inches above her knees, a white V-necked silk blouse with navy blue buttons down the front, and her characteristic black Burberry high heels that made her seem taller than she was. He also liked the fact that she was totally oblivious to the effect she had on men. As moths are drawn to a flame, so too were most of the men who fell within her orbit. And, Sam being Sam, she was totally unaware that she left a trail littered with male stares and broken dreams in her wake.

Clarke tore his gaze from Sam and motioned at the table.

"Everyone? Jake? Let's go ahead and take our seats so we can get started."

Hearthstone immediately pulled out their chairs and sat down, leaning back comfortably while they waited for the briefing to begin.

Clarke took a chair between General Gray and Director Jefferson, then grabbed one of the carafes and poured some coffee. After taking a quick swallow, he placed his briefcase on the table, clicked open its latches, and pulled out a thick sheaf of papers.

"Now, before we begin," he said with a look at Hearthstone, "I understand that Lieutenant Commander Stoneman has briefed you in on what's happened in Pakistan. So, you're all aware that the Taliban have stolen two, one-hundred-kiloton warheads from the Pakistan Air Force, and where they are now is anybody's best guess. But we think they're hidden somewhere in the border region between Pakistan's northern tribal areas and Afghanistan. Now, the challenge we face is, how can we make sure they're destroyed? Or at least rendered inoperable? As your commander may have told you, President Taylor was given several options that ranged from inserting a large force of our own into Pakistan, to infiltrating smaller teams into the area. For various reasons those scenarios all had a low probability of success, and probably would have gotten a lot of our own people killed, not to mention the problems it would have caused with the Pakistanis. We also realized we'd most likely get only one shot at trying to take out these warheads. It also goes without saying that we can't involve the Pakistanis. You know better than we do that as soon as the Pakistanis know what we're up to, so would the Taliban. Sympathizers within their government and military would see to that. So, of the options available, the one that had the highest probability of success, was to have you men work in conjunction with a project called Gabriel."

Clarke paused and took another swallow of coffee, wishing it had been a stiff shot of bourbon, then glanced at General Gray and Director Jefferson who nodded for him to continue.

"Commander Stoneman was told the other night by Director Jefferson a little bit of what Gabriel entails, but not any of the particulars. So, please, I'm just asking that you all have an open mind and listen to the briefing, because what you're going to hear will sound pretty goddamned farfetched, but I've seen it with my own eyes as has Director Jefferson and President Taylor. What we're talking about, gentlemen, is inserting you men into Pakistan or Afghanistan, once we have a better location on the nukes, utilizing a process known as Molecular Displacement."

Clarke paused when he saw his mentioning of Molecular Displacement—MD for short—had gone right over their heads. *Maybe I'll get off easier than I thought,* he hoped.

"Molecular Displacement, which Dr. Johnson will explain in more detail, was an unforeseen by-product of Project Gabriel. And, if we can use this new found capability, we should be able to place you in very close proximity to the warheads once they're located. But more importantly, we can extract you at a moment's notice. Nor will you have to infiltrate the area, this capability reducing your exposure to possible enemy action. To be absolutely clear, your job will be to act only as spotters, to get in to verify the location of the nukes. And, once located, to direct standoff weaponry to take them out, either with B-2s, F-117s, or cruise missiles. To reiterate gentlemen, your job will only be to verify the location of the nukes, not to get into a firefight with the Taliban. So—"

Petty Officer Third Class Steve Martinez hesitantly raised his hand as if in a classroom, cutting off Clarke in midstatement.

"Sir, Petty Officer Third Class Steve Martinez. I'm sorry to interrupt, but just what is this Molecular Displacement? I don't think I've ever heard that term before."

Steve saw the same confusion on his fellow team members' faces, in particular Chief Moczarny and Squealer whose brows were furrowed with doubt, both on the verge of having asked the same exact question.

Clarke bent his head and looked at the table, his hands clasped together. *Okay, now it starts.* Taking a deep breath, he looked up at the third class petty officer.

"Well, Mr. Martinez, Molecular Displacement is just a fancy term for teleportation. That's the reason—"

Steve Martinez shot out of his chair, abruptly cutting Clarke off a second time, unable to believe what he had just heard.

"Teleportation? You mean like Star Trek, sir?" he asked incredulously. "I'm sorry, sir, no disrespect intended, but you gotta be kiddin' me! This sounds more like science fiction or something!"

"I can assure you, Mr. Martinez," Clarke said, his face flushed and about to lose his temper, "that we are not kidding! Not kidding at all! That's the reason for this briefing! To bring you up-to-date on the project; to show how you can best make use of it. But again, I suggest we let Dr. Johnson conduct her briefing, then you can ask all of the questions that you want. Does that seem fair?"

Chief among Steven Clarke's faults was his inability to be questioned or brought to task in an open forum.

Jake could tell that Clarke was about to blow it, his face reddening with his lips compressed into a narrow white line. He didn't want things to get out of hand before the briefing had even started, so he motioned to Clarke by waving his hand from side to side a couple of inches above the table, just like a Black Jack player would do to decline a hit from the dealer. Without saying a word, he silently asked Clarke to back off. From the corner of his eye, Clarke caught Jake's signal and curtly nodded back. Jake knew he needed to get his team back on track as he rapped his knuckles on the table.

"At ease!" he bellowed. "Settle down and be quiet! The reason we're here is to listen to the briefing, not to shoot down the project before we've even heard anything! So, for right now, you men got two choices—either listen up or get the hell out of Dodge! Personally, I'd like to hear what the good doctor has to say. So what's it gonna be?"

One by one the Hearthstone team members looked at one another, completely caught off-guard by Jake's response. Without a word said, they all arrived at an unspoken consensus and slowly gave him a thumbs up.

"We're good-to-go, Skipper," Lieutenant Thompson chimed in.

If the truth be known, Brett was more than a little intrigued and wanted to hear more about the project, in particular teleportation. Although it did sound more like science fiction, the fact that they were all sitting here in the bowels of the CIA listening to this briefing meant there oughta be something to it.

With a sense of relief, Jake nodded at Clarke to continue and settled back in his chair.

"All right, then," Clarke said, visibly relieved. "Dr. Johnson will brief you in on the details of Gabriel, and how we think it can best be used to take out the warheads."

Knowing it was time for him to butt out, and for Sam to do her thing, he caught her eye.

"Dr. Johnson, you all set to go?"

With a slight nod, Sam picked up her briefing papers, trying to think of how she could make true believers out of these skeptical and obviously dangerous men, but she was more than ready to go.

"Okay," Clarke announced, "let's go ahead and get started."

"Thank you, Mr. Clarke," Sam said as she made her way toward the head of the table.

"Jesus Christ, Boss," Steve mumbled under his breath, not wanting to take his eyes off Dr. Johnson. "Man-oh-man! Sure hope this briefing takes a couple of hours! I sure as hell never had a teacher like that! Kinda restores your faith in the good old US of A, don't it?"

Jake leaned over and whispered out of the side of his mouth.

"Down boy, down! But I gotta agree, I never had a teacher like that either. Now, listen up to what she has to say and see if you can learn something for once."

"Good afternoon, gentlemen," Sam began pleasantly, her forearms resting on the lectern. "I apologize for not greeting you earlier, but my name is Samantha Johnson and, as Mr. Clarke just indicated, it's my job to bring you up-to-speed on Project Gabriel."

Sam picked up a laser pointer and clicked it on and off a couple of times just to make sure that it worked, then pushed a button on the control module built into the top of the lectern. Immediately, a large four-by-six-foot section of the back wall came to life, looking not unlike a flat-screened LCD monitor one could find in almost any home, but this one was of much higher definition than anyone could purchase on the open market. Once the display was on, she picked up the pointer, clicked it back on, and looked at Hearthstone, making sure to make eye contact with each team member while she unconsciously pushed a wisp of blonde hair out her eyes and tucked it neatly behind her ear.

"Okay, gentlemen, as I said before, this briefing is to give you a better understanding of Project Gabriel. But more importantly, Molecular Displacement. And, for those of you unfortunate souls not well-versed in scientific terminology, better known as teleportation."

With that pronouncement Jake laughed, and heard more than a few chuckles from his men. He felt better knowing that his team would now give Dr. Johnson a fair shot.

"Now, Mr. Stoneman? Gentlemen? Just one more thing before we get started. Even though my name is Samantha, I'd appreciate it if you called me Sam. That's what all my friends call me."

"Excuse me, Sam," Jake interrupted, smiling up at Dr. Johnson. "But I'd like it if you called me Jake. Makes me feel too old and decrepit when you call me Mr. Stoneman," he added good-naturedly.

"Okay then, Mr. Stoneman, Jake it is," she said with a warm smile that displayed a set of perfectly aligned white teeth.

"But for now, getting back to the subject matter, if you could please take a look at the outline I've put up on the monitor," she continued, with the red dot of the laser placed on an outline depicted on the screen, "I've divided today's briefing into several sections so that you can better understand how Gabriel and teleportation came about. As you can see, the first section deals with introducing you to the different scientific members who comprise the Gabriel team. Who they are, what their specialties are, and the contributions they've made to the project. And, please remember, these are the same scientists you'll be working with if you come onboard and join us.

"The second section deals with a brief history of Gabriel. Why it was started and who sponsored it. The third section deals with an overview of quantum computers, the true heart of the project, including how they differ from today's computers. And lastly, we'll get into what's called Superposition and Entanglement, the two quantum theories that made teleportation possible."

Sam lowered the pointer and paused.

"Any questions so far? No? All righty then, let's get into the meat of it. But I warn you, you need to pay attention. There *will* be a written exam you'll need to pass in order to leave this facility."

All of the men at the table grinned at that remark, General Gray included. Unknown to Sam, Hearthstone now looked forward to learning more about quantum computers and teleportation. *Whatever the hell a quantum computer was,* they all thought.

"I also have to confess that today's briefing will be somewhat dry and scientific, so I ask in advance for your patience. And should any of you have a question, or if I say something that you don't understand, please, just stop me and ask."

Sam paused and picked up a glass of water, taking a small sip. She could tell they were still with her as they nodded in agreement.

"Anyway, I know teleportation sounds a lot like Buck Rogers. Hard to believe. A difficult concept for anyone to get their arms around. But remember what people first thought of radio at the end of the nineteenth century, and then later with the development and transmission of television signals. It was all thought to be magic. The same thing with today's conventional electronic computers. And the majority of people today can't tell you how computers work, much less radio and television, but they live with radio and television and computers every day of their lives. It's now taken for granted. So, please believe me when I tell you that teleportation is completely possible and, most importantly, safe. In fact, through our experiments, we've refined the process to where we now have a ninety-eight point nine percent success rate in being able to safely teleport both animate and inanimate objects."

Hearing this statistic Hearthstone perked up noticeably, having honed in on that ninety-eight point nine percent success rate.

"Now, before I get into the basics of quantum computing, its history, and how it relates to teleportation, I would like to briefly tell you more about myself and my other colleagues who have worked so diligently on Gabriel. First, a little about myself. I have doctorates in both Quantum Physics and Advanced Computer Theory. I'm also a professor of Quantum Physics at the Massachusetts Institute of Technology where, for the last eight years, I've conducted extensive research into the Bose-Einstein theorem as it relates to subatomic structures, and how it can best be applied to real world applications."

Jake just sat there feeling more than a little stupid. He had no idea in hell what she had just said. He could also tell the other team members had no clue as to what she did. Even General Gray, Director Jefferson, and Steven Clarke looked puzzled.

Sam noted everyone's perplexed looks, and knew she needed to clarify what she had just said.

"Okay, let me try to explain that another way," she added quickly, never having had to explain what she did to laymen. "Basically, what I do is study the interaction of atoms at their lowest quantum level, to try and understand their quantum relationships with respect to micro-atomic structures."

There! That's much better. Much more clear, she smugly thought as she adjusted a rheostat on the console to dim the ceiling lights, completely missing the still baffled looks on the men's faces. Then she picked up the laser and placed its small red dot on the name of a Dr. Kenneth Williams.

"Dr. Kenneth Williams," Sam continued, "is also at MIT. He's been at the forefront of Project Gabriel for the last five years, and also holds advanced degrees in Quantum Theory and Quantum Mechanics. In addition to being a world renowned theorist in these fields, he's also pioneered the development of quantum algorithms that are synonymous to written code for today's computers."

Then she highlighted the name of a Dr. Richard Ross.

"Dr. Richard Ross is a professor at Cal Tech. He's our expert on super-cooled gaseous condensates. Now, that's a big title and I don't expect you to know what that means, but in a nutshell, Dr. Ross works on being able to bring gaseous states, such as chloroform, to a temperature of near absolute zero without solidification. That's minus 459.7 degrees Fahrenheit, gentlemen. He's also developed a methodology to have a large fraction of these gaseous atoms collapse down into their lowest possible quantum state, namely electrons, for further manipulation. Later on you'll see the significance of Dr. Ross' work."

Sam next pointed to the name of Dr. Ted Angstrom, the last scientist on the list.

"Our final team member is Dr. Ted Angstrom from the University of Chicago. Dr. Angstrom has spearheaded our understanding of quantum theory and how it can best be applied to the real world. But most importantly, he's also developed a means of utilizing Nuclear Magnetic Resonance—what we now call NMR—for manipulating gaseous subatomic particles, in particular electrons, at their most basic quantum level."

Sam stopped and busily began to type something into the console.

"Dr. Johnson?" Chief Moczarny asked with his hand raised. "Chief Petty Officer Moczarny, ma'am. Not to sound stupid or anything, but what's a. . . . whatever you called it, a Nuclear Magnetic something? What's it do?"

Sam looked up and gazed at Moczarny for a second, digesting his question.

"Nuclear Magnetic Resonance, Mr. Moczarny, or NMR," she re-iterated, then stared at the far wall to try and think of how best to answer his question.

"An NMR, Mr. Moczarny, basically allows us to determine what state an electron is in at any given moment, and to change that state if needed by measuring it electronically. Try to think of it this way," she continued with a slight tilt of her head, seeing he was still confused. "Think of it like an oversized magnetic magnifying glass, so we can determine what state an electron is in at any given moment and, if need be, to apply a magnetic charge to have it do something else. Does that help?" she asked hopefully.

"Okay, I think I got it, ma'am," Chief Moczarny said, no way in hell understanding what she had just said. "Thank you, ma'am."

"You're welcome, Mr. Moczarny. And, please, remember that my name is Sam, not ma'am," she added with a slight chuckle as she again brushed aside that nagging wisp of hair that just wouldn't stay put.

"So, continuing on, the purpose of this meeting is to familiarize you with Project Gabriel, how it came about, and what we do. Now, historically speaking, Project Gabriel was approved and set up in 1987 by President Ronald Reagan via Presidential Decree. Its original intent to research alternatives to standard microchip computing technology, all with an eye towards developing ultrasecure encryption algorithms."

Sam paused to see if there were any questions. Not hearing any, she continued.

"So, to get back to the basics, Project Gabriel evolved over time into the development of the first quantum computer. Again with the express purpose of creating more secure encryption codes for ourselves and to break enemy codes. It's also pertinent to know that we're not the only ones in the race to develop the first quantum computer. As we speak, Russia, China, and the European Union are sinking billions of dollars into quantum research and development. They too understand the ramifications of quantum computing. It's almost analogous as to who was going to be the first to develop the atomic bomb during World War II. But what you need to understand, is that the development of a quantum computer far outstrips that of having been the first to build a nuclear weapon."

Sam waited to see if they were following along at this point.

"Gentlemen, any questions?"

She heard only silence.

"Okay, then it's time for us to get into the basics. First, what is a quantum computer and how do they differ from today's computers?"

Not waiting for a response, Sam answered her own question.

"Basically, the answer is very simple. Today's computers—you may or may not know—use microprocessors on silicon chips for processing data in their CPU, or Central Processing Unit, with bulk memory storage accomplished by recording magnetic impulses on metallic discs called hard drives. In our quantum computer, instead of using microprocessors or magnetic impulses on discs, we use electrons in a gaseous state, at or near absolute zero temperatures, that act as both the microprocessors and means of memory storage."

"Excuse me, ma'am," Lieutenant Brett Thompson interrupted. "Lieutenant Thompson, ma'am. Did you say electrons? Like the electrons that go around an atom?"

"Yes, Lieutenant, electrons," Sam answered firmly.

"But, ma'am? How's that possible? I mean, electrons are even smaller than an atom. I didn't even know we could see electrons since they're so small."

"Well, Lieutenant, you're correct. We can't see them, but we know they're there because we can measure them scientifically. But I'll get into that later when I talk more about quantum computing, I just don't want to jump the gun right now. And if you still have questions about electrons at the end of the briefing, I'll try to answer them at that time. Would that be okay?" she asked nicely, flashing the lieutenant one of her most dazzling smiles.

"Yes, ma'am. Thank you, ma'am."

"And please, Lieutenant, remember my name is Sam. You don't need to call me ma'am. Makes me feel too old and decrepit," she added with a mischievous glance at Jake.

"Yes, ma'am, uh, I mean, Sam. Thank you, ma'am," Lieutenant Thompson said, feeling more like a stupid dumbshit.

Sam couldn't help but smile at her conversation with the young lieutenant as she directed her comments back to Hearthstone.

"Okay, now getting back to current computer technology, today's computers utilize physical electronic processors that operate on a binary system."

At the end of that statement, she clicked the laser back on and pointed it at a depiction of the binary system on the monitor.

"As you can see, by a binary system, I mean that today's data storage, software, and data manipulation are done through the use of binary digits, or what we call bits. Either a one or a zero. So a conventional computer stores and manipulates data by the use of ones and zeros. Eight bits strung together is called a byte, with bytes being the standard building blocks for conventional computer code. But the most important thing you need to remember is that conventional computers can only process and store data in a *linear* way, and can only work on one outcome at a time."

Sam searched the faces of Hearthstone to see if they were still with her. *So far so good!* she thought. *They must have had exposure to conventional computers and had heard the terminology before.*

"Anyway, the quantum computer we've developed uses gaseous chloroform electrons that act as both the primary memory chips and data processors for the system, each of which we now call a qubit. That stands for Quantum Binary Digit, gentlemen, at near absolute zero temperatures. Through our research, we've found that electrons, at the quantum level at least, can be in two states simultaneously through the application of what we call Superposition. Now, please let me restate that, because this is a key concept for you to understand and is one of the two theorems that made teleportation possible. The electrons can be in two states at the same time. So, what that means is, the electrons can be both a zero and a one at the same time due to Superposition."

Sam could see the confusion and frowns that instantly clouded the faces of Hearthstone, but before they could ask a question she quickly jumped in.

"Now, I know your questions pertain to Superposition. How can something, an electron let's say, be two things at once? Sounds impossible, doesn't it? Well, this isn't the best answer, but you'll just have to take it on faith that at the quantum level we've found this to be true. We've proven it time and time again in our experiments."

Sam could see they were still having a problem with the concept, so she raised a hand to capture their attention.

"Okay, gentlemen, try to think of it this way." Sam knew, more than anyone else, what a difficult theory it was to understand. "Try to imagine a qubit as an electron in a magnetic field. The electron's spin can either be in alignment with the field, which we call the spin-up state or a one, or opposite to the field, which we call the spin-down state or a zero. The same as in a conventional computer where a bit can only be a one or a zero. We can also change the electron's spin from one state to another through the application of a pulse of energy. In this case, through the use of the Nuclear Magnetic Resonator developed by Dr. Angstrom. But we also discovered that if we only used a half pulse of energy, we could completely isolate the electron from all external influences. This is the point at which Superposition occurs. According to quantum theory, the electron then enters a Superposition of states where it behaves as if it were in both states at the same time, each qubit taking on the Superposition of both a zero and a one simultaneously!"

Using the pointer, she highlighted a summary of the primary differences between conventional and quantum computers.

"Now, I warned you this was going to be a dry subject and difficult to understand. But bear with me, I'm almost to the punch line here," she added with a quick smile.

"Given that a qubit can be both a zero and one at the same time, the computative power and storage capacity of a quantum computer is not a *linear* function as in today's computers, but rather a *factorial* function. That's a mind boggling difference and the key to everything. This is the concept you have to understand, *factorial* versus *linear* functions. Now, *factorial* functions look at all possible states that can exist simultaneously at any given time. This is what gives us the storage capacity to be able to scan and store the more than seven to the twenty-seventh power of atoms found in a typical human body. And, gentlemen, that's a gigantic number! A number with twenty-seven zeros trailing after it!"

With an impish smile, Sam looked at Jake.

"Jake, you're going to be my guinea pig today. Ready to do a little math? To put the difference between current computer storage capacity and quantum computers into perspective?"

Jake was game for the challenge.

"Sure, Sam. But I gotta warn you, I was never very good at math, but go ahead and give me your best shot."

"Okay," she replied playfully. "Let's assume we have ten bits in a conventional computer, one of today's computers. How many simultaneous states can they be in at any given time?" Sam was confident he would most likely get it wrong.

Jake frowned and thought for a few seconds, thinking through the problem, then he looked up and guessed, "ten?"

"No, Jake, I'm sorry. But don't feel too badly, that's the answer given by most people when asked that question. But remember what I said before, that conventional computers are linear. So a string of ten conventional bits can only be in one state at a time, no matter how the individual bits are arranged. So, the answer is only one. Try to think of it this way, if all ten bits were one's that would be one state, and if they were all zero's that would be a second state. So the formula for ten bits would be *one raised to the tenth power* or one. One times one equals one, times one equals one, and so on ten times. But now, how many simultaneous states can we have with ten qubits?"

Jake, more than a little embarrassed at being wrong, saw the humorous smiles plastered on Hearthstone's faces when he was put on the spot. As he drummed his fingers on the table trying to think, he suddenly reached out and grabbed a pencil and a pad of paper and furiously did some calculations. After a minute or so, he looked up and tentatively answered, "a hundred?"

Sam chuckled as humor danced in her eyes.

"Please don't take offense, Jake; I'm not laughing at you, but that was kind of a trick question. What you have to remember is that a quantum computer's qubit can be in two states simultaneously, not just one state like a normal computer. So, the quantum function is *factorial* in nature. That is, computing all possible states or permutations at the same time. Therefore, the math for a *factorial* function would be ten times nine, times eight, times seven, all the way down to one. Now, you may not believe this, but the resulting product for ten qubits would equal three million, six hundred and twenty-eight thousand, eight hundred states. And for each additional qubit added, the number of states would rise exponentially by a factor greater than ten. For example, eleven qubits would result in over thirty-nine million states, twelve qubits would exceed four hundred and seventy-nine million states, and thirteen qubits would have over six billion states. Given the math, you can see the computational power and data storage of a quantum computer is astronomical! Numbers so large they're hard to imagine!"

Sam suddenly thought of a better way to drive home her point.

"Gentlemen," she continued, seeing they were on the verge of understanding, "to really put this in perspective, consider a quantum computer that had five hundred qubits. It would have the ability to do *500 factorials* of calculations in a single step. Believe it or not, that number would exceed the total number of atoms that exist in the known universe."

Everyone sitting at the conference table, including Steven Clarke, General Gray, and Allen Jefferson, was thunderstruck, not able to grasp a number so large.

"You gotta be shi . . . uh, kidding me, Sam. That many?" Jake asked disbelievingly.

"Yep, that many. Now think of how fast qubits can store and process data. So far, my colleagues and I have perfected a quantum computer that utilizes thirty-five qubits. Pretty unbelievable, isn't it? You have to remember that qubits process data, using Superposition, from both ends simultaneously. All possible quantum states at the same time. This is what allows us to scan the trillions and trillions of atoms found within a human body, store them within the quantum computer, and then project and reconstitute those atoms at some distant location."

Director Jefferson, so far quiet throughout the briefing, spoke up.

"Sam, I think now's a good time to go into more detail as to how the quantum computer allows you to teleport objects. You know, what happens durin' the process."

"Of course, Director, but right now I suggest we take a brief break. I don't know about you, but I need to visit the little girl's room."

Chapter 16

DAY SIX, 1145 HOURS
THE FARM
OUTSIDE QUANTICO, VIRGINIA

FIFTEEN MINUTES LATER, everyone filed back into the conference room while Dr. Samantha Johnson once again positioned herself at the head of the table.

"Now, I need to get into the second quantum principle you need to understand. It's called Entanglement and, I'm afraid to say, this concept may be a little harder for you to grasp than Superposition."

Sam knew her task was to at least give Hearthstone a broad overview of Entanglement, the second theorem that made teleportation possible. She stood stock-still for a few moments to gather her thoughts.

"Basically, the concept of Entanglement essentially means that once quantum particles have interacted, they retain a kind of *nonphysical* connection to one another. Why? Well, frankly, we don't know. But we do know that quantum components are entangled in pairs, complete duplicates of one another. That's a proven fact. And once entangled, one particle will always assume a spin-up orientation while its partner assumes the opposite, or spin-down orientation. This happens when the entangled pairs are measured by a pulse of energy. To be honest, we haven't quite figured out why this occurs. Even Einstein was aware of this phenomenon which he called '*Spooky action at a distance*'. But what quantum Entanglement *does* allow is the instantaneous, nonphysical interaction between two particles that are separated by great distances."

Sam paused and took another sip of water, pleased to see that Hearthstone was hanging on her every word.

"Now, if you can bear with me a moment, I think the best way to view this interaction is to think of it being more along the lines of telepathy. Telepathy exists as we all know, and telepathy does not have a physical connection between two people's thoughts. We also know that telepathy, or the exchange of thoughts, has supposedly occurred between individuals who were literally worlds apart. Scientists have also theorized that telepathic thought travels instantly with no constraints as to the speed of light limitation. Without going into a lot of detail, just know that all entities that possess mass are dependent on some physical force to move them. That being the case, the speed of light restriction applies to the fastest speed capable for that moving force. However, and we still don't know exactly why, but with Entanglement, as with telepathic thought, quantum systems are correlated in some way that does not involve a physical force for transport. What that means is, regardless of what Einstein's Theory of Relativity tells us, if there is no *physical* force involved that has its own inherent speed limitation, then the speed of light restriction goes right out the window."

Jake, surprised that he understood what she had just said, leaned forward and planted his elbows on the table.

"Sam, even I know enough about Einstein to know you can't exceed the speed of light. Are you telling us that Einstein was wrong? That something can go faster than the speed of light?"

"Well, I guess you can say that, Jake. We believe that to be true of telepathy, and at least theoretically at the quantum level with Entanglement. We still have a lot of research to do to try and understand this phenomenon. But please note, at least presently, we can't exceed the speed of light in delivering an object or entity via teleportation. We're limited by the actual speed of the delivery system, for example, the speed of a laser. But once an object or entity has been teleported to some distant location, there is no speed of light limitation for its return; its return would be instantaneous. Does that help?"

"Okay, Sam, if you say so," he said doubtfully, not believing a word she had said.

"Now, I know I've hit you gentlemen with a lot of information today, and Entanglement is a very difficult concept to understand, so let me try to explain the mechanics of how we actually accomplish teleportation within the framework of Project Gabriel. If you would please take a look at the flowchart displayed on the monitor, as we experimented with the Nuclear Magnetic Resonator developed by Dr. Angstrom, and the quantum algorithms developed by Dr. Williams, we've been able to scan both animate and inanimate objects down to the smallest subpart of an atom. In the case of animate objects, or living organisms, we've even captured and reconstructed brain wave patterns all the way down to their chemical syntax level between neurons. And, with the use of the NMR, have stored both sets of a living organism's entangled particles within the core memory of our quantum computer. That is, the object or entity scanned having been reduced to its lowest possible quantum state. In effect, having ceased to exist in our physical world, just like in Star Trek," Sam added with a quick smile directed at Petty Officer Third Class Martinez.

"Then, using the laser projection techniques we've developed, one set of the entities entangled particles is incorporated into a focused laser beam, while the other duplicate set remains stored within the computer. Once that's accomplished, we can project that one set of particles—those incorporated in the laser—at the speed of light, or at least at the speed of the laser, to any three dimensional point on or above the earth's surface. And since one set of particles is retained within the core memory of the computer, the teleported particles can be instantly recalled from their location to remerge with its partner.

"Now, the next question I'm sure you're thinking is, how do we return the teleported particles to join back with their partners? Just remember, all we need do is remeasure the set of particles that still reside in the computer, that one set of stored particles always knowing the location of its partner, no matter where they're located in this universe. At the exact moment that measurement occurs, the teleported particles, now in physical form at some distant location, will collapse down to their lowest possible quantum state and remerge instantly with those stored within the computer. No laser or other artificial means of transport is required. And this remergence, as I said before, occurs faster than the speed of light, just like with telepathic thought. Once the entangled particles are reconstructed as pairs, all we need to do is reverse the NMR scanning process to bring them back to their physical state. That's about it, gentlemen. Are there any questions?"

Sam waited for a multitude of questions, but was greeted only by silence. Finally, she laughed at Hearthstone's quizzical expressions and slapped the top of the lectern.

"Oh, come on guys! Help me out here! You have to have at least one question! Lieutenant Thompson?" she asked hopefully. "I can tell by the look on your face you're aching to ask at least one, so go ahead and ask!"

"Well, okay, ma'am," Lieutenant Thompson replied reluctantly. "What I was thinking about was being stored away in some computer. I guess as some kind of an electrical impulse or something. That's really kind of hard to swallow, if you want to know the truth. But what really bothers me is, assuming this thing works, what happens if there's a power outage or something? What happens then? Do we just kind'a blink out and cease to exist?"

"Well, Lieutenant, that's a great question, and one I should have addressed during my briefing. Now, I know this all sounds kind of scary. Quantum computers, teleportation, and entangled particles. Never been done before. And, believe it or not, my colleagues and I all had the same concern."

Not able to restrain a devilish urge, Sam thought she would have a little fun with the lieutenant and the rest of the Hearthstone team.

"So, just to let you know, my colleagues and I will be taking turns pumping gas into our backup electrical generator, to keep the juice going so you don't blink out as you so eloquently put it. Okay?" she finished, flashing Hearthstone a wicked smile.

The silence was now thunderous. Hearthstone just sat there with blank looks on their faces, not knowing how to react to what she had just said. They knew it had to be a joke, but they weren't exactly sure.

"Gentlemen! Gentlemen! Please!" Sam said, her eyes twinkling with mirth. "I'm just kidding! We have thought of that! First off, our primary power source is the nuclear reactor at Los Alamos; and secondly, we've developed numerous backup electrical systems for just such an eventuality. There's never been an issue to date regarding power to the computer. I should also let you know that you will not be the first to teleport; I've reserved that honor for myself. I've always planned on being the first person to actually teleport."

With that statement, Sam could see Hearthstone deflate like old party balloons as they relaxed back into their chairs, the pressure having been lifted from their shoulders. But they also wore guilty looks when they realized a woman would take their place as the guinea pig. But she also saw she had gained a great deal of respect in their eyes and appreciated that. They'd just needed to know it was her project to run and, come hell or high water, she would be the first to make history. *Well, maybe I just made the team,* she thought candidly as she gazed at the rugged men seated around the table.

"Sam," Steven Clarke said, interrupting the discussion, "I think now's the time to show Hearthstone exactly what we're talking about."

Clarke sat back with a look of confident expectation on his face, this demonstration being his ace in the hole. He just hoped to hell that it worked.

Sam nodded and smiled, then flicked a yellow switch and said in a Scottish brogue, "Beam me down, Scotty."

With the use of a fibre optic cable secured in the ceiling, since a true laser couldn't penetrate the building, a pencil-thin-beam of orangish-white light suddenly flashed downwards and hovered just inches above the table.

Hearthstone, taken completely by surprise, inadvertently drew back while their eyes snapped in on a wavering, opaque distortion that floated ghostlike before them. An entity that quickly grew in size that measured roughly six feet in length by one foot in height.

With a look of pure wonder on their faces, they stared at the apparition as it undulated and rippled as if alive, surrounded by a soft, muted, bluish-white light as it continued to grow in size and solidify in form. Then, with a final snap that caused the men to jump in their chairs, the distortion disappeared, replaced by Jake's .50-caliber, Mark-107 sniper rifle that floated unbelievably—for just a microsecond or two—a couple of inches in the air, then clunked solidly onto the table's surface complete in all respects.

"Holy Mother of God," Steve Martinez murmured as he anxiously crossed himself.

The other team members sat silent as chunks of granite, unable to believe what they had just seen, not daring to blink as they stared at the massive rifle that lay on the table.

With the unbelievable now a reality, Jake tentatively nudged the rifle with his fingertip and quickly snatched it back, acting as if he had just touched a piece of red-hot, molten steel. *Sure feels like my rifle,* he thought sheepishly.

As everyone continued to stare, Jake took the bit in his teeth and abruptly stood up, throwing caution to the wind as he grasped the rifle with both hands and—in a Pavlovian response—pulled its charging handle to the rear to make sure it was unloaded. Then he flipped it on its side with the shell-casing ejection port face down and carefully read the serial number stamped into its barrel, the same serial number he knew better than the back of his hand.

Jake placed the rifle back upright with a thud and stared hard around the table. First at Steven Clarke, then Director Jefferson, then General Gray, and finally back at Sam. Turning toward his own men he could tell they were convinced.

"Well, Mr. Clarke, I guess you've got yourself a team!"

Chapter 17

DAY SEVEN, 0725 HOURS
THE OVAL OFFICE

PRESIDENT GARRETT TAYLOR looked up expectantly from the paperwork that littered his desk, smiling as Karen Dodds—his longtime secretary—ushered Steven Clarke into the Oval Office. Taylor gratefully removed his elbows from the desk and leaned back good-naturedly.

"Good morning, Steven."

"Good morning, Mr. President," Clarke said as he angled toward the office couches with a sheaf of papers clutched in his hand. "Sir, I've got the latest intel briefs on Afghanistan and Pakistan. Thought you'd want to see them now, rather than wait for the eight o'clock briefing."

"Thanks, Steven, and you're right," Taylor said, throwing his pen down in disgust on the pile of papers he'd been reviewing, shaking his head in frustration as he stood up and made his way to the couch opposite from Steven's.

"I was just going over the new Defense Appropriations Bill. And you know what, Steven? I don't think I'll ever understand Congress," he said, jerking his thumb at the six-inch stack of papers that sat on his desk. "They just don't get it, do they?" he continued as he plopped comfortably into the thick, soft cushions of the couch.

"The one thing we can't do is continually gut the military! Been going on for too damned many years! And yes, I know the military overspends sometimes, like spending four hundred bucks for a toilet, but you don't throw the baby out with the bathwater. What they don't get is that the military secures their liberty so they can pursue their other agendas. They can't keep robbing Peter to pay Paul; it just doesn't work."

President Taylor knew that he had a battle on his hands with the Defense Appropriations Bill, but there was no way in hell he would go along with further reductions in military spending, much less those recommended cuts that sat on his desk. In fact, he was going to push for a significant increase in the defense budget.

"Steven, please excuse me, just letting off a little steam. But, by God this job can be frustrating!"

"No problem, sir," Clarke said, handing President Taylor the latest intelligence summaries.

"Well, at least this gives me an excuse to put that damned Defense Bill aside."

President Taylor took a minute or so and slowly flipped through the report, but he didn't see any mention of the Taliban nukes, much less their location.

"Any update on the nukes?" he asked hopefully.

"No, Mr. President, absolutely nothing. Not even a peep."

"Well, what of the NSA (National Security Agency) or CIA? What the hell are they doing? Don't they realize this is their top priority? I know it's only been a week, but we gotta get a handle on where those nukes are hidden," he said, closing the report and tossing it on the coffee table.

President Taylor unbuttoned his suit coat and draped both arms casually across the back cushions.

"Would a direct call from me help? Shake things up a little bit? Maybe light a fire under them, so to speak?"

"Mr. President, I'm convinced the NSA and CIA are doing everything they can at this point, but the Taliban are being very smart. They're not communicating with their hijack team. No radio, cell phone, or even satellite calls. A complete communications blackout on their part. You know that's the best way for us to locate them, through their communications. The Taliban, I'm sorry to say, have finally figured that out."

"I know, I know," Taylor said wearily as he rubbed the back of his neck. "It's just that it's frustrating as hell to know those damned things are on the loose and can come back and bite us in the ass."

"The other problem the NSA and CIA have," Steven continued, "is the region between Afghanistan and Pakistan where the nukes are hidden. That's some of the roughest country in the world. It's like trying to find a needle in a haystack in the middle of the Rocky

Mountains. And remember, sir, those folks have been traipsing around those mountains for generations, and know 'em like the backs of their hands. They also know how good our satellites and drones are."

"Okay, okay, I understand," President Taylor agreed, his hands raised as if in surrender. "So, all we can do is wait at this point."

"Sir, that's about the size of it. All we can do is hope that the Taliban makes a mistake, and that we're ready to move when that happens."

With a nod of agreement, Taylor sat silent for several moments, then reached for the coffee service with a brief glance at Steven.

"Yes, sir, thank you."

After he poured, Taylor settled into the couch and quietly sipped his coffee.

"So . . . changing the subject, how'd the briefing go with Hearthstone?"

"Well, sir, to tell you the truth, I think it went very well," Clarke replied, thinking back to Sam's briefing. "We had a few bumps in the beginning, but it looks like they're fully onboard. They had a hell of a lot of good questions, and Dr. Johnson did a great job in explaining how it all works."

"How'd they strike you? Hearthstone, I mean. Think they're up to the task?"

President Taylor wanted Steven's input on what he thought of the men.

"Sir, we couldn't have picked a better group of men," Steven answered flatly. "Lieutenant Commander Stoneman is smart, dedicated, and completely focused on taking out Islamic militants, as are the rest of his team. They know better than anyone the threat posed by those guys. They've lived it day in and day out over the past few years in Iraq and Afghanistan. They totally understand the position we're in, and know what's at stake here, Mr. President."

"Good," Taylor said flatly. "I value your judgment, Steven, and if you think these are the guys we need, then I'll go with that."

"Thank you, sir. And just to let you know, Stoneman and his men will head out to Los Alamos in the next day or so with all of their gear. Dr. Johnson wants them out there for on-site orientation and what she calls 'Realistic Training'."

"Good, sooner the better! And Steven, keep me up-to-date on their progress. I hope they know we're running out of time."

"Yes, Mr. President, they do," Clarke confirmed. "But, sir, before I forget, there's one of the team members I just *gotta* tell you about," he said with a shake of his head.

With a come-on gesture, President Taylor smiled in anticipation and sank back further into the couch. He could use a good story today.

"Well, sir, there's this great big black guy on the team named George Tolman, Petty Officer First Class George Tolman, United States Navy SEAL. And when I say big, I mean this guy is fucking huge, excuse my French!" Clarke said with a grin that split his face.

"Just picture a guy that stands at least six-foot-five, weighs around two hundred and sixty pounds of pure muscle, and looked to be the meanest guy on the team. Anyway, sir, this guy's nickname was Squealer which I thought was a little odd. So, after the brief, I took Commander Stoneman aside and asked him how a guy like Tolman got stuck with a name like that."

Steven leaned back and chuckled, then he relayed the trials and tribulations of Petty Officer First Class George Tolman and the camel spider.

When he had finished, after adding a few embellishments of his own, both he and the president had laughed so hard that tears filled their eyes. President Taylor even had to put out a hand to keep from falling off the couch. All he could picture was this huge Navy SEAL jumping up and down, squealing like a little girl, while he tried to get that big damned spider off himself. And when told the spider in its last ditch attempt not to be shaken loose had chomped onto Tolman's most sacrosanct body part, the president lost it.

After a few moments, Taylor straightened back up, digging deep in his coat pocket for a handkerchief to dab at his eyes.

"God, Steven! I sure needed that! Funniest damned story I've heard in years!"

Chapter 18

DAY NINE, 1820 HOURS
GENGI KEL TRAINING CAMP
WAZIRISTAN PROVINCE, PAKISTAN

THE SUN WAS just beginning to set below the ridgelines of the ten thousand foot Tipakai Mountains, mountains whose slopes shimmered in the golden glow of dusk that abutted Afghanistan.

Fingers of darkness marched rapidly over the cluster of mud-daubed, cinder-blocked structures that occupied a narrow valley between the Tipakai Mountains to the east and the Shinkai Mountains to the west. A camp called Gengi Kel whose sole purpose was to train Taliban terrorists. A small, unobtrusive compound that consisted of twenty, single-storied dwellings set out in a grid pattern of four rows of five buildings each, with each dwelling separated by a two-meter-wide dirt path piled high with garbage and split by an open-trenched sewer. Through the center of the camp was a hard-packed dirt road that bisected the structures from south to north, with ten dwellings arranged on each side of the road.

To the north of the camp were training fields. One relatively flat, barren piece of land speckled with small stones and pebbles that was used for early morning physical conditioning; and adjacent to the field was an obstacle course that mimicked those found on any United States Marine Corps base made up of log towers, low wooden walls, and heavy ropes for the recruits to climb. Further north still was an entanglement course strewn with barbed wire that measured thirty meters in width, by one hundred meters in length, with eight designated corridors where the trainees were forced to crawl on their bellies—loaded down with full field packs and weapons—under the supervision of Taliban instructors who set off explosive charges to simulate mortar impacts and randomly sprayed AK-47 automatic weapons fire in their path. Five hundred meters to the south was a firing range with primitive target butts pounded into a low sandy berm where marksmanship was taught; and to the east of the camp was a special compound set aside by itself, comprised of three cinder-blocked structures surrounded by a chain-link fence topped with coiled razor wire. A compound that housed the faithful who were being indoctrinated into the company of martyrs—suicide bombers—most of them very young who ranged in age from only seven to twelve years old.

Gengi Kel, at an elevation of six thousand six hundred feet, had cool evenings and daytime temperatures that rarely exceeded eighty-five degrees in the blistering heat of the Pakistan summer. Small by most standards, the camp was home to a permanent cadre of thirty seasoned fighters whose main task was to train the Islamic faithful in the art of war; trainees who had been recruited from devout Muslim communities that included Chechens, Saudis, Afghanis, Syrians, Pakistanis, and a myriad of other nationalities who hated the west—even a few Americans—whose common bond was their own feudal interpretation of the Qur'an. But what was most important to the Taliban leadership was not the camp itself, but the myriad of deep tunnels that had been physically hacked into the hard granite of the mountains four kilometers to the north.

The first complex of tunnels had been started in 1979 by Mujahedeen fighters at war with the Soviets across the border in Afghanistan. The tunnels, initially meant to be weapons storage depots, were later used as sanctuaries for exhausted Taliban fighters. And, as the war progressed, the complex of tunnels had been dug deeper and broader with crude shafts drilled to the outside for ventilation; and low-wattage bulbs, strung from bare electrical wires hammered into their jagged ceilings, provided whatever meager illumination existed. But of most importance to the Taliban was that the tunnel complex had been kept secret for such a long period of time. Although rumors had run rampant within the Soviet Military, and later within the coalition forces of the United States, that such a stronghold existed, the location of the tunnels had never been compromised. All attempts by the infidels to locate its whereabouts going for naught. Even the Taliban volunteers who underwent training at Gengi Kel were ignorant that four kilometers to their north there existed such a massive complex.

Qudos Mehsud—commander of the Tehrik-e-taliban, a force of ten thousand fanatic jihādist fighters spread over the FATA of Pakistan—leaned tiredly back from the worn wooden table, rubbing his eyes with rough, dirty hands. He was alone in the room which he preferred when he needed to think, and right now he didn't need any distractions. With a brief look around the sparsely furnished room, he resignedly stood up and walked over to an old, battered, kerosene lantern to pump life into its fuel container—that sole lantern providing whatever scant lighting existed within the dingy structure.

Qudos, who was not a tall man, stood no more than five-foot-six in height, and at thirty-six years of age was young for the position he held. He was also diabetic which only his closest advisors knew, his weight having always been a problem throughout his life. He now weighed more than two hundred and forty pounds and had a fat, chunky body rather than the lean, rangy look of his Taliban fighters.

He walked back to his desk and sat down, then picked up a cheap ballpoint pen and tapped it absently against the table. He was worried about Mahmood and the fighters he had sent to ambush the Pakistani transport. If they did not arrive soon he would have to assume they had been intercepted, and that would cause a major problem with the Taliban Council of Elders, the same council that had elevated him to his present position. He knew if he could not make good on his promise to fatally punish the infidel Americans in their own homeland, the reins of power he now held would be in jeopardy.

It had been nine long days since the hijacking had taken place, and he knew that Mahmood and his men should have arrived the day before yesterday, the plan having allowed seven days for the fighters to make their way north through the Afghanistan mountains that paralleled the Pakistan border to the FATA. As the crow flies, it was only a little over one hundred kilometers distant, but given the rugged terrain and many obstacles that needed to be traversed, the actual walking distance was closer to three hundred kilometers. Seven days, he knew, should have been plenty of time for the ambush force to make its way back to the camp. Communications had also been strictly forbidden. He knew all too well how good the infidels were at intercepting radio and cellular phone calls, and then using those signals to locate their source.

Although informants within the Pakistan military had kept him abreast of their own search operations, he was unsure of the Americans. He didn't know if his men had been spotted by their cursed American satellites and then attacked by Predator aircraft, or intercepted by one of their Special Forces teams that were regularly inserted into the mountain passes.

In the distance, the rippling crack of AK-47 automatic weapons fire suddenly shattered the calm evening air. Many more soon joined in adding their own rifle fire to the first, their combined sounds swelling more and more into a deafening crescendo multiplied many times over by the delayed echoes that reverberated off the nearby mountain cliffs. It sounded as if a massive firefight was taking place.

Startled by the gunfire, Qudos jumped up and grabbed his AK-47, his heart pounding within his chest, convinced that the camp was under attack as he desperately thought of a way to escape. But where could he go? He knew if he stepped outside unsure of where the enemy was located he could be shot, and what use would he be to the jihād dead? Breathing heavily, sweating, he edged closer to the door and listened intently—silent as a stone—fearing the worst when he was rewarded with what sounded like the muted cheers of men in the distance. With his tensed shoulders now relaxed, and angry at himself for having been afraid, a hint of a grim smile crossed his face, for in his heart he knew it had to be Mahmood. Finally! By Allah's grace!

Limp with relief, he quickly opened the door and stepped onto the road, oblivious to his four bodyguards who nervously fingered their weapons. Instead, he looked northwards where he could hear the cheers and sounds of rifle fire. With his AK-47 hastily slung over his shoulder, he impatiently motioned for his guards to follow as he ran awkwardly towards the sound of gunfire. To his rear his men followed, their boots crunching loudly on the hard-packed earth.

No more than two hundred meters from where he had begun, Qudos topped a low rise and saw more than seventy trainees and cadre members packed tightly in a circled mass, shouting and laughing as they jerked their rifles over their heads and emptied their magazines into the sky. He quickly moved toward the clump of men who opened a lane for him to pass, the fighters becoming quiet and respectful as they knuckled their foreheads, or pulled on stringy forelocks, in a gesture of respect.

In the center of the men stood Mahmood, accompanied by several of his fighters, all of them thickly layered with dirt and grime. He could tell they were exhausted as they smiled broadly and slapped men that they knew on their arms and chests, acknowledging their shouts of praise. Through the haze of dust kicked up by the men's rejoicing, he strode toward his lieutenant with his arms outstretched.

Mahmood saw his commander approach and hurried towards him with a broad smile on his dark, dirt-encrusted face. Clasping one another in a brotherly embrace, they pounded each other on the back to enjoy their moment of victory.

"Allah be praised, Mahmood! He has brought you back to us victorious! Welcome! Welcome!" Qudos shouted.

"Thank you, Hakim," Mahmood tiredly said, beaming with pride at the compliments paid to him by his leader. Hakim being an honorific term for "ruler" or "commander" in Pashtu.

Finally, when the jubilations had ceased, Qudos motioned for Mahmood to follow as he turned back towards the camp. When they topped the low rise, he wrapped an arm tightly around his lieutenant's waist and hugged him close to his body.

"And the warheads my friend? They are safe?"

"Yes, Hakim, they are safe," Mahmood answered, unable to break eye contact with his commander. "As you told me to do, they have been placed deep within the tunnels, along with those we brought with them. Except for the men I brought with me here, the rest of our fighters guard the bombs as we speak, including our guests who know about such things. I left Qasim in charge."

"Good! Very good, Mahmood! You have done well! Now, come with me! You and your men need something to eat and to rest! And in the morning, after we give thanks to Allah, we will go to the tunnels to see the weapons. But for now, tell me everything that happened."

Chapter 19

DAY TEN, 1127 HOURS
LOS ALAMOS NATIONAL LABORATORY
LOS ALAMOS, NEW MEXICO

THE UNITED STATES Navy C-37B, better known throughout the world as the Gulfstream G550 twin-engine executive jet, sliced through the crisp mountain air as it made its final, straight-in GPS approach to runway Two-Seven of the Los Alamos Airport.

Although the instrument approach plate correctly showed an airport elevation of 7,171 feet above mean-sea-level, the latest calculations performed by the young copilot—incorporating the current airport temperature of 86 degrees Fahrenheit, a barometric setting of 30.32 inches of mercury, and a dew point of 48 degrees—had resulted in a higher density altitude of 10,157 feet. That is, even though the true altitude of the airport was just over seven thousand feet, the aircraft felt and performed as if it were being operated at an altitude of over ten thousand feet.

The pilot, knowing the higher density altitude would result in a much greater landing speed, canceled his instrument flight plan with Albuquerque Center and throttled back early, coming in low and slow under visual flight rule conditions given the runway was only a little over five thousand feet in length. He just wanted to make sure he had enough runway on which to plunk down the large business jet and, better yet, stop.

After the sleek aircraft turned off the one and only active runway, the grizzled, gray-haired, full-boat Navy captain turned to his young copilot.

"Just remember, Lieutenant," the captain said gruffly, "and you can write this on your forehead if you want. The most important thing about flying is that your landings equal your takeoffs!"

The captain laughed openly at his own wit and pointed at the control yoke.

"You've got the aircraft, son. Just take us over yonder to the transient ramp where we can off-load our passengers."

Yonder? the copilot thought, glancing at the old dinosaur that sat in the left seat.

Lieutenant Commander Jake Stoneman had never been to Los Alamos before, and had peered curiously through the small plexiglass window adjacent to his seat. As the Gulfstream swiftly shed altitude in preparation for landing, he had tried to get his bearings with respect to the layout of the town and adjacent laboratories. Being on the left side of the aircraft, he could barely make out the actual town of Los Alamos to his front, and what could only have been the large laboratory complex spread over the countryside to the south and west of town.

Before they'd left Washington, D.C., he had studied up a little on Los Alamos, more than surprised to learn the town and laboratories were located at an elevation of over seven thousand feet, and situated on a high, broad, volcanic plateau known as the Pajarito rim. For some reason he'd always thought Los Alamos was in the desert. But he'd been even more surprised to learn that the laboratory complex was scattered like a shotgun blast over more than forty-three square miles of rolling, pine-tree-dotted mesas and arroyos, with most of the lab's buildings congregated in clumps—like little villages—and fairly isolated from one another.

Jake had also discovered that the laboratory had originally been built during World War II as a secret, isolated facility known as Site Y12—Site Y12 having coordinated the scientific research for the development of the first atomic bomb. *Well,* he thought as he leaned back from the window, *this place is fucking huge!*

When the aircraft pulled into the transient parking area and stopped, he unbuckled his seat belt and stood up, careful not to bang his head on the overhead. The one thing he'd learned the hard way about these types of aircraft was their limited head space. To get out of the damned thing you had to walk down the aisle all hunched over.

Jake slid into the aisle while the rest of Hearthstone busily unbuckled their seat belts and retrieved whatever meager personal effects they had brought onboard. Unlike most commercial jets, the

Gulfstream didn't have overhead storage bins where you could place smaller carry-on bags. All of their gear had been stowed in the aircraft's baggage compartment.

Hearing a smacking thump to his rear, he turned and saw Squealer furiously rubbing his head after he'd slammed it hard into the aircraft's overhead.

Embarrassed, Squealer scrunched down onto almost all fours and began to make his way laboriously down the aisle toward the front of the aircraft. Jake thought he looked more like some big old Grizzly bear waddling down a forest path. Petty Officer First Class Jung-su Pak—directly behind Squealer and with more than enough clearance to stand fully erect—had a shit-eating grin plastered on his face, and then to Squealer's annoyance slapped him hard on the ass.

"Sometimes it pays to be short and deadly, Squealer!"

Once the aircraft door had been opened and the stairway extended to the ground, Jake poked his head into the cockpit.

"Captain, I just wanted to thank you for the ride. I know we're not the VIPs you normally haul around, but we sure do appreciate your getting us here on time."

"No problem, Commander," the captain replied jovially. "Enjoyed flying you boys out here. Besides, Junior here," the captain said, with a jerk of his thumb at the copilot who looked to be no more than fifteen years old, "needs all the time he can get flying one of these things. He's still trying to figure out what all the knobs and switches are for."

Jake laughed and shook the captain's hand, then waved nonchalantly at the copilot and exited the cockpit.

Pausing on the stairway, Jake breathed in the crisp clean air of northern New Mexico. *Damn it's clear!* he thought, his eyes almost aching as he looked at the Pajarito Mountains just to the north of Los Alamos; mountains that seemed close enough to touch, but in actuality were more than six miles away. Mountains whose summits soared to over twelve thousand feet and pierced the dark-blue New Mexico skies like the serrated edge of a steak knife. Los Alamos proper, he could see, was snuggled up comfortably against their foothills.

Hearing someone call out his name, he turned and curiously looked toward the terminal. Two white SUVs, which looked to be

Ford Excursions, and a large, beige, Econoliner cargo van, were parked sixty yards to his front next to one of the hangars. Four men, who he correctly guessed to be military given their short haircuts, ramrod postures, and camouflaged BDUs, stood in front of the vehicles. Then he saw Dr. Samantha Johnson standing to their left as she continued to wave and call out his name. He smiled, waved back, and rapidly made his way down the stairs.

"Good morning, Dr. Johnson," he called out.

"Good morning, Jake," Sam replied, gracing him with one of her typical, dazzling smiles. "Welcome to Los Alamos. And please, my name is Sam."

"Okay, Sam," he said, thinking she was just as beautiful as he'd remembered.

Sam was dressed casually in a pair of dark-brown, ankle-high, calf-skinned boots with heels, tight-fitting designer blue jeans, and had everything topped off with a cream-colored silk blouse that buttoned up the front with small wooden buttons. She also sported a matching cream-colored scarf she had used to tie up her blonde hair into a ponytail.

Jake, as usual, was dressed in a faded pair of scruffy old Levi's, brown ripstop nylon combat boots, and a yellow pullover golf shirt he had bought on sale at Walmart.

"Well, Sam, sure is beautiful country, isn't it?" he said, turning back to the mountains, thinking the scenery more than reminded him of western Montana. Although not as lush and green as the Bitterroots with their carpet of towering pine and larch trees, the sight still made him more than a little nostalgic. Being a very private person, he had never told his team—or anyone else for that matter—that he had been born and raised in a small town nestled in the foothills of the Bitterroot Mountains.

Jake's hometown of Victor, located thirty-eight miles south of Missoula and seven miles north of Hamilton, had been, and still was, little more than a gas stop on State Highway 93. The downtown section had only one bank, the Farmer's State Bank; one Exxon gas station with six older-style pumps; a relatively newer, single-storied, red-bricked post office; and a small but well-kept park behind the post office equipped with swing sets for the kids and a couple of gray-colored porta-potties. And directly across the highway was the local watering hole called *The Long Branch Saloon*—a weathered, single-storied, wood-framed building with split-planked floors and log-beamed ceilings, a building that looked as if it had been time warped from the 1880s where the locals hung out for their afternoon beers and bullshit sessions.

The son of a rugged mountain logger, Jake's dad had worked—at just a notch above minimum wage—for a company that cut and supplied raw logs to the local log home building industry. But he knew he couldn't have asked for a better place to have grown up. From an early age, he had been taught by his father to be an avid fly fisherman and hunter as had his two younger brothers. He had also spent many peaceful summer days fishing the Bitterroot River for trout and whitefish just across Highway 93 to the east. It was a rare day that he failed to catch his limit.

Another fond recollection was of hunting geese and ducks in the fall with the Winchester 20 gauge, double-barreled shotgun he had excitedly received on his twelfth birthday. He also had vivid memories of silent, stark-freezing winter dawns with the ground covered in a crusty sheath of sparkling white snow, snow that would crunch and crumple beneath his Sorel snow boots.

Winter had also been the time of year when he and his father would climb into their dirty-old-gray 1952 Chevrolet pickup, a truck that had definitely seen better days, and drive to their special spot at the base of the mountains. Once parked, they would hike up Sweathouse Creek into the steep Bitterroot foothills armed with their matching Remington 7mm magnum rifles in search of deer and elk during the hunting season. Not hunting for the sport of it, but to stock the family larder for the coming year.

Given his father hadn't been a wealthy man, their home had been a twenty-year-old double-wide trailer that occupied the corner of North Blake Street and Sixth Avenue just three short blocks west of Highway 93, its once white exterior streaked red with rust stains. But his father had more than provided for his mother, himself, and his two brothers.

"Yes, yes it is Jake," Sam replied as she followed his gaze toward the mountains. "Of course, being so high—we're at over seven thousand feet you know—it does make the winters rather interesting. But right now I really think you're seeing it at its best."

Jake inhaled another lungful of fresh air.

"Okay, Sam, so what's on the schedule?" he asked as they both turned and walked back towards the Gulfstream.

"Well, first off, we need to get your equipment loaded into the van, then get everyone over to the lab. Our area is what's called TA-53. TA stands for Technical Area, Jake, and there's over seventy TAs within the boundaries of the lab complex. Anyway," she continued, "we've arranged quarters for you and your men within TA-53 itself. I have to admit they're not fancy, but they oughta do, and that was hard to pull off, to say the least."

Sam remembered the shouting match she'd gotten into with the Los Alamos Lab's overall director of security; the security director's stance being that he would never, ever allow what he called knuckle-draggers and their weapons to gain access to the facility, much less remain overnight.

"But when you have direct access to the president's Director of National Security, who can make a quick phone call, it sure smooths out the rough edges."

Sam had been present when the Los Alamos lab's director of security had had his ass royally reamed-out by Steven Clarke.

"The only other alternative would've been for you and your men to stay at one of the motels in town. And given the security for the labs, you'd have had to go through three separate security checkpoints every morning and afternoon, what they call Vehicle Access Portals. That would've been a major hassle since you never know when they'll perform a full-on security search," she stated flatly.

As they approached the side of the aircraft, they pulled up short and watched as the balance of Hearthstone made their way down the flight stairs.

"Excuse me, Sam," Jake said with a brief touch to her arm. "Let me get the team squared away and I'll be right back, okay?"

"No problem, Jake."

While Jake made his way to the team, Sam waved to get the attention of one of the men standing beside the vehicles. When he waved back, she cupped her hands and shouted, "Major Davidson! We need the cars over here!"

With a thumbs up from Davidson, the men who had been standing in front of the vehicles loaded themselves up, fired up the large SUVs and van, and drove slowly toward the Gulfstream.

Jake stopped in front of the team who were now aligned alongside the aircraft's fuselage.

"Okay, men, listen up! We've got transportation to the lab." Then hearing vehicles approach, he watched as the two Excursions and van slowly pulled up and parked close to where they were standing. Turning back to Hearthstone he gestured at Sam.

"I'm sure you all remember Dr. Johnson. She'll be taking us into the facility today, and she's also arranged quarters for us on-site. So, what we need to do is off-load the equipment, get it stowed in the van, and head on out. Brett?"

"Yes, sir."

"See to the off-loading of the gear, then divvy up the team into the trucks. I'll get back to you in just a minute, okay?"

"No problem, Skipper."

With everything well in hand, Jake stepped up to Sam who was standing next to one of the men who had driven over in the vehicles, an army major by the golden oak leaves pinned to the collar points of his uniform. But before he could say anything further, the major bellowed, "Sergeant Ferguson!"

"Yes, sir!" one of the men replied.

"Take your men and help with the unloading. Report to the lieutenant."

"Yes, sir!" the sergeant said, motioning for the other two soldiers to follow as he headed over to Lieutenant Thompson.

"Sorry to butt in, Commander," Major Davidson said, "but from the looks of all that gear, it looked like your men could use a little help."

Before Jake could answer, Sam spoke up.

"Jake, this is Major Thad Davidson, United States Army, and the head of security at TA-53. Major, this is Lieutenant Commander Jake Stoneman, United States Navy, and a former troop commander with SEAL Team Three."

Jake thrust out his hand.

"Good to meet you, Major."

Caught with a large, thick, manila folder in his right hand, Major Davidson quickly transferred it to his left and shook Jake's hand.

"Same here, sir," he responded.

Major Davidson, as the head of security for TA-53, had been able to review Stoneman's and his team's nonconfidential personnel files prior to their arrival. To say the least, he'd been more than impressed with Stoneman's combat record and that he had been a troop commander with SEAL Team Three. Although he wasn't sure why they were here, or who they even reported to, he knew they were classified way the hell above his pay grade. It was a rare day indeed to see a "Top Secret–Presidential" security classification assigned to a particular group of men. But he could tell that Stoneman and his team were operators—trigger pullers as they were called in the military—just by the way they moved with that well-deserved swagger customary to Special Ops troops who had seen a lot of combat in the Middle East.

"Commander Stoneman?" Major Davidson asked. "Before you get back to your men, there's some admin stuff we need to get out of the way."

Davidson stepped over to one of the Excursions and laid the thick manila folder on its hood, then opened the folder's side flap and pulled out six sets of paperwork all neatly paper-clipped together.

Jake followed, curious as to what all the paperwork was for.

"What I have here, Commander, are your security badges for the lab. These badges will allow you and your men access to the general laboratory grounds, and authorize your admittance into any building within TA-53. And, please note, Commander, whenever you or your men enter, leave, or are on the lab grounds, they have to be on your person at all times. Either clipped to your shirt or worn around your neck; your choice. But most folks just wear 'em around their neck," the major explained, pulling out his own badge that dangled from a thin black cord. "All I need for you and your men to do is sign for their badges."

"Okay, Major, you got it."

Jake took the first set of paperwork that had his security badge—including his photo—already clipped to the front, and quickly scribbled his signature on three sheets of paper and handed them back.

"Thanks, Commander. Now, if you could send your men over here one at a time, I'll go ahead and get them signed up and their badges issued."

"No problem," Jake said, catching Jung-su's eye and waving him over to the vehicle. After each team member had signed and received their badges, they went back to work and continued to sort out their gear.

With all of their equipment finally loaded in the Econoliner, Chief Moczarny claimed "Shotgun" for the van and climbed into the passenger seat, the chief never wanting to be far from the team's weapons. The rest of Hearthstone split-up fairly evenly between the two Excursions with Jake, Sam, Major Davidson, Jung-su, and Sergeant Ferguson—who served as the driver—climbing into the first vehicle while Brett, Steve Martinez, and Squealer—along with the vehicle's driver—climbed into the second.

With Jake's Excursion in the lead, they all headed out of the terminal area and turned right on Trinity Drive, then drove three miles north as the small downtown section of Los Alamos passed by slowly on their right. In just a few minutes, they stopped at the main checkpoint into the Los Alamos Laboratory complex where everyone was made to get out of their vehicles to have their badges checked. Once that was completed, they all piled back into the vehicles and drove another four miles where they hit the second checkpoint.

But at checkpoint three, just prior to entering TA-53, the security personnel went apeshit when they checked the contents of the van. Major Davidson had to spend over ten minutes in a vain attempt to try and explain why the carryall was crammed full of weapons and military gear, including the largest goddamned rifle the security guards had ever seen. Finally, after a phone call had been placed to the Los Alamos Laboratory's director of security, who unpleasantly recalled his disastrous conversation with Steven Clarke, the caravan of vehicles was quickly passed through with no further delay.

Minutes later, they pulled up in front of a decrepit, two-storied stuccoed structure about a half mile from the main portion of TA-53's labs. The building, looking kind of lost and forlorn, reminded Hearthstone of a particular low-budget motel they knew of located ninety-five miles south of Las Vegas in the barren desert outside Baker, California.

As the vehicle's tires crunched loudly on the crumbled, asphalt parking lot shot through with tall weeds, Major Davidson apologetically turned and looked at his passengers.

"Hate to say it, gents, but here's home sweet home!"

Chapter 20

DAY TEN, 1138 HOURS
TUNNEL COMPLEX, GENGI KEL
SOUTH WAZIRISTAN PROVINCE

AFTER WHAT SEEMED like an eternity of climbing, Qudos Mehsud—commander of the Tehrik-e-taliban—finally reached the top of a steep, shale-strewn trail that spilled onto a bowl-shaped opening wedged between two mountain cliffs. Completely out of breath, he stopped and leaned over with his head bent between his knees, his calves and back muscles burning from exertion, a reminder as to why he rarely liked to visit this place; the path was just too rough and steep.

The opening had a rock-strewn floor forty meters in width that gently sloped upwards for another two hundred meters to his front, then narrowed to a point where it ended in a jagged cleft clogged with boulders. He had always imagined, in the haze of the far distant past, the deluge of water that must have poured through the cleft from seasonal summer rains and scoured out the crevice from the hard native rock. He also knew the Mujahedeen could not have picked a better place to build the tunnels. Sunlight could only strike the complex at noon when the sun was directly overhead, but at all other times was screened with gloom and shadow by the mountain walls that rose starkly on each side. Qudos knew they made the tunnels almost impossible to be seen by drones or space-based satellites.

When he first visited the complex many years before, he had been impressed that no tailings from past excavations could be seen to give away their location. Each shovel full of dirt and rock laboriously hacked from the mountain had been hauled down to the valley floor by either beasts of burden, or on the backs of the workers themselves, and then carefully scattered throughout the countryside to blend in with their surroundings.

The fruits of their labor were evident. On the left mountain face were four tunnel openings, each approximately three meters in height and two meters in width, with two additional tunnels carved into the right mountain wall. Each entrance guarded by a sand-bagged revetment set in a semicircle at waist height manned by two Taliban fighters armed with AK-47s.

Qudos looked to his front and saw several men, who had just rounded a tall, fingerlike outcropping of rock, walking rapidly towards them. In the lead was Mahmood's second-in-command, Qasim Wassan, who excitedly shook an AK-47 over his head in greeting. Quickly forgetting his aching muscles, Qudos ran up to the men with Mahmood following to his rear.

"Allahu akbar!" he called out loudly, smiling a large, toothy grin as he hurried his steps still more.

"Allahu akbar!" Qasim responded with a broad smile that almost split his sunburned face in two.

Qudos quickly closed the distance and hugged Qasim close to his chest.

"You look well, Qasim! You look well!" Qudos exclaimed, pounding him on the back.

"Thank you, Hakim! Allah, in his infinite wisdom, watches over us all."

"And Allah, in his wisdom, has brought you, and Mahmood, and all of our fighters back safely to us, including the means to punish the infidel Americans," Qudos said. "Come, I cannot wait another minute. Take me to see the warheads."

They all turned as one and walked up to the outcropping of rock, then quickly rounded its corner. Not twenty meters to their front right was another tunnel opening, separate and hidden from the others, guarded by two fighters who quickly stepped aside, knuckling their foreheads in a sign of respect to their supreme commander.

Qudos briefly waved a hand in gruff acknowledgment as he hurriedly walked into the tunnel entrance, then paused to allow his eyes to adjust from the outside glare. In the distance, he could hear the muted throb of a gas-powered generator that provided power for the low-wattage bulbs that hung loosely from the ceiling, lights that glowed dully down the tunnel and imbued the rough-hewn walls with an eerie golden glow of shadows.

Qudos walked quickly down the tunnel as the sound of the generator grew louder. When he reached the end of the tunnel, he stepped into a large gallery where five smaller tunnels branched out in a circle like the spokes of a wheel.

In the center of the gallery he could see ten old, wooden tables constructed of thick planks, flanked by sturdy benches, where thirty members of Mahmood's ambush force sat and ate an early midday meal. The rest of the ambush force, he knew, were scattered in the mountains to provide additional security.

When the men saw their commander approach, they stood as one and cheered him with shouts of "Allahu akbar! Allahu akbar!" that rang throughout the great cavern.

With a broad smile on his face, Qudos reveled in the adulation of his men, his face alight with passion as he waved for them to be seated.

"Please! Please, my friends!" he yelled. "Please sit down! You must still be tired from your journey!"

But the men would have none of it, their shouts of welcome undiminished as Qudos walked among them, greeting those he knew with a slap to the chest while congratulating them on their victory.

Ten minutes later, Mahmood spoke quietly in his ear.

"Hakim, the prisoners are in tunnel two, and the warheads are in tunnel three."

"Good! Let us go see the warheads first, then I will see to the others," he said excitedly.

Qudos left the cheering fighters and walked quickly into the entrance of Tunnel Three. Once inside the much smaller chamber, he stopped when he saw two large, olive-drab metal containers that rested on granite ledges carved into the far wall. With reverence in his heart, he mumbled a thankful prayer as he stepped up to the one nearest him and placed his hands firmly upon it, convinced he could feel its power surge throughout his body.

One hundred kilotons! he giggled with relief, having done his own research to know the power he now commanded. *He, Qudos Mehsud, the commander of the Tehrik-e-taliban, was now a nuclear power!* And he knew exactly which American cities would feel the wrath of his God. New York first, with its financial centers, would be gutted like a stinking fish as if cast upon a shoreline. Then Washington,

D.C., to send their leaders to cower before Allah's wrathful judgment. Both attacks, he hoped, to happen on the same day.

Qudos reveled in the thought that he alone would be given the honor of plunging the stake of jihād through the heart of America, ripping out her guts as if she were a lamb to be slaughtered for Eid al-Adha—the Feast of Sacrifice. He knew attacks such as these would far surpass anything Osama bin Laden could have imagined, attacks that would make him the undisputed leader of the entire Islamic jihād.

He lifted his hands from the container and looked toward the ceiling, his eyes closed with both arms raised as if in prayer, to once again give thanks for his merciful bounty. After several silent moments, he lowered his arms and turned to Mahmood.

"Now, take me to our guests so that I can make them more welcome."

Qudos entered Tunnel Two whose gallery had been originally constructed as an explosives bunker, but was now used to hold Taliban fighters who had broken their faith with Allah; the gallery sealed off by a large iron door surrounded by a thick, black-iron frame set permanently into the native rock. And the small smithy's forge, tucked away into a far corner of the room with its fire-blackened walls, gave more than ample testimony to its current use.

While he waited impatiently for the guard to open the door's ancient lock—a lock that looked more reminiscent of those found in old English dungeons—he took his time to view the prisoners through the door's steel mesh window. He could see the prisoners, the pilot included, shackled hand and foot to thick wooden chairs placed in the center of the room, each with a hood of black gunnysack draped over their heads and drawn tightly around their necks with lengths of thin hemp rope. The hoods, since their capture, having been removed only when the prisoners had needed food or water. Additional shackles, embedded in the stone walls of the chamber, hung limply towards the floor.

The guard—to his profound relief—finally succeeded in getting the stubborn lock to open, then swung open the massive door on its well-oiled hinges.

With his head lowered, Qudos stepped into the room followed closely by Mahmood and two of his fighters. Once inside the much smaller gallery, he eyed the prisoners as if they were unclean lepers, but he knew they were the key to unleashing the might of the weapons he now possessed. He could also tell which was the traitorous pilot by the torn and filthy flight suit that he wore.

Qudos had thought long and hard about the pilot. *What should I do with him?* On the one hand, he knew the pilot could be useful, particularly with regard to the operations of the Pakistan Air Force. He also hoped the pilot would have knowledge as to how to defeat the unmanned drones or, at the very least, to give him a better understanding of when and how these aircraft were used. In addition, when it came time to deliver the weapons to America, the pilot could be extremely useful. He knew that he had been trained in America, knew their customs, spoke their language, and had even met with some of their military higher-ups. What he did know for certain was that the pilot would never again fly.

But can he be trusted? he had thought these many days. *Absolutely trusted? If he had turned traitor once, he could turn traitor again. And if he did, he would know not only the location of the tunnel complex, but that of the warheads. Information that could easily be bartered with the Pakistanis or the Americans.* That was why he had told Mahmood to treat the pilot exactly like the other prisoners, including the use of a hood. *Once a traitor, always a traitor,* he had to constantly remind himself.

Laying those thoughts aside, he studied the other two prisoners in more detail, the technicians who could arm the weapons. He could see they were scared beyond belief and this warmed his heart. The little one to the right literally shook like a leaf and, given the smell of shit that surrounded him, had soiled his trousers. *Good!* he thought smugly. *This will be like pulling the wings off flies.*

The prisoners, soaked in their own sweat, exuded a thick cloud of stinking fear one could almost taste, their heavy breathing causing their hoods to balloon in and out in rhythm like children blowing up paper bags to use as toys. Qudos brusquely pointed at the most right-hand prisoner.

"Mahmood, remove his hood so we can have a little talk."

Without a word, Mahmood pointed at Riyad and Gamal, two of his best fighters who stood by his side, and motioned them forward. As they approached the prisoner from behind, Gamal roughly grabbed the technician's shackled arms and pinned them firmly behind his back. But at the touch of the fighter, Jamel Syed screeched in fright and smashed his head violently into the back of his chair, jerking and thrashing about in his chains.

Riyad quickly walked to the prisoner's front and punched him solidly in the face. As Jamel's head rocked backwards from the blow, Riyad shouted, "Stay still, you son of a whore!" Then he reached to his belt, deftly extracted a long sharp knife, and neatly sliced the hemp twine that secured the gunnysack around the technician's neck.

When the hood was jerked free Jamel sat stunned—cowed like a rabbit caught in the hypnotic gaze of a snake—his eyes squinted shut from the dim glare of the overhead lighting; his hair disheveled and caked with dried sweat as if cast in concrete. The beginnings of a stubbled beard from ten days growth also gave a dark, dirty cast to his face while a small trickle of blood dribbled down his chin.

With a grim smile, Qudos brusquely pushed Riyad to the side.

"Well, my little friend?" he asked softly, gazing at the downcast head of the prisoner. "What is your name?"

Jamel, frozen in terror, quietly whimpered, unable to focus his eyes on the apparition from hell that stood before him. But instead of answering, he cast a sidelong glance around the room, not seeing the anger build within his captor's eyes. He only knew he was in some kind of a cave with his supervisor and the pilot chained to his right.

After several moments of silence, Qudos silently stepped forward and roughly grabbed a fistful of Jamel's hair, gripping the hair so tightly that it began to rip from his head, then punched the technician hard in the face. He savored the feel and crunching sounds of smashed bone that had given way beneath his fist. With a quick flash of a smile, and seeing the technician's nose smashed flat against his face, he released the prisoner and stepped back to avoid the torrent of blood that exploded from Jamel's mangled nose. Blood that gushed down the prisoner's chest and pooled on the uneven stone floor beneath him.

Breathing heavily, Qudos relished his power over this piece of camel shit as he again grabbed the technician's hair and punched him squarely in the mouth, shattering Jamel's front teeth that slashed through his purpled, swollen lips.

"Now, my little friend," he continued softly, rubbing his bruised knuckles on his trousers, "you must learn to answer when I ask you a question. And you will answer immediately!" he roared, slapping this shitty excuse for a man hard across the face. "Now, what is your name?"

Jamel sagged forward restrained only by his chains, feeling as if he was climbing a steep mountainous slope through a thick fog of pain. With visible effort, he raised his battered face and mumbled through his crushed mouth.

"My name, uh . . . my name is Jamel Syed, Saaqhib." Saaqhib meaning "master" in Pashtu.

"Good, very good!" Qudos said, smiling as he softly stroked Jamel's head. "See? That was not so hard to do. And what is your job, Jamel? What do you have to do with the warheads?"

"I am first assistant to Abdul," Jamel answered immediately, risking a quick glance at his supervisor. "I am only a junior nuclear technician and work for Abdul, Saaqhib."

"Ah, you work for Abdul," Qudos repeated, his brow furrowed in thought as he scratched absently at his beard. Then he glanced quickly at the second technician while he paused to think of his next question.

"Now, do you know how to arm the warheads? To make them work?" he hissed, coiled in anticipation at Jamel's answer.

Jamel once again sagged against his chains, and replied without thinking.

"No. No, I do not, Saaqhib. I am only a junior technician. I only know how to store the weapons and to perform minor maintenance on them, that is all," he managed to croak with a quick nod at Abdul. "Abdul is the only one that can make them operational."

Finished, Jamel grimaced at the pain that throbbed through his nose, mouth, and teeth. Little did he know that his answer was the worst he could have given.

Qudos gently raised Jamel's battered face and peered deeply into his eyes, as if he could see into the depths of his soul.

"Well, my little friend, that may be just too bad for you."

Jamel stared in horror when he finally understood that death stood before him. His body wracked by sobs that caused his chest to heave in and out, his eyes clenched shut that forced tears down his cheeks to mingle with the blood on his face. He could not imagine what lay in store for himself.

Qudos released Jamel's chin and glanced at the other two

prisoners.

"Mahmood, remove their hoods so that we can continue our little talk."

Not having to be ordered to do so, Gamal and Riyad at once moved toward the middle prisoner, grabbing and pinning the second technician's arms as they quickly cut the hemp twine of his hood and jerked it free.

Abdul Farooqi, his knees weak with fear, remained silent as the hood was ripped from his head, not able to bring himself to look at his tormentor. He had heard everything that had happened to Jamel and, as with Jamel, his eyes were squinted shut against the dim glow of the room's lighting. With all his might he prayed for deliverance.

Gamal and Riyad next stepped over to the pilot and cut free his hood.

While the hoods were being removed, Qudos strode to a corner of the room and grabbed a heavy wooden chair, placing it squarely in front of Abdul while eyeing the prisoners as a jackal would do its next meal.

To the right of Abdul the pilot was silent, his head lowered, but to his left Jamel continued to sob and snuffle as if something was caught in his throat; unable to control his utterances as warm urine erupted against his inner thighs, his trousers now stained by piss that trickled down his legs.

Qudos looked irritably at Jamel, feeling nothing but contempt for the cowardly technician who sat there whimpering like an old feeble woman, even pissing and shitting his pants. As his anger continued to simmer, he stared hard at the junior technician. *What a weakling! No pride! He would not last a single day with his fighters!* Suddenly, he stood and slammed an iron hard fist against Jamel's temple.

"If you continue to cry and whine and piss like a woman," he shouted, "you will be treated like a woman! Is that what you want, my little friend?" he spit out leeringly. "To be used as a woman? Because if that is what you want, then that can be arranged! My men have not had the company of a woman for many days. They would enjoy bending you over a table and spreading open your backside. Is that what you want?"

Jamel weakly shook his head.

"No, Saaqhib, that is not what I want. I will try to remain silent."

Qudos glared at the technician for several more seconds, then roughly slapped him in the face.

"Mahmood, if he continues to carry on like this, have him stripped and given to the men."

Mahmood smiled.

"It will be done, Hakim."

Qudos turned back to Abdul and lightly patted his knee.

"So, my friend, look up at me."

Abdul slowly raised his head and looked into the lifeless, dead eyes of the man before him, but could see that only death and misery lurked there. He knew he must do anything this man asked of him.

"My name is Qudos Mehsud, the leader of the Tehrik-e-taliban. Do you understand this?"

"Yes, Saaqhib, I understand," Abdul answered, his head lowered once again toward the floor.

"And what is your name?"

"My name is Abdul Farooqi, Saaqhib," Abdul answered instantly.

"Good! Very good, Abdul!" Qudos said, pleased that the technician had answered so quickly. "Now, I understand that you are the senior technician. Is that true?"

"Yes, Saaqhib," Abdul responded dully.

"And what is your position, Abdul? What do you have to do with the warheads?" he asked in a soft, conversational tone. The same question he had asked Jamel.

Abdul quickly blurted out, "Saaqhib, I am responsible for making sure the warheads are functionally operational. By that I mean, testing their electrical components and updating any software changes within the weapon's programming."

"Ah, I see," Qudos said with a nod, not really understanding Abdul's answer. *What the hell is he talking about?*

"And what are these, what did you call them, programming changes that you do?" he asked, his hands clasped together as if in prayer.

"Saaqhib, each warhead has small programmable computer chips within their warhead housing. Whenever programming updates to the computer chips are required, I download those changes into the weapons, and then test them to make sure that they work," Abdul answered quietly. "To make sure the changes were properly entered," he added hastily.

"And how do you do this?" Qudos asked, his chin cupped in both hands as he awaited the technician's answer.

"My equipment was in a red toolbox in the aircraft, Saaqhib."

Qudos jerked up and quickly looked at Mahmood.

"Did you bring the technician's toolbox?"

"Yes, Hakim! We brought all of the equipment we could find on the airplane. The toolbox is on the floor next to the warheads."

With relief, Qudos turned back to Abdul.

"Now, my friend, and please answer me truthfully. Can you arm the warheads? This is what I want to know."

With his head raised in fear, Abdul looked into the bottomless black eyes of the Taliban commander. He could see the eagerness on his captor's face and knew the answer that he wanted, but it was an answer he could not give. He could not arm these particular weapons, not without their PAL codes. These weapons were of a newer design that required an eight-digit alphanumeric code to be entered for arming. The older weapons he could have easily armed; they had mechanical safeguards he could have overcome, but these weapons required PAL codes, and if the wrong code was entered they would become useless. Their internal microchips would shut down and not allow any additional arming sequence until replaced, and the PAL codes were kept under strict security within the presidential palace. The only person authorized to release the nuclear codes was the president of Pakistan himself.

Panic-stricken, he chanced a brief glance at Jamel who sat immobile to his right, his mangled face lowered toward his chest. Then he looked at the pilot, and then quickly back at Qudos who impatiently awaited his answer. He could not bring himself to answer the Taliban commander.

"Well?" Qudos asked, his patience wearing thin. "Can you arm the warheads or not?"

Tears streamed unbidden down Abdul's cheeks as he shrugged pathetically within his chair, the chains clinking around his chest.

"Saaqhib, I am sorry!" he blurted out, staring into Qudos' eyes. "You have to believe me! As Allah is my witness, if I could arm the weapons I would! But I cannot, Saaqhib!"

Qudos felt as if he had been kicked square in the balls, unable to comprehend what he had just been told.

"What do you mean you can't arm the warheads!" he roared, abruptly standing up, his chair crashing over backwards. Then he grabbed a fistful of Abdul's hair and slapped the technician hard across his face again, and again, and again, all the while screaming, "That is not the right answer, Abdul! That is not what I wanted to hear!"

Finally, with spittle dribbling down his beard, he slapped Abdul once again. "So! You think to play games with me! To play me for the fool! Well, my little friend, we will see who is the fool!"

"Saaqhib! Saaqhib!" Abdul screamed in stark terror. "What I tell you is the truth! I am not lying! These weapons can only be armed by using a PAL code! A code that has to be entered into the weapons to make them operational! And the only person who can release those codes is the president of Pakistan!"

Qudos, his breath labored with his arms hanging limply by his side, turned to Mahmood.

"Find Faisal! Have him come and start the forge! We will have the truth shortly!"

With a whisper of a cruel smile on his face, he locked his eyes on those of the terrified technician.

"I think we will have some fun, Abdul. You, me, and Jamel. For you see, I do not believe you. I think you are lying. Trying to be the clever person. Well, we will soon know if you are trying to be the clever person," he stated flatly. "So, too bad for you, Abdul." Then he stared hard at Jamel. "And too bad for you."

"No, no, Saaqhib! I am not lying!" Abdul screeched as he jerked against his chains. "Ask the pilot, he knows!" Abdul begged with a frantic look at Zalmay. "Please, ask him, Saaqhib! He will tell you I am not lying! He is military! He knows about these things!"

"Pilot! Look at me!" Qudos commanded, desperate to know the truth.

Zalmay slowly raised his head and looked directly at the Taliban commander with calm eyes.

Qudos was surprised to see the pilot was not afraid, but looked at him with confidence and courage, things he had not seen in either Jamel or Abdul. *Well! Maybe Zalmay will be useful after all,* he thought, gaining a measure of respect for the pilot.

"Zalmay?" he asked harshly. "Does Abdul tell the truth? Do I need these things called PAL codes?

Zalmay continued to look at the Taliban commander as if cast in stone, then slowly nodded his head.

"Abdul tells you the truth, Saaqhib," he said in barely a whisper. "PAL codes are needed to arm these weapons."

"Well," Qudos said resignedly, "we will soon find out." But deep inside he worried that what Abdul and the pilot had told him about needing PAL codes was the truth.

Qudos sat down heavily and waited for Mahmood to fetch Faisal. He knew Faisal well and respected his skills. He was their smithy who was gifted in being able to repair all things made of steel and iron. Much older than most of his Taliban fighters, Faisal had long stringy-white hair that framed a weathered, wrinkled face that looked like an old rotten apple with all of its moisture sucked out; the smithy's fingers gnarled and misshapen from having handled too many molten metals throughout the years. But Faisal was uncommonly good with the forge, and even better at pulling the truth from those who were reluctant to answer questions or confess their sins against Allah. Faisal, if it be known, thoroughly enjoyed his job of extracting information from prisoners, and took pleasure in the pain he could inflict on the helpless.

Qudos sat quietly and contemplated what Abdul and Zalmay had just told him, surprised and angered by the warhead's complexity. *PAL codes? By Allah! What in the hell are PAL codes?* As with any bomb he had thought they would be simple to arm, and if they could not be armed without these PAL codes, then he would have to think of a way to get these codes. There was no way he could go back to the Council of Elders and tell them he had stolen useless weapons. He would look the fool.

Suddenly, he made an abrupt decision.

"Mahmood, release the pilot and have him taken to a different cell. Have his shackles removed, and make sure that he has food and water. I will want to speak with him later."

Chapter 21

DAY TEN, 1345 HOURS
TUNNEL COMPLEX, GENGI KEL
SOUTH WAZIRISTAN PROVINCE

THE RANK SMELL of burnt flesh, singed hair, and acrid smoke permeated every crevice of the small cave-like cell. Faisal roughly grabbed the technician by his blistered scalp and lifted his head, then used his right thumb and forefinger to pry open the eyelid of Jamel's one remaining good eye, the other being nothing more than a smoldering crater cauterized black by his red-hot metal probes. Removing his fingers, he pressed an ear to the blackened chest to see if he could hear a heartbeat or any other signs of life. Not hearing any, he stepped back and looked disgustedly at the charred body that hung limply from the wall's shackles. With a slight gesture to Qudos, he bowed his head deferentially.

"Hakim, I am sorry, but this one is dead."

Qudos Mehsud stepped forward and gazed dispassionately at Jamel's tortured body, his nose crinkled in distaste at the corpse's stench. *He lasted much longer than I thought,* he mused, reliving the shrieks and pleadings of the junior technician with satisfaction, having thoroughly enjoyed watching Jamel's torment. *Too bad he is dead, but the one who learned the most from this piece-of-shit's agony was Abdul. Just as I had hoped.*

Abdul, chained to the wall next to his assistant, had been forced to watch Jamel's torture to ensure his complete cooperation.

Qudos then smiled, thinking of the soft, decadent Americans. *A weak and spineless people used to hiding behind their technology. A people who shamelessly paraded their women about practically unclothed and who worshipped pornography. A godless people made up of mongrel races whose men were as soft as women. Not willing* to make the sacrifices he and his fighters knew were necessary. *Not willing to be hard and ruthless when it was necessary to be hard and ruthless. That is why they will lose this war of religion, and the black banner of Islam will fly over all of the countries of the world. Even their own laws can be used against them. By Allah's grace, how naïve and stupid they are!*

He even remembered when the American leaders had been upset at something called "Water Boarding", thinking it outrageous and inhumane. He had laughed when he heard of it. *Their own leaders are their worst enemies. Weak and self-centered. Only seeking godless pleasure and power for themselves. No, they do not have the stomach for this kind of war. They do not understand that one must do many unpleasant things in order to be victorious. And he, Qudos Mehsud, was Allah's most steadfast warrior on earth, willing to do anything within his power to ensure the jihāds' victory. How many American leaders could have stomached watching Faisal flay the living flesh from Jamel's naked body strip by strip with red-hot irons? Or have him brutally emasculated with a white-hot rod that immediately cauterized what was left of his male member and shriveled sack? Or endured the endless screams and pleadings until Jamel's tongue had been roughly torn from his mouth just to shut him up? No, this they could not have done. They are weak and soft like women. That is why they will lose.*

Qudos snapped back into the reality around him, his nose still wrinkled in disgust at the nauseating odors that permeated the cell. With a coarse hack deep within his throat, he spat a large chunk of greenish-red phlegm directly into what used to be Jamel's face, then watched indifferently as it oozed down the body's scarred chest. *So much for Jamel, and so much for the godless infidels.*

"Mahmood," he said absently, wiping some spittle from his beard with the back of his hand, "have this camel turd taken outside and burned."

"Yes, Hakim," Mahmood answered, gesturing at Gamal and Riyad to take care of the body.

Qudos stepped back while Mahmood's fighters unlatched the chains from Jamel's limbs, the body falling to the floor like a limp bag of wheat. When Gamal and Riyad had rolled Jamel's body tightly within a large, filthy, tarp-like piece of canvas, he watched as they dragged it from the cell.

After the body had been removed, he stepped in front of Abdul who was still chained to the wall. But Abdul had not been hurt. Even he understood that the services of this man would be needed to arm the weapons when, and if, the PAL codes were obtained. He had just wanted to make sure the senior technician had been truthful about the codes. It had also been good to let him see what would happen if he tried to sabotage the weapons. He could tell that Jamel's agony had made a raging true believer out of Abdul.

"Well, Abdul? Jamel was not that helpful, was he," Qudos sighed as he lightly patted the technician's cheek. "I hope you now understand that I need you to be helpful. That I will not tolerate anything less. Do you understand?" he gently asked as a flicker of a smile crossed his face.

"Yes, Saaqhib, I understand," Abdul stammered, his mind and senses numb from the butchery he had just witnessed. "I understand completely, Saaqhib."

Chapter 22

DAY TEN, 1422 HOURS
THE TUNNEL COMPLEX, GENGI KEL
SOUTH WAZIRISTAN PROVINCE

SQUADRON COMMANDER ZALMAY MahMund sat on a dilapidated wooden bench and looked tiredly around the hand-hewn cave, a cave similar to the one where he, Abdul, and Jamel had originally been placed, but this one was much larger; its ceilings were five meters in height and had a breadth of almost twenty meters. To him it looked more like a barracks.

There were rusted metal bunk beds arranged on both sides of the room with several large, well-used, wood-planked tables scattered haphazardly about its center, and toward the rear of the room was a small etched-out alcove that served as a latrine. He could tell that it had been well-used from the foul smells that emanated from it.

Inside the primitive latrine he could see dented metal basins set at waist height used to wash one's hands, and above the basins were small tin cisterns attached to the rock wall that held water. Opposite the basins were large wooden buckets, overflowing with excrement, that served as toilets.

Zalmay had been led to this room by a fighter named Hafiz who had motioned for him to sit so that his chains could be removed. Once freed from his chains, the thought of escape never entered his mind. Unfamiliar with the labyrinth of tunnels, he never would have made it past the guards. And besides, he had cast his lot with the Taliban.

With his elbows set firmly on the table, he had silently endured the unending litany of Jamel's screams that had reverberated throughout the tunnel walls. He had even tried clamping his hands over his ears in an effort to shut them from his consciousness. Finally, when the screams had mercifully stopped, he knew he would soon be visited by Qudos.

Qudos Mehsud slowly entered the room flanked by Mahmood and his two fighters.

"Gamal, Riyad, go get something to eat," Qudos gruffly ordered. "Mahmood and I will speak to the prisoner alone."

As soon as Gamal and Riyad had left, Qudos tried to think of what he should do with the pilot. *This man has courage,* he thought again. *Had he not delivered the weapons? Had he not severed all ties with his past life and the Pakistan Air Force? Had he not shown strength, this pilot?*

"Well, Zalmay, have you eaten?" he inquired to break the silence.

"Yes, thank you, Hakim."

Qudos plunked himself down on a bench opposite from Zalmay's and stared hard at the pilot, drumming his fingers lightly on the table.

"Zalmay? Why do you bring me weapons that do not work? That need these things called PAL codes?"

Zalmay did not break eye contact with the Taliban commander, but shrugged his shoulders slightly.

"Hakim, not all of the nuclear warheads require PAL codes, only the newer ones. I am sorry, but I did not know what type of weapons were to be flown to Samungli. If these had been the older warheads we would not have needed PAL codes. In this we were just unlucky. Inshallah," he said with his gaze lowered to the floor, his hands spread outwards before him. Inshallah meaning "As Allah Wills".

Qudos pondered the pilot's answer.

"Was Abdul telling the truth? When he said that only President Chutto could release these codes?"

"Yes, Hakim, unfortunately he was telling the truth. The codes for these types of weapons can only be released by the president. They are intended as a fail-safe feature so they cannot be used by anyone not authorized to commit nuclear weapons."

"But what if we could somehow get these codes? Do you think Abdul could arm the warheads?"

Qudos hoped the pilot would answer in the affirmative.

"Yes, Hakim, I am sure that Abdul could arm the weapons. He is a Senior Nuclear Technician. He has his tools. He has the training. This is what they do."

"Well, my friend," Qudos sighed, relieved by the pilot's answer while he gently patted Zalmay's hand. "Then we must find a way to get these codes. But how can this be done?"

"Hakim, I have been thinking on this for the last couple of hours. The codes cannot be stolen; they are too well guarded. So we must think of a way to force President Chutto into giving them to us. How do we do this? The only way would be to kidnap President Chutto or members of his family, to hold as ransom for the codes. But he and his family are heavily guarded, and there is no way to storm the presidential palace. They are too well-protected and if attacked, the presidential bunker is all but impregnable. But sitting here, I think I have found another way. With your permission, Hakim, I will briefly outline this way to you."

Five minutes later Qudos smiled. What the pilot had told him made sense. It was a bold plan and workable, a plan worthy of his Taliban. And, better yet, it had a high probability of success. It could even enlist the support of the western powers, most notably the Americans, to apply pressure on the Pakistan government to give him the codes. The more he thought of the pilot's plan the more he liked it. It was simple, direct, and could be carried out somewhat quickly. It would also solve his problem with the Council of Elders. A bold stroke that would shore up his support within the Taliban and show the Americans to be the spineless country that they were. It would also disgrace the Pakistan president. Successful or not, it would only make his power greater within the jihād. Either way he would win.

Chapter 23

DAY ELEVEN, 0430 HOURS
TECHNICAL AREA 53
LOS ALAMOS NATIONAL LABORATORY

LIEUTENANT COMMANDER JAKE Stoneman tossed and turned on the lumpy queen-sized bed—his head pressed into the cold, sweat-drenched pillow—mumbling unintelligibly into the darkened recesses of the room. But no one was there to hear, his struggle for breath coming in short, small, uneven gasps as if he were being physically held underwater on the verge of drowning. Then, as they always did, the images exploded within his head like a freight train of unwanted fireworks set off on the fourth of July, his subconscious mind consumed by the blinding nightmare.

A massive fireball expanding in the heavens. Tendrils of red flame and acrid white smoke that arched gracefully through an azure blue sky. His eyes seared red by a kaleidoscope of colors that marched disjointedly across his line of vision. The gut-wrenching stench of death and the sickly sweet odor of burned flesh clinging to his nostrils. Bright shards of aluminum, twisting and falling, flashed streaks of sunlight off an unrelenting sun as they slowly drifted toward the green earth below. He remembered someone in the distance, a small child he thought vaguely, calling for his daddy. The sound of ambulances that pierced the stillness of what had once been a pleasant and beautiful spring day.

As the images and deathly smells faded from his tormented dream, Jake abruptly jerked awake and pushed himself upright, propped up on his elbows while he stared with sightless eyes into the black void of the room, not daring to move as he recalled random flashes of the nightmare.

Now fully awake, he lurched to the side and threw off the wet, tangled covers, then swung his legs outwards and placed his bare feet on the cold linoleum floor. He could feel the grit of sand that must have blown under the door during the night. Reaching up, he vigorously rubbed his stubbled face. *Well, at least that dream doesn't come as often,* he numbly thought.

For several moments he sat silent, thinking of how much he missed his wife and son, missing them to the core of his soul. Less than four years ago he had had a family; and Jennifer, his wife of what would have been nine years, and Todd, a son who would have been all of four years old, were gone. Dead and buried. And Todd's casket had been so very small. You just didn't need that big of a casket for an eight-month-old child.

The bomb had gone off three hours into their flight just north of Midland, Texas, at an altitude of thirty-eight thousand feet. When the emergency crews had arrived, the debris field had looked more like the tons of confetti strewn up and down the streets of New York City after the Macy's Thanksgiving Day parade, with large and small chunks of the aircraft and passengers scattered over more than fifty square miles of the Permian Basin. They did find some remnants of Jennifer and Todd, but nothing that could be identified as once having been human. Just some bits and pieces.

As he did every day, he tried to shake off his feelings of guilt for their deaths. He was the one that had convinced Jennifer to fly out with Todd to visit her parents in Washington D.C. while he attended some meetings at the naval base in Little Creek, Virginia. It was he that had put them on the flight that would never arrive home in San Diego. It was all supposed to have been a short, fun trip for Jens and Todd.

It had been a terrorist bomb; an indiscriminate, but well thought out action on the part of al-Qaeda. Only one day after their loss, al-Jazeera had interviewed the smug and sanctimonious jihādist leader who squatted on a Persian rug before a white linen background—an AK-47 assault rifle cradled in his lap—while he calmly and dispassionately informed the world that the killing of three hundred and twenty-five innocent men, women, and children was to show their continued displeasure with the United State's involvement in Afghanistan.

But what had been burned into his memory were the news broadcasts that had been shown across the world, showcasing the thousands of Muslim extremists, and just plain ordinary citizens of Islamic countries—many who professed to be our allies—as they rejoiced at the bombing. Their faces joyfully alive as they danced in the streets. Their eyes ablaze with religious fervor as they chanted an unending litany of "Death to America" and burned the American flag. God how he hated them! Hated them with a passion that encompassed his very being. He longed to kill every one of those sadistic, half-human assholes. Hate is what kept him alive.

With a mournful sigh, he pushed off the bed and headed for the bathroom dressed only in his military boxers. Clicking on the light, he stepped up to the sink and splashed some cold water on his face, then grabbed a hand towel and dried off. With his forearms resting on the basin, he studied his reflection in the mirror. *Well, today's a new day,* he thought, seeing a few more lines etched into his rugged face. *Time to buck up and stop feeling sorry for yourself. Besides, today should be an interesting day. We finally get to see Gabriel in action.*

Feeling somewhat better, he brushed his teeth but didn't shower or shave; he'd do that after his morning workout. Back in the bedroom, he picked up his gym bag and rummaged around in it for a second or two, pulling out his running shorts, red "SEAL Team Three" T-shirt, and Nike running shoes. Now dressed for his workout, he tossed the bag on the bed and stepped outside into the cool mountain air that was tinged with the sharp smell of pine.

With a quick glance to the east he could see Venus—the morning star—that shined brightly above the horizon, surrounded by its halo of millions of stars that burned fiercely across the heavens; the stars undiminished by the first streaks of dawn. Nearby he heard what had to be Mountain Quail as they scurried through the low-growing bracken. He couldn't see them, but he could hear them as they called out to one another.

With a smile once again on his face, Jake embraced the new day and stepped over to a small patch of grass to begin his daily warm-up exercises. Ten minutes later, he slowly kicked off on his daily six mile run, thinking he would first head west on La Mesita Road that bisected area TA-53, then pick up East Jemez Road and head out towards the main gate.

Chapter 24

DAY ELEVEN, 0910 HOURS
TECHNICAL AREA 53
LOS ALAMOS NATIONAL LABORATORY

THE FORD EXCURSION screeched into the parking lot of the Baker Hilton as the team now called their humble abode. Hearthstone had been told they would be picked up at 0830 hours sharp and driven over to the lab that housed the guts of Project Gabriel for their initial orientation. With that thought in mind, they had all rushed through their breakfast at the facility's cafeteria, and then hightailed it back to their quarters to dress for the day. As usual, dressed in their well-broken-in, chocolate-chip-camouflaged BDUs, brown ripstop nylon combat boots, and soft-covers—all psyched up to see the actual mechanics of Gabriel in action. But it was now well past 0900 hours.

The Excursion slammed to a stop, rocking back and forth on its chassis. Lieutenant Commander Jake Stoneman could tell that Sam was upset when she jammed the vehicle into "Park", hurriedly unfastened her seat belt, and threw it off her shoulder.

Thinking to have a little fun, he snapped off a quick salute after she jumped out of the vehicle and slammed shut the door.

"Well, gee, Sam, glad you could make it! We were all starting to wonder if it was something we said yesterday! We even took our weekly shower four days early just for you!"

"I'm so sorry, Jake!" she said as she ran quickly up to him.

Jake couldn't help but smile as he watched her run. Like most women he knew, whenever they ran, they almost always kept their elbows locked down by their sides, looking more like a penguin trying to run on hard-packed snow.

Sam looked past Jake's shoulder and saw the rest of Hearthstone waiting patiently on the sidewalk.

"Guys, I'm really very sorry," she called out, but to her relief she saw them smile back. She even heard Jung-su and the chief say, "No problem, ma'am" and, "Don't worry about it, ma'am."

Feeling slightly better, she turned back to Jake.

"I swear I'd left in plenty of time to pick you all up, but they had a full-blown security shutdown at the main gate, and it took me close to an hour to get through. They searched every car and even slid mirrors underneath, looking for what I don't know! And to top it all off, they did a full ID check. It was a nightmare! They even had M16s. The last time this happened was a couple of years ago when we had a terrorist threat," she said breathlessly, a sheepish grin on her face as she reached up and fooled around with her scarf, trying to knot it tighter around her ponytail.

At the word "terrorist" Jake tensed and looked instinctively into the distance; his eyes narrowed as he scanned the horizon for jihādist assholes. But then he kicked himself mentally when he remembered he was in the land of the free and not the badlands of Afghanistan. Now relaxed, he chalked up the tightened security to some crazy nut who had probably called something into the facility, like a bomb threat or something.

"No problem, Sam. Don't worry about it. And I'm sorry you got stopped, but you're here now and we're all set to see what you've got lined up for us today."

At Jake's statement Sam brightened. She couldn't wait to take them over to the lab to show them what she really did.

"Okay, then, let's get everybody loaded up and head on over to the Sector M Building. That's where the project's located. And I'm sorry I only have one truck, but I think we can all squeeze in."

"Not a problem," Jake said as he turned toward the team. "Okay, Brett, let's get everybody loaded up."

The Excursion, with all six team members scrunched up uncomfortably inside, pulled out of the Baker Hilton parking lot and turned right on La Mesita Road that ran down the center of TA-53. To Jake's left was one building that immediately caught his attention, parallel to their route on the left-hand side of the road, one of the longest damned buildings he'd ever seen.

"Sam? What's that really long building over there?" he asked curiously, leaning forward to get a better look out of her driver's side window.

Sam glanced to her left to see what he was talking about, then grinned with a brief peek back at Jake.

"That's the Linear Particle Accelerator Building, Jake. It houses one of the largest and most powerful accelerators in the world. And just to let you know, that building is almost a mile long."

Sam could see the obvious curiosity in his eyes, and even heard Chief Moczarny mutter from the rear, "What the hell's a particle accelerator?"

Well, she thought, *now's as good a time as any to start Hearthstone's orientation to TA-53.*

"The reason that building's so long, gentlemen," she continued, "is it houses a long hollow pipe about ten inches in diameter, sealed under vacuum, that runs the entire length of the building. Within that pipe they can accelerate subatomic particles, like electrons and protons, up to two million volts down the tube to hit different targets for their experiments. And when I say volts, I'm talking about the amount of energy delivered to the magnets that line the tube. Most often, the target for their experiments is water-cooled tungsten so they can measure the particle's impact. But what's really interesting is that the particles within the accelerator can sometimes approach the speed of light."

Sam looked at Jake to see if she had lost him.

Jake didn't say a word, but just nodded in silent acceptance wondering what the hell water-cooled tungsten had to do with anything. Finally, he settled back and looked towards his front. He could see they were approaching an area with a hell of a lot more buildings.

"Seems to be a pretty big place, Sam. Just how big is TA-53?"

"Well, in size it's pretty large," she began. "Just over seven hundred and fifty acres and occupies the entire top of Mesita Mesa. It's one of the largest facilities within the whole Los Alamos complex. It has over four hundred lab buildings and about eight hundred full-time staff. But when the accelerator is in operation—it's closed now for maintenance," she explained, "there could be as many as three hundred additional folks here, mostly visiting scientists wanting to conduct their own experiments with the accelerator."

The Excursion continued down La Mesita Road, passing Alvarez Road on their right as Sam continued to act as tour guide.

"Now, that big three-story building coming up on our right is the Accelerated Test Building, and the one just further down is the Accelerator Technology Lab. Where we're heading is that larger building way up there to our left, the one that caps the end of the Particle Accelerator."

When Sam approached the end of La Mesita Road, she turned left into a broad parking lot situated in front of a large, two-storied, white-sided metal building.

"Well, here we are gentlemen. Welcome to the Sector M building."

Major Davidson, who had been waiting patiently for the last forty-five minutes outside the main entrance, watched as the Excursion pulled up and parked.

"Good morning, Commander!" he called out when Jake exited the vehicle.

"Good morning, Major!" Jake replied.

"Didn't know if you and your team was going to make it," Davidson joked.

"Neither did we for a while," Jake said, returning the major's crisp salute. "So, what's the routine, Sam?" he asked when she joined them.

"Well, first off, let's get everyone inside so Major Davidson can show you how to get through security. From there we'll head on down to the lab so I can introduce you all to Dr. Angstrom, Dr. Ross, and Dr. Williams, the other project scientists I told you about in Virginia. They flew out a couple of days ago to show you how Gabriel works."

"Okay, Sam, sounds good to us," Jake said while the rest of the team piled out of the truck.

With Hearthstone trailing behind, Major Davidson opened the main door to the facility and held it open until everyone had passed on through.

Once inside, Hearthstone saw they had entered a medium-sized room with what looked to be several glass-enclosed security checkpoints similar to what one would see at an airport, but these looked to be a hell of a lot more sophisticated and intimidating.

"Now," Major Davidson began, getting everyone's attention, "this is the primary security checkpoint for entering the Particle Accelerator. That's what's housed in this building, along with the Los Alamos nuclear power plant. Another security checkpoint, just like this one, but smaller, is located at the far end of the building about a mile down the road. But this is the checkpoint you'll use to access Dr. Johnson's lab. As you can see, there are four entry portals. Doesn't make any difference which one you use, but when you enter or leave the building you'll need to use one of them. They're pretty straightforward."

The team curiously checked out the portals. They could see each entry station was faced front and rear with thick glass doors embedded with steel mesh, and to the right of each door was what looked to be a credit card reader one would find at any ATM.

"For today we'll enter through the first portal—I've had its security system disabled—and as we go through I'll tell you what you need to do," Davidson continued, directing everyone over to the first entry port.

"The first thing you do is swipe your security badge through the reader. At this point the door should open. Once open, just step inside and shut the door; it'll lock automatically. Then, just like at an airport, stand still for a few seconds with your arms raised above your shoulders. Once the scanner's finished and a security guard has reviewed the images, and assuming everything's okay, he'll pop open the retinal scanner located to the right of the exit door. Just look into the scanner, press the scan button, and wait a couple of seconds for the scan to be completed. At that point the door should open. It's that easy. So, for right now, what we need to do is get retinal scans from each of you so they can be downloaded into our security mainframe. There's also retinal scanners to gain entrance into any of the labs, and the computer keeps track of which labs you're authorized to enter. Any questions, gentlemen?"

"Nope," Jake said, "seems pretty simple."

"Okay, let's go ahead and get your scans out of the way. Once that's done, you folks can head on down to Dr. Johnson's lab."

After the retinal scans had been completed and downloaded into the security computer, Major Davidson wished everyone well and shook hands with Jake. He wasn't authorized access into the Gabriel lab located in the depths of the facility.

Sam led Hearthstone down a short hallway and turned into a small alcove that had an elevator set into its far wall. Above the elevator was a steady red light where one would normally see the floors an elevator serviced, and to the right of the door was a retinal scanner in lieu of a call button. Sam flipped open the scanner, looked steadily into the opening, and punched the scan button. After just a couple of seconds, the light above the elevator changed from red to green with a soft gonging sound.

"Once through security," she explained, "just use this scanner to activate the elevator. Once the doors open the elevator will operate automatically, no buttons to push, and this elevator goes nonstop straight down to our lab."

"How far down's the lab?" Jake asked as they all stepped into what was obviously a large freight elevator.

"Well, it's more than ninety feet down," Sam answered, making sure to include everyone in her explanation. "Gabriel's located in what used to be an old uranium centrifuge room, back when they did nuclear weapons development in the 50's and 60's. We picked this location for three reasons: first, the security for the particle accelerator is the tightest within the whole Alamos complex; and secondly, the old centrifuge room is isolated with only one entry point, and had the necessary work space required for the project; and, last but not least, Gabriel requires enormous amounts of power, as does the particle accelerator. So, we're just able to tap into the accelerator's nuclear power source."

Twenty seconds later the elevator stopped and its doors slid silently open. Jake and the rest of Hearthstone followed as Sam stepped through a small entry area and up to a set of aluminum pneumatic doors that hissed quietly open.

Hearthstone stopped in amazement. Spread before them was a large, open, airy room roughly sixty feet wide and ninety feet deep. A room that had been carved out of the living rock of Mesita Mesa jammed full of technical looking equipment. The ceiling, they could see, was at least twenty feet high and studded with numerous banks of fluorescent lights that marched down the length of the room, each suspended by thin metal rods. The lab's walls were also painted in a nonreflective light-green paint, and the floors were surfaced with a thick, hard, black-rubber matting one would find in most upscale gyms. The matting, they assumed, to eliminate any vibrations from the lab's equipment.

On the right side of the room, separated by a floor-to-ceiling glass wall partition, was what looked to be banks of computers that stretched down the right sidewall almost to the end of the room, and on the left side of the lab were several glass-enclosed offices and three large conference rooms. Two individuals, wearing white lab coats, were in the right-hand conference room leaning over a table littered with papers.

But what really caught their attention was an enormous, black, monolithic-looking machine that dominated the center of the lab. Ceramic encased, the NMR scanner resembled a large doughnut set on its side and squashed flat on the bottom. From what they could tell, it looked to be almost ten feet in diameter and fifteen feet in length, more than resembling a huge hospital-type MRI that had been fed a steady diet of powerful steroids. They could also see countless cables that protruded from its sides like scrambled piles of spaghetti, dangling down its curved surface where they entered numerous openings in the floor.

Flanking the machine on each side was an elevated stainless steel table set at waist height, and above each table was a highly-polished round metal hood suspended by rods. The balance of the room was occupied by a mishmash of randomly scattered desks and work stations covered with computer displays and various types of testing equipment.

Dr. Ted Angstrom, busily adjusting some settings at the rear of the scanner, looked up when he heard the pneumatic doors open. He saw Sam and what could have only been the Hearthstone team standing quietly at the entrance to the lab.

Quickly wiping his pudgy hands on a clean rag, he called out brightly, "Good morning, Sam!", then tossed the rag onto a nearby workstation as he made his way to where Sam and Hearthstone waited.

Jake watched as the heavyset scientist waddled his way toward them, kicking his thick legs laboriously out to the sides. From what he could tell, Dr. Angstrom was an extremely portly man who stood no more than five-foot-six and guessed his age to be around sixty or so. With a broad smile on his face, the scientist also sported a ruddy, Scottish-highland complexion as if he had just finished a bout with a large bottle of single-malt scotch whiskey. Jake thought the scientist looked more like a monk. He had a thick wad of medium-length gray hair that encircled his bald crown, and his white lab coat, obviously too small to cover his large stomach, was just left unbuttoned. He couldn't help but smile when a picture of Friar Tuck popped into his mind.

"Well, I was getting a little worried you weren't going to make it,

Sam!" Dr. Angstrom said, patting her paternally on the arm. "And this must be the Hearthstone team!" Not having known what to expect, he clinically appraised the six rugged SEALs who stood before him, all dressed in their brown, chocolate-chip BDUs and combat boots.

"Morning, Ted." The one thing Sam always liked about Dr. Angstrom was that he was always upbeat and jovial. "And you're right, this is Hearthstone. Ted, this is Lieutenant Commander Jake Stoneman who heads up the team. Jake, this is Dr. Ted Angstrom."

"Pleased to meet you, Commander Stoneman," Dr. Angstrom said, vigorously shaking Jake's hand. "But, please, call me Ted. No need for formality since we'll all be working together."

"Thanks, Ted, and you can call me Jake." Then Jake quickly introduced the rest of his team.

"Okay, Sam, why don't you take these gentlemen into the first conference room and get them settled in. There's fresh hot coffee on the back table and some really good jelly doughnuts I brought in just this morning. While you're doing that, I'll get Richard and Ken to join us, so we can get everyone introduced and go over the project in more detail. To answer the many questions I'm sure these gentlemen must have."

"Will do," Sam replied, all too aware of Ted's penchant for jelly doughnuts. When it came to jelly doughnuts, she knew that Dr. Angstrom was the proverbial jelly doughnut gourmet.

"Later on I thought we could show them a demonstration of Gabriel, to show them what it can do, if you think that would be all right."

"Sounds good to me, Ted," Sam answered brightly. "Gentlemen? If you'll follow me, please?"

While Sam settled the team into the first conference room, Dr. Angstrom walked as fast as his short, stout, stumpy legs would take him over to the adjacent conference room and rapped twice on its window.

Drs. Richard Ross and Ken Williams looked up expectantly and saw Dr. Angstrom motioning for them to come outside, then they spotted Sam and what had to be the Hearthstone team filing into the adjacent room. With their schematics put aside, they quickly joined Ted and stepped into the main conference room.

"Good morning, Sam," they both said as they curiously checked out the Hearthstone team.

"Good morning, Richard. Morning, Ken." Then she directed her attention at Hearthstone. "Gentlemen, please let me introduce Dr. Richard Ross and Dr. Ken Williams. Richard? Ken? This is Lieutenant Commander Jake Stoneman and his Hearthstone team."

Jake, having just poured some coffee, introduced himself and the other team members. After the introductions had been made, everyone took a seat at the conference table with the exception of Dr. Angstrom who was grabbing a jelly doughnut and pouring some coffee at the back table.

Jake was curious about the other two scientists. When he looked at Dr. Ross, what he saw was a tall man with a lanky build and a youthful, clean-shaven face that belied his forty-five years of age. At just over six feet tall, Ross had short light-brown hair parted from the left and inquisitive blue eyes set in a drawn intelligent face. The scientist reminded him of a runner with his sunken cheeks.

Dr. Williams, on the other hand, stood no more than five-foot-eight and wore thick, black-framed eyeglasses that gave him a bookish look, all topped off with a neatly trimmed Van Dyke beard. He could also tell that Dr. Williams was higher strung than Dr. Ross. Williams was reluctant to look a person in the eye and nervously picked at his fingernails. Jake just thought he hadn't spent that much time around military men before, much less Navy SEALs, and was probably a little intimidated, or shy, or both. He couldn't tell which. But he knew if he had been a professorial type person like Dr. Williams, cooped up in a room with six strange guys he'd never before met dressed in battle cammies and wearing combat boots, he would've been a little intimidated himself.

Jake also reasoned that the Gabriel staff had to have been briefed on their backgrounds and knew what they did for a living—the efficient elimination of jihādist terrorists with extreme prejudice, preferably with a 5.56mm round placed right between their eyes. But Dr. Williams and Dr. Ross seemed friendly enough and eager to show them what Gabriel was all about.

"Gentlemen," Sam began, getting everyone's attention, "if we're all ready, we can begin the orientation. Ted? Could you go ahead and start us off?" she asked with a quick look at the back table where the portly scientist was wolfing down a particularly large jelly doughnut.

"By all means, Sam," he mumbled through his full mouth, having just taken a huge bite of his doughnut.

The heavyset scientist made his way back to the front of the room while he continued to chew on his pastry, the corners of his mouth now decorated with large globs of red filling and powdered sugar.

When the scientist approached the head of the conference table, Jake heard a muffled, snorting sound to his left. Turning, he saw Jung-su and Steve had their heads lowered as they snickered at one another, both doing a bad job of shielding their faces as they watched the chubby scientist chow down on his jelly doughnut. Jake knew all too well they needed to get off on the right foot, so he surreptitiously rapped a knuckle on the table and gave them a hard stare that meant, "Knock that shit off or I'll kick your ass!"

Jung-su and Steve caught Jake's pissed-off look and immediately wiped the smiles from their faces; both straightening up in their chairs as they made a concerted effort to try and be more attentive—looking as if they had just been plunked down in some principal's office to await punishment.

Almost finished with his doughnut, Dr. Angstrom pushed the last large morsel into his mouth and wiped his mouth daintily with a napkin.

"Jake? Gentlemen?" he began, his arms raised to encompass all of Hearthstone. "Welcome to project Gabriel and, needless to say, we're very glad to be working with you. Dr. Johnson, Sam I mean, has already told us about your meeting with Steven Clarke, the president's Director of National Security. And, just to let you know, the day before yesterday we had a televideo conference with Mr. Clarke where he outlined the challenges facing us all. I can assure you, gentlemen, even though still experimental at this point, my colleagues and I are more than sure that Gabriel will be up to the task."

Dr. Angstrom paused at that point and took a healthy swallow of coffee to wash down the remnants of his doughnut. Not a split second later, his eyes almost burst from their sockets as he frantically tried to spit the scalding hot coffee back into his cup.

"GODDAMN, THAT'S HOT!" he shouted, fumbling with the cup and managing to spill most of the burning hot liquid down the front of his lab coat. With a quick transfer of the burning cup to his other hand, he hastily set it on the table and picked up his discarded napkin clumped thick with raspberry jelly, then wiped vigorously at the stain on his coat. After a moment or two, all he had managed to do was leave large smears of bright-red jelly streaked across his chest. Finally, giving up in disgust, he smiled plaintively at Hearthstone.

"Please, you'll have to excuse me," he said apologetically, his face having turned several shades of red. "But, believe it or not, I tend to be a little messy at times. But, BY DAMN that coffee was hot!"

At this point everyone laughed, the ice having been broken.

"Ted?" Jake said aloud. "I can't tell you how many times I've done the same damned thing. Nothing worse than a mouthful of hot coffee, then trying to figure out how to get rid of it!"

"Thank you, Jake, for that kind sentiment. I appreciate it. But I must say it did take me somewhat by surprise!" Dr. Angstrom said, chuckling along with the others while he continued to wipe haphazardly at his lab coat. "Now, where were we before we were so rudely interrupted? Oh, yes, the teleconference with Mr. Clarke.

"Mr. Clarke told us about the hijacking of the Pakistan nuclear weapons, and outlined the various strategies available for trying to locate and destroy them. I also need to tell you that my colleagues and I agreed with Mr. Clarke, that the only alternative that may work is to utilize Gabriel. That is, as Mr. Clarke explained it to us, to place two or more of you men in the vicinity of the weapons once their hiding place is discovered. It's also our understanding there would be two objectives: one, to verify the weapon's location; and two, to call in outside forces to destroy them. Of course, there's a third objective we suspect would be high on your priority list—to successfully return you men back to your point of origin, namely, this laboratory. Now, as you're all aware, Gabriel is in its final development stage, but please rest assured that the utilization of the quantum computer and its teleportation properties has so far been successful. Very successful indeed! Over ninety-eight percent to be precise. So, our objective during your stay is to have you become more familiar with Gabriel, to get more comfortable with the project. Once we're done with that, we'll have you individually, and then later as a team, make actual jumps outside this facility."

Brett raised his hand.

"Go ahead, Lieutenant."

"Sir, Lieutenant Thompson. What jumps are we talking about?

"Well, Lieutenant, I don't know if Sam told you or not, but we've done teleports using animals within this lab. With the use of a fibre optic cable and our own internal laser. But I'm not sure if she explained that jumps to an outside coordinate requires the use of a much larger laser and an orbiting space mirror. If you recall, the demonstration with Commander Stoneman's rifle didn't utilize a laser, just a fibre optic cable. Teleports outside this lab will need to use the Los Alamos Free Electron Laser located in TA-46. Once you're more comfortable with the process, we'll proceed to the next step and use the big laser and an NRO (National Reconnaissance Office) space-based mirror for jumps outside this facility."

"Sir, Petty Officer First Class Pak. So, what you're telling us is, you've never teleported using a laser outside this lab? Is that correct, sir? That we're going to be, uh . . . the guinea pigs?" he asked nervously.

"Well, no, not really, Mr. Pak," Dr. Angstrom countered. "You're not going to be the guinea pigs as you so aptly stated. But please let me explain, and if I get too technical stop me at any time. I sometimes have a tendency to go into way too much detail," he said warmly.

"In any event, as far as the space mirror jumps are concerned, we'll probably start with inanimate objects, with such things as pieces of your equipment, weapons, etc., to validate the process. Basically, this will involve using fibre optics to transfer one set of entangled particles scanned into our quantum computer over to the Free Electron Laser facility, the one in TA-46 I just mentioned, where the particles will be incorporated into the laser beam. Then, using one of our space-based mirrors in geosynchronous orbit, we'll be able to determine the parameters needed to successfully project those particles outside the boundaries of this lab. But of course, as Sam told you before, returning the teleported objects is much easier. It just requires us to electronically measure the duplicate set of particles stored within the computer's core memory. So, once we become more proficient here at the lab, we'll proceed to the next step of projecting and reconstituting living organisms outside this facility. Now, within the Los Alamos complex, we've identified an area that's perfect for our needs. Out in area TA-70. It's really very simple when you think about it," Dr. Angstrom finished.

"Thank you, sir," Jung-su said, unconvinced as he looked inquiringly at his teammates.

Seeing the discomfort in his team's eyes, Jake raised his hand.

"Ted?"

"Yes, Jake?"

"We were under the impression you'd already been able to teleport using a laser. I mean, outside this lab. I think what would help us feel a lot more comfortable would be to see a demonstration of how the laser works. First here inside the lab, and then outside."

"Well, as a matter-of-fact, Jake, that's exactly what we had in mind. But first, we want to take you on a tour of our facility to explain the different components that make up Gabriel, to give you and your men a better understanding of how everything works. You know, how all the pieces fit together. From there we'll go on to the demonstration stage by showing you a living animal being teleported here within the lab. Then later, maybe tomorrow or the next day, we'll teleport outside the facility. We'd just hoped that would be okay with you and your team," Dr. Angstrom explained anxiously.

Before Jake could respond, Sam placed a hand gently on his forearm and gave it a little squeeze.

"Jake?" she said softly.

Jake turned when he felt her hand on his arm, and then gazed uncomfortably into her bottomless blue eyes. All he could see was warmth and the hint of a smile that lurked beneath her open expression. Frozen to his chair, he tried to understand the feelings that coursed through his mind, his arm seeming to burn from her touch.

"Jake," Sam continued, "we've set up a temporary test facility out in Technical Area 70, just as Ted said. TA-70's located in the lowest southeast quadrant of Los Alamos. It's basically an abandoned area that's miles away from any other active site. After your orientation here at the lab, and having actually seen teleportation work, we'll all head out to TA-70 in the next day or so to see the laser and mirror in action. Hopefully, that'll eliminate any of the doubts you and your men may have about teleports outside of the lab. Does that sound okay?"

Jake found it difficult to break his gaze from her eyes, and then he looked at the rest of his team. They were all hunched over the table awaiting his decision with smiles plastered all over their faces. He didn't know what the hell they had to smile about, but he could tell they were willing to carry on.

"Well, Sam, that sounds good to us."

Five hours later, Hearthstone—Jake included—was about ready to go out into the parking lot and slash their wrists, or scream, or just put a pistol to their heads and pull the trigger. They'd just spent those last five hours with Dr. Williams and Dr. Ross who had tried to explain the intricacies of the quantum computer. Although they were sure both scientists were brilliant men, and knew of what they were talking about, Hearthstone was bored out of their minds; their eyes glazed over as everything the two scientists told them went right over their heads. The team now ready for anything that was tangible and solid, something they could actually put their hands on. Quantum theory and hypotheses and qubits and algorithms were all well and good, but to their frame of mind the theories the scientists had tried to explain was like trying to teach differential calculus to an Australian aborigine.

Truth be told, they didn't give a shit how it worked, just that it did. Dr. Williams had spent over three hours with schematics and graphs explaining the ins and outs of quantum algorithms, and after Dr. Williams, they had spent another couple of hours with Dr. Ross who had tried to explain gaseous condensates. At the end of that session they still didn't know what the hell gaseous condensates were, or how they related to the inner workings of the quantum computer.

But Dr. Angstrom had finally saved the day. When it was his turn, he guided them over to the huge doughnut-shaped NMR that squatted in the middle of the lab. Up close it was even more intimidating than from a distance. As far as Hearthstone was concerned, it looked like something that had just come straight out of the 25th century. But to be honest, this was more to their liking. This was something they could see with their own eyes, something they could touch and feel. Tangible and solid. Even they understood this was what made teleportation possible.

Dr. Angstrom had taken about half an hour to go over the basics of the NMR, explaining in simple terms what it did and how it interfaced with the quantum computer. Totally surprised, the things he'd told them seemed to make sense. They still didn't understand the theories and underlying mechanics, but they did get a general sense of how the thing was supposed to work. At the end of his explanations, Dr. Angstrom had the team stand in a semicircle roughly ten feet in front of the massive machine. From where they now stood, they could see directly into the interior of the NMR and the steel tables that flanked its sides.

Sam, having excused herself a few minutes earlier, walked slowly back from the rear of the lab with a small brown rabbit that kicked frantically in protest against her chest. Dr. Angstrom, with a warm smile, took the terrified rabbit and placed it gently on a table.

"Sam?" he asked easily, "could you hold this little beastie down for a second?"

"Of course, Ted."

Sam moved quickly to the table and pressed both hands firmly against the rabbit to keep it immobile.

While Sam took care of the rabbit, Dr. Angstrom picked up a small hypodermic syringe filled with 3cc's of a clear fluid and injected the rabbit with a mild sedative. After a minute or so, with the rabbit now inert and docile, he picked up its limp body and gently placed it on a ceramic table that protruded from the interior of the machine. Then, with the flick of a switch, the table moved silently rearward into the NMR's cavernous opening.

When the table was fully retracted, Dr. Angstrom moved to the right side of the machine and looked at Dr. Ross and Dr. Williams who were ensconced in the large glass enclosure that housed the quantum computer. With a thumbs up from the two scientists, they indicated the computer was ready to go. Dr. Angstrom nodded, and with the rabbit fully enclosed within the NMR, he flipped a final switch.

A low-frequency humming sound—at first barely noticeable—resonated from the interior of the machine, a sound that quickly increased in intensity and filled the room. Hearthstone could actually feel the low-frequency waves pass through the fillings of their teeth and the soles of their boots, even though they stood on the floor's rubber matting. Chief Moczarny and Steve became slightly nauseous while Jake had a twinge of vertigo.

As they continued to peer into the NMR, the team could see the body of the rabbit enveloped in a vacuous glow, the rabbit becoming more and more translucent as if it were a thin piece of rice paper with no substance. Suddenly, with no warning, the rabbit disappeared, the table within the NMR now vacant and empty.

In the blink of an eye, taking all of Hearthstone by surprise, a barely discernible, pencil-thin-beam of orangish-white light shot out from the large round metal hood suspended above the table to the right of the scanner. The beam, however, didn't hit the table, but stopped—suspended in space—approximately an inch or two above its surface. Within milliseconds, the team saw a small opaque distortion about the size of a basketball beginning to take form, mimicking exactly what had happened with Jake's rifle as it rapidly undulated and coalesced about itself. In the next instant, the laser snapped off as if someone had clicked off a searchlight, and in its place the body of the rabbit seemed to float in space just above the table. Then, no longer supported by whatever had kept it hovering there, the rabbit plopped softly to the table's surface.

Hearthstone remained rooted to their spot. Steve, in a repeat of what he had done at the demonstration at the Farm, unconsciously crossed himself and mumbled a quick prayer. Petty Officer First Class Jung-su Pak and Lieutenant Thompson stood frozen in place, staring at the rabbit that lay peacefully on the table. Squealer just found it hard to believe what he had seen. Sure, he'd seen the rifle appear at the briefing with the director of national security, but this was different. Deep within his subconscious mind he had thought the appearance of Jake's rifle could have been a magician's trick, but an actual living, breathing creature had just been teleported before his very eyes. Jake and Chief Moczarny stole unbelieving glances at one another, then looked back down at the table in disbelief.

"Holy shit, Skipper!" the chief whispered.

"Holy shit is right, Chief!" Jake whispered back.

Sam, totally focused on the rabbit and not having heard Jake's or the chief's comments, gave Hearthstone a few moments to absorb what they had seen. The first time she had witnessed the actual teleport of a living organism had shocked her senses to the core. It had taken her days to come to grips with what they had accomplished. Then she placed a hand lightly in the small of Jake's back.

When Jake turned towards her, his face could be read like an open book—doubt, disbelief, and wonder was written across his weather-beaten face. As she smiled up at him, she knew full well the emotions he must be feeling. She even saw a whisper of a smile crack the edges of his mouth; his eyes glowing with the possibilities.

"Gentlemen, what you have just seen is the product of over twenty-five years of applied research," Dr. Angstrom stated proudly as he walked over to the rabbit and gently stroked its fur. "Now, as I'm sure Sam explained in your previous meeting, please observe that the NMR is now empty. The result of every subatomic particle of this little beastie having been scanned into the memory of the quantum computer, at which point the physical being of the subject ceased to exist. But its memories, feelings, electrical and chemical structure, and physical properties, down to the syntax level between neurons, was stored within the qubit memory banks of the computer. Now, if you recall what Sam told you before, the entangled particles of the rabbit, or any other entity scanned, can be separated. So, we took one set of the rabbit's particles, bundled them into our lab's laser, and projected them to another point on earth; namely, this table outside the NMR, replicating in every detail the characteristics of the remaining—or what we call host—set of particles that still reside within the computer. In effect, gentlemen, reconstituting a complete mirror image of the subject at its destination. So, for right now, there's one complete set of the rabbit's particles still contained within the computer's core memory, and the second set you see before you."

"Dr. Angstrom?" Steve Martinez asked quickly, unable to tear his eyes off the rabbit. "Petty Officer Third Class Martinez, sir. Is the rabbit still alive?"

"Oh, very much so, Mr. Martinez," he replied with a slight chuckle. "Come on over here and touch it."

Steve tentatively stepped up to the table and began to stroke the rabbit's fur. He could tell that it was still warm and breathing; its whiskers even twitched at his touch. With his hand resting lightly on the rabbit's side, he flashed Dr. Angstrom a relieved smile.

At this point the other team members pressed forward and took their own turns stroking the sides of the animal. As far as they were concerned, seeing and touching was believing.

"The reason he's not jumping around," Dr. Angstrom explained, "is due to the sedative I gave him. We couldn't very well have had this little fellow jumping around inside the NMR. Now, if you'll please step back a little, we'll demonstrate the return of this little beastie back to the NMR."

Hearthstone once again took up their positions in front of the scanner while Dr. Angstrom walked back to the machine's control panel.

"Now, to bring this little guy back involves measuring the set of entangled particles stored within the quantum computer. As Sam told you in her briefing, when we take a quantum measurement of the host set of particles that reside within the computer, this will cause the second set of teleported particles—more specifically, the rabbit laying on the table over there—to collapse down into its lowest possible quantum state and instantly remerge with the set of particles still contained within the computer. Once both sets of particles have merged, we use the NMR to reconstitute the subject."

Dr. Angstrom once again signaled to Dr. Williams and Dr. Ross. The team wasn't sure what the other two scientists did, but the NMR came back to life with the same low-frequency sound waves filling the lab.

An opaque, translucent glow appeared above the vacant table that rested inside the NMR. At that moment, Dr. Williams triggered the measurement energy pulse, the pulse measuring the quantum state of the host set of entangled particles that still resided within the quantum computer. At the exact moment of measurement, the rabbit abruptly disappeared from the outside table and instantly reappeared on the ceramic table within the NMR. As the machine silently wound down, the scanner's table, with the rabbit resting quietly upon it, slowly moved into the lab.

Chapter 25

DAY THIRTEEN, 1118 HOURS
TECHNICAL AREA 70
LOS ALAMOS NATIONAL LABORATORY

TECHNICAL AREA 70 lay at the extreme southeast portion of the Los Alamos Laboratory Complex, flanked by State Highway 4 to the east and Pajarito Road to the north. The terrain characterized by an unending series of hidden arroyos, small dry mesas, and wide, deep-cut gullies, all interspersed with a sprinkling of stunted pine trees and low-lying native bushes. At an elevation of six thousand nine hundred feet, the morning air was cool and dry and would reach a daytime temperature of no more than seventy-nine degrees.

The sky, brilliant blue with the slightest whisper of clouds far overhead, more than reminded one of the red rock country of Sedona, Arizona. TA-70 was also known as the Rio Grande Site, most likely due to the Rio Grande River being located a few miles further east outside the town of White Rock, New Mexico; and, as it had done for countless millennia, the Rio Grande continued its slow, unhurried journey south to the Gulf of Mexico.

A large, female, red-tailed hawk, rudely interrupted in her search for food, hunched down and suddenly exploded upwards, thrusting with powerful legs as she launched herself from one of the upper branches of a scrub pine, the powerful sweeps of her four foot wingspan leaving invisible vortices in her wake as she slowly propelled herself through the thin, crystalline air. When she caught a whiff of a strong late morning thermal, she spread her wings wide—banking steeply into the rising column of air—and then looked irritably back at the offending creatures who had caused her to take flight.

Lieutenant Commander Jake Stoneman, who sat in the front passenger seat of the lead Excursion, watched as a red-tailed hawk slowly circled away to the south; its wings fully outstretched as it climbed swiftly into the morning sky. As it climbed higher and higher, it became no more than a distant speck on the horizon, a speck that he quickly lost as it merged with the rays of the sun. With his eyes squinted almost shut to try and reacquire the hawk, both Excursions slowed and made unhurried right-hand turns onto a deeply-rutted, unmaintained dirt road with large rocks that pushed through to its surface.

Dr. Ross, the driver of the lead Excursion, slowed so as not to bounce his passengers around in the back, then reached for the dashboard and engaged the vehicle's four-wheel drive, making sure to take his time as he crawled over the many dips and washed-out gullies that lay in their path. Jake, thinking discretion the better part of valor, tightly grasped the handhold above his window and placed his other hand against the dash. Seated uncomfortably in the middle row of the Excursion was Jung-su Pak and Steve Martinez.

The second Excursion that followed was occupied by Chief Moczarny, Lieutenant Brett Thompson, and Squealer; the chief driving as usual with Brett sitting in the front passenger seat. Squealer, however, had taken advantage of having the entire middle row to himself and had splayed his body out along its entire length.

"Jake?" Dr. Ross said with a quick glance to his right. "We've only got about three miles on this road to the laser site. It's pretty rough going, but as you can see, it's secluded and we've never had any visitors. This was the best place we could find in the entire Los Alamos area for our experiments.

"No problem, Richard," Jake said, when he was suddenly catapulted a foot out of his seat and slammed down hard by a particularly nasty pothole.

Dr. Ross, hearing muffled grunts and a couple of "shits!" from his rear passengers, shouted over the grinding roar of the engine.

"Sorry about that guys! Missed that one! Just hang on! We oughta be there in the next ten minutes or so!"

As they continued down the bumpy, derelict road, Jake wondered why Sam hadn't come along. She'd met them earlier for breakfast at the facility cafeteria, and then driven everyone over to the lab. He had thought that with today being their first demonstration to see something teleported using a space mirror, she'd have wanted to be on hand. But after they'd received an overview of what was going to happen out at TA-70, he was surprised when she had suddenly excused herself and joined Dr. Williams and Dr. Angstrom in the computer room. He knew the two scientists were needed to run the equipment, so maybe they'd needed her to help out.

Several minutes later, Dr. Ross shifted the Excursion into four-wheel-low and pulled the large SUV up a steep thirty degree incline, its tires digging into soft dirt as it hauled itself onto a flat, rock-encrusted mesa. Once atop the mesa, followed closely by Chief Moc-zarny, he braked to a stop just short of a large, round, concrete plat-form that measured twenty feet in diameter and three feet in height.

Dr. Ross shifted the Excursion into "Park" and turned off the ignition. "Okay, everyone! We're finally here! Welcome to Technical Area 70!"

Everyone unfastened their seat belts and exited the vehicles, slamming their doors shut as Dr. Ross continued his description of the area.

"TA-70," he began, waving his arms in a wide arc, "was originally a high explosives test area, but it's quite safe now. This is pretty much an abandoned site and there hasn't been any testing here for the last few years, but it's perfect for what we need. No obstructions and no prying eyes," he finished with a small laugh.

Hearthstone, freed from the confines of their trucks, stretched out their arms and backs while they took a moment to look about themselves. They could see the site was surrounded by scrubby pine trees and thirsty, dried-out chokeberry bushes that dotted the land-scape. And directly to their left, less than a quarter of a mile away, was a barren plateau—flat as a pancake—that loomed over the site. To their front the land sloped downwards for many miles cut through by deep culverts and dried-out stream beds. Dr. Ross had been right: TA-70 was isolated and in the middle of nowhere, with no buildings or any other kind of structure visible in the distance.

At the conclusion of his brief description, Dr. Ross popped open the rear cargo doors of his Excursion and rummaged around in its cargo bay. With a quick look around the vehicle's fender, he saw Jake and Lieutenant Thompson checking out the area.

"Jake? Could a couple of your men help me out with this stuff?"

Jung-su and Steve Martinez, standing to Jake's left, overheard Dr. Ross and walked over to help.

"What'cha need done, Doc?" Steve asked with a quizzical look at the jumbled pile of equipment stuffed in the back of the vehicle.

"Oh, thanks, Steve. You too, Jung-su," Dr. Ross said, pulling at a large leather camera bag. "If you guys could help me out with these cameras and tripods, I'd sure appreciate it. We need to set 'em up over there in front of the platform. This is the stuff we're going to use to video the teleport."

"No problem, Doc," Jung-su said as both he and Steve pulled out the remaining tripods, camera cases, and coils of tangled cables from the truck's cargo bay. With a raised brow, Steve silently asked where all the stuff needed to go.

"Just pile it up over there about ten feet in front of the platform. There should be three video systems in here. Once we sort this stuff out, we'll set up a camera on each side of the platform and one directly in front. Sound okay?"

"Okay, Doc, no problem."

Squealer and Chief Moczarny also joined the group as everyone grabbed an armful of gear and trudged over to the platform where, under Dr. Ross' supervision, they began to sort and set up the equipment.

Jake and Brett, left to themselves, briefly watched as the men tried to figure out how to set everything up.

"Well, Skipper," Lieutenant Thompson said, scooping up a handful of sandy dirt and pouring it absently back and forth between his hands, "looks like this oughta be an interesting day."

"Sure does, Brett. So . . . what do think of all of this?"

Jake wanted to get a better feel for what Brett thought about Gabriel.

"Well, I think today'll show us just how safe all this teleportation stuff is," he answered honestly. "You know, using a space mirror to reflect that beam down here."

"Yeah, I know," Jake agreed, smiling when he saw Chief Moczarny scratching his nearly bald head in confusion, the chief having a little difficulty as he tried to figure out how to attach what looked to be a large, complicated video camera to one of the tripods. "Sure hope this thing goes off without a hitch."

Brett shrugged.

"Well, Skipper, I guess we'll find out if those space mirror things really work."

Brett tossed the dirt to the ground and absently wiped his hands on his trousers.

"You know, this whole thing about teleportation is still hard to believe. At least for me it is. I know what we've seen so far, and I have to admit it's a great way to fuck with the Taliban. And it's probably the only way to get those nukes back without getting a lot of our own people killed. So I'm like you, Skipper; I really want this thing to work. I've also been thinking how nice it would be to just zap into any place, pop the fuckers, then zap out. You know? No muss, no fuss! It's Miller time!"

"Yeah, I know," Jake agreed. "That's why I hope everything goes okay. Well, let's go see how our intrepid warriors are doing setting up those cameras. Looks like they could use a little help."

"Yeah," Lieutenant Thompson said with a chuckle, "sure looks like they do."

When they were no more than halfway to the platform, Brett suddenly laughed out loud.

"Man! Can you believe this shit? What I just said? All this talk about zapping here or zapping there? Sometimes, you know, I feel like we're all in the goddamned Twilight Zone. That we'll wake up and this was all a dream."

"Brett?" Jake said with a slap to his lieutenant's back, "I know just how you feel."

Dr. Ross, satisfied the camera systems were set up where they were supposed to be, and more importantly worked, moved from camera to camera to make doubly sure their batteries were fully charged and placed in standby mode. Finished with those tasks, he turned back to the team.

"Okay, guys, looks like we're good-to-go," he said, stepping back about fifteen feet to critically assess the camera's placements and angles. He couldn't see anything wrong.

"Now, gentlemen, just to reiterate, what's supposed to happen is at exactly one o'clock a living object will be teleported from the lab to that raised platform in front of us, just as Dr. Angstrom explained this morning. This'll also be the first time we'll be using the Free Electron Laser in conjunction with an NRO space mirror parked over the western United States."

Dr. Ross paused and looked at his watch, then peered into the sky as if he expected to see the laser shoot down at any moment.

"Looks like we've got about thirty minutes to wait, so we may as well make the time productive. Now, are there any questions you have while we're waiting? Something we haven't covered?"

"Richard? I have a question," Jake said. "At the meeting in Virginia, and also in the lab, we all noticed the laser never actually touched the surface of the table. I mean, both my rifle and the rabbit were suspended in the air about an inch or two. Why exactly was that?"

"Jake, that's a damned good question! And to be honest, I'm embarrassed we didn't address that earlier without your having to ask! But this is really important, so thanks for asking," Dr. Ross replied truthfully. "Basically, the answer to your question is that we need to make sure there's free space, just air if you will, available for the teleported entity to reconstitute itself. We found through our experiments that should the laser's beam, or fibre optic beam for that matter, interact with anything solid like the ground or a table, the teleported particles would become embedded in the atomic structure of whatever solid matrix it encountered."

"By embedded, do you mean like stuck in mud or something like that?" Chief Moczarny asked as the rest of Hearthstone gathered around to listen to Dr. Ross' answer.

"No, Chief," Dr. Ross replied soberly, trying to figure out the best way to answer the chief's question. He didn't want to scare the shit out of them. Then he looked at Jake, and finally at the rest of Hearthstone in an effort to convey the seriousness of the chief's question.

"Have any of you ever heard of the Philadelphia Experiment? The one that supposedly happened during World War Two?" he asked in general.

"As a matter fact I have," Jake said, briefly searching his memory banks. "Didn't it have something to do with trying to make a destroyer disappear? But I heard it was all a hoax, an old wives' tale."

"Well, Jake, there's been a lot of theories about what they were trying to do. And yes, most people think it was a hoax, or an old wives' tale. But the underlying problem that supposedly occurred with that ship *absolutely* applies to quantum teleportation."

Dr. Ross paused to let that statement sink in.

"It was believed the primary purpose of the Philadelphia Experiment was to come up with some kind of a cloaking device to render the ship, I think it was the USS Eldridge by the way, invisible. Without going into all of the details, supposedly the experiment worked and the ship did become mostly invisible. But when it reappeared, some of the crew members had become embedded in the metal structure of the ship . . . and killed. The importance of what I'm trying to say is, whatever is being teleported *will*, not maybe, but *will* become intermingled with that solid object's molecular structure if they come into contact with one another. The worst case scenario being death in the case of a human subject. Although we've made tremendous strides in GPS location, particularly with respect to height above the ground, our team will always err on the side of caution. That's why all teleported entities are suspended above any solid matrix when beamed to their destination."

Jake dipped his head and thought through what Dr. Ross had just said, then he glanced at the team. He could see the scientist's explanation had gotten their full and undivided attention. *Well, shit! But what the hell! They all needed to be aware of the risks associated with Gabriel.*

"So!" he said suddenly, "sounds simple enough to me. What do you think, Chief?"

"Makes no never mind to me, sir," Moczarny said indifferently.

"Everybody else okay with this?" Jake asked.

"I would also like to add, gentlemen," Dr. Ross interrupted quickly, "except for the first couple of experiments, we've never had any of the problems I just described. The odds of that situation occurring are minuscule, less than one in ten thousand. All I can say is, please rest assured that we know what we're doing."

Hearthstone relaxed at that statement, once again upbeat to see what was going to happen.

"Now," Dr. Ross continued as he motioned for everyone to follow him back to the platform, "it's almost one o'clock. So I suggest you all stand over there," he said, pointing to an area ten feet in front of the platform. "I'm going to turn on the cameras and then join you. I don't know if you realize this yet, but you're now a part of history, and hopefully you'll be impressed with what you see today."

Jake smiled as he watched the team bob their heads up and down in unison like ducks in a feeding pond, first looking down at their watches, and then lifting their heads to stare skywards for the first telltale sign of the laser. As the second hands of their watches swept past 1300 hours, and though prepared for the event, they all pulled back when a very large, translucent distortion—just under seven feet in height and four feet in width—flashed into existence on the platform.

Seven pairs of eyeballs—Dr. Ross' included—immediately clicked forward and zeroed-in on the apparition, none of them having any idea the lab would try to teleport something so large. Above the distortion they could also see the faint outline of an orangish-white laser that disappeared into the distant heavens. The laser, as it had done in the other demonstrations, stopped just short of the platform and hovered barely inches above its surface.

The opaque distortion undulated and roiled about itself like the rapids in a swift mountain stream, whipping about itself as it finally began to solidify into something of substance. Then, with a muffled snap of white light, the laser disappeared as if it had never existed. In its place a human figure, crouched over and centered in the middle of the platform, suddenly let out a shrill scream of, "Oh, shit!"

In disbelief, everyone watched as Sam stumbled onto the platform with her arms outstretched to break her fall, obviously having lost her balance while a large rip split the right knee of her designer blue jeans.

Jake, unable to move, stood frozen in place like the other men clustered around the platform. In his wildest dreams, Sam was the last person or object he thought would be teleported. As the men stood there dumbfounded, she used her forearms to push herself upright, then rolled onto her butt, her hair all askew—looking more like a bedraggled Samantha Stevens of "Bewitched" fame who had just fallen off her broom—but nothing could suppress the beatific expression that enveloped her face as she flashed them all a dazzling smile.

Jake, the Hearthstone team, and Dr. Ross—in that order—broke out from under their spell and ran up in a herd to the platform, vaulting onto its surface in a rush to help her out. Chief Moczarny and Brett were the first to arrive and gently lifted Sam to her feet. As they helped her to stand up, she threw back her head and shouted at the top of her lungs like a banshee, "We did it! We did it! Oh, my God! We did it!"

Dr. Ross, standing just a few feet to her right with a shit-eating grin plastered on his face, ran over and lifted her off her feet in a huge bear hug, then twirled her around in a circle.

"You're damn right, Sam! We did it!" he yelled, stunned as

everyone else. He'd had no idea that she was to be the first test subject teleported outside the lab, the plan agreed upon to use the same sedated rabbit they had teleported within the lab. All he could think was, by hook or crook, she had somehow convinced Dr. Angstrom and Dr. Williams to use her for the test. And besides, she was the project director and would have had the final say.

When Sam finally calmed down, she grabbed Chief Moczarny around the waist and hugged him tightly to her breast, then planted a big smack on his cheek. With the chief blushing red from embarrassment, she did the same to Brett and every other Hearthstone team member when they came up to give her their unbridled congratulations, hugging and kissing them all in turn.

Almost worn out from her rejoicing, and with the adrenaline rush of being the first human to teleport still coursing through her veins, she spotted Jake—standing all by his lonesome near the edge of the platform—staring at her in disbelief. With a sexy smile on her lips, she peered deeply into his eyes and slowly stepped forward, then drew his head to hers and planted an enormous kiss full on his lips. Still staring deeply into his eyes, accompanied by the loud whoops and whistles from Hearthstone, she backed up a couple of steps, dropped her hands slowly to her sides, and then thrust them skywards in triumph, spinning and dancing with uncontrolled joy.

As Hearthstone and Dr. Ross watched, they were more than reminded of Rocky Balboa doing his victory dance on the steps of the Philadelphia Museum. Jake, however, just stood silent; his heart racing more than a thousand miles per hour.

Chapter 26

DAY SEVENTEEN, 1017 HOURS
SECTOR M BUILDING
TECHNICAL AREA 53
LOS ALAMOS NATIONAL LABORATORY

DR. SAMANTHA JOHNSON leaned casually against the edge of a computer table with coffee cup in hand, watching as Hearthstone laid out their weapons and gear, on the lookout for any signs of nervousness on their part since today was to be their graduation ceremony. The team about to make their first jump into TA-70.

Over the last three days Hearthstone had become much more familiar with the lab's equipment, and she was confident they now had a strong foundation in the basic mechanics of Gabriel. She could also tell they were more comfortable with her scientific colleagues: Dr. Ross had even joined Hearthstone on their early morning runs.

She had to smile when she remembered what Jake had told her about their first run with the intrepid doctor. At first, he had told her, the team was pissed that he had allowed Dr. Ross to join them. They didn't want to have a civilian entering their inner sanctum sanctorum. But, boys being boys, Hearthstone had finally relented as they warmed up to the idea of running the good doctor into the ground. Just to make a point. Particularly since SEALs were noted for being the most physically fit, conditioned men in the military. "Lean and mean" as they say in military parlance.

But what Hearthstone didn't know was that Dr. Ross was a fitness freak who ran like the wind and had the stamina of a Zulu warrior. Sam knew he was an internationally ranked amateur runner, and participated in as many organized marathons that he could sign up for. She also knew he had run the Los Angeles marathon the previous March. Predictably, the Kenyan runners had been the fastest, but

Dr. Ross had logged a time of just over three hours that had placed him three hundred and thirty-second in the overall competition. To most folks that may not sound very good, but given there were over eleven thousand registered participants, three hundred and thirty-second place was very respectable, to say the least. She also hadn't let on that Dr. Ross was what you called a "Ringer". So, she hadn't been surprised at how subdued Hearthstone had been after their first morning's six mile run with Richard.

Jake had told her that as Hearthstone huffed and puffed their way up and down the undulating asphalt road—the team battling the unaccustomed seven thousand foot altitude more than anything else—Dr. Ross had easily kept pace while he ran most of the way backwards, all the while delivering an unending discourse on the mechanics of Project Gabriel. He hadn't even broken into a sweat. Unbeknownst to the good doctor, Hearthstone had silently wished he would just shut the fuck up so they could concentrate on finishing their run. If they could've put a bullet through his head they would've done it. But after all was said and done, Dr. Ross had ended up gaining the respect of the entire Hearthstone team.

Sam also thought fondly back to the previous evening. Although she'd only known Jake for less than two weeks, he'd caught her eye ever since they'd first met in Virginia. She didn't know what it was, couldn't put her finger on it, but there was something about him that made her want to know more about him. Of course, his rugged good looks, muscular frame, piercing blue eyes, and sense of command—in addition to having a very dry, boyish sense of humor—had nothing whatsoever to do with it.

Normally cautious in any relationship she had with the opposite sex, she had always adhered to the rule of never getting involved with someone with whom she worked, but Jake wasn't a co-worker she'd convinced herself. So, yesterday, when he had asked her if she would have dinner with him, she had leapt at the chance. She had also asked Dr. Angstrom if he knew of a place they could go, since there was a real scarcity of good restaurants in the Los Alamos area.

Ted had recommended the Paragua Mexican Restaurant located in Espanola, a larger town situated twenty miles to the northwest of Los Alamos. He had told her that the Paragua had excellent Mexican food, terrific atmosphere, and was easy to find. She knew if Dr. Angstrom thought it was good, then it had to be good.

Jake had thought it was a great idea and told her that he loved Mexican food. But of course, Jake being Jake, he'd felt obliged to ask the other team members to come along. The team wasn't stupid, however, and opted instead to go to a highly-recommended BBQ place they'd heard about and leave Jake and Sam to themselves.

Unknown to Jake, Hearthstone couldn't have been dragged by a team of wild horses to go to the Paragua Restaurant. They thought the boss deserved to have a nice night out and besides, they liked Sam. So all of the other team members had piled into the second Excursion and proceeded posthaste to the Bandelier Bar & Grill located in beautiful downtown Whiterock, New Mexico, just a few miles south of Los Alamos. In the meantime, Sam had picked up Jake at the team's ramshackle Baker Hilton in the lab's other Excursion.

As Sam drank her coffee and watched Hearthstone at work, she fondly remembered back to the previous night's dinner. The restaurant had been just what the doctor had ordered. It had been easy to find, just as Ted had told her, located off State Route 30 to the north of Los Alamos. She had also been pleased that the restaurant had had that old Mexican flavor to it with its dark-brown cobble-stoned floors, hand-distressed beamed ceilings, adobe brick walls with flecks of straw visible, and a myriad of potted cactus plants—from beautifully blooming barrel cactus to seven-foot-tall Arizona saguaros. The restaurant's walls, of course, graced with the obligatory black velvet paintings that depicted Mexican dancers, half-nude, large-breasted Mexican maidens, bullfights, and native village scenes. An added bonus was that the restaurant hadn't been crowded, since it had been a weekday night.

Their waiter had escorted them to a booth tucked away in a far corner of the main dining area where they sat across from one another on red-leather-benched seats, the table's lighting provided by an old, battered, brass miner's lamp that sat on the right side of the table with the condiments; the lamp's flickering candle providing just enough light to read the menu.

After a couple of margaritas, and sampling some of the restaurant's homemade tortilla chips and salsa, they had both ordered soft-chicken tacos accompanied by a side of steaming chili relleños covered thickly with melted cheddar cheese. While they waited for their main entrée to arrive, Sam had finally gotten Jake to open up a little about his past.

Extremely reticent at first, Jake hadn't wanted to talk about himself and deflected most of her questions back, then asked questions of his own. But as their conversation continued, she came to understand that Jake was a very private person, almost to the point of having built an armored wall around his emotions. But she was gently persistent and wanted to know more about him. After a couple of more margaritas, he had finally loosened up and the barriers began to fall. She now knew he had been born and raised in a small town called Victor in the Bitterroot valley of Montana, and when he had talked about his boyhood home, she had seen the longing in his eyes for a period in his life that could never be relived.

Later, when she had asked him if he'd ever been married, he'd flinched as if he'd been physically struck in the face; his eyes reflecting a depth of sadness she had never before seen. At that point she had reached across the table and softly taken his hand in hers, squeezing it gently, silently urging him on until he had finally recounted in graphic detail the horror of that fine spring day four years before, thirty thousand feet over Midland, Texas.

"Well, I think this is all the gear we're going to need," Jake finally said, more to himself than anyone else in the room, standing up from the tables where six neat rows of combat gear were laid out. With a quick smile at Sam, he looked at the chief. He could see that Moczarny had just finished ticking off each item of equipment on a metal clipboard he held in his hands.

"So . . . what's the word, Chief?"

Moczarny flipped the clipboard's cover over and pocketed his pen.

"I think we're good-to-go, sir," he answered matter-of-factly. "We've got everything proscribed for our CQC."

CQC was the acronym for "Close Quartered Combat" that outlined the basic tactical gear normally worn by SEALs for a fight, a fight in which they could be expected to engage an enemy at close quarters or in hand-to-hand combat. The CQC, however, was just a guideline and could be modified by each individual SEAL with the approval of his team commander, to suit the needs of the individual SEAL with respect to the area of operations, terrain, and the scope of their mission.

In this case Hearthstone had elected to go into Pakistan light. They knew they didn't need all of the gear for an extended operation, each of them hoping that the actual mission would be quick—in and out—and last no more than an hour or two.

For today's training session, their first actual, honest-to-god teleport out to Technical Area 70, Hearthstone would insert with the actual weapons and equipment they would take into Pakistan, the weapons they had selected being the new Colt M4A1 SOPMOD 5.56mm Integrated rifle and the MK23 semiautomatic .45-caliber pistol.

The Colt M4A1 rifle was an interesting weapon. Just fielded into the United States armed services to replace the older version of the M4A1, the Special Ops units were the first to receive it. It was called "Integrated" because this version of the rifle had the SOPMOD Block 3 upgrade, meaning that the optics and lasers and sights that usually hung off carrying rails had been incorporated into the weapon's structure. As far as Hearthstone was concerned, it sure made the rifle's various functions easier to operate. Also new to the rifle was a state-of-the-art thermal imaging system that could detect the slightest heat sources at night, sensitive enough to pick up the latent heat impressions of someone who had lain or walked along the ground, or had left a handprint against a building's wall.

To facilitate the use of the rifle's various functions, mode switches had been built into the weapon's pistol grip. An operator could now activate, with the touch of his thumb, the various lasers, visible light, thermal imaging, and other optical sights incorporated into the weapon. The rifle could also be fired in one of two modes, either semiautomatic or fully automatic, and spit out a high-velocity 5.56mm round from its thirty round magazine. A round that could easily defeat terrorist body armor that had an effective range out to six hundred meters. The entire rifle, fully loaded, weighed only six and a half pounds. There was also a newly developed, experimental KAC sound-canceling suppressor Hearthstone would be using for the first time. A sound suppressor so effective that when the rifle was fired, all one could hear were the muted click-clack sounds of the weapon's action as it cycled new rounds into the firing chamber.

The MK23 Mod O semiautomatic .45-caliber pistol closely resembled the frame of the older M1911 Colt .45-caliber pistol, the M1911 having been the standard issue pistol used by the United States military since the early 1900s. But there the resemblance ended. Developed by Heckler & Koch out of Germany, the MK23 was an offensive handgun designed specifically for the United States

Special Operations Command.

What Hearthstone liked most about the pistol, and needed for this mission, was its ruggedness, knock-down power, and match-grade accuracy. Although heavier than their standard sidearm, the M11 Sig Sauer P-228 semiautomatic 9mm pistol, Hearthstone wanted to err on the side of caution. They knew that no matter where a person was hit with a .45-caliber, 185 grain hollow-point round, they went down and stayed down.

The MK23 also incorporated a newly developed laser aiming module—called a LAM—that could operate in one of four selected modes: visible laser, visible laser with flashlight, infrared laser, and infrared laser illuminator. All one needed to do was place the projected laser on the target and pull the trigger; the twelve shot pistol would take care of the rest and, most importantly, very quietly. As with the M4A1 Integrated rifle, the pistol was also equipped with a smaller, cut-down version of the sound-canceling KAC suppressor, the KAC reducing the sound of the pistol's firing to little more than the sound of its action.

"Okay, Chief. Thanks," Jake said. "Sam? What's next?"

Sam put down her coffee and pushed off the table.

"Well, anybody a little nervous today?" she asked playfully, her head cocked to the side as she looked from one team member to another. She could tell by their manner that they were, Jake included. *Well,* she thought, recalling how she had felt when she had taken that first big step into the NMR, *that's understandable. This isn't something you did every day.* Then she took pity on the team and continued in a more serious vein.

"Okay, gentlemen," she said with her hands placed on her hips, "just to let you know, there's nothing to it. It's so easy that even a girl can do it!"

That statement brought smiles to the faces of the stoic, and obviously nervous Hearthstone team.

"You won't feel a thing," she continued seriously. "And you know I speak from experience. All that's going to happen is you'll feel as if you've been instantly transported to some other place which," she said, smiling at the Catch-22'edness of her statement, "will be exactly the case. One moment you'll be in the lab, and the next moment—Poof!—you're somewhere else. Now, you've all seen over the last few days how Gabriel works, and hopefully we," she continued with a gesture at Drs. Ross, Williams, and Angstrom, "have answered all of your questions."

When Jung-su looked as if he wanted to say something, she paused and inquired in a soft, low voice.

"Jung-su? Anything you want to ask?"

Sam wanted all of Jake's team to feel free to ask anything at anytime from either herself or one of her colleagues.

Jung-su, uncomfortable at having been singled out, just shook his head.

"No, ma'am," he said with a look down at his feet. "Everything's good-to-go."

"Okay, then," she said firmly. "Any questions from anyone else? No? Then I'm going to turn this over to Ted. He'll outline the rest of today's agenda."

"Good morning, gentlemen! And how are we all feeling this bright and glorious day?" Dr. Angstrom asked as jovially as he could, rubbing his hands together in anticipation as if he had just seen a huge lobster dinner spread out before him. He could also feel Hearthstone's tension flow over him as if the Mississippi had just burst through a levy.

"Sorry I couldn't meet you when you all arrived, but we just wanted to make sure that everything was in sync with Gabriel. And, just to let you know, she's operating at one hundred percent. No problems at all. Gabriel's ticking along just as she should. So," Dr. Angstrom continued, "it's time to get down to the nitty-gritty as they say. Jake? I see you and your team have all of your equipment. Sure you've got everything you need?"

"No problems, Ted," Jake answered with a quick look at their gear. "We've got everything we need, including our basic ammo load."

Then he looked at the rest of his team members.

"Just one thing, though. When we actually go on the mission, we want to go in with weapons loaded. Ready to respond to any situation. Once on-site we don't want to take the time to load up. Who knows? We could end up being inserted right next to some bad guy. Any problem with us going in tactical today? I mean with weapons loaded?"

Dr. Angstrom thought through Jake's request, but he had to agree. Whether loaded or not, their ammunition was going with them. Besides, Jake was the professional in this line of work.

"Jake, that's a good idea. No problem with that at all."

"Okay, Ted, thanks."

"All right then, gentlemen. Richard and Sam will head out to TA-70 and set up the cameras just like you did the other day for Sam. Once they have everything set up, they'll let us know by radio."

With a quick look at his watch, Dr. Angstrom paused.

"It's almost noon. We plan the insert taking place at one thirty. Since that gives us roughly an hour and a half here in the lab, I suggest you men check over your equipment and get suited up. Oh, and just to let you know," he said, smiling as he absently flicked a doughnut crumb off his lab coat, "there's fresh jelly doughnuts in the conference room. I brought 'em in just this morning."

Chapter 27

DAY SEVENTEEN, 1305 HOURS
TECHNICAL AREA 70
LOS ALAMOS NATIONAL LABORATORY

DR. SAMANTHA JOHNSON stood up after she made the final connection to the last video camera. It had taken her and Dr. Ross just over thirty minutes to set up the equipment exactly as it had been done for her own teleport. She had also changed clothes before leaving the lab, now dressed in Levi blue jeans, a pair of sturdy brown hiking boots that laced up the front, and topped off with a red- and black-checkered, long-sleeved, woolen Pendleton shirt—its shirttail knotted across her stomach with the sleeves rolled up to her elbows.

With one final look at their morning's work, and satisfied that everything was set for Hearthstone's teleport debut, she knew they couldn't have asked for a better day. There wasn't a cloud in the sky as she gazed upwards. All she could see was a canopy of blue faintly marred by the distant, billowing white contrails of a northbound airliner that etched a lazy path across the horizon. *Betcha they're heading for Denver*, she thought.

There was also a light warm breeze from the south filled with the pungent scent of sage and piñon pine. Feeling completely alive, she inhaled deeply and stretched out her arms to savor the smells. From her work at Los Alamos she'd come to love the high-country of northern New Mexico—its solitude, openness, and stark, barren beauty.

A door slammed shut on the Excursion that jostled her out of her daydream. Turning, she saw Dr. Ross heading her way fiddling with something in his hands. When he got closer she saw it was the two-way radio they would use to contact Ted back at the lab.

"Well, Sam, looks like we're all set. Anything else you can think of? Anything we forgot?"

"Nope," she replied matter-of-factly. "Nothing I can think of, Richard. The cameras are all set to automatic and I checked their batteries. We're good-to-go as Hearthstone would say."

"Okay, then. I'll get on the horn and let Ted know we're all set."

Dr. Ross faced where Technical Area 53 was located, just a few miles northeast as the crow flies.

"Ted? This is Richard."

After a few seconds, and not hearing a response, he keyed the transmit button again.

"Ted? This is Richard. Can you hear me? Come in, over!"

There was still no response. Dr. Ross looked down and double-checked to make sure the radio was turned on. He saw that it was. Then he keyed the transmit switch a third time and saw the red diode illuminate. The radio was working. With a deep sigh, accompanied by a shake of his head, he spoke slowly and distinctly.

"Ted! This is Richard! Come in, over!"

Back in the lab, Dr. Angstrom had heard the first two transmissions, but for the life of him he couldn't locate the damned radio. With Dr. Ross' third transmission, he hastily scrambled over to an adjacent table where he thought he'd heard his voice, digging through a stack of papers until he finally found the radio.

"Richard? This is Ted! Richard? This is Ted! Can you hear me?"

When Dr. Angstrom's voice came over the radio, Dr. Ross answered.

"Ted, this is Richard! I read you five-by-five!"

"Richard? Sorry about that, but it took me a bit to find the damned radio."

"No problem, Ted," Dr. Ross said with a chuckle. He knew that Ted was a brilliant theoretician, but sometimes he couldn't find the forest for the trees. He remembered one time when Ted had been totally frustrated when he thought he'd lost his reading glasses, spending almost an hour tearing the lab apart looking for them, only to be totally embarrassed when he realized they'd been perched on top of his head the entire time. Now that he had Ted's full attention, he continued. "I just wanted you to know we're all set up out here."

"Okay, good," Dr. Angstrom replied. "Hearthstone's almost set. When we're ready to teleport we'll let you know."

"Okay, Ted, thanks. Sam and I will be standing by."

Dr. Ross lowered the radio.

"Well, you heard the man. I guess right about now they'll begin scanning Hearthstone into the computer. My best guess is they'll be ready to teleport in the next twenty minutes."

"Sounds about right," Sam agreed with an uneasy look at the concrete pad. "But I gotta tell you, Richard, I'm glad I'm out here and not back at the lab. I just don't think I could've taken it watching them go through what I did."

With her troubled gaze directed at the southern horizon, she spotted a distant hawk that glided effortlessly through the sky. After several moments, she shrugged her shoulders ever so slightly.

Dr. Ross could see her concern, and had a pretty good idea why she was acting the way she was. He knew that she had gone to dinner with Jake Stoneman last night, a dinner of which he had heartily approved. It was about time she'd gotten out of the lab and started to have a life, one that didn't revolve around Gabriel every minute of every day. And he, along with Dr. Angstrom and Dr. Williams, had seen the marked interest she'd shown in the Navy SEAL commander. It didn't take a rocket scientist to figure out that she was smitten with Jake and concerned for his safety. He reached up and lightly placed a hand on her shoulder, giving it a gentle squeeze.

"Oh, come on, Sam. Snap out of it. There's nothing to worry about. Jake and his team will be fine. You know Gabriel's safe. And if it can help us recover those Pakistani nukes, then you know it's well worth it. It'll save lives. Let's just be glad we're at the point where we can use it."

"I know, Richard, I know," she said softly, totally in agreement with what he had said. "I guess I'm just being silly, but do you know how scared I was to step into that NMR? Even though I knew, or thought I knew, what was going to happen?"

Sam blushed as a smile flickered at the edge of her lips.

"I have to confess I almost peed my pants I was so scared, but right now we have six men taking it on faith that we know what we're doing."

She looked pointedly at Dr. Ross as she tried to shake off her negative feelings.

"Don't get me wrong, Richard, I know Gabriel will work. I've been there and done that. But I just can't help wondering what's going through their minds right now."

Dr. Angstrom placed the radio back on the stack of papers. *Good!*

Sam and Richard are ready. Then he looked at Dr. Williams who was making some last minute tweaks to one of the monitoring modules.

"Ken? Sam and Richard are all set to go. How's everything look?"

"No problems, Ted. The NMR is up-to-speed and all computer functions are normal. We can start scanning at any time."

With one final adjustment to the monitoring module, Dr. Williams stepped away from the work station and joined Dr. Angstrom.

"Okay, Ken, I think it's time to get Hearthstone out here and set up," Dr. Angstrom said. "Jake? You and the team ready to go?" he shouted across the lab. "I just heard from Richard. He and Sam are all set to go."

"Yeah, I think we're about set," Lieutenant Commander Jake Stoneman answered from the conference room. "Just give us a second to double-check things and we'll be right out."

Jake critically eyed each member of his team. He could see that Hearthstone had unconsciously slipped into what he called their mission "Persona", what others called putting on your "Mission Face". No smiles, no fidgeting, no emotions whatsoever, just trying their best to look detached and calm as if they did this every day.

Jake, however, could feel the tension that filled the room. It was so palpable he could almost cut it with a knife. His men understood this was unlike any other mission they'd been on, missions that had been strictly focused on placing rounds in the heads of jihādist assholes, something they were very good at doing. No muss, no fuss. Sure, they knew those missions had entailed risk, but they were measurable risks they could accept. They were familiar with the enemy and confident in their own abilities. They also knew how the Taliban would react in most situations, but this time it was different. Really different.

Even though today was just considered a training exercise, they were about to place their lives into the hands of men they barely knew and in a technology they didn't fully understand. That was hard to do, just going on faith—particularly for this group. Hearthstone was used to working with other professional warriors who could cover their backs, on call with support should they need the help. But this support team was made up entirely of civilians whom most warriors loathed. Folks who had never experienced the uncertainties of combat, or knew the stark terror that it sometimes entailed. And they were going to attempt something that only one other human being—Sam to be more specific—had ever done before. To say their pucker-factor was straight through the roof was the understatement of the century.

All Jake knew was to lead by example, knowing his men trusted him as he had come to trust Sam, the other scientists, and their machines. But what really motivated him was his firm belief that if this exercise was successful, then he and Hearthstone's ability to kill a whole shitload of jihādist terrorists would be increased a thousand fold. He liked that. The odds were in their favor.

"Okay, before we move out, everyone make sure your weapons are on safe," he ordered.

Each team member immediately unslung their rifles, looked down, and double-checked to make sure their firing selector switches were set to the safe position. Reslinging their rifles, they unsnapped the retaining clips of their drop-leg holsters, extracted their MK23 pistols to confirm they were on safe, then reholstered the pistols and snapped their retaining clips back in place. Once that was done, they tightened the slings on their rifles and maneuvered their muzzles downward across their chests.

With the team all set to go, Jake led them out of the conference room into the main portion of the lab.

As they slowly emerged and stood silently side by side, Dr. Angstrom and Dr. Williams were more than a little shocked as they stared at Hearthstone in silence, both men feeling small and inconsequential.

Hearthstone, sure they would be inserted at night, were dressed in their black-camouflaged BDUs; Pro-tec ballistic helmets with its built-in communications package; insect-like AN/PVS-15 night vision goggles—NVGs—attached to the front of their helmets; body armor-plate carrier harnesses front and rear; ABA tactical vests fitted with numerous pouches that held additional ammo magazines; and, of course, their weapons. Jake had also insisted that each team member apply camouflage greasepaint on all exposed body parts. Each man, using sticks of black, dark-green, and dark-brown greasepaint, had applied random zigzagged patterns that completely covered their faces, necks, and hands. Camouflage paint that made them look like creatures that had just emerged from the Black Lagoon.

Dr. Angstrom couldn't help but be afraid of these men, what little hair he had beginning to bristle and rise. Instead of the polite, young, well-spoken men he had met just a few days before, he was now face to face with the United States most lethal antiterrorist killing machine. America's assassins. Stone-faced with unfeeling fish-dead eyes. To him they seemed as if they had just stepped out of the pages of a Stephen King horror novel.

Dr. Williams shared the same thought as a primordial fear clutched at his guts, making him inadvertently step backwards a foot or two, feeling more like the proverbial deer cornered in the woods by a pack of ravenous killer wolves. *Jesus Christ! These gotta be the scariest damned dudes I've ever seen!*

Unknown to each of them, they silently agreed they were lucky to be on Hearthstone's good side. They sure as hell didn't want to be on their dark side.

Dr. Angstrom tentatively stepped up to these formidable men and asked softly, "Jake? You and your men all set to go? Any questions before we start?"

"We're good-to-go, Ted," Jake said unemotionally in his low-key mission voice. "And no, no questions. We just want'a get this show on the road."

"All right, then. Gentlemen?" Dr. Angstrom said as he pointed to an area just in front of the NMR. "If you'll just step over here, we'll go ahead and start the scanning process. Shouldn't take more than thirty seconds per man."

Hearthstone followed Dr. Angstrom's directions and placed themselves directly in front of the NMR. The team could see that the NMR's ceramic table had been removed as it had been done for Sam, the interior of the machine now looking more like the open gullet of some large, black, predatory beast.

"Okay, Jake," Dr. Angstrom said, motioning for him to stand at the lip of the machine. "When I tell you to, just step inside, center yourself in the middle, then turn and face me. And remember to stay as still as possible with your arms down by your sides. Once I start the scanning process it should take less than thirty seconds. As Sam told us before, you shouldn't feel a thing. The next thing you'll know you'll be out at TA-70. Once you're scanned, I'll go ahead and scan the other team members just like we discussed this morning."

Earlier they had decided to start the scanning process in rank order. Jake first, followed by Lieutenant (j.g.) Brett Thompson, Chief

Petty Officer Walter Moczarny, Petty Officer First Class George Tolman, Petty Officer First Class Jung-su Pak, and lastly, Petty Officer Third Class Steve Martinez. Given the storage capacity of the quantum computer, there would be more than ample room to store all six men's quantum components and, once everyone had been scanned, the laser inserts would also occur in rank order. The one limitation to the laser system, the scientists had explained, was their inability to teleport more than one person at a time. So each insert had to be done individually, with each teleport taking anywhere from ten to fifteen seconds. As a result, it would take more than two minutes to have the entire team placed on-site.

"Questions, anyone?" Dr. Angstrom asked with a grave look.

There were no questions.

"Okay, then. Once everyone's on-site, we'll reverse the process and bring you back to the lab. As you already know, the laser won't be needed for the extraction. Now, Jake, go ahead and step in."

Jake did as he was told.

Chapter 28

DAY TWENTY, 0558 HOURS
TALIBAN SAFE HOUSE
GOLRA ROAD, SECTOR E11/1
ISLAMABAD, PAKISTAN

MAHMOOD TAHQI EXITED the doorway of the ramshackle house and stepped quietly onto the flagstoned courtyard. As the door closed softly behind him—extinguishing the light that had spilled from the dwelling—he stood silent for several moments and listened to the hushed sounds of morning, relishing the rich, earthy smells of the countryside.

With his coat pulled tightly about his shoulders, he absently reached into his pocket for a pack of Gold Leaf cigarettes and pulled out a crumpled smoke, then lit it with a cheap plastic lighter; the flame briefly illuminating a face that had been ravaged over the years from having lived in the Northern Pakistan tribal areas. Stuffing the pack back in his pocket, his gaze swept around the courtyard searching for anything out of the ordinary. In the distance, through a sheen of ground fog, he could barely make out the huddled form of one of his sentries who stood guard at the northern entrance to the compound.

With a brief blessing to Allah, relieved they had not been discovered by the Pakistan ISI, Mahmood knew he needed to make sure his men were up and about, but for now he looked east over the dim outline of Islamabad. He could see the first soft blushes of dawn that silhouetted the distant Shîn Mahinyu Mountains to the west, mountains that overshadowed this Taliban compound of innocuous huts surrounded by a thick, two-meter-high stone wall constructed of gray native rock and dried clay. Structures and compounds such as these being common in the rural areas of Pakistan.

Located off Golra Road in the lightly populated southeast section of Islamabad, the few ancient, flat-roofed, single-storied dwellings were grouped together within the twelve hundred square meter confines of its walls, structures constructed of weathered pucka bricks that occupied the most southern portion of the complex.

In the northwest corner of the compound grew a large stand of poplar trees whose leaves shimmered in the slightest of winds, trees that effectively screened the Taliban dwellings from the curious eyes of their neighbors. One overly pushy passerby—a local Pakistani adamant in his efforts to seek menial work—had been insistent on trying to gain entry into the enclave, his body now buried beneath a deep pile of manure adjacent to the south wall. No one could know that Taliban fighters occupied this group of shabby structures. The passerby, Mahmood had thought, may have been one of the faithful, but he had not been one of them.

It had taken eight days to infiltrate his fighters into the area by ones and twos as they had made their way across the farmlands of the Pothohar plateau, the last contingent of men having just arrived the day before yesterday. As he exhaled a lungful of harsh tobacco smoke, he glanced at the parked vehicles arranged in front of the dwellings. What he saw were five old Chevrolet delivery vans in various states of disrepair, but the vans were mechanically sound and of a type commonly used to make deliveries within the boundaries of the city.

Originally painted in what used to be a light-tan color, the vehicles were now faded and pockmarked with dents, and had dark patches of rust around their wheel wells and side-entry doors. Each van also sported the unique logo of Golden Harvest Foods—Islamabad's largest provider of bread products—that catered to the many schools and universities within the capital. As far as he could tell, critically eyeing the vehicles for flaws but not finding any, everything about them was perfect. They would easily blend into the morning traffic of similar trucks making their deliveries about the city.

With one last drag of his cigarette, he dropped the smoldering butt to the stone floor of the courtyard and ground it out with his boot, thinking that today should be a very good day. Stepping back inside the house he saw Qasim, his second in command, pulling on a pair of old, cracked leather boots.

With a grin splitting his face, Qasim asked excitedly, "Well,

Mahmood? Today is the day, is it not?"

"Yes, Qasim, it is that. And Allah has given us a glorious morning for today's work," he replied quietly. Then hearing his fighters rustling about in the back rooms, he looked at his watch.

"Qasim, have the men assembled and ready no later than eight. Make sure the section leaders have inspected their men's weapons and equipment packs. And I want you to personally check the bomb vests and special weapons."

"It will be done," Qasim said as he leaned over and pulled his trouser cuffs over his boots. "Do you want the men here or next door?"

"Have the men assembled here."

"Yes, Mahmood," he said, standing up and stomping his boots one by one against the wood-planked floor. "All weapons and equipment packs. I will see to the loading of the vests and special weapons."

"Thank you, Qasim. Now, it is time for me to get ready."

Two hours later, Mahmood stood before the assembled men and could see that his fighters were ready. Some stood casually with their backs against the wall, but most were seated on the floor with their legs crossed, each sporting a look of determination and totally focused on what he was about to say. He felt a swelling of pride when looked at these men, knowing they were hard and tough. A few of them, Qasim included, had been with him when he captured the Pakistani transport and its cargo of nuclear warheads.

Mahmood lifted his chin toward the ceiling and spoke in a low, fatherly voice, as if he were a Mullah speaking to his flock of faithful.

"May Allah cast his blessings on us all. May he bless this day's holiest of tasks. We are but the servants of Allah. May we be victorious in his righteous name and of his one true prophet, Muhammad. Today we will strike a blow for all of Islam. We will plunge our swords into the chests of our enemies and tear their living hearts from their bodies. We will show the Pakistanis how weak they are, and will show no mercy to our enemies, just as Muhammad showed no mercy to the enemies of the one true faith."

Mahmood turned, his eyes alight with fire, and pointed outside.

"Now is the time, Qasim!"

"Yes, Mahmood," he answered. Then he motioned at the section leaders. "You know what to do. Get your men loaded, and may Allah guide us this day."

The men silently got to their feet, secured their weapons, picked up their equipment packs, and marched outside. Ten minutes later the five vans, each stuffed with ten fighters, quietly pulled out of the enclave and turned left on Golra Road.

Chapter 29

DAY TWENTY, 0815 HOURS
ISLAMABAD PREPARATORY ACADEMY
KHAYABAN-E-JOHAR ROAD
ISLAMABAD, PAKISTAN

PAMELA RAYNOR, THE new superintendent of the Islamabad Preparatory Academy, turned right on Khayban-e-lqbal Road and mashed the accelerator of her beat-up black Volvo to the floor, quickly covering the two miles down to Service Road E one block south of Ninth Avenue.

Caught by the stoplight, she slammed on the brakes and stopped, fuming to herself as she nervously chewed her lower lip and tapped her nails against the steering wheel. *Damn, I can't be late for the assembly! Not today of all days!* The new school year was about to start and today's assembly was important; it would be the first time all of the students and faculty would be gathered as one group to go over the goals for the coming year. But of more importance, it would be her first opportunity to address everyone as the new superintendent of the academy.

When the light finally changed she tromped on the gas, the Volvo's tires squealing as she made a hard left turn onto Service Road E and flew down the remaining three miles to Khayaban-e-Johar Road. At Khayaban-e-Johar Road, she made a sharp right turn and almost plowed into an old derelict truck piled high with used tires that chugged down the middle of the street.

With a quick swerve to the left, barely missing the truck, she was thankful she hadn't wet her pants as the Volvo straightened out and barreled down the last two miles to the academy's main gate. With a huge sigh of relief, she knew she would make it with only minutes to spare.

Thirty seconds later, the Volvo lurched to a stop in front of a thick metal pole that barred the entry into the school parking lot. Within seconds, one of two armed guards exited the cinder-blocked security shack and made his way toward her car. The guard's partner, however, remained inside the hut and scrutinized the Volvo from the shadows.

When the first guard approached to within thirty feet, he recognized Pamela for who she was and returned her hurried smile with a hand raised in greeting, his smile showing off two large, gold front teeth prominently displayed in his mouth. Turning to his right, he quickly stepped over to the barrier and pushed down hard on the weighted end of the pole to allow her to enter.

With a nonchalant wave at the guard, Pamela drove directly across the packed lot and nosed her car into the slot marked "Superintendent". Turning off the ignition, she unfastened her seat belt and grabbed a scruffed-up brown leather satchel that rested on the passenger seat, the same satchel she had dragged around throughout her college days eleven years before. But before she opened the door, she paused and rummaged around in her purse and pulled out a small hairbrush and a tube of lipstick. With the visor flipped down, she peered into the vanity mirror and quickly brushed her shoulder-length blonde hair back into place, then touched up her lipstick and blotted her lips with a Kleenex.

Thinking she now looked somewhat more presentable, she threw the makeup back in her purse, opened the car door, and with the battered satchel and purse clutched in her hands, slammed the door shut with her hip. *God!* she thought wearily. *Time to get a new car! That's the second time this week that old clunker's taken forever to start. No wonder that embassy asshole reassigned to Baghdad gave me such a great deal on it.*

With her usual athletic strides, Pamela stepped briskly across the parking lot and up the steps to the auditorium front doors. One of two Pakistan Secret Service agents stationed at the main entrance opened the left-hand, metal-framed door and stood aside for her to enter. With a thankful nod, she graced him with a smile and stepped into the building's foyer.

As the door closed with a gentle hiss, cutting off the humid glare of morning, she was grateful for the building's air conditioning as she tried to suppress her excitement. She could hear the swelling chorus of children's shouts and laughter that came from within the main hall, and knew she would most likely be the last to enter, but couldn't care less. With a brief wave and a smile at the two additional Secret Service agents who stood sentry inside the foyer, she stepped toward a second set of doors that led directly into the main auditorium.

The Secret Service agents were different from the school's regular security guards. Much larger than most Pakistani men, they stood well over six feet in height and had thick necks with well-muscled frames, each wearing identical black suits and white shirts below wary eyes. Their arms crossed over their chests—silent as sentinels—like two Egyptian statues whose sole purpose was to guard the entrance into the auditorium proper.

The agents ignored Pamela's greeting and, like the two agents outside, were tasked to provide security for President Assif Chutto's two young sons, Vahe and Nasim—aged seven and nine—this being the boys' first year to attend the school. A total of ten agents had been assigned to their security detail and this morning, during the assembly, two of the agents stood guard at the auditorium's main entrance, two more guarded the rear entrance adjacent to the amphitheatre, two guarded the foyer, and four more were stationed within the main hall itself.

Pamela briefly thought back to when she had met with President Chutto's Administrative Assistant, having come away with a better understanding as to why the president of Pakistan had chosen the Islamabad Preparatory Academy for his boys. The administrative assistant had told her the president felt that his sons would benefit from interacting with children from different cultures, and thought their attendance at the school would improve their foreign language skills. Of course, the fact that the academy had the highest academic rating within the city had made the president's decision all that much easier. The youngest boy, Vahe, was to start the second grade while his older brother, Nasim, had been placed in the fourth.

Well aware of the school's history, she knew it had been founded in 1957 as an American chartered educational institution that catered to the children of American and foreign diplomats, as well as to the elite of Pakistan society. But the student body was small, totaling only three hundred and ten children for grades kindergarten through senior high school. Surprisingly, only eighty-nine of the students were American nationals, with the bulk of the student body coming from Islamabad's more affluent Pakistani families, or from families whose members were high-up in their government. The Pakistani children numbered one hundred and thirty-five, with the remainder of the students being the dependents of British, German, French, and Canadian diplomats, to name a few.

The Islamabad Preparatory Academy was situated at the corners of Johar Street and Khayaban-e-Johar Road in the extreme southeast corner of the capital, four miles from the Islamabad International Airport and six miles from the diplomatic enclaves. The academy's school grounds, rectangular in shape, encompassed over twenty-five acres that measured five hundred yards in length by two hundred and fifty yards in width; its perimeter enclosed by a red-brick wall five feet high and three feet thick breached in three places as vehicular entry points—two on the south side of the academy used by service workers and the main gate through which she had entered—with each entry point manned by two civilian school guards armed with 9mm semiautomatic pistols.

Pamela had at first been troubled that the school needed to have armed guards, but she knew the history of Pakistan and the recent Taliban terrorist attacks that had taken place within the city. So she could understand why the school would be cautious, even more so with President Chutto's children in attendance, but now she hardly even noticed the guards or that they were armed.

Attached to the rear of the auditorium was a small, semicircular, outdoor amphitheatre used for evening plays in the Roman tradition, and dominating the central portion of the school were three single-storied, flat-roofed quads each of which enclosed a small grassy courtyard. The quads—one each for the elementary school, the middle school, and the high school—were set in a triangular pattern flanked by the school cafeteria to the east and by the auditorium to the west. Centered between the quads was the school gymnasium, and slightly to the northeast was an Olympic-sized swimming pool. Due east of the cafeteria was a large soccer field surrounded by a running track that marked the school's easternmost boundary, the soccer field now used in the mornings and early afternoons as a landing zone for the presidential helicopter that ferried President Chutto's sons to and from the palace.

As she was about to enter the main auditorium, she heard

someone call out her name.

"Pamela! Ms. Raynor! Good morning!" Bruce McAllister shouted as he cheerfully waved a hand effusively in the air.

Shit! Pamela thought. Bruce was the last person she wanted to see, and it was just her bad luck to run into this obnoxious asshole.

Bruce, a British citizen on contract to the school, was one of the academy's instructors who taught intermediate math to the seventh and eighth graders. He had also been the first person to volunteer to show her around Islamabad and, not quite so subtly, the first male who had tried to hit on her.

She hadn't taken him up on the invitation, although she had to admit that Bruce was a good-looking man, tall at six-foot-three with a slim athletic build. But she just couldn't get over his carefully coiffed hair with wisps of gray at the sides, his perfectly white teeth thanks to the efforts of his dentist, and his somewhat effeminate, condescending British manner that screamed to the world he was god's gift to the female gender. He was also forty-four years old and that made him twelve years her senior. *No thanks,* she had thought determinedly. If she had one firm rule set in concrete, it was never to date a man who thought he was prettier than you, especially one she thought was an obnoxious asshole.

When Bruce made his way toward her, Pamela's shoulders slumped while she gritted her teeth.

"Oh . . . good morning, Bruce," she answered with absolutely no enthusiasm.

"So, ready for the assembly?" he warmly asked, his hand placed possessively on her shoulder.

Pamela turned and lowered her shoulder to shrug off his touch.

"Yes, Bruce, I am. But I really have to go. I'm late and the assembly's about to start. Aren't you going?" she asked pointedly.

"Oh, you're right as usual. It's about that time, isn't it? Can't be late now, can we? After you, Mademoiselle," he said with a brilliant display of his perfectly manicured white teeth, mimicking a slight bow while making a broad sweeping motion with his arm.

Leaving Bruce abruptly in her wake, Pamela strode through the foyer doors and made her way into the main hall.

The auditorium was large, with three seating sections that could accommodate up to five hundred people. The largest section, flanked by a narrower section on either side, was centered in the middle of the hall with each seating area separated by a dark, maroon-carpeted aisle. With a quick glance down at the stage, she could see that fifty metal folding chairs, with bright-yellow-cushioned inserts, had been arranged in five rows of ten and set in a broad semicircle that faced the main hall. The chairs, intended for teachers and staff, located to the rear of a tall, well-used wooden lectern.

As she made her way down the aisle, she saw that most of the faculty had already taken their seats where they animatedly discussed the school, family and friends, or just plain gossiped. The few faculty members not yet seated were gathered at the rear of the stage in front of a large, black, floor-to-ceiling stage curtain edged with maroon piping. When those staff members saw her approach, they broke out of their groups and began to drift toward their seats.

She could also see the different grades had been placed well up front with the elementary school students seated in the centermost section closest to the stage. The kindergartners in the first row, followed by each additional elementary school grade stacked behind the other with the sixth graders bringing up the rear.

Seated in the right-hand seating section were the middle school students—seventh and eighth graders—who talked and laughed animatedly, but with more restraint than their elementary school counterparts; and in the left-hand section were the high school students, quiet and sedate, content to remain aloof from the other grades as if it was beneath their dignity to join in the revelry. The high schoolers more than aware they were at the top of the academy's food chain.

Pamela reached the end of the aisle and turned in front of the stage, waving at several of the teachers seated in the front row of faculty chairs. Once up on stage, she stepped to the lectern and placed her purse and satchel on the floor, then she spotted Ned Thumel—the academy's assistant superintendent—sitting quietly to her rear.

"Good morning, Ned," she said, gracing him with a brilliant smile.

"Good morning, Ms. Raynor," Ned barely choked out.

Ned Thumel, a small, quiet, thirty-eight-year-old bachelor with stooped shoulders who barely stood five-foot-four, had a sparse head of dark-brown hair well advanced into the final stages of male-pattern baldness, hair he had let grow to over six inches in length on the sides so he could swirl it across the top of his bald head. Pamela remembered seeing Ned just the other day when it had been windy, unable to stop from laughing when the wind had pushed his flap of hair straight up like a rooster's comb. Ned had looked like an overgrown chicken.

Pamela continued down the line of chairs greeting the other teachers and staff. Once done, she stepped up to the lectern filled with anticipation, thinking *Her students!* as the auditorium finally quieted down. Behind her, she could still hear some muffled conversations taking place between faculty members, but that didn't bother her. She savored every moment as she leaned over the lectern's microphone.

"Good morning, students!" her voice boomed throughout the hall. "And good morning to this year's graduating class!"

The seniors, who totaled only twenty-eight students, immediately stood up, whistling and clapping as they acknowledged her greeting. They knew this was their year and they were going to make the most of it.

With a huge grin on her face, Pamela waved for them to be seated. The seniors, once again having established their priority in the school's pecking order, slowly sat down.

Enjoying the moment to its fullest, she gripped the lectern and looked expectantly at the students seated before her.

"I wanted to take this opportunity to let you know how honored I am to be the new Superintendent for the Islamabad Preparatory Academy. And, during this, our first assembly of the student body, I would like to outline the ambitious goals we have set out for the coming school year."

Chapter 30

DAY TWENTY, 0837 HOURS
KHAYABAN-E-JOHAR ROAD
ISLAMABAD, PAKISTAN

THE CARAVAN OF five dilapidated vans slowed to make right-hand turns from Ninth Avenue onto Khayaban-e-Johar Road. It was just past eight thirty in the morning and Mahmood Tahqi could see that the road was clear to the school. With a quick look in the outside rear-view mirror, he saw the fifth and final van begin its own turn. When the last van completed its turn, he picked up a cheap portable radio and keyed the transmit switch.

"Now, listen to me. We are less than a kilometer from Gate Three. Just a little further up we will pull off to the side of the road. Once stopped, have your men prepare their weapons and make sure that everyone has their balaclava on. When completed let me know. Then, as planned, I'll continue with my three vans to the main gate. Nayid? Hammid? Stay in place until you see us make our turn. At that time head to your own gates and begin your attacks."

Mahmood tapped his driver on the arm and pointed to the right.

"Slow down and pull over."

The driver put on the brakes, pulled over to the right side of the road, and stopped. Unsure of what to do next, he glanced at Mahmood.

Mahmood ignored the driver and looked at the men seated on the cargo bay.

"We're almost there. Make sure your weapons are loaded and your backpacks secure, and put on your balaclavas. When I hear from the others we will continue to our target. May Allah bless us all."

Two minutes later his radio crackled to life.

"Mahmood, this is Qasim, we are ready."

"Thank you, Qasim."

Soon thereafter he answered three more times, each van indicating they were ready to go.

"Understood! We are leaving now! Allahu akbar!"

With another tap to the driver's arm, Mahmood pointed straight ahead.

"Okay, my friend, take us up to the main gate."

Mahmood's van, followed by Gamal's with the weapons van in trail, pulled onto the road and made their way toward the main gate. When they were no more than fifty meters from making their turn into the Islamabad Preparatory Academy, the weapons van—as planned—pulled off the road just out of sight of the main gate's security shack, the fighters crammed inside its cargo bay waiting expectantly for the first shots to be fired. When Mahmood's van began its turn into the academy, he once again looked in the side-mirror and saw the fourth and fifth vans pull onto the road, each headed for their own targets.

Mahmood's van stopped in front of a thick metal pole that blocked the entrance into the school parking lot. With his elbow planted casually on the passenger door windowsill, Mahmood watched as a guard, with his pistol snapped down tight in its holster, exited the security hut and approached his side of the vehicle. He could see a second guard had stayed inside the shack, eyeing them suspiciously from its doorway. Across the lot, planted in front of the main entrance doors to the auditorium, he saw what he assumed were two members of the Pakistan Secret Service detail, their attention focused on the vans as one of them lowered his head and spoke quietly into a lapel microphone. Mahmood slowly pulled his arm inside the van and grasped a 9mm semiautomatic pistol that lay on his lap, its hammer already cocked and ready to fire.

"Good morning," the guard said gruffly. The guard had noted the Golden Harvest Foods logo on the sides of both vehicles.

"Good morning," Mahmood said with an open smile.

"Deliveries are to be made through Gate Three," the guard sternly said.

"I know," Mahmood replied, "but we were told to make today's delivery to the auditorium. They told us there was a school assembly and wanted the pastries delivered to the auditorium kitchen. I guess as a treat for the children."

The guard grunted and looked down at his clipboard, thumbing through the sheets of paperwork. A frown creased his brow as he flipped back and forth several times through the various sheets.

"I am sorry, but you are not on today's list for deliveries," the guard bluntly announced.

When he looked up from the clipboard, all he could see was the dark, deadly bore of a 9mm semiautomatic pistol pointed no more than twelve centimeters from his head. With his face blanched white with fear, and before he could take a single step backward, a bright-red hole appeared in the center of his forehead, followed immediately by the booming explosion of Mahmood's pistol.

The guard's head, slammed backwards by the impact of the round, exploded as if it were an overripe watermelon. The ground to his rear sprayed with a reddish-plume of blood and brain tissue. Mahmood quickly changed targets, gripping the pistol in both hands with its butt resting on the windowsill, and lined up on the second guard still silhouetted in the security hut's door. With his aim now steadied, he cranked off three more quick rounds as the guard fumbled to pull his own pistol from its holster. But the guard was slow, way too slow as Mahmood grinned when he saw his second round had hit the guard square in the chest just above the heart.

At the sound of the first shot, the fighters in the back of his van burst through its side-entry door with screams of "Allahu akbar" on their tongues, fanning out into the parking lot and firing their AK-47s at the Secret Service agents stationed outside the auditorium. The teams from the second and third vans also erupted from their vehicles and quickly joined the fighters from the first, spreading out to the right and left as they formed up into a loose skirmish line, ducking and weaving their way between parked cars while they fired their weapons from the hip; their 7.62mm rounds impacting the front of the building and gouging deep pockmarks into its red-bricked walls.

As soon as he shot the second guard, Mahmood jumped out of the van and sprinted across the parking lot, his heart pounding from excitement where he soon found himself squatting behind an old, dented-up black Volvo. When he raised his head to get a better look at what was going on, he frantically jerked it down, flopping behind the car as a line of submachine gun fire riddled the Volvo from front to rear.

Now covered with shards of glass from the Volvo's shattered windows, he silently cursed the agent who had shot at him with an Uzi. Tentatively, he again raised his head and watched as the Secret Service agents threw themselves behind two large, concrete planters that flanked the auditorium entrance, the agents firing frantically at his men who were still scrambling their way across the lot.

In the distance, he welcomed the sounds of explosions and automatic weapons fire that came from the other two service gates. *Good!* he thought excitedly. *The other vans have attacked their targets!*

Mahmood squatted behind the Volvo with his head bent well below the trunk, his body hunched forward with his right hand resting lightly on its bumper. With a quick look around, he could see that his fighters had gone to ground, fearful of the Secret Service agents' accurate submachine gun fire.

When he turned back to his front, the auditorium doors unexpectedly burst open. Two additional Secret Service agents, with Uzi submachine pistols gripped in their hands, were trying to exit the building to join their comrades behind the planters. At this point every Taliban fighter brought the agents under crippling AK-47 rifle fire, the front doorway sprayed with hundreds of rounds as if squirted through a water hose.

The two agents, repeatedly hit by the withering fire, jerked back and forth from the impact of rounds, looking more like puppets on a string being slammed by sledgehammers.

Mahmood smiled at their deaths. *Two less sheep turds to worry about!* Then he reached into his pocket and pulled out his radio.

"Gamal! Gamal! Come in!"

There was no response.

But before he could key the transmit switch a second time, his radio burst to life.

"Mahmood! Gamal here!"

"Good!" he said relieved. "Gamal, there are two more guards behind some planters near the front doors! Below those two that were just killed! They have us pinned down! Can you see them?"

Gamal, roughly thirty meters to Mahmood's right, quickly popped his head around the fender of a car and stole a quick glance at the building's entrance. He could see the two dead agents wedged in the doorway of the auditorium. Then he looked to their left and saw the movement of legs from behind one of the planters. Suddenly, a plume of dirty-gray smoke spewed into the morning air accompanied by the high-pitched staccato sounds of Uzi submachine gun fire. One of the Secret Service agents had just let go a long burst at the right side of the parking lot. Turning, he saw that one of their fighters was down, screaming and writhing on the asphalt in a spreading pool of blood.

"Yes, Mahmood! I see the guards!"

"Good!" Mahmood yelled. "See if you can get closer to the building! To get a better shot at those two damned goatherds! Get them in a crossfire! We can't let them hold us up!"

"Yes, Mahmood! It will be done!"

Gamal stuffed the radio in his trousers and waved at two fighters who had followed him to the car, both fighters trying their damndest to stay out of the line of fire.

"You two! Listen up! See those trees on top of that wall?" he said, pointing at a five-foot-tall concrete retaining wall that separated the parking lot from the front of the building.

Both fighters looked to their front, and quickly pulled their heads behind the car, nodding affirmatively.

"Okay! What we're going to do is make our way to that wall. Once there we'll climb over it and hide behind those trees. From there we can shoot straight down the sidewalk and kill those two damned camel turds! Understood?"

Both fighters nodded as they prepared themselves for the mad dash.

"Okay, let's go!" Gamal shouted as he scurried around the right side of the car and sprinted madly for the wall.

Mahmood, still covered by the bulk of the Volvo, watched as Gamal and two of his fighters ran as hard as they could across the parking lot. When they made it unscathed he breathed a short sigh of relief. After a moment or two, he watched as they clambered over the wall and threw themselves behind some trees, then crawled on their bellies toward a sidewalk that ran parallel to the front of the auditorium.

Gamal hunched up on both knees to get a better angle of fire, his AK-47 sighted down the concrete walk. His patience was rewarded when the remaining two Secret Service agents—still screened by the planters—desperately tried to scuttle backwards through the open entrance doors. But all the agents had managed to do was to become entangled in the bodies of their dead compatriots who now blocked their path.

When the agents rose partially up to try and crawl over their dead comrades, Gamal pulled the AK-47's trigger and emptied its magazine, his rounds thunking into their bodies and blowing off small chunks of their flesh. *Don't have to worry about those two camel turds anymore,* he thought, exulting in the deaths of the guards.

Seeing that all four Secret Service agents were down, Mahmood stood up, screamed "Allahu Akbar" at the top of his lungs, and then charged the last few meters up to the building. With his back pressed against the auditorium wall, still breathing heavily with excitement, he ejected his spent magazine and slammed a new one home. When the rest of his men finally joined him—now massed on both sides of the entrance doors ready to storm the interior of the auditorium—he cautiously stepped through the doorway threshold, but then tripped on one of the dead agents' bodies that littered the entryway. With a silent curse on his tongue, he looked down at the dead agent and kicked him roughly in the face.

Chapter 31

DAY TWENTY, 0837 HOURS
ISLAMABAD PREPARATORY ACADEMY
ISLAMABAD, PAKISTAN

BRUCE MCALLISTER PICKED at his newly manicured nails as he leaned nonchalantly against the foyer's back wall, still miffed by Pamela's standoffish manner and less than warm greeting while he listened to her words that echoed throughout the auditorium. *Well, you always did like a challenge old boy.*

As he tried to think of a way to get Pamela to go to out with him, he was startled by what sounded like large firecrackers going off outside in the parking lot. *What the hell?* he thought, pushing off the wall, thinking it had to be kids or something. With his head canted curiously to the side, he walked toward the entrance doors to see what the hell was going on.

The rippling crack of Uzi submachine gun fire suddenly exploded right outside the front of the building, the earsplitting burst of noise ringing in his ears as he stumbled backwards confused and frightened. But before he could take another step back, he was roughly thrown to the floor by one of the two Pakistan Secret Service agents who stood sentry in the foyer.

Bruce looked up in shock as the agents, with Uzi submachine pistols grasped in their hands, ran up and kicked open the front doors; the agents frantic to help their comrades stationed outside.

As soon as the doors crashed open, a deluge of 7.62mm rifle fire smashed into and around the front entrance, kicking up cyclones of dust and pieces of brick as several rounds passed through the opening and snap-cracked over his head. Frozen in place, he watched as the two agents, now silhouetted in the doorway, were torn to pieces by AK-47 automatic weapons fire and blown backwards across the doorway threshold. *Jesus Christ! We're under attack!*

Bruce rolled onto his back and lifted his head in panic—his eyes wide with fright—staring at the bodies of the two agents that were now no more than a grotesque tangle of arms and legs, their bodies wedged in the entryway that kept the doors from closing. One agent, just moments from death, groaned loudly as he tried to push the dead body of his fellow agent off his own.

As he stared at the gruesome scene, Bruce felt something warm and sticky trickle down his face. In a panic, he quickly wiped his cheek with the back of his hand and pulled it in front of his eyes, faint with revulsion when he saw it was covered with blood and pieces of flesh. *My God! I've been shot!* Frantically, he ran his hand over the rest of his face searching for a wound, but when he couldn't find one he collapsed with relief, realizing he must be covered with blood that had sprayed from the exit wounds of the agents who had just been killed.

Now in full flight mode, and knowing he needed to get out of the line of fire, he pushed back to the foyer wall. As he tried to regain his senses, he stared over the dead agents' bodies. He saw two other agents stationed outside, scrunched up behind a couple of planters, popping up and down as they furiously returned fire. The sidewalk around them covered with brass shell casings as incoming rounds blew off pieces of concrete from the planter's tops and sides. One of the agents then looked quickly at his partner and shouted something unintelligible.

As if caught in a slow motion nightmare, Bruce watched as the agents scuttled backwards on their stomachs, trying to seek safety inside the foyer. But in their haste to abandon their position, they got hung up on the dead agents' bodies that blocked the doorway. When they partially rose up to try and squirm their way through, their movement attracted another onslaught of automatic weapons fire from their right.

Bruce dumbly watched as the fusillade of bullets tore into the agents again, and again, and again, the exit wounds exploding through their bodies looking like someone had taken a large butcher knife and cut three-inch jagged holes into their flesh. At that moment, one of the agents' heads exploded into a halo of misting blood when it was hit dead-on by a 7.62mm round. He shrank from the ghastly scene as bile surged within his throat, and then vomited his morning's breakfast onto the carpeted floor.

With a final heave of his stomach, dazed and not knowing what to do, he pushed himself upright and stumbled toward the main auditorium hall. With a final look back, his numbed brain saw many men running across the parking lot screaming and yelling, all carrying assault rifles with black masks pulled over their heads. One of the men suddenly stopped and, with a flick of his wrist, casually tossed what looked to be a small backpack through the open doorway of the guard shack. Within seconds, a deafening explosion ripped through the small building, spewing glass and cinder-block across the main entrance driveway. As the concussion rolled over the school, he watched as gouts of red flame shot through the security shack's shattered windows—twisting as if alive—and then quickly retreated inwards to be replaced by thick, dark, oily tendrils of smoke.

"My God, my God," he moaned as he bolted for the main hall, making low mewling noises to himself when he tripped on the foyer threshold and fell face downwards to the floor.

Pamela Raynor had also heard what sounded liked muffled firecrackers going off outside. With a puzzled expression, she turned from the lectern and looked at the staff, then back at the student body. *Are the seniors up to something? Some kind of a prank?* A brief flash of light from the foyer lobby suddenly caught her eye, as if someone had opened the main doors to the parking lot. At that moment the high-pitched bark of rifle fire was unmistakable.

Not understanding what was going on, and frozen with fear, she noticed some movement below the lectern. Two of the four Secret Service agents who guarded the aisles had leapt into action as they frantically jumped over students and seat rows to get to President Chutto's sons. The agents, completely indifferent to the screams of the children, threw several of the students to the floor like so much garbage in their haste to make it to Vahe and Nasim.

Stunned by what was happening, she watched as the other two agents pulled Uzi 9mm submachine pistols from under their coats and sighted down their short stubby barrels at the upper end of the hall. One of the agents then grabbed a hand-held radio from his suit coat and pressed it to his lips, yelling something she couldn't understand. The two agents tasked with securing Chutto's sons finally made it to the boys and jerked them out of their seats, then stumbled their way back toward the aisle, each with a boy gripped tightly under his arm.

In the distance, she could now hear screams of "Allahu akbar" from outside the hall. Not two seconds later, a massive explosion rocked the building that caused the ceiling's chandeliers to sway and chatter, dislodging a cloud of dust particles that filled the air like dirty-brown snowflakes. Most of the children, still rooted to their seats, erupted as one as they cried out in fear. Up on stage most of the faculty members had also risen from their chairs, their panicked screams adding to the ensuing melee.

In the upper reaches of the hall she saw Bruce McAllister, his face covered with blood, stumble through the left-hand foyer door, and then fall face forwards to the aisle. *My God! He's been shot!* Pamela thought as she clutched the lectern in a death grip, but was relieved when he slowly staggered to his feet.

As Bruce wobbled one or two more steps down the aisle, his eyes suddenly bulged open in shocked disbelief—his arms splayed outward to the sides—when several rounds slammed into his back, and then burst through the center of his chest like a scene from "Alien".

The rest of the faculty now stood up en masse, screaming and shrieking in terror as their chairs clattered across the stage, trampling one another like a herd of spooked cattle in their haste to escape. A few of the teachers didn't panic. They were scared to death, but gathered fearfully around Pamela to see what they could do to help.

Pamela desperately grabbed the microphone and screamed, "Everyone on the floor! Get under your seats NOW! GET UNDER YOUR SEATS NOW!" With her command echoing throughout the great hall, the children not already on the floor frantically threw themselves under their chairs, twisting and wiggling their bodies under their seats as they continued to cry out in fear.

The two Secret Service agents who had remained in the aisle could now see masked heads at the foyer doors. With their Uzi's still raised, they sighted down their barrels and sprayed the doorway openings with rippling bursts of 9mm submachine gun fire, their spent shell casings smoking as they arched through the air, and then tinkled with bell-like sounds when they hit the metal frames of the chairs. At the upper end of the hall, pieces of drywall and brick filled the air from the impact of their rounds.

The senior Secret Service agent hastily turned and shouted at the agents who held Chutto's boys within their arms, ordering them to take shelter on the floor in front of the stage. Not five seconds later, two more explosions rumbled in the distance that caused the building to sway once again.

The agents who held Chutto's sons abandoned the aisle and sprinted toward the stage, shoving Vahe and Nasim under the front row of seats while they tried to shield them with their bodies. The other two agents slowly backed up, covering the foyer doors to their front, their weapons still smoking and sighted-in when they hurriedly ejected their spent magazines and slammed new ones home.

The senior agent knew that the front of the building had been lost to the attackers, and that their only hope of escape—and to prevent Vahe and Nasim from being captured or killed—was to escape through the back service entrance into the amphitheatre. If they couldn't do that, their last option was to barricade themselves in the small kitchen next to the backstage dressing rooms and wait for reinforcements.

Those hopes were instantly dashed when screams and wails of confusion erupted from the faculty members who had tried to escape backstage, their screams accompanied by the sharp crack of automatic weapons fire that came from directly behind the stage curtain.

Chapter 32

DAY TWENTY, 0852 HOURS
THE PRESIDENTIAL PALACE
ISLAMABAD, PAKISTAN

"SCHOOL FIRE! SCHOOL Fire! I say again, School Fire!" The code name pounded and crackled through every headset of every Secret Service agent stationed within the presidential palace. Mustaffa Kardar, chief of the Presidential Security Detail, stopped dead in his tracks and pushed his radio earpiece further into his ear, unconsciously holding his breath when he once again heard the panicked call along with what sounded like automatic weapons fire in the background.

"School Fire! School Fire! Allah, please help us! School Fire!"

Mustaffa immediately reacted to the call, his mind going into hyper drive.

"Central Control, this is Mustaffa! Central Control, this is Mustaffa!"

"Mustaffa, go ahead!" came the hurried response from a senior agent located in the security detail's underground headquarters. He too had heard the code name and knew exactly what it meant.

"Launch the Ready Reaction Force! I say again, launch the Ready Reaction Force!" he screamed.

"Acknowledged!" the rattled agent shouted as he quickly toggled a radio directly linked to the Ready Reaction Force, the Ready Reaction Force made up of two Mi-171 helicopters fully armed with 3.5-inch rocket launchers and miniguns with two squads of SSW troops stationed on twenty-four hour alert.

In less than five minutes the high-pitched screams of jet turbines could be heard from the palace heliport, the Mi-171's rotors turning slowly as two squads of troops—dressed in full battle gear—hastily split themselves between the choppers and loaded onboard.

With their rotors now fully engaged, blurring with speed, the pilots jerked their machines straight up from the pad and hovered briefly for a moment in ground effect, then kicked in right-full rudder to turn their choppers into the wind, dropped their noses, and skimmed the ground as they raced to pick up airspeed. Once sufficient airspeed had been achieved, the pilots pulled full collective and pointed their Mi-171s almost straight up in an effort to gain altitude as quickly as possible. At the apex of their climb, they nosed over and made wide, sweeping, left-hand turns to the southeast headed directly for the Islamabad Preparatory Academy, barely missing the arrays of antennas that speckled the palace rooftop.

Mustaffa ran down the hall toward President Chutto's office, then briefly looked up as the choppers thundered by overhead, the ceiling shaking with their passing. Fearing the worst, and knowing the two squads of SSW troops onboard were no longer available for perimeter defense, he keyed his radio a second time.

"All agents! All agents! This is Mustaffa! Implement Plan Blue! I say again, implement Plan Blue!"

Plan Blue was the security detail's standard operating procedure that called for whisking President Chutto to his underground bunker in case of an attack on the palace, with other agents tasked with taking Mrs. Chutto to the same bunker. At the same time the palace grounds would be sealed off, its perimeter manned by the remaining company of troops and Secret Service agents.

Mustaffa raced down the corridor when he saw the doors to the presidential office burst open. Two of his agents had President Chutto firmly in their grasp as they literally dragged the confused president into the hallway. Two other agents provided cover front and rear with their machine pistols drawn. As the entourage cleared the doorway, they stopped when they saw him approach.

"What in the name of hell is going on?" President Chutto shouted, his face bloated with rage when he recognized Mustaffa running towards them. "Why are your guards manhandling me?" he screamed, trying to shrug out from under their grasp.

"Mr. President!" Mustaffa replied breathlessly, pulling up short in front of Chutto. "I am sorry! But there has been an attack on the Preparatory Academy!"

"What?" President Chutto asked thunderstruck, the rage on his face instantly replaced with the ashen look of fear. "What do you mean an attack on the school?"

Mustaffa saw the change in his president's face and that he understood what he had just been told. Suddenly, Chutto's shoulders visibly sagged. Had he not been supported by the two Secret Service agents he would have collapsed to the floor.

"Sir! Not more than a minute ago we had an emergency call from your sons' security detail! School Fire was the code name given! I have also implemented Plan Blue for you and Mrs. Chutto's safety until we can figure out what's going on!"

President Chutto knew the code name School Fire and what it meant. He had been briefed just last month by Mustaffa and the minister of defense when he had decided that his sons could attend the academy, the same meeting where he had raised questions concerning their security. But he had been fully assured by the minister of defense that they would be well protected, the only objection having come from Mustaffa.

His director of security had wanted his sons to remain within the palace grounds and be taught by tutors, but he, in his stupidity, did not want his boys to feel as if they were caged animals. He had wanted them to experience as normal a childhood as possible. He knew how paranoid his security detail was, that they would prefer that he and his family never venture from the palace grounds; and if they did venture out, to have at least an army Brigade in attendance, preferably accompanied by tanks. But bolstered by the assurances of the minister of defense, and in a moment of fatherly weakness, he had discounted the concerns of his security chief. He was the one who had given in to the pleadings of his cherished sons to attend the school.

"My sons! How are my sons?" he asked, the anguish on his face plain to be seen.

"Sir, all we know is that the school is, or was, under attack. The Ready Reaction Force is already on its way. We'll know more once they're on station."

Mustaffa paused and looked hard at his president to see if he was being understood. All he could see was grief and fear written on Chutto's face.

"Sir, your sons' security detail are the best men we have. I handpicked them myself. They will lay down their lives for your boys.

But for now we need to get you and Mrs. Chutto into your bunker. We don't know if the school attack is isolated, or if there will be an attack on the palace."

The last thing President Chutto wanted was to be cooped up in the presidential bunker where he knew the communications gear was meager. He needed to know what was going on.

"No, Mustaffa," he firmly said, regaining his composure and shrugging off the holds of the two agents. "I can't . . . I will not go to the bunker! Not while my sons' lives are in danger!"

"But, Mr. President, I must see to your safety!"

"You can see to my safety in the Situation Room," President Chutto bluntly replied. "I will not be isolated. I need to know what's going on and I can only do that from the Situation Room. Take Mrs. Chutto to the bunker, but I will be in the Situation Room!" he declared flatly.

Mustaffa thought quickly, knowing the Situation Room was located two stories below ground level. Although not as secure as the bunker, it could still be defended. He nodded slowly in agreement, not wanting to argue with his president. With a quick nod at the elevator, he looked at the agents who flanked the president.

"Okay, take the president to the Situation Room, but let me know when Mrs. Chutto is in the bunker. And sir, these men will remain with you at all times. I'll let you know more when I have a better idea where we stand. I'll be in security headquarters and you can monitor our transmissions from the Situation Room. Right now I need to get into communication with the Reaction Force."

"Okay," President Chutto agreed. "But let me know what you find out as soon as possible!"

"Don't worry, sir, I will!"

Chapter 33

DAY TWENTY, 0840 HOURS
ISLAMABAD PREPARATORY ACADEMY
ISLAMABAD, PAKISTAN

MAHMOOD TAHQI HEARD the sharp crack of rifle fire that came from the rear of the building. He could also see the teachers running around and screaming in panic like a gaggle of wild geese, pushing and shoving at one another as they desperately made their way from the back of the stage to its main floor. He grinned when many of them stumbled over the collapsed chairs that lay in their path.

Qasim! Qasim must have taken the rear of the building! he thought when two of the teachers suddenly crumpled to the floor, hit by gunfire from some of Qasim's fighters.

Further movement in the hall caught his eye. He saw four Secret Service agents crouched down behind the front row of theatre chairs. Two of them had President Chutto's boys tucked close by their sides while they all held submachine pistols at the ready, the agents looking panicked as they jerked their heads back and forth between the stage and foyer doors.

Thinking of what to do next, Mahmood turned to the fighters arrayed on both sides of the main hall entry doors, the men firing their weapons wildly into the chamber. Angry for the wasted ammunition, and angrier still that they could hit Chutto's sons, he shouted for them to stop firing, but the fighters—consumed by bloodlust—continued to empty their magazines into the hall.

Not wanting the lives of President Chutto's sons jeopardized, he pointed his rifle at the ceiling and ripped off a long burst, stitching the overhead with 7.62mm rounds that showered the men with shredded pieces of drywall, chunks of mortar, and shattered glass from the lighting fixtures, but now he had their full and undivided attention.

"Stop firing! Stop firing!" he shouted again. "The next one of you goatherds that fires I will shoot through the liver!"

The fighters, looking dazed, pulled back with their rifles pointed toward the floor, awaiting their commander's orders.

Mahmood jerked off the now useless Balaclava, his face bathed in sweat that had cut dirt-encrusted rivulets down his face. With his attention once again focused on the presidential guards, he made an abrupt decision. Slinging his rifle, he stepped partially around the doorway with his hands cupped around his mouth.

"You, the guards! You, the guards!" he shouted.

The guards, he saw, couldn't hear over the gunfire that came from the rear of stage and the screeching cries of the children.

"Guards! You, the guards! Up here!" Mahmood bellowed again, this time waving his arms over his head.

The agents had heard someone shout, but couldn't make out who was saying it.

As the agents searched for the source of the shouting, Mahmood once again cupped his hands and shouted, "You! The guards! Up here!"

All four Secret Service agents looked in the general direction of the foyer, then zeroed-in on an individual half-crouched in the left-hand foyer door—their machine pistols pointed in his direction—but they withheld their fire.

"Yes! You!" Mahmood shouted, standing fully erect when he saw he had finally gotten their attention. "Lay down your weapons! You cannot escape! You are surrounded! The boys will not be hurt, by the grace of Allah! But they will surely die if you do not do as I say! You have fifteen seconds before we open fire!"

The agents paused and looked at one another. They knew their situation was futile. With their comrades killed and the militants occupying the front and rear of the auditorium, there was no chance of escape. Reinforcements could not possibly arrive in time to save them. And if they continued to resist, not only would President Chutto's boys most likely die, but so would many of the children who cringed beneath their seats.

The senior agent looked at his men and acknowledged their silent nods of agreement, and then made long eye contact with the one he assumed to be the leader of the attack. With nothing further to do, he tossed his Uzi into the aisle.

"Don't shoot! Don't shoot! We give up!" he yelled as he motioned for his fellow agents to do the same.

One by one the other agents stood and, as their leader had done, cast their weapons into the aisle. The two agents tasked with protecting Chutto's sons, in a reflexive action, shoved the boys behind them to try and screen them from harm. With their arms now raised, they locked their hands behind their heads and silently prayed for deliverance.

With the presidential agents now disarmed and their hands clasped behind their heads, Mahmood stepped fully into the aisle, ignoring the dead body of Bruce McAllister that lay at his feet. Then, with a gesture at his men, he watched as they ran down the aisle in triumph and brutally knocked the agents to the floor with the butts of their rifles.

President Chutto's boys, terrified by the onslaught, screamed and tried to flee down one of the seat rows, but were roughly grabbed by their necks and jerked back.

As his men continued to beat the agents with downward slashing butt strokes to their heads and shoulders, Mahmood raised his AK-47 and fired a full clip into the ceiling, screaming "Allahu akbar!" to rejoice in his victory.

Slowly he lowered the rifle, wiping some sweat from his brow as the rest of his fighters boiled into the assembly hall. With a look toward the stage he saw Nayid, one of his lieutenants, directing a group of men who were beginning to corral and secure the panicked teachers.

"Nayid!" he shouted. "Here! Come here!"

Nayid quickly looked up and stepped off the stage, a smile of victory on his face.

"We have done well, have we not?" he asked, his eyes shining brightly from the battle. "The teachers should be taken care of in just a few minutes, Mahmood."

"Yes, yes, Nayid. We have done well," he agreed with a hard slap to his lieutenant's shoulder. "But now, my good old friend, how many of those do we have?" he asked, pointing at the white nylon handcuffs held in Nayid's hands.

"About a hundred I think."

Mahmood gazed around the auditorium and saw the number of

children and teachers present.

"Make sure to use what we have on the teachers and older children first. When we run out, we run out, and that will be Allah's will. Just make sure that anyone who can cause us trouble has those placed on their wrists, and have the teachers gagged with duct tape. I don't want them speaking to one another or calling out to the children."

"It will be done," Nayid said as he jogged back to the stage to make sure the teachers were securely cuffed and gagged, then directed more of his men to cuff the high school students who cowered behind their seat rows.

As the older students were cuffed, they were roughly herded back to their seat rows and admonished to keep quiet, but many of the younger children continued to cry and scream. These children were harshly slapped in their heads, or kicked by their Taliban captors who forced them back into their chairs. The teachers, however, were made to sit on their butts in three rows on the forward portion of the stage with their hands zip-cuffed tightly behind them.

"Mahmood," Qasim stated breathlessly, having made his way to the aisle. "The rear of the auditorium is in our hands. I have also stationed several fighters and an M60 machine gun with Gamal in the amphitheatre for security. The rest have been sent out to the cafeteria and classroom areas. Hammid is now taking control of the security gates, including the main gate out front."

"Thank you, Qasim. You have done well," he said magnanimously, impressed that his lieutenant had done so much in so short a time. "Later I want to walk the perimeter, to see where the men are positioned."

"Yes, Mahmood, but we have some other problems," Qasim said as he reached up and tore off his own sweat-stained Balaclava. "As you told us to do, Shafiq has been listening to the Pakistani radio frequencies. As we speak, soldiers are on their way in trucks, probably no more than twenty or thirty minutes away. From what he could tell it must be at least a company, but he also heard them talking to some helicopters. He thinks at least two are on the way."

Mahmood scrunched his brow in thought, absorbing what he had been told, surprised that the Pakistanis had reacted so quickly. He had hoped they would have had at least an hour to get ready before their soldiers arrived, but everything was in Allah's hands and they were but the instruments of his will on earth. He also knew the main cafeteria building, located at the easternmost boundary of the school, provided the best view of the soccer field where the Pakistani helicopters would most likely try to land.

He placed a bony hand on Qasim's shoulder and squeezed it tightly.

"Okay," he said curtly. "This is what we must do. There are only two places where their helicopters can land—in the fields in front of the school and the soccer field. But I think they will head for the soccer field. Much more room for them to off-load their soldiers. But just in case, send two missile teams to each place. Make sure they are well-hidden and stay out of sight."

Suddenly he laughed and punched Qasim in the chest.

"It is time to see if those damned missiles work," he said with a wolfish smile. "And if they work, it will be a big surprise for the Pakistanis. We can watch them all shit their pants!"

"It will be done!" Qasim replied, returning Mahmood's smile. He looked forward to seeing the Pakistanis shit their pants.

"When I'm done here I will join you at the soccer field. Now go," he said with a light push to Qasim's shoulder, "and make for a big surprise for the Pakistanis."

"Yes, Mahmood!"

Mahmood briefly watched his lieutenant tend to his task, then he looked down with hate at the semiconscious Secret Service agents that lay spread-eagled at his feet. *Now, time to teach the infidels a lesson in obedience.*

"Take this trash up to the stage. Place them in front of the teachers," he ordered several of his fighters.

The Secret Service agents were picked up like sacks of wet flour and dumped roughly in front of the teachers. Mahmood almost laughed when the infidels scuttled backwards in fear like crabs on a beach. He was going to relish what he was about to do and wanted to savor the moment. With his rifle slung, he casually walked up the steps to the stage floor while the teachers' terrified eyes washed over him. He just glowered back at this mostly bedraggled group of infidels.

Pamela Raynor, who sat at the rear of the group, stared at him with revulsion, still sick to her stomach when she remembered how two of the Taliban terrorists had wantonly groped and fondled her breasts while she was being cuffed and gagged. One had even reached under her skirt and shoved his hand up between her thighs, while the other had placed his face next to hers and breathed a warm, sour stench in her face, and then slowly licked her right cheek as he muttered something in Pashtu. She had trembled in their grasp. She knew all too well what would happen if they were given half a chance.

Mahmood planted himself squarely in front of the teachers and unslung his rifle.

"My name is Mahmood, of the Tehrik-e-taliban, and you are our prisoners. If you do as you are told, you will not be harmed. But if you do not do as you are told, this is what will happen to you."

As the teachers watched in disbelief, Mahmood stepped up to the agents who had been forced to sit upright on their knees; their wrists zip-tied tightly behind their backs—the agents oblivious to what was going on as they wobbled from side to side as blood coursed down their faces.

The teachers and faculty just stared as if trapped in some ghoulish play, unable to comprehend what the Taliban leader was about to do. Mahmood pressed the muzzle of his rifle firmly against the back of the first presidential guard's head and pushed it forward. When he was satisfied he had the infidels' full attention, he smiled and pulled the trigger.

The explosive crack of the rifle caused the bound teachers to jerk back as one as the round exploded into the rear of the agent's head, then exited just above the bridge of his nose; the teachers showered with thick stringers of blood, brain tissue, and fragments of skull.

Stunned by what they had seen, and covered in bloody gore, they were unable to fathom the deep crater where the agent's face used to be. Once over their initial shock, the captives flopped onto their sides and pushed with their legs, desperate to escape the horrific scene. The agent, as if in slow motion, slowly crumpled sideways to the floor.

Mahmood was humored by the infidels' feeble attempts to try and wriggle away. He could even see where several had wet themselves, leaving small puddles of light-yellowish urine that glistened dully on the wooden floor. In quick succession he stepped over to the remaining agents and blew their heads off one by one.

Disappointed there had been so few to execute, he sighed as he confronted his shocked audience. "This is what will happen if you disobey! So please, my dear friends, do not disobey."

To his delight, he actually saw several of the stupid infidels nod their heads in agreement. *By Allah's grace! What a gutless people these are,* he thought with a shake of his head.

With no further use for the teachers, he dismissed them from his thoughts. It was time to check in with his lieutenants.

"Hammid, Mahmood here!"

"Yes, Mahmood," came the scratchy reply.

"Are the entrance gates secured?"

"Yes, Mahmood. Men are stationed at all three gates."

"Very good. Qasim!"

"Yes, Mahmood," came the immediate reply.

"Are the missile teams in place?"

"Mahmood, only the team at the front gate is ready. I am now heading over to the cafeteria with the second team."

"Very good! I will see you there shortly!"

Stuffing the radio back in his pocket, and satisfied that every-thing was under control, he paused and deeply inhaled the smell of gunsmoke that wafted thickly throughout the large chamber. As he exhaled a long, low, breath of relief, he once again pulled his bala-clava over his head, grateful that their mission had been successful with the capture of Chutto's boys. He knew that Qudos would be pleased. Qudos now had his bargaining chips for the nuclear PAL codes.

Ten minutes later, Mahmood squatted on a concrete walkway next to one of the missile teams protected by Qasim and several of his fighters. When he looked about the position he was pleased. It was situated on the edge of the southeast corner of the cafeteria with perfect missile fields of fire toward the soccer field, the position shielded by low-slung hedges.

When he had approached Qasim's position, he also noticed an-other building just to the left of the cafeteria. Unknown to him this was the changing room for the school's Olympic-sized swimming pool. But what had caught his attention were the front corners of the two buildings that almost met at a forty-five degree angle to his front, the two buildings forming a natural funnel whose end pointed toward the soccer field. A perfect place to set up the M60.

"Qasim?" Mahmood said, his hand raised to shield his eyes from the sun as he searched for the inbound helicopters. "Call back and have the M60 moved up from the amphitheatre. I want it positioned between these two buildings before our guests arrive."

"Yes, Mahmood," Qasim answered, keying his radio to carry out Mahmood's order.

"And again you have done well," he said in praise of his lieutenant. "This position is perfect for the missiles. Qudos will know how well you have done this day."

"Yes! Thank you, Mahmood! Thank you!" Qasim replied, his face beaming with pride. "I also think we will give the Pakistanis a big surprise," he added hopefully.

"I think you are right. Their machines will not help them today. And, with Allah's guiding hand, we will kill them all."

Two minutes later he heard the distant thump of rotor blades to the northwest.

Chapter 34

DAY TWENTY, 0850 HOURS
MI-171 HELICOPTER
FOUR KILOMETERS NORTHEAST

"SERVICE SIX, SERVICE Six, this is School Fire One!" the command pilot called out.

The Mi-171s, one thousand feet above the ground, were proceeding southwest at 120 knots indicated as they passed over the intersection of Faisal Avenue and Kashmir Highway, more than halfway to their destination and just minutes from the school.

"School Fire One, this is Service Six! I read you loud and clear!" Mustaffa Kardar responded.

"Service Six, we're approximately four kilometers northeast of the school. We can see three columns of smoke near the Khayaban-e-Johar Road entrances. We do not see any personnel outside the buildings. How would you like us to proceed?"

"School Fire One, be advised that two companies of troops are en route by truck at this time. Colonel Solangi is in command and will coordinate all ground troops upon arrival. Standby, please!"

Mustaffa paused and hastily consulted a school map that showed the layout of the school grounds, his finger resting on the soccer field.

"School Fire One, see if you can off-load your troops to secure the soccer field east of the cafeteria. Have the platoon commander set up a perimeter. Once on the ground, have him contact Colonel Solangi on one-two-one point eight. I'll let the colonel know to rendezvous with some of his troops at the field."

"Copy that, Service Six. Understand our troops are to secure the soccer field east of the cafeteria, set up a perimeter, then have Lieutenant Waseer contact Colonel Solangi on one-two-one point eight, is that correct?"

"That is correct, School Fire One!"

"Copy that!" the pilot replied.

The pilot faced rearward, making eye contact with the SSW platoon commander who sat in a fold-down seat centered between himself and the copilot.

"Did you catch all of that?"

"Yes, sir, I did."

"All right, standby!"

The pilot keyed his radio and called back to the second chopper.

"School Fire Two, Fire One! Did you copy the last?"

"Fire One, affirmative!" the second pilot answered.

"Okay, Two, standby!"

The pilot switched back to intercom.

"Okay, Lieutenant, here's what we're going to do. Do you see Iqra University there to our front?" he asked, pointing at a clump of buildings in the distance.

Waseer craned his neck to get a better view outside the cockpit where he could just make out the university.

"Yes, sir!"

"Okay. With School Fire Two in trail, we're going in just over the university into the academy's soccer field. Do you see it?"

Lieutenant Waseer looked southeast of the university and saw an expansive field surrounded by a running track adjacent to a grassy athletic field.

"Yes, sir."

"Okay." the pilot said again. "You've got about two minutes to let your men know what's going on!"

Without a word, Waseer unbuckled his seat belt, stowed his seat against the fuselage, and made his way back to the troop compartment.

"Service Six, Service Six, this is School Fire One."

"School Fire One, Service Six, go ahead!" Mustaffa answered.

"Service Six, we should be on the ground in the next couple of minutes."

"Understood, School Fire One. Be advised that Colonel Solangi and his ground troops are ten minutes outbound!"

"Copy that, Service Six. We're making our approach now, out."

"I've got the aircraft!" the pilot announced, shaking the stick a couple of times to let his copilot know he now had control of the chopper.

"You've got the aircraft!" the copilot said.

"Fire Two, take up a trailing position just below and to our left! We'll go in over the university at six hundred feet and land due south into the soccer field! How do you copy?"

"Fire One, I copy. Follow in trail over Iqra at six hundred and land due south into the field."

"Copy is correct, Two. Here we go!"

Both Mi-171s—one after the other—abruptly pitched their noses down, descending rapidly to six hundred feet off the deck where they quickly leveled off. In the middle of sweeping, right-hand power turns over the university, the lead pilot looked down and to his right. He could see that hundreds of university students had spilled from their classrooms, confused as they shaded their eyes and stared at the low-flying helicopters, justifiably curious as to what the hell was going on. All of them had heard the explosions and gunfire that had come from within the Islamabad Preparatory Academy.

As the Mi-171s completed their turns and approached the soccer field, a sudden flash of fire burst from within the confines of the school. Not a split second later a second flash quickly followed the first. The lead pilot, startled, looked to his right, stunned to see two plumes of milky-white rocket exhausts streaking toward his chopper.

"Holy fucking Allah!" School Fire One's pilot screamed. "Flares! Flares! Release flares now!" he shouted as he jerked the chopper abruptly down and to the left, banking the Mi-171 nearly perpendicular to the ground in an effort to get away from the inbound missiles.

The copilot mashed down hard on the flare release button, pumping out a curtain of magnesium flares to the Mi-171's sides and rear; flares that resembled small incandescent suns that slowly drifted toward the ground. The pilot kept his eyes locked on the missiles, then breathed a sigh of relief when both missiles angled toward the rear of his aircraft.

School Fire Two, however, was not so lucky. Still in trail to School Fire One, its pilot was taken completely by surprise when the lead chopper had suddenly pitched over and banked wildly to the left across their flight path. Fearing a collision, and wondering why the hell School Fire One was dispensing flares, the pilot of School Fire

Two—ignorant of the Taliban missile launch—desperately jerked his Mi-171 up and steeply to the right, directly into the path of the incoming missiles.

The two FIM92E Stinger missiles, each packed with a 6.6 pound blast fragmentation warhead, sensed the burgeoning heat signatures of School Fire Two's red-hot turbines and turned from the flares, their seeker heads petulantly locked onto School Fire Two's engines.

In less than the blink of an eye, both missiles slammed—one after the other—into the starboard engine of School Fire Two and exploded in a massive fireball. The helicopter's five-bladed rotor hub, now unbalanced, immediately separated and whizzed off into the sky like a child's toy. Several of School Fire Two's onboard SSW soldiers, sitting in the open side hatches in preparation for landing, were blasted into the blue void like so much deadweight from the chopper's fuselage, their screams swallowed by the death throes of the Mi-171.

Now fully engulfed in flames, School Fire Two tumbled through the sky as if someone had kicked over a trash can stuffed with burning straw, then plummeted straight down and slammed hard into the dry grass of the soccer field; its grave marked by a funeral pyre of blinding, orange-red flames and mushrooming clouds of dark, oily smoke; its resting place easily marked by the spreading pools of burning JP-5 jet fuel and the numerous secondary explosions that wracked its hull as onboard rockets and ammunition cooked off.

Holy shit! the pilot of School Fire One thought as he unconsciously jerked his chopper to the right to put the burning hulk of School Fire Two between himself and any additional missile attacks. Now leveled off, he stared in shock at the shattered remains of School Fire Two.

"Lieutenant!" the command pilot shouted in a shaken voice.

"Yes, Commander!" Lieutenant Waseer answered from the troop compartment.

"We've just lost School Fire Two! They were hit by missiles and went down in the field! I don't see any survivors! I'm going in behind their crash site to off-load your men! We'll hit the LZ in about thirty seconds and the LZ is hot!"

"Got it, Commander!" Waseer shouted with a nervous glance at his men. "I understand!"

The pilot of School Fire One racked the Mi-171 onto its side and then leveled off, skimming the field just inches above the ground, its rotor wash creating hurricane winds that flattened the grass beneath it. When the pilot approached to within two hundred feet of the burning carcass of Fire Two, he pulled up hard on the collective and twisted down on the throttle, the chopper instantly flaring nose high and stopping its forward motion.

With its tail rotor just inches from scraping the dirt, the Mi-171 nosed over as it lost all lift and dropped heavily to the earth. The SSW troops, all primed and ready to go, burst from both sides of its fuselage to establish defensive positions on each side of the burning remains of School Fire Two. Once all of the troops had been off-loaded, the lead pilot hastily pulled the Mi-171 into the air, pivoted 180 degrees to the northeast, twisted in full power, and departed the field as fast as he could go. Once clear of the field, he pulled the chopper up into a steep, left-hand climbing turn as he passed over Iqra University, unaware that the landing gear of his aircraft was within inches of scraping its rooftops.

As the soccer field receded quickly to his rear, the pilot keyed his radio.

"Service Six! Service Six! This is School Fire One!"

"School Fire One, this is Service Six, go ahead!" Mustaffa anxiously replied.

"Service Six, be advised that we just lost School Fire Two! I say again, we just lost School Fire Two! He was knocked down by a couple of goddamned missiles!"

Mustaffa stood transfixed, not wanting to believe what he had heard. When it finally hit home, he gripped the microphone and pushed the transmit button.

"Understood, School Fire One! Understand School Fire Two is down! What's the status of its troops?" he asked, hoping for the best.

"Sir! There were no survivors as far as we could tell! It was blown out of the sky during our approach and crashed hard into the middle of the soccer field! I just off-loaded Lieutenant Waseer and his troops next to the crash site! They are now forming a defensive perimeter as ordered!"

"Understood, School Fire One," Mustaffa answered, saying a brief, silent prayer for School Fire Two. "I understand Lieutenant Waseer and his troops are now on the soccer field."

"Sir, that is correct! Do you want us to remain on station or return to the palace?"

"School Fire One, maintain station to the northeast. I say again, maintain station to the northeast and contact Colonel Solangi. He now has operational control and may need your firepower. Do you copy?"

"Copy that, Service Six. School Fire One to maintain station to the northeast and contact Colonel Solangi."

The pilot released the radio transmit switch and stared once more in helpless rage toward the rear of his aircraft. He could see the plumes of fire and smoke that marked the gravesite of School Fire Two. Smoke and fire that rose high into the air like giant storm clouds that had gathered over a dark and forbidding place.

Chapter 35

DAY TWENTY, 0905 HOURS
ISLAMABAD PREPARATORY ACADEMY

MAHMOOD TAHQI LAY sweating on the burning concrete walk feeling more like a sacrificial goat skewered over some fire at a religious feast, thanking Allah with all his might that the missiles had worked. He had never seen how a missile could pluck an aircraft from the sky, much less understood how they worked. Initially, he had felt a pang of fear pierce his guts that the missiles would miss, but now his jubilation was complete, rejoicing in the pyrotechnic display that was unfolding before him.

He had watched as the helicopters tracked rapidly across his front at an altitude of less than two hundred meters. But once the missiles had been launched, the lead helicopter had somehow picked up the inbound missiles and pumped out many, many burning flares that streamed outwards from its sides; flares that looked like miniature suns as they arched gracefully across the morning sky, and then drifted lazily down to earth trailed by ghostly-gray wisps of smoke.

His frustration knew no bounds when he saw the missiles turn from the first helicopter and head for the flares. He knew they only had three missiles left and could not afford to have these two miss. Unconsciously, he had pounded his fist on the concrete walk, muttering over and over, "No! No! No!", but suddenly he stopped his antics and became hopeful. The missiles had caught the scent of the second helicopter.

Mentally he had urged the missiles on as if he were watching a soccer match, thankful that the second helicopter had been stupid in failing to throw out its own flares. As he watched in morbid fascination, both missiles abruptly turned left and slammed into the side of the trailing helicopter, resulting in the most glorious of glorious explosions.

"Yes! Yes! May Allah be praised! May Allah be praised!" he shouted as several of the hated SSW troops were thrown bodily from the flying machine, looking more like rag dolls as they plunged to the earth, screaming and flailing their arms about until they hit the ground. Seconds later he cheered when the loathsome helicopter smashed to a fiery death on the newly mown grass of the soccer field, engulfed by flames and boiling clouds of dark smoke as it burned furiously with abandon.

Reluctant to tear his gaze from the blazing wreck, he quickly looked to his front and picked up the first helicopter as it made a steep, circling, right-hand turn to the north, the pilot using the burning hulk of the second helicopter as a shield. Then it pivoted in midflight and came in quick and fast and low behind it, its skids just inches above the field when it suddenly flared nose high and thumped hard to the ground to off-load its soldiers.

The M60 machine gun to his left immediately opened up in a booming, staccato-like rhythm that echoed off the walls of the cafeteria. With a cyclic rate of over five hundred rounds per minute, the M60 raked the ground in front of the Pakistani soldiers, knocking several of them back while hundreds of puffs of dirt and clumps of grass stitched a line across their front. The remainder of his fighters quickly joined in, adding their own firepower to that of the machine gun.

Taken totally by surprise, the SSW troops recoiled backwards as if they had stuck their hands into liquid pools of fire, shocked by the unexpected volume of fire that came from within the confines of the school—desperately back-peddling as the rate of Taliban fire increased. The soldiers, many of them panicked and frightened, tried to seek cover behind the shot down helicopter, or make their way to the hedgerows located toward their rear.

With the Pakistanis having gone to ground, and their attack stopped dead in its tracks, Mahmood slapped Qasim on the shoulder.

"Stay here! Keep the Pakistanis pinned down!"

He knew he needed to contact the Pakistan president as soon as possible to open up negotiations, for only President Chutto could keep the SSW at bay to prevent them from storming the school. Besides, Chutto was the only one who could give them the PAL codes.

It was time to lay down the law to the Pakistanis.

Mahmood used his forearms and rifle to push back from the sporadic SSW rifle fire that was beginning to impact their position. Finally, he made it to the corner of the cafeteria and stood up, steeling one more cautious look at his hated enemy. The SSW, he could see, continued to maneuver backwards in the hope of finding a more defensible position.

"Qasim!" he shouted over the high-pitched cracks of rifle fire. "I'm going to check the other positions, then head back to the auditorium! Call me if they try another attack!"

"Yes, Mahmood!" Qasim shouted. As far as he was concerned, he was having the time of his life. For once they had the Pakistanis on the run and he could see many of their lifeless bodies lying motionless beside the destroyed helicopter. Several of the soldiers, badly wounded, screamed in pain with their hands raised in a futile gesture as if praying to Allah. *By Allah's grace,* he thought excitedly, *let them continue to attack so that we can kill them all!*

Mahmood looked back at Qasim, but flinched when a Pakistani round blew off a small chunk of the building's corner, peppering his face with stinging fragments of brick. With a curse stifled in his throat for the Pakistani shit that had shot at him, he again looked at Qasim. "It is time for me to call the president! Remember, let me know what the soldiers do here!"

"Yes, Mahmood!" Qasim shouted back, now hugging the earth to shield his body from the increasingly accurate SSW rifle fire that plunked into the ground around him.

With one final look at the battle scene, Mahmood ran toward the middle school to check on his men stationed at Gate Two. Minutes later, he squatted in the dirt next to several of his fighters. He could tell that all was quiet and that the Pakistan infantry had not yet arrived. As he looked across Khayaban-e-Johar Road toward Service Road N fifty meters to his front, he could see the roads were separated by a fairly flat expanse of ground covered with low-growing weeds and split down the center by an abandoned railroad track. *Yes! Yes! Perfect fields of fire! Allah, in his wisdom, graces us with his guiding hand!*

He slapped one of the fighters on the knee, then sprinted across the width of the school to the northern side of the campus. When he reached the perimeter wall, he could see this position was even better than the middle school. It had wide, flat fields of fire to his front with few places for the Pakistanis to hide. His men who manned this side of the school also told him there had been little sign of the Pakistan infantry. They had seen a couple of military six-by-six trucks drive down Street Six two hundred meters to their front, but the Pakistanis, it seemed, had not yet had enough time to set up a perimeter to seal off this side of the school.

Satisfied that his men were well positioned, Mahmood pulled back and left the perimeter, jogging through the amphitheatre where he greeted two more fighters who stood guard at the rear entrance to the auditorium. With one final look around the campus, and hearing the continued crackle of gunfire from the soccer field, he opened the building's rear door and stepped inside.

As he walked rapidly down the short hallway at the rear of the stage, he was suddenly brought up short by a woman's piercing scream. Startled, he was sure the scream had come from an office just five meters to his front. A second blood-curdling scream quickly followed the first, filling the hallway as he ran up and looked through the office window. He saw two of his fighters grappling with one of the women hostages.

Mahmood kicked open the door and immediately recognized the woman to be the superintendent of the school, being slapped around by one of his fighters while the other tried to pull her up on a desk. He was furious at his men for their stupidity, not because they wanted to rape the infidel whore, but because he still needed her to keep the other hostages in line and to possibly speak with the Pakistani bastards.

The first fighter, his arm wrapped tightly around the infidel's shoulder, looked up and immediately froze when he saw Mahmood, then released the woman and stepped back in fear toward the rear of the office.

The second fighter, unaware that his commander stood behind him, grunted in satisfaction when he finally pushed the bitch's skirt high above her thighs and ripped off her panties. But before he could reach down to unbutton his trousers, Mahmood lifted his unslung rifle and crashed it down hard on the man's skull, splitting the fighter's scalp with a jagged gash and knocking him to the floor.

"I need this woman, you pieces of camel shit!" he screamed. "She's in charge of the school, by Allah's grace! What do you mean doing this now? Why are you not guarding the hostages?"

The fighter who had been butt-stroked, with blood pouring from a four-inch slash to his scalp, crawled painfully on all fours around the desk toward his companion. Pamela Raynor, in an attempt to stifle her screams, bit down hard on her fist, then lurched off the desk and ran to a corner of the office—slowly sliding down the wall to try and make herself as inconspicuous as possible.

With his face swollen in anger by their idiocy, Mahmood continued to rage. "If you have to rape someone, there are plenty of old women out there!" he shouted, his finger pointed toward the stage. "Go get one of them if you must! But if you want this one, you will have to wait until she is of no further use to me!"

Both fighters, fearful of Mahmood's anger, quickly looked down, not wanting to make eye contact with their commander. They knew what had happened to other Taliban fighters who had done some deed that had not met with his approval. Both remembered all too well the fate of one fighter who had repeatedly angered Mahmood. In a fit of rage at the man's insubordination, Mahmood had had the man summarily beheaded in a public square and his limbs hacked off one by one, then had his carcass disemboweled to be used for a tribal game of Buzkashi.

Buzkashi, somewhat similar to polo in the west, was made up of two teams of eight men mounted on horseback that used a gutted, headless goat in lieu of a small ball. The goal of Buzkashi was for one team to grab the goat from the ground using only their hands and race full tilt across the field in an effort to pitch the carcass across their opponents' goal line. The other team tried to prevent this by whipping their opponents across their faces and shoulders with lengths of hemp rope, or crashing into their opponents' horses with their own. All in order to gain possession of the prize.

In the game remembered by the two fighters, the Taliban's disemboweled torso had been flung up and down the field from one team member to another, many times hitting the ground only to be trampled into the dirt by the horses' hooves. At the end of the match, the Taliban's headless, limbless corpse had been reduced to nothing more than broken, protruding rib bones and long stringers of flayed meat.

"Yes, Mahmood," they both stammered.

But Pamela shook with fear when she heard those dreadful words from the Taliban leader. He had basically told these men they could have her once her usefulness was at an end. She knew that her nightmare was far from over, but lingered in the not too distant future.

With a disdainful look at the superintendent, Mahmood spat out, "Make yourself decent you infidel bitch!" Then he turned to the two fighters. "And you two, when she is ready, take her back out to the stage. Make sure her arms are cuffed and her mouth taped shut. I am making you both responsible for her safety."

At that moment he smirked, just to let his men know he was no longer angry. They could have their fun with the infidel when she was no longer needed.

"Yes, Mahmood," the first fighter answered, a cautious smile on his lips while his eyes pierced Pamela with a leering glance.

Once back in the hallway, Mahmood made his way to the auditorium manager's office, but before he entered he saw Nayid standing at the rear of the stage.

"Nayid, I am not to be disturbed. It is time to call the Pakistanis. Interrupt me only if something happens."

"Yes, Mahmood."

Mahmood opened the office door and made his way to a large, cushioned, wood-framed swivel chair placed behind the manager's desk. With his rifle set aside, he sat down heavily and leaned forward with his elbows resting on the desk, trying to think everything through. His fighters had secured the perimeter and the Pakistanis had not yet deployed their soldiers, except for those at the soccer field. But he knew that more soldiers were on the way, and would shortly arrive to seal off the outer perimeter of the school.

Mahmood, however, smiled. He knew he had the upper hand and the arrival of additional Pakistani troops did not bother him, not while he had President Chutto's boys as hostages. While he tried to think of what he had forgotten, and before he placed his call to the president, he was startled to see Nayid running down the hall.

"Mahmood! Another helicopter is coming! Heading for the front gate!"

He instantly forgot his call to the president and jumped out of his chair, running down the hall toward the main auditorium.

"What kind of helicopter?" Mahmood shouted as he jumped off the stage and made his way up to the foyer, fearful that the Pakistanis were about to attack the front gate.

"I'm not sure!" Nayid shouted back as he struggled to keep up with his commander. "Hammid just called and said he could hear one coming! I thought you should know!"

"You're right, Nayid! Let's go and see what the Pakistanis are up to!"

Exiting the building, Mahmood stepped over the bodies of the Secret Service agents that still littered the entryway. When he heard the distinctive thumping sounds of an approaching helicopter, his first thought was that these sounds were very different from the helicopters at the soccer field. With his eyes shielded from the glare of the sun, he searched the sky to the north.

A much smaller helicopter slowly swept into view at no more than one hundred meters in altitude. As he watched it approach, he was sure it was not military. It had a full, glass, bubble-nosed cockpit, and alongside its fuselage were large red letters that spelled out "CNN". Its small side door was also slid back and a man, with what looked to be a large video camera cradled in his arms, leaned precariously outside.

The helicopter slowed even more and slewed to the right, to try and give the cameraman a better shooting angle. Within moments, several AK-47s set on full automatic opened up from the main gate's security shack, riddling the cockpit so that it looked more like a transparent slice of Swiss cheese, the inside of its windscreen immediately streaked with smears and splotches of blood when the pilot and copilot were hit. More automatic weapons fire swept down the helicopter's fuselage, stitching the cameraman with 7.62mm rounds that blew him back inside the passenger compartment. Other rounds sliced through the chopper's single in-line engine, causing it to spew out clouds of dirty-gray smoke and flames through its exhaust.

With its engine shrieking in protest, and pumping out darker and darker clouds of smoke, the helicopter twisted out of control and smashed violently into the school's northwest parking lot, its impact marked by a huge explosion that shot a fireball high into the air. As smaller secondary explosions wracked its frame, Mahmood and Nayid ran down the auditorium steps and looked to their right. Both could see the helicopter crumpled up like an accordion, engulfed in flames along with two school buses that had been hit, the buses' own smoke added to that of the crash site.

Mahmood spat and dismissed the conflagration as unimportant, then pulled from his jacket a small set of binoculars to scan the area directly in front of the school. He was much more interested in the Pakistanis rather than the burning civilian helicopter to his right.

With the binoculars raised to his eyes, he could see several army trucks, no more than five hundred meters to his front, slowly pull into view followed by numerous large vans. The vans, however, he could tell were not military, but had to be civilian news trucks given the network logos splashed across their sides and the large, telescoping antenna dishes bolted to their rooftops. Several other news vans that had arrived prior to the soldiers were already stopped in place, busily deploying their own satellite dishes.

Once the dishes were locked in place, he could see several individuals standing cautiously around the vehicles with what looked to be microphones in their hands, pointing and gesturing wildly at the academy and the burning helicopter. *Allah be praised! Those news people will broadcast what it means to defy the Taliban!*

Before he headed back to the auditorium, Mahmood walked casually to the main gate and gave explicit instructions to Hammid not to fire at, or molest in any way, the news vans to their front. He wanted their cameras to show the world the resolve of the Tehrik-e-taliban. He would twist the news media around his finger and let them be his propaganda machine from a distance. As far as he was concerned, they could broadcast all the images of the school that they wanted, to be witness to what needed to be done.

After making his way back to the manager's office, he sat down and stretched his arms toward the ceiling. He knew he was tired. The day had started very early and there were many more hours left before he could sleep. Absently, he reached into his filthy shirt pocket and pulled out the piece of paper that had the presidential palace phone number on it. Sitting forward, he grabbed the desk phone to make his call to the Pakistan president, but then he changed his mind. He knew he had better call Qudos first.

With the paper placed on the desk, Mahmood hit the speed dial button of the satellite phone given to him at Gengi Kel. As he sat back to gather his thoughts, he could hear the various clicks and clacks that told him the call was going through. He knew that Qudos would be pleased.

Chapter 36

DAY TWENTY, 0953 HOURS
GENGI KEL TRAINING CAMP
NEAR WANA, PAKISTAN
SOUTH WAZIRISTAN PROVINCE

QUDOS MEHSUD GREW more anxious as each moment passed. The attack had been planned for eight thirty and Mahmood should have called over an hour ago, but it was now almost ten. He knew that Mahmood would have a lot on his hands, assuming the attack had been successful, but many things could have gone wrong. The security detail that guarded President Chutto's sons could have been increased, or maybe the sons were not even there, or the fighters had been intercepted on their way to the school. He just didn't know at this point. But everything told him by his military informants indicated the boys should be there with a security detail of ten Secret Service agents. By Allah's grace, he hoped that everything had gone according to plan. His position with the Council of Elders depended upon it.

Qudos paced the dirt floor of his headquarters, stopping and turning occasionally to frown at the obnoxiously silent satellite phone that sat on his desk, praying that it would ring. Behind him, sitting in a rickety wooden chair, was the Senior Nuclear Technician Abdul Farooqi guarded by the pilot Zalmay MahMund. Abdul to verify the PAL codes they received were valid and Zalmay, with his knowledge of weapons systems, to make sure that the tech told him the truth.

Abdul watched as Qudos glowered about the room, knowing full well that his life depended on the Taliban leader getting the correct codes. He prayed with all his might that President Chutto would authorize their release.

Qudos continued to pace an unending circle within the narrow confines of the room, his hands locked behind his back when the satellite phone began to ring, its strident tone ripping through the silence of the room. Stopped in midstride as if he had run into a brick wall, he stared at the phone as it continued to ring and bounce on the table.

Qudos thanked Allah for his providence. If something unplanned had taken place, the phone would have remained silent. He had told Mahmood to destroy his phone if it looked like he could be captured or killed.

Scrambling to the side of the table, he snatched up the phone and smiled when he recognized the incoming phone number.

"Mahmood, can you hear me?" he asked anxiously.

"Yes, Hakim! I can hear you!"

"Good! Good! So where do we stand? Have you taken over the school? Have you captured Chutto's boys?"

"Hakim, all has gone as we planned. As we speak, our fighters guard the perimeter of the school. And yes, we have Chutto's sons, and all the other children and teachers as hostages. They are all bound up in the auditorium. But the Pakistanis reacted much faster than we thought. They have the school surrounded and we had to fight two of their helicopters at the soccer field. We destroyed one of their machines with missiles, but the second helicopter was able to off-load its soldiers. But we pushed them back and managed to kill many of them. For now they are content to remain where they are and have made no further attempts to enter the school. We also shot down a news helicopter trying to get pictures of the school grounds, and there are a lot of news vans across the field in front of the school. We can see their reporters walking around reporting on our attack, but I have told our fighters not to shoot at them."

With a brief prayer to Allah for their providence, Qudos pulled out a chair and sat down.

"Very good, Mahmood! Very good! Now, listen to me. Keep to the plan. Call President Chutto. Tell him his sons are being held hostage and that we have the warheads. And for the return of his sons he is to give us the codes, by no later than eight o'clock tomorrow morning. He is also to provide you and your fighters a plane when you leave the school. Also tell him if his soldiers attack the school his sons will die. Stress that point with him. Then after his sons, the rest of the hostages. They are to make no attempts to take back the school."

"Yes, Hakim, I understand. But I still think we should kill some of the students, to put pressure on the Pakistanis to release what we want."

"No! No! I have explained that to you! If we do that the Pakistanis may attack! Or the Americans! They would think they had no choice! It is better to let Chutto simmer in his own shit and think of his sons. Remember, this president is weak. By Allah's grace, he will not run the risk of losing his boys. I am sure they will give us the codes by tomorrow morning. But if not then kill a student, an American student, every hour beginning at nine. Do you understand?"

"Yes, Hakim."

"But make the demand for the codes now! This I know they will not do; it is still too soon and they will try to stall, to try and think of a way to rescue Chutto's boys. So do as we had planned. Make an example of one of the American students to show them we are in charge. And make sure it is public and in full view of the reporters. I am sure that Chutto will be watching from his palace. He will not want the same thing to happen to his boys. This will also give the Americans time to apply pressure on the president. Remember, the Americans are also weak. I am sure they would rather let us have the codes than watch their children die. Do you understand?"

"Yes, Hakim, I understand!"

"Good! Now, when you have the codes, call them in to me by radio. Do not use the satellite phone. Destroy it. They could trace another call back to this camp. Once you have radioed in the codes I will have the technician make sure that they work."

"It will be done, Hakim!" Mahmood responded.

"When the warheads are armed, I will radio you back. This will be the time for you to demand that you and your men be taken to the plane. Then release the hostages except for the president's boys. Tell him you will keep his sons to ensure your safety. That his sons will be released unharmed once you have arrived." *Or maybe not?* Qudos mused, smiling into the phone. *Those boys could come in handy.* "Do you understand?"

"Yes, Hakim! I will do as you say! Allahu akbar!"

Chapter 37

DAY TWENTY, 0955 HOURS
THE SITUATION ROOM
PRESIDENTIAL PALACE
ISLAMABAD, PAKISTAN

SYID BULEDI, THE Prime Minister of Pakistan, ran down the ornate hallway that led to the presidential palace Situation Room. Not twenty minutes earlier he had been briefed by one of his security people that a Taliban attack had taken place somewhere within the city. He had thought no more of it at the time, terrorist attacks having become more common within the city limits, and they had always turned out to be small, isolated affairs. But when he had received an urgent call from President Chutto, with the sound of near panic in his friend's voice, he had instantly suspended his morning advisors meeting and bolted from the Ministry's conference room—his aides left confused and looking awkwardly at one another. He knew the president, only under the direst of circumstances, would tell him to drop everything and get over to the palace as quickly as possible.

When he exited the Ministry building he suddenly stopped—his security detail almost ramming him from behind—and looked across Constitution Avenue, searching the broad expanse of the city to see if anything seemed out of the ordinary. The only thing he could see was several thin pillars of dark smoke that rose languidly into the sky far-off in the distance, already mixing with the hazy smog layer that was beginning to form over the city. The smoke seemed to be in the southeast portion of the city less than ten kilometers away. *Looks to be Sector H9.*

Hurriedly buttoning his suit coat, he walked down the Ministry's broad marble steps and was immediately ushered into his armored Mercedes limousine, and then driven rapidly down Constitution

Avenue to the presidential palace less than a kilometer away.

Dressed in his usual light-gray suit, conservative blue tie, and black wing-tipped shoes, Syid waved aside the Secret Service agents who guarded the entrance to the Situation Room. After an agent opened one of its two large, double doors, he stepped into the room and saw President Chutto with a phone glued to his ear, hunched over the conference table with a bleak look on his face—the sleeves of his shirt rolled up to his elbows with his suit coat draped carelessly over the back of his chair. *That is very unusual,* Syid thought.

Normally fastidious in appearance, Chutto's disheveled look was totally out of character and gave the prime minister pause for thought. The president's eyes were also red-rimmed and burned brightly like two incandescent wicks, accenting a face weighted down by discordant, wrinkled folds as if he had just been in an auto wreck. Syid was shocked. His friend looked as if he had aged twenty years from yesterday.

President Chutto looked up and hastily waved him over to the table. As he made his way across the room's thick carpets, he approached his friend in confusion, wondering what in Allah's name had made him so troubled.

"Okay, Mustaffa, thank you for the update," he heard Chutto say, then watched as his president listened for several more anxious moments. "Yes, Director General Pasha and Marshal Khattack are already on their way. They should be here at any moment. Have them come directly to the Situation Room. Prime Minister Buledi has just arrived."

President Chutto listened for several more seconds.

"Thank you. And I know . . . I know. And yes, when you can, join us here. Sooner the better. And be sure to bring the maps."

Chutto nodded several more times in silent agreement, his lips compressed into a hard, white, bloodless straight line.

"Yes, I agree! Whoever has done this evil thing will pay with their lives! And may Allah guide us all through this terrible day!"

At the end of the conversation, President Chutto placed the phone in its cradle and tiredly leaned back in his chair, staring off into nothingness.

"Assif? What is wrong? I came over as quickly as I could! I also heard there has been a Taliban attack within the city! What can you tell me?"

Syid had never seen his friend act this way, not even during their brief war with India.

President Chutto motioned for him to remain silent as he slumped deeper in his chair, his chin tucked into his neck. After several moments, he gruffly rubbed his face and then spread his arms, choking back a sob.

"The Taliban! They have attacked and taken over the Islamabad Preparatory Academy! The same school my boys attend!"

"What? The academy? When did this happen?" Syid exclaimed, shocked by Chutto's statement.

"Sometime around eight thirty this morning, my friend. Mustaffa received a garbled message from the agents in charge of Vahe and Nasim's detail. They said they were under attack by Taliban militants and, after that one call, there's been no further word. Nothing. Mustaffa ordered in the Ready Reaction Force by helicopter, but one of them was shot down with no survivors. By a goddamned missile no less!" he said, unaware that his nails were cutting deeply into the palms of his balled fists.

Syid did not take offense at his friend's belligerent tone, knowing better than most the stress his president had to be under. It was common knowledge that he worshiped the ground those boys walked on, how he doted on them and bragged they would extend the Chutto family line far into the distant future. Those boys were his life, his reason for being. Syid calmed himself as he waited for Assif to continue.

"Ground forces under the command of a Colonel Solangi are now surrounding the school."

"But why would they do this?" Syid asked, having no idea what the Taliban had to gain. "Didn't they know your boys attended the school? What this would mean to their cause and their people?"

"I have no idea," Chutto replied heavily. "It makes no sense. It's crazy! They have just pissed away all the gains they have made with my government over the last few years, especially regarding the FATA. And to jeopardize the lives of my sons is unforgivable! It's insanity!"

President Chutto paused, his face flushed red with unbidden anger, his well-known temper about to explode to the surface.

"I'll tell you this! If just so much as a hair, just one fucking hair is hurt on my boys, I swear before Allah and all of my ancestors that

I will have every Taliban scum in Pakistan tracked down and killed! And their families! All of them! With no mercy! They will all be killed!"

Then, as if a light switch had been thrown, his anger vanished, his face once more crumpled by grief as he thought of his two young boys—his two precious sons—whose lives were now fully at stake. Unable to contain his despair, he held his head between his hands and began to sob.

Syid watched his friend's pain in silence, not knowing what to do. Though normally never at a loss for words, now he could only place a hand firmly on his president's shoulder. He knew that Assif needed to get this out of his system. It was one thing to be the target of an attack—they were both used to such things; it came with their positions of power—but when they attacked your children that was something entirely different. They were trying to kill off your future heritage!

"We will get them back! Don't fear my friend! We will get them back!" he said with as much determination that he could muster.

The intercom suddenly came to life.

"Mr. President?" his secretary said. "Director General Pasha and Air Chief Marshal Khattack have just arrived. May I send them in?"

President Chutto slowly lifted his head and stared at the phone in stone-like silence, the muscles of his face set in rigid hate, trying to mask his fear. Reaching into his trousers, he pulled out a hand-kerchief and wiped at his eyes. Then, with a quick glance at Syid, he nodded and stuffed the handkerchief back in his pocket.

Syid abruptly flicked the intercom switch.

"Yes, please, send them in at once!"

Director General Umar Pasha, the current head of the ISI, and Air Chief Marshal Anwar Khattack, the chairman of the Pakistan Joint Chiefs of Staff, followed each other stoically into the room, both men distraught as they stepped up to their president and perfunctorily shook his hand. Both were well aware of what he must be going through.

"Mr. President," Director General Pasha began in a soft, gravelly voice. "We know," he said with a gesture at Marshal Khattack, "what has happened at the academy. We want you to know we will do everything in our power to see that your boys, and all of the children, are released unharmed. I make this pledge before Allah the Merciful," he finished, grasping Chutto's forearm and squeezing it tightly.

"I too, Mr. President, make that pledge before Allah," Marshal Khattack added, giving President Chutto a firm hug. "This is an insult to God to attack children! And to do so within the boundaries of our capital is unforgivable! The Air Force and Army are united, sir! Please rest assured, we will punish those who have done this evil thing!"

"Thank you, thank you both," President Chutto said emotionally, gaining strength from the words of these two men. "Now, please. Please be seated."

As they approached the table, the intercom once again came to life.

"Mr. President? Mustaffa Kardar has just arrived."

"Good! Send him in!" Chutto said, looking eagerly at the room's main door.

Mustaffa Kardar, with maps rolled into long tubes clutched in his hands, hurriedly made his way to the table.

"Mr. President, I have an update on the school situation, and maps of the academy grounds and surrounding areas!"

"Good! Very good, Mustaffa!" he said. Here was something tangible he could work on, feeling more energized as he stepped up to his security director. "Just spread them out on the table so we can all see. Gentlemen? Please gather round. Mustaffa, bring us up-to-date on what's going on."

Mustaffa leaned across the broad table and unrolled a map of Sector H9 that showed all of the roads and buildings within six kilometers of the academy. With the map about to roll back upon itself, Director General Pasha and Marshal Khattack reached over and held it in place while Mustaffa grabbed two heavy ashtrays and placed them at the map's top and bottom. With the first map anchored to the table, he unrolled a second map that was much more detailed of the school grounds, a map that showed all of the academy buildings, entry points, athletic fields, and maintenance facilities.

"Mr. President, Mr. Prime Minister, gentlemen," Mustaffa began, pointing at the H9 map, "Colonel Solangi is now completing his encirclement of the academy. Bounded by Kirthar Road to the north, Street Three to the east just below Iqra University, by Service Road N to the south, and to the west by the International Islamic University."

With a quick look at President Chutto he continued.

"As it stands right now, sir, the perimeter should be secured in the next ten to fifteen minutes. Colonel Solangi has also established his headquarters here," he said, pointing to a location on the western side of the academy, "at the International University located across these fields, not far from the main entrance to the school. This location also gives them a direct line of sight into the academy. From what we can tell, it looks like the attack took place during a school assembly in the auditorium. And, sir, it looks as if all of the students and faculty were present at this assembly. That's a little over three hundred students, with many of them being the children of American and foreign diplomats. But the majority of the students, I'm sure you already know, are the children of some of our more prominent citizens."

"Shit" was all President Chutto could say as he turned from the map. "Syid, we need to put out a statement concerning the attack, to let the embassies know what's going on. That we're doing everything within our power to resolve the situation."

"Yes, Mr. President," he said, turning toward a second bank of phones at the far end of the table.

"Sir," Marshal Khattack interrupted, "as for the disposition of our troops, I spoke with Colonel Solangi not five minutes ago. He has two companies of SSW special forces now forming his perimeter. I also directed that a battalion of regular army troops be placed under his command. This will give him over one thousand men to surround the academy. In addition, I have placed the 22nd Helicopter Gunship Company at his disposal. These forces should give him more than enough firepower to contain the militants and to make an assault if needed."

"Thank you, Anwar," Chutto said gratefully. He knew he could count on the military to take decisive action.

"Mr. President," Director General Pasha interjected, "I hate to say this, but we have another problem. One we need to deal with right now, sir."

"And what is that, Umar?" President Chutto asked, staring at the school map and burning the location of the auditorium and his sons into his memory.

"The press, sir! When I was coming to the palace I was told that word of the attack has already spread to the media. I would assume they are descending on the school like a swarm of locusts. That makes it even more important to get out a statement about the attack, but that leaves us with the Americans. They are going to be very upset and I don't know what they will do. I suggest you call President Taylor as soon as possible to let him know what's happened. That we are doing everything within our power to resolve the situation."

"Okay, point well taken," President Chutto said. He hadn't even thought of the American president at this point, or how he would react to the attack, but he agreed with the wisdom of the director general's statement. "As usual, you're right again, Umar."

"Mr. President," the intercom blared, "I have Colonel Solangi for you. He's being patched through by radio. Shall I put him on?"

"Yes! Yes! Put him on now!" he shouted as he quickly hit the speaker button.

"Mr. President? Colonel Solangi here, sir!"

"Go ahead, Colonel!"

"Sir, we just had an incident occur that I thought you should know about. A media helicopter, we think it was from CNN, just overflew the school trying to get some pictures. Anyway, sir, it was just blown out of the sky with automatic weapons fire. No survivors and it crashed into the northern section of the school parking lot. I have now ordered the 22nd Helicopter Gunship Company to enforce a three kilometer no-fly zone over the school. But I thought you should know about the helicopter. And, sir, just to let you know, we have a whole armada of news trucks trying to enter the area. Many of them have already set up, but I am not allowing them to get any closer than five hundred meters to the school."

Well, now it starts, President Chutto thought glumly.

"Colonel Solangi?" Marshal Khattack interrupted. "Marshal Khattack here. You are to keep the media away from the school. I say again, you are to keep the media away from the school! And I concur with the no-fly zone. Now, have you determined how many Taliban are in the school?"

"Sir, right now we don't have a firm estimate, but we are taking sporadic rifle fire whenever we try to approach the school. So I have ordered all troops to stand fast, to concentrate on just securing the perimeter, but the Taliban are well-hidden behind a perimeter wall that surrounds the school. I'm sorry, sir, I just don't have any more information at this time."

"Okay, thank you for the update, Colonel. And I agree, just secure the perimeter and stand fast. Mr. President? Any further questions for the colonel?"

"No, not now," Chutto said with a shake of his head.

"Okay, Colonel. Keep us informed of anything, and I mean anything, that goes on at that academy. And do not attempt any assaults at this time. Just stand fast and secure the perimeter. Do you understand?" Marshal Khattack commanded.

"Yes, sir, I understand!"

After the call was disconnected, the marshal shrugged and stated the obvious. "Well, Mr. President, I suggest you make that call to President Taylor. The sooner the better."

Resigned to his fate, President Chutto was about to have his secretary place the call to the White House when he paused.

"Marshal? What's the time in Washington right now?"

"Sir, there's a ten hour time difference between Islamabad and Washington, D.C. Right now it's almost midnight Washington time."

"Well, I guess it can't be helped," he said dejectedly. "Better to wake him up and let him know what's going on, rather than see it on the morning news."

President Chutto reached for the handset when his secretary's voice once again came over the intercom.

"Mr. President? I have a call from the Islamabad Preparatory Academy. Do you wish to take the call, sir?"

Chutto jerked his hand from the receiver as if it were a coiled Cobra ready to strike and fell heavily into his chair, feeling as if a vise had grabbed his heart. He knew he was in no condition to speak with the other person on the line, the person that held the lives of his precious sons within his grasp. His advisors stood frozen, mute and unsmiling, but he knew he had to come to an immediate decision. With his heart racing at breakneck speed, he gathered up his courage and punched the button for the active line.

Chapter 38

DAY TWENTY, 2348 HOURS
THE WHITE HOUSE
WASHINGTON, D.C.

A LATE EVENING storm slowly passed overhead as the black armored Suburban turned out of the West Wing parking lot onto Executive Avenue NW, the street lights glinting off its rain-streaked windows while its windshield wipers thunked rhythmically from side to side. Thunder rumbled in the distance while lightening flickered overhead, briefly illuminating the vehicle as it completed its turn and drove half a block north toward Pennsylvania Avenue.

Steven Clarke, the president's Director of National Security, tiredly closed the file on his lap and pushed back in the soft leather seat. It had been another long day, one that had started at six in the morning and ended at ten that night with the conclusion of the White House State Dinner for the prime minister of Great Britain. Oddly enough he had enjoyed the dinner. Normally, he hated these types of functions for visiting heads of state, but he was a big fan of the older gentleman and always enjoyed the Brit's stories about World War II when he had been a child during the London blitz. He also knew the old man was astute and had a good take on world events, the prime minister's predictions—more often than naught—eerily coming to pass. He was one of those folks you listened to.

And so, after a long tiring day, he had said good night to the president and first lady who had retired to their quarters a little after ten, and then trudged diligently back to his office—still dressed in his formal tux and black tie—to spend another couple of hours going over some paperwork for tomorrow morning's meetings.

The Suburban made a left-hand turn onto Pennsylvania Avenue, headed for 17th Street NW where it would turn right and then make another left-hand turn onto K Street—the quickest way out of the District and into the area around Falls Church, Virginia, where Clarke lived.

Before the mesmerizing sound of the windshield wipers put him to sleep, Clarke glanced outside the driver's side window and idly watched as the Eisenhower Executive Office Building—illuminated by spotlights that seemed to cause the old building to shimmer in a dark cloak of rain—slid by in all its erstwhile grandeur. Previously known as the State, War, and Navy building earlier in the century, he never tired seeing the grand old structure. With his eyes now closed, ready to take a quick nap on the ride home, the Suburban's communications console unexpectedly burst to life.

"Cement Mixer to Hawkeye! I say again, Cement Mixer to Hawkeye!"

Jarred from his near sleep, Clarke's eyes popped open. The driver, a Secret Service agent who doubled as his bodyguard, immediately snapped the phone from its cradle and extended the handset.

Cement Mixer, Clarke knew, was the Secret Service code name for the White House Situation Room, the perfect moniker as far as he was concerned. Whenever he attended meetings there, the constant comings and goings of aides, support staff, and just the hangers-on gave it a churning, rolling feel. Hawkeye, he also knew, was his Secret Service code name. He didn't know how they had come up with the name, but he kind of liked it. It reminded him of his favorite character on MASH.

Jesus Christ! Now what the hell's going on! he thought, pressing the handset to his ear.

"Cement Mixer, this is Hawkeye," Clarke curtly answered.

"Major Walton, sir. Situation Room Watch Team Duty Officer. We've just received a flash message from our embassy in Pakistan."

That got his attention. Flash messages were rare, and to have one come in from Pakistan couldn't be a good sign. But he was tired; he'd already put in a full day at the office. All he wanted to do was get home, take a quick shower, and then crash until his alarm went off at five the next morning. The last thing he wanted was to go back to the White House.

"Major, can't this wait until morning?" Clarke asked hopefully. He could see they were about to turn right on 17th Street NW. "I'll be back in the office in less than six hours."

"Sir, I think this is something you need to see right away," the major said.

Clarke thought for a couple of seconds. He knew the type of message traffic received by the Situation Room, and they were just minutes from the West Wing. The watch commander would have only recommended his return for something very important. Then a thought suddenly flashed through his mind. *The Pakistani nukes! By God! I bet they've found the nukes!*

"Okay, understood!" he replied excitedly. If this was about the nukes, he couldn't wait to head back and read the message. And whatever the major had, he was sure it had to do with the nukes. Couldn't be anything else.

"Okay, we're on our way back! I'll be heading directly to the Situation Room. Please have the message available when I get there!"

"Yes, sir. It'll be waiting for you, sir!" Major Walton said, and then hung up.

"Okay, Jim," Clarke said, hooking his thumb back at the White House. "Time to turn this thing around and head back to the barn!"

"You got it, sir!" the driver said. With a quick scan of the mostly deserted streets to his front, and seeing the road was clear, the driver jammed on the brakes and made a tight u-turn at the intersection of 17th Street NW and Pennsylvania Avenue, then mashed down hard on the accelerator; the rear-end of the Suburban fishtailing on the wet pavement as he flipped a switch on the console. Immediately, red and blue flashers concealed under the Suburban's front grille and rear bumper flashed wildly across the rain-soaked street.

When the Suburban screeched to a stop in front of the West Wing, Clarke retrieved his discarded folder and jogged briskly through the light falling rain to the West Wing entrance. When he reached the basement level, he vaguely acknowledged the uniformed Secret Service agent who stood adjacent to the Situation Room's entry door.

Entering the facility, he made his way directly to the primary conference room, inadvertently ignoring the staff members who manned the Watch Center Command Room, totally focused in thought as he stepped up to his chair that was set in the middle of a long, oblong table that dominated the center of the room.

The Situation Room complex was large, much larger than most people thought, over five thousand square feet in size with three adjoining conference rooms of varying size. In addition, there were separate offices for White House staff members, and one special soundproofed room that could be used by the president for confidential calls with heads of state. Adjacent to the conference room was the two-tiered Watch Command Center that bristled with computer monitors and communications equipment.

Run by the National Security Council staff, the Situation Room's various functions were overseen by thirty individuals equally divided between the intelligence community, Homeland Security, and the various branches of the military. The Watch Center's mission—manned twenty-four hours a day, seven days a week—to keep the White House up-to-date on significant events that took place throughout the world.

Now settled into his well-worn black leather chair, Clarke grabbed a doughnut and poured some coffee from one of the carafes that sat on the table, the pastries and coffee placed there minutes earlier by naval stewards who also manned the facility twenty-four hours a day. Stirring in some cream and sugar, he cupped the hot navy mug in both hands to relish its warmth, then blew on it lightly to cool it down and took a small sip. He needed the caffeine. He knew this could turn into a long night.

To his right, Major Walton exited the Watch Command Center with an 8½- by 11-inch buff-colored envelope that had "TOP SECRET" stamped in red, two-inch-high letters across its front.

"Good evening, sir," Major Walton said. "Sorry to have you turn back, but I thought this was something you should see right away."

"Good evening, Major. Or is it morning yet?" Clarke asked with a humorous, tired smile.

"Uh, I think it's still evening, sir. But just barely," Major Walton replied, handing over the message.

"Okay, so what have we got here?" Clarke said, more to himself than the major as he opened the envelope and pulled out the message. After reading halfway through, he looked at the watch commander with a puzzled expression. The message had nothing to do with the Pakistani warheads.

"Major? I don't understand. Why would we get a message about some militants attacking a school in Islamabad? That's bad, don't get me wrong, but that happens all the time over there, doesn't it? Why would the ambassador send us a flash message about this?"

"Sir," Major Walton answered grimly, "prior to calling you back

I had the same question. So I pulled up data on the school. What I found out is that the Islamabad Preparatory Academy is an American chartered school that has a large contingent of American students. Sir, there are over three hundred children in that school, with close to a hundred of them being the dependents of our diplomatic corps."

Clarke sat heavily in his chair, taking a second to absorb the importance of what he had just been told.

"Well, Jesus Holy Shit!" he said vehemently, planting his elbows on the table to reread the message.

"And, sir," the major plowed on, "it gets worse. The only two sons of the Pakistan president, President Chutto, also attend the school. One in the first grade and the other in the fourth."

"Well, hell!" Clarke exclaimed. "This just gets better and better, doesn't it?"

Goddamned Pakistanis! First they lose two nukes to the Taliban which neither of us can find, and now this. He knew this attack had all the markings of a first scale, A-1, international cluster-fuck, and was sure the media would have it plastered all over the airwaves first thing in the morning. He also knew that all hell was going to break loose when the American public found out about it. Compounding the problem, he was sure the Pakistanis wouldn't let them get anywhere near the academy, much less try to help out. Not with Chutto's kids being in there.

"Major, we need to get the boss down here right now! And I mean ASAP! I have a bad feeling this is going to turn into one huge, goddamned furball! We also need SecState, the DCI, and General Gray here! Sooner rather than later!"

Clarke paused at that point and raised a hand to get the major's attention. He'd just remembered that SecState wasn't available. He was out of the country attending one of those stupid, meaningless, never-ending Middle East peace conferences between the Israelis and the fucked-up Palestinians.

"Major, forget SecState. He's out of the country. But give him a heads-up. President Taylor may need his input. But let's get Director Jefferson and General Gray over here as soon as possible."

"Yes, sir!" Major Walton said as he turned and strode hurriedly back to the Watch Center, then marched down the row of watch-standers and pointed at his most senior person.

"Master Sergeant Wilson, get the DCI and General Gray on the horn. Tell 'em the director of national security requests their presence in the Situation Room. Also let 'em know that President Taylor will be attending. Then get a hold of SecState and ask him to stand-by. Tell him the president may need to speak with him."

"Yes, sir!" Master Sergeant Wilson said as his fingers flew across the communications console.

While Master Sergeant Wilson placed his calls, Major Walton picked up a red phone that connected directly to the president's sleeping quarters.

Chapter 39

DAY TWENTY, 1010 HOURS
THE SITUATION ROOM
PRESIDENTIAL PALACE
ISLAMABAD, PAKISTAN

"PRESIDENT CHUTTO," HE said emotionlessly as he stabbed the speaker button so that everyone could hear what the Taliban leader had to say; his advisors clustered around the phone.

"Ah, Mr. President! Thank you for taking my call!" Mahmood Tahqi crowed, wishing he could see how his call was being taken. He knew there had to be more people present than just the president, but he didn't give a shit. He was the one that dealt from strength.

"Who is this? Who am I speaking to?" Chutto demanded.

"Mr. President, that does not matter. But by now, I am sure, you know that we have taken over the school. Do you not?" Mahmood replied easily, leaning back in his chair.

"Yes, I am aware of it!" Chutto spat out curtly. He knew he had to keep his temper in check and force himself to listen to this Taliban pig's condescending tone. Then he thought of his sons, worried if they had been hurt in the clutches of this madman. He couldn't stop from asking the one question that tore at his soul. "But what of the children? Are they okay? Are my sons okay?"

President Chutto despised himself for having asked. He knew this showed weakness on his part.

Mahmood smiled when he heard the question. Had he been in Chutto's place, he would have thought nothing of sacrificing his own sons for the jihād, to be honored as martyrs for the cause. Qudos had been right. He had told him this spineless Pakistani would do anything to get his sons back alive.

"Mr. President, all of the children live, including your sons, but for how long will depend on you."

By Allah, he wanted this Pakistani shit to squirm and grovel! It was not often that a Taliban from the FATA had the chance to speak with the president of Pakistan, the person who had persecuted his people for so many years—much less be able to grasp his balls and squeeze them slowly and firmly, and then mash them together until he squealed like a stuck pig. Mahmood knew he had his hands firmly planted on President Chutto's balls.

"However, Mr. President, several of the teachers were not very cooperative, I am sorry to say. They were killed. And to let you know, the guards who protected your sons were not very good, not very good at all. You must do better next time. Four of your guards did manage to live by giving up without a fight," he lied, "but I executed them. Personally! To set an example for the others."

Mahmood waited for Chutto to respond, but he only heard labored breathing on the other end of the line.

"They died bleating like lambs being taken to slaughter," he goaded, rubbing salt into the president's open wound. "I thoroughly enjoyed watching them in their final moments, groveling on the floor for their lives until I placed my rifle against their heads and pulled the trigger, seeing their brains splatter from their heads. But why speak of such messy things?"

President Chutto's rage burst to the surface as he lost all control, a rage that briefly overcame his grief and fear. With the phone grasped tightly in his hand until his knuckles turned white, he lashed out at this Taliban scum.

"Now, you listen to me you piece-of-shit!" he demanded shrilly, twisting his body roughly to the side to shrug off Syid's hand that had suddenly gripped his shoulder, Syid trying to keep him from saying something he would regret.

"If you do anything to the remaining hostages, or to my sons, you will pay! I swear to Allah you will pay! And your people will pay! Do you understand?" Chutto screamed, shooting out of his chair and glaring at the far wall.

Mahmood pulled the phone from his ear and laughed. This turd of a president was so predictable.

"Oh, Mr. President, you disappoint me. You make threats? I hold the power here, not you, you Pakistani piece-of-shit! But listen to me very closely. We, the Tehrik-e-taliban, are the ones who stole your nuclear bombs, and they are well-hidden in a place you will never find. But let me get to the point; the lives of your sons depend upon your releasing what you call PAL codes that are needed to arm the weapons. On this we will not negotiate. You must give us the codes by no later than eight o'clock tomorrow morning. Use this number at the school; I will be waiting. You will also give us a plane to take me and my men wherever we wish to go. Once you have done that the hostages will be released, but not your boys. We will keep them until we are safe. At that point your sons will be released. Those are our terms. And remember, we have your bomb technician to make sure the codes you give us are correct, so do not be stupid and try to trick us. If you do, you will not like the results."

Mahmood heard nothing but silence from the presidential palace.

"Also know if your soldiers attack the school your sons will die. It will not be a pretty death, but it will be quick and merciful. For you see, each of your sons now wears one of our martyr's vests and I have the detonator. If any of your soldiers attack I will push the button, and then we will kill the rest of the hostages. Your men will not have time to save them. And I and my fighters will die a glorious martyr's death. So, Mr. President, the lives of your sons and all those within this school now rest in your hands. I would think carefully about that and choose wisely."

Chutto was shaken to the core by the Taliban demand, a searing pain ripping through his heart as if someone had driven a white-hot poker through his chest. With a desperate look at Syid, then Director General Pasha, and then Marshal Khattack, he knew he could not release the codes. It was impossible! The demand from this Taliban scum was no more than a death sentence for his two boys, but he had to respond, and he had to respond now.

President Chutto choked back a sob and answered in a defeated voice, "This you know I cannot do. It is impossible! All I can offer you, as Allah is my witness, is if you release my sons and the other hostages unharmed, I will personally guarantee you and your men safe passage out of Islamabad. To anywhere you wish to go."

"Well, Mr. President," Mahmood said disquietly, "that is not the answer I wanted to hear!"

Qudos had told him this would be their first answer, but he was prepared.

"If that is your answer, then maybe it is time for you to learn who holds the power here! So, please, turn on one of the news channels! To see what will happen to your sons if you do not change your mind! Also know if I have not received the codes by eight tomorrow morning, a student will be killed every hour until the codes are given to us, and lastly your sons! As for me and my men, we will gladly sit at the foot of Allah!"

With nothing further to say, Mahmood slammed the phone into its cradle.

President Chutto heard a click and then the buzz of a dial tone.

"Mustaffa! Turn on one of the monitors! Get one of the news stations covering the school!"

When the monitor flickered to life, he saw that Mustaffa had chosen al-Jazeera where one of its reporters was talking excitedly about the standoff between the Taliban terrorists and Pakistani troops. As they all watched in rapt silence, the camera suddenly swept to the right and zoomed-in for a close-up on the entrance to the auditorium. The newsman, with his microphone held close to his lips, breathlessly told his audience that something was going on.

The world paused, not daring to breathe, when the front door of the auditorium slowly opened. A terrorist, with a black balaclava pulled over his head, peered cautiously outside, then roughly grabbed what looked to be a young blonde girl of about six years in age. With her arm gripped tightly in his hand—a grip that left deep impressions in her flesh—he pushed her through the door onto the concrete sidewalk.

The little girl didn't move, but just stood silently as she cried and looked back at her captor. Now impatient, Qasim jabbed the muzzle of his AK-47 painfully into her back and pushed the little infidel bitch toward some steps that led to the parking lot. Still crying, the little girl finally understood what her captor wanted her to do, then stumbled her way down the steps to the parking lot.

President Chutto stood frozen before the monitor, his hands sweat-soaked while saliva flooded his mouth. He knew what the Taliban had in mind.

"Allah, the merciful! Please! Please! Please, don't let this happen!" he groaned.

Unable to tear his eyes from the monitor, he watched as the camera suddenly zoomed-in closer, the girl's tiny body now centered on the screen as she made it to the bottom of the stairs and stepped shakily onto the parking lot. After one or two steps, however, she suddenly jerked in fright and stared at the CNN helicopter that still burned furiously some distance away. *A small explosion or something must have gotten her attention,* Chutto thought. The little girl twisted back, looking toward the main entry gate no more than sixty meters to her front, and began to walk haltingly towards it.

The worldwide audience could see that she was scared and helpless as tears streamed silently down her unblemished cheeks. Blue-eyed, with her long blonde hair pulled back into a ponytail and tied-off with bright-pink ribbons, she looked to be calling out for her mother. The viewers could also tell that she wore some kind of a black, bulky vest over a soft-pink dress as she wiped her eyes with tiny clenched fists.

Finally, when she reached the center of the parking lot, she stopped and dropped silently to her knees, her head bent down with both hands placed on the burning hot asphalt. As she continued to cry, the cameraman quickly turned when he heard a commotion to his rear. He saw a man, armed with what looked to be an M16 rifle, struggling with some of the soldiers. With his camera swiveled to the rear, he focused-in on the fight just as the man broke through the line of troops.

The field news director who sat in the al-Jazeera van immediately switched to a split-screen picture, ordering the first cameraman to stay on the little girl while he told the second to keep the armed man in focus. Now in split-screen mode, with the little girl on the right side of the picture and the man carrying the M16 to the left, they watched in silence as the interloper ran straight across the field headed for the school's main gate, the man screaming "Emily! Emily!" at the top of his lungs.

The little girl, hearing a familiar voice, looked up expectantly from where she kneeled, her clear blue eyes illuminated by a spark of hope when she recognized her father in the distance. Pushing herself upright, she began to stumble her way towards her father, her arms outstretched as she cried out shrilly, "Daddy! Daddy! Daddy!"

The monitor instantly flashed white accompanied by the sharp, crackling boom of an explosion. When the scene reappeared, a fireball roughly ten meters in diameter exploded outwards from where the little girl had been running, its outer fringes tinged with a reddish, misting fog surrounded by small body parts.

While the ground rumbled and shook, the camera slowly zoomed-in on where the little girl had once stood. All that could be seen were the blackened pieces of a small pink dress that drifted lazily through the air like soot-covered snowflakes.

A blood-curdling cry of "no!" exploded from the man who had been running across the field. The man, now stopped in midstride, stared hopelessly at where his daughter had once stood, his mouth opening and closing silently in despair. Within seconds, a line of M60 machine gun tracer fire lanced outward from the confines of the school.

The television audience, knowing the man could only have been the little girl's father, watched in silent horror as the machine gunner calmly adjusted his aim—the line of red tracers bending slowly to the left—and impacted the father's body, stitching him from groin to chest.

Blown backwards to the ground from the impact of rounds, the father—ever so slowly and obviously in agony—rolled onto his chest, then used his M16 rifle as a makeshift crutch as he lurched to his feet and feebly staggered across the field, still crying out the name "Emily". Two more lines of automatic weapons fire licked out from the school, riddling his body a second time as the M16 slipped slowly from his hands. With his face creased in anguish, his chest pumping out a thick torrent of bright-red blood, the father dropped to his knees and looked one last time for any trace of his little girl, then fell face forwards to the earth.

President Chutto stumbled from the conference room table and made his way drunkenly to the Situation Room's bathroom. With not a second to spare—his face ashen and devoid of color—he dropped to his knees and gratefully rested his head on the cold porcelain bowl; his stomach heaving as he puked out his guts. Syid, who had quickly followed behind, gently patted his president on the back.

Chapter 40

DAY TWENTY, 2345 HOURS
PRESIDENTIAL SLEEPING QUARTERS
THE WHITE HOUSE

THE BEDSIDE PHONE continued to warble its low, obnoxious tone. On its fourth ring, President Garret Taylor groaned and rolled over, then grabbed his down-filled pillow and mashed it over his head. Moments later he jerked awake when he finally recognized the phone's distinctive ring. With his pillow thrown to the side, he grabbed the handset off the end table. He knew this particular tone was never the harbinger of good news, only bad. With a quick glance at the bedside clock, he could see it was only eleven forty-five.

"Taylor here," he answered tiredly, wishing he hadn't drunk as much as he had during the evening's state dinner for the British prime minister, but he couldn't help himself. He always enjoyed the sprightly old prime minister's company, and the dinner had been a huge success. *Nothing's too good for our cousins across the pond,* he thought. *Best damned allies we've ever had. Even if we did have to kick their ass in 1776 and again in 1812.*

"Sir, Major Walton here. I'm the Situation Room Watch Team Duty Officer. We've just received a flash message from Pakistan and Mr. Clarke requests your presence."

"Okay, Major," he said halfheartedly. "Tell Mr. Clarke I'll be down in a few minutes." He knew if Steven thought he oughta be there, then he oughta be there.

"Yes, sir," the major said, and then hung up.

President Taylor softly placed the handset back in its cradle.

"What is it Garret?" his wife asked sleepily.

"Nothing much, sweetie. Just something I have to go look at. Now, go back to sleep and I'll be back in just a bit. Okay?" he said, rubbing her thigh affectionately through the covers.

"Okay," she mumbled as she rolled over, managing to tug most of the covers with her.

President Taylor slipped his feet into his favorite sheepskin slippers and made his way carefully in the darkened room to the bathroom. Turning on the light, he pulled off his t-shirt and spied the clothes hamper in the far corner. With a grin, he made an overhead jump shot directly into the hamper. *Two points!* Then he ran his tongue around his mouth, thinking he'd better brush and take a quick shower. Flash messages were important and he didn't know how long this would take.

With his late night ablutions completed, he pulled on a pair of old sweatpants and a well-used, olive-drab sweatshirt with the USMC Globe and Anchor splashed across its front. He had to smile when he remembered how many times he'd had to save it from the trash bin. For the life of him, he couldn't understand why his wife kept trying to throw it away just because it was torn and ripped in a few places. *Gotta be some kind of female thing,* he thought humorously, but he loved her anyway. After pulling on a pair of old Reebok running shoes, he stepped quietly into the corridor.

President Taylor acknowledged the two Secret Service agents who stood post in the broad hallway. One of the agents remained at his post while the other escorted him to the elevator to take him down to the main level, and then over to the Situation Room. As they walked down the broad corridor, the agent who accompanied the president spoke softly into his lapel mic, "Shooter's on his way to the Mixer."

President Taylor stepped into the conference room and saw Steven Clarke, still dressed in his tux minus the black jacket and bow tie that lay heaped on the table, scribbling away on a pad of paper.

"Good evening, Steven," he said pleasantly.

Clarke looked up and immediately pushed himself erect.

"Good evening, Mr. President," Clarke said, handing over the message slip. "Sir, we just received this from Ambassador Jenkins in Islamabad."

President Taylor took the message slip and sat down, but before he could begin to read Major Walton stepped up with a fresh mug of hot coffee, a mug emblazoned with the Presidential Seal.

"Thought you could use this, sir," the major said.

"Oh, thanks, Major. Don't mind if I do," Taylor said, smiling up at the young watch commander.

"You're welcome, sir," Walton responded with a slight grin.

One thing Major Walton knew was that the staff really liked this guy. He was unassuming, tough as nails, and asked good questions when in doubt. And he was not a bullshitter. When he didn't know something he wasn't afraid to let you know, he would just ask the right questions to come up-to-speed. Much better than most of his predecessors who were deathly afraid of appearing stupid, or ignorant, or both. And the fact that he had been an infantry company commander in the Marine Corps wasn't held against him. The staff had already made allowances for someone whose previous job in the military had been to charge machine gun nests while throwing hand grenades. But given that he had actually seen combat, and had been awarded the Silver Star for valor, was far more impressive to the "Midnight Gnomes"; "Midnight Gnomes" being what the staff called themselves who manned the graveyard shift.

"Okay, let's see what we got here," President Taylor said as he took a sip of the blazing hot coffee. Once through the message, he went back and read it more closely a second time. When he had finished, he looked at Clarke with a question in his eyes.

"So? What's the big deal? This happens all the time over there, doesn't it?" he asked a little bewildered, asking the same question that Clarke had asked earlier. "Why would the ambassador send us a flash message about this?"

"Mr. President," Clarke began softly, "the school is basically American. Of the three hundred some-odd students attending, close to a hundred of them are American dependents, mostly the children of our diplomatic corps. And to make matters worse, the Pakistan president's two sons also attend the school."

"Jesus H. Christ," Taylor whispered, lowering his eyes to read the message a third time, this time in much greater detail. With a quick glance at Clarke he ordered, "Steven, get Director Jefferson and General Gray over here right now! Also notify SecState to standby . . . shit!" he said. *Now where in the hell was he?* "Oh yeah, he's in Egypt," he finished out loud.

"Sir, they've all been notified. SecState should be standing by and Director Jefferson and General Gray are already on their way. They should be here in the next few minutes."

"Good, good," he said absently as he turned back to read the message a fourth time. With a shake of his head, he pinched the bridge of his nose as if he had a headache.

"Jesus H. Christ!" he said again. "We've got close to a hundred American kids being held by goddamned Taliban terrorists? Plus another two hundred or so from other countries?"

President Taylor fully understood the urgency of the situation.

"Major, I need to speak with Ambassador Jenkins right now!"

"Yes, sir!" Major Walton replied as he pivoted and hurried back to the Watch Command Center.

Taylor leaned back and stared at the ceiling, inadvertently letting the message slip drop to the table. *Shit! And I thought today was going to be a great day.*

Within moments the major's voice came over the intercom.

"Sir, Ambassador Jenkins is on the line. I've set up a televideo conference, encryption level three. He'll be on monitor two, sir."

"Thanks, Major."

President Taylor swiveled to his left and looked at the monitor built flush into the mahogany-paneled wall. It immediately snapped to life.

"Good morning, Mr. President . . . and to you, Mr. Clarke," Ambassador Jenkins added when he saw the director of national security was also in attendance.

The ambassador, Taylor could see, looked frazzled and under a great deal of strain.

"Well, here it's just a little past midnight, Mr. Ambassador," the president said a tad too shortly. He had to remember that Islamabad was ten hours ahead of Washington. "But we just received your message. So, what the hell's going on?" he asked, getting right to the point. "I also have Allen Jefferson and General Gray on their way over here to go over this situation."

"I understand, Mr. President," Jenkins replied heavily. "Anyway, sir, around eight thirty this morning our time, a group of Taliban militants, numbers unknown at this point, attacked and took over the Islamabad Preparatory Academy. I don't know if you're aware, sir, but the academy is an American chartered school that caters to our diplomatic personnel, and to the children of other foreign diplomats. And to the Pakistanis for that matter. That's the reason for the message. Right now there are over three hundred children and teachers being held hostage, with close to a hundred of them being

American nationals. But what you may not know is that President Chutto's two sons also attend this school who—"

"Mr. Ambassador," President Taylor interrupted, cutting him off in midstatement, the full import of what had happened in Pakistan chewing into his guts, "just so we don't duplicate our efforts here, my staff has already briefed me in. And yes, I'm aware that Chutto's sons attend the school. What I want to know is, what the hell's going on right now?"

"Okay, Mr. President. The situation can only be described as very tense. From what we can piece together, the attack took place less than ninety minutes ago, during a school assembly in their auditorium. As far as we can tell that's where the hostages are being held."

The ambassador hastily turned from the camera, cupping his hand over the desk's microphone as if trying to squelch out the sound, and acknowledged an assistant who stood anxiously by his side. President Taylor and Steven Clarke watched as the ambassador listened intently for a moment, and then looked startled and asked a couple of quick questions. Taylor and Clarke strained to hear what was being said but couldn't make it out.

Jenkins finally dismissed the aide and turned wearily back to the camera, shaking his head in resignation.

"Excuse me, Mr. President, sorry for the interruption, but I've just been told that a news helicopter was shot down about ten minutes ago over the school. Preliminary reports indicate it was a CNN helicopter."

"Shit!" was all that Taylor could say, his knuckles whitening as he gripped the edge of the table. "Steven, we've got to get ahead of this damned thing. I'm sure this'll be all over the news first thing in the morning. Get the press secretary out of the rack and bring him up-to-speed on what we know. Tell him to prepare a statement I can put out now."

"Yes, Mr. President!"

"Now, Mr. Ambassador, not to go off on a tangent, but that brings us back to the press. What's been their reaction so far?"

Taylor knew the media would go into a feeding frenzy over the attack.

"Mr. President, every major news agency in Islamabad is either at the school or on their way. CNN, ABC, CBS, Fox News, you name it. It's just a little after ten in the morning our time and the satellite feeds are going out as we speak. I suggest you tune in to either CNN or Fox to see what they're saying."

"Okay, we'll do that in a minute, but what other resources do we have at the school? To let us know what's actually going on? I don't want to have to rely on the Pakistanis for updates."

"Mr. President, our military attachés are on their way right now, if they're not there already. They also have secure communications back to the embassy. Once they get a handle on things, they have orders to call me immediately."

The ambassador paused at that point. As much as he regretted doing so, there was another problem he needed to tell the president.

"Mr. President, I need to let you know we may have a problem with one of our staff, Mr. John Bradsen, who's our CIA station chief. He headed over there less than thirty minutes ago with six of his men loaded for bear. They took several M16s from our Marine detachment and should be there right about now."

The ambassador could see the confused look on President Taylor's face.

"What I'm trying to tell you, sir, is I ordered Bradsen not to go. But he ignored me. Basically told me to shove it up my ass. And to tell the truth, sir, I couldn't really blame him. He reminded me in no uncertain terms that I didn't have any jurisdiction over him or his men, that he took his orders only from Langley, sir."

"Disobeyed your orders not to go?" President Taylor asked, getting pissed, his face beginning to turn beet red. "Just who the *hell* does this guy think he is?" The one thing he couldn't afford right now was to have a loose cannon rolling around the deck.

"Mr. President," the ambassador answered sadly, "just to let you know, Mr. Bradsen's daughter, Emily, aged six and the cutest little thing you ever saw, just began the first grade at the academy. Today was her first day."

Taylor's anger vanished instantly as if someone had thrown a glass of cold water in his face. *No wonder he headed to the school. I'd have done exactly the same damned thing, and taken as many men and weapons as I could lay my hands on. Jesus! What that guy must be going through!*

"Okay, I understand, Mr. Ambassador," President Taylor said now calm. "But I hate to say this, we can't worry about Mr. Bradsen right now. What we need to do is figure out a way to save those kids."

At that moment, Allen Jefferson and General Gray walked grimly into the Situation Room, both having been briefed by their aides on the academy.

"Good mornin', Mr. President," Director Jefferson softly said as he made his way to the conference table. "We got here as soon as we could."

The director couldn't help but see that the president was dressed in a pair of well-worn sweatpants and an old Marine Corps sweatshirt covered with little tears and holes in it. Given he'd dressed in the same old rumpled suit he'd worn all day, he suddenly felt a lot better about how he looked. But of course, General Gray looked as if he had just stepped off the parade ground at 8th & I, impeccably turned out in his Marine Corps uniform and spit-shined shoes.

"Good morning, Allen, General," President Taylor said.

"Good morning, Mr. President," General Gray said, bringing up the rear.

"Ambassador Jenkins? Allen Jefferson and General Gray just arrived. Please bring them up-to-date on what you've told me and Steven."

"Of course, Mr. President. Good morning, Director Jefferson, General Gray."

"Morning," both men said as they sat themselves down and reached for the coffee, their attention riveted on the video monitor.

One minute later everyone was on the same page.

"Okay," President Taylor said finally. "Recommendations?"

"Mr. President," Steven Clarke began, "as far as I see it, we don't have enough information to plan anything at this point. I recommend we go ahead and put out a press statement just as you suggested, then see what our people on the scene and the Pakistanis can tell us. I also suggest we try to get a roster of the kids at that school. I'm sure the embassy's going to be getting a lot of calls from parents. This would also help us in trying to figure out how many kids were in that assembly."

"Mr. President," General Gray interjected, his fingers steepled in front of his face, "I agree that we need put out a press statement, the sooner the better. And getting a handle on how many kids are in there will tell us the scope of what we're looking at. But we also need to prepare for the worst."

"What do you mean by the worst?" Taylor asked, but he knew

exactly what the general had meant. He just didn't want to go there right now.

As they watched General Gray sit there, President Taylor, Allen Jefferson, and Steven Clarke saw a side to the old Marine warhorse few men ever wanted to see; the muscles in his jaws flexing unconsciously; his face furrowed with a malevolent, violent look of death to it. If one thing really pissed-off the general, it was the way these jihādist terrorists went after the kids.

"I'm just saying, sir, that we gotta be prepared when those sons-of-bitches start killing the kids!" he said, pounding his fist unconsciously on the table. "And I can almost guarantee, gentlemen," his anger getting the better of him, "that those ragheads will start killing the kids, especially the American kids, when they're damned good and ready. And it's not gonna be pretty. No, sir, not pretty at all. So we gotta be prepared to deal with that when it happens. What with all those news stations being on-site, you know as well as I do how the American public's going to react when they see the killings begin. They're gonna go apeshit, gentlemen! And want those kids rescued, come hell or high water! And to hell with the consequences!"

Silence filled the room as President Taylor recognized the truth in what the general had just said, but there was no way American kids were going to be slaughtered on his watch. He would do everything in his power, up to and including sending in the Third Marine Division out of Okinawa, to get those kids back.

"General, I agree. But what I need you to do, for all of us to do, is to come up with a plan. To put boots on the ground if and when that becomes necessary. I don't care if that means pulling troops out of Afghanistan, or Okinawa, or sending in a Delta team. But we need to come up with a plan to take down that school. In the meantime, I'll speak with President Chutto to see if he'll let us help out."

"Mr. President," General Gray said reluctantly, "I don't want to contradict you, sir, but I don't think sending in troops or a Delta team's gonna work."

Taylor sat back and made a hasty come-on gesture.

"Explain that, General."

"What I mean, sir, is I can't see us using troops to get those kids out. Remember what happened to the Israeli's just a few years ago? When one of their schools in the Golan Heights was taken over by Hamas? As soon as their troops went in those kids were hosed down with machine gun fire. It was a goddamned blood bath, sir. Out of forty or fifty kids, they only managed to save seven or eight. The rest were chewed to pieces. And we've got over three hundred kids in that school. Besides, we're also gonna have a lot of trouble with the Pakistanis if we try to do this on our own."

President Taylor disgustedly threw his pen across the table.

"Well, shit, General! If you don't think we can use troops, then what the hell can we do?"

"Mr. President!" Ambassador Jenkins shouted. "You need to turn on one of the news broadcasts! Something's happening at the school!"

"Major Walton! Get one of those news channels on the other monitor!"

"Yes, sir! Monitor one, sir!"

It was the Fox news channel, the news anchor in the middle of describing the same scene being watched by President Chutto.

The school looked to be less than half a mile away with the main gate clearly visible. They could also see smoke curling into the air from what looked to be a blown-out guard shack, and a much larger plume of black smoke where the CNN chopper must have crashed.

The camera panned over the newsman's shoulder and zoomed-in on the entrance to the auditorium. Everyone watched as a little blonde-haired girl was shoved through the auditorium door, then roughly jabbed in the back by the muzzle of an AK-47 toward some steps that led to the parking lot. When the little girl finally made it to the bottom of the stairs she looked about in confusion—crying softly as she wiped at her eyes—then haltingly made her way toward the main gate. About halfway across the lot she fell to her knees and lowered head to the asphalt.

The camera wiggled back and forth as if being jostled, then finally settled on a man dressed in civilian clothes carrying an M16 rifle. A man who had just broken through a line of Pakistani troops and was now running across the field directly toward the school's main gate. They could clearly hear him screaming "Emily!" over and over again at the top of his lungs. When he made it roughly halfway to the gate, a bomb vest that had been strapped to the little girl exploded.

Everyone in the Situation Room jerked back in revulsion as the picture divided itself into split-screen, the left half showing the man stopped in midstride with the second half focused on a billowing ball of fire where the little girl had once stood. Abruptly, the sound of machine gun fire came clearly over the Situation Room's monitor as the scene changed from split-screen back to single-screen. The machine gun fire initially kicked up small puffs of dirt in front of the man, but then lifted and struck his body, causing him to jerk back and forth from the impact of rounds. They all watched as he sank slowly to the ground, tried to stand once again, and was then hit by a second stream of automatic weapons fire.

"Jesus H. Fucking Christ," President Taylor murmured, snapping a pencil he hadn't known he had been holding, sickened and shocked by what he'd seen. After several moments, having silently spoken a brief prayer for the little girl and the man who surely must have been Mr. John Bradsen, he lifted his head; the revolting image of Bradsen and his little girl burned into his brain. As he tried to tune out the comments from the dazed newscaster, he shifted his stone-like countenance to General Gray, then Steven Clarke, and lastly to Allen Jefferson, each of them feeling the same as he did. He knew what had just taken place confirmed everything that General Gray had just said.

"Mr. President?" Ambassador Jenkins said softly as soon as he could find his voice. "I'm not sure if you're aware, but that was John Bradsen and his daughter Emily. I just thought you oughta know."

President Taylor, still shaking his head disgustedly, didn't tell the ambassador he had already figured that out. Turning from the loathsome image, he stared at his advisors, his face hardened by angry eyes.

"All right, gentlemen, now we know what we're dealing with! I want options, and I want to hear them now!" he said with bloodless lips.

"Mr. President," General Gray began solemnly, "I hate to say this, but this is just the beginning. They popped that little girl to make a point. To show they hold all the cards and control all of the lives in that goddamned school. As I said before, sending in troops will only get the rest of those kids killed."

"I know that!" President Taylor shouted angrily, pissed at hearing the obvious. "But I'll be goddamned if we're just going to sit here with our thumbs up our asses and do nothing!"

"Excuse me, Mr. President," Allen Jefferson said softly, "but I was thinkin' on that on the way over heah. You see, suh, we're goin' to have the same problem if the Pakistani troops go in, just like the general said. And the Pakistanis will go in. Maybe not today, maybe not tomorrow—they don't have enough intel right now—but eventually they will. And I can assure you, suh, the Pakistanis' prime mission will be to free Chutto's boys. Those other kids will be as expendable like ticks on a dog."

"So you're telling me we can't do a goddamned thing?" Taylor asked, feeling hemmed in with no way out.

"No, suh, I'm not sayin' that a'tall. Now, please, just hear me out. 'Cause that brings me back to what I was a thinkin'.'"

The director knew the president was upset, and that his first knee-jerk reaction would be to do anything to save those kids. But he knew the president had to stay calm; his job was to give Taylor options for dealing with the terrorists.

"Suh, it seems to me that when the 'coon's in the henhouse, what we need to be doin' is figurin' out a way to chop off his balls and shove 'em down his throat."

Director Jefferson paused and turned toward Steven Clarke, asking in that low, soothing, Alabama drawl of his, "Steven? What's the status of Hearthstone? Are they all trained up and ready to go?"

Steven looked quickly at President Taylor, and then back at Director Jefferson. He could see what the director was getting at. *Jefferson just may have something here!*

"Yeah, Allen, they're all trained up and still at Los Alamos as we speak. With all of their equipment and weapons just waiting for the nukes to be found."

Director Jefferson saw a flicker of hope in the president's eyes.

"Suh, I can't think of a better time to use the capabilities of Gabriel and Hearthstone. The school has the same target limitations of ingress and egress, and the same requirement for surprise. Just like goin' after the nukes. Hearthstone could arrive unannounced, penetrate the school, do their business, and then, as they so eloquently say, get the hell out of Dodge."

President Taylor cupped his chin in his hands and thought through the director's proposal. He couldn't see any downside, except for the risk to Hearthstone, and a damned good chance of Gabriel's cover being blown. *But damnit! Those children had to come first, even before the nukes. Everything else paled in comparison to getting those kids out of that shithole.*

"General? What do you think?"

"Sir, I think Director Jefferson's recommendation is shit-hot! And he's right. It's almost the same parameters for going after the nukes, and probably the only chance those kids'll have. It's low profile, under the horizon, and, most importantly, doesn't involve the Pakistanis. They could be ready to go in just a few hours. Our only time constraint is to get more intel and come up with a plan."

"Steven?" President Taylor asked hopefully.

"Sir, I agree. I think this is the only way we can go with this."

"Okay, gentlemen," Taylor quickly decided, "that's what we'll do. Allen? General? I'll leave it up to you to brief in Hearthstone and coordinate the mission. Tell 'em to be ready to go as soon as possible, preferably when it's dark over there. Steven? I want you to know I'm not pulling you off Hearthstone, but this is now a military operation. Director Jefferson and General Gray will have the point on this."

"No problem, sir. I understand."

"What I do want you to do, however, is coordinate our activities here at the White House. Okay?"

"Yes, sir!"

"And General?"

"Yes, sir!"

"This'll be our primary plan, but I still want you to come up with a contingency plan. To go in with troops if this thing falls apart."

"Will do, Mr. President. And Sir, just to get ahead of the curve here, I suggest we contact the NRO and have them reposition one of their KH-12S satellites smack-dab over that goddamned school. They could probably do that within a few hours by moving the one they have parked over Afghanistan. That would give us surveillance capability. And sir, this particular satellite has a new, very effective thermal imaging system in addition to its daytime optics, but its real advantage is its real-time video capability. Now, the resolution for video isn't quite as good as photos, but it's still damned good. It would give us the ability to watch everything that happens on that campus. So, whether day or night, we'll be able to count the number of pimples on each gomers' ass when they take a shit."

"Good idea, General," President Taylor agreed, smiling at Gray's colorful analogy. He just had to give it to the general, he sure had a way with words.

"Allen? Call the NRO and have them reposition one of those

satellites over that school ASAP. Tell 'em you're speaking with my authority."

"Yes, suh, Mr. President," Jefferson said with the sparkle of a gleam in his eye.

"Ambassador Jenkins? I want you to forget anything you've heard us discussing right now. Just suffice it to say that we may have another way of getting into that school. But what we really need is for your assets to keep us up-to-date on what's going on."

"Yes, Mr. President."

"Allen, after you call the NRO, get a hold of whoever's now in charge of our Islamabad station. Tell 'em we're working on a way of getting those kids out of that school and that we're going to need the support of his people. Also let 'em know they're not to initiate any action whatsoever without our prior approval. Make 'em understand that would just make it a hell of a lot harder for us to go in there and rescue those kids. Understood?"

"Yes, Mr. President, understood. I'll get a hold of him as soon as possible."

"Mr. President?" Major Walton's voice interrupted, breaking into President Taylor's train of thought. "Excuse me, sir, but the president of Pakistan is on the line. Do you want to take the call?"

Taylor looked around the conference table, and then motioned for everyone to keep their seats.

"Ambassador Jenkins, please stay with us a moment longer. I want you to hear what Chutto has to say."

"Of course, Mr. President."

"Major, go ahead and put him on."

"Yes, sir. He'll be on monitor three, sir."

Chapter 41

DAY TWENTY, 1035 HOURS
THE SITUATION ROOM
PRESIDENTIAL PALACE
ISLAMABAD, PAKISTAN

PRIME MINISTER SYID Buledi picked up a pitcher of ice water and poured a glass halfway full.

"Here, Assif, take this," he said, handing the glass to President Chutto. Syid felt much better now; Assif seemed to have regained his composure after having watched the debacle with the little girl and his brief, embarrassing sojourn to the bathroom. Cleaned up now, with his suit coat back on to cover his sweat-stained shirt, the president looked and acted more like himself.

With a perfunctory nod of thanks, Chutto popped a couple of heart pills into his mouth and took a large swallow of water, clucking his head up and down like a bird to wash down the pills.

"Thank you, Syid," he said, wiping his mouth with a napkin.

"Mr. President," Marshal Khattack said, "that was Colonel Solangi. He wants us to know the school is now cut off and the perimeter secure. I also reiterated they are to do nothing without your prior approval. To stand fast until further ordered."

"Good! Thank you, Marshal! Now, if you would please join us, I need to make that call to the White House."

"Yes, Mr. President," Khattack said as he picked up his notepad and made his way back to his chair.

"Mustaffa, please set up the video call to President Taylor."

"Yes, Mr. President."

Silence blanketed the room as they waited for the call to go through. Director General Pasha looked dour as he fiddled with an ink pen in his hand, twirling it absently around his fingers. Marshal

Khattack, on the other hand, sat stern-faced and immobile, his hands clasped together and motionless. Syid glanced at Assif and hoped that he was up to the task. After just a minute or so, the video monitor came to life with a blank screen.

"White House switchboard," a melodic female voice announced.

"President Chutto of Pakistan calling for President Taylor," Mustaffa said.

"Just one moment, please."

Several seconds later the operator came back on the line.

"President Taylor is in the Situation Room. I'll put you right through, sir."

With that response Chutto looked surprised.

"It seems that President Taylor is not asleep. If he's in his Situation Room, he must already know about the attack."

He had assumed they would have had to wait several minutes for President Taylor to be awakened, or schedule a later time to call back.

"I would guess that he has," Syid said, nodding in agreement.

The monitor burst to life that showed President Taylor sitting at a table over eleven thousand kilometers away.

President Chutto noted how Taylor was dressed, not in a suit and tie, but in a ragged shirt with some kind of military symbol splashed across its front. This suggested he had been in a hurry to make it to his meeting room, and the only thing that could have caused that would have been his knowledge of the attack on the academy. He also saw that Taylor's face was grim and drawn, his eyes tired but penetrating with an air of menace that seemed to float around him.

"Good morning, Mr. President," Chutto said as he pushed himself straight up in his chair. "Or should I say good evening?"

"Good morning, Mr. President," Taylor replied matter-of-factly. "And here it is just past midnight."

"Yes, of course, Mr. President," he replied to President Taylor's emotionless answer. "Please, you will have to excuse me, but I always get mixed up with the time differences between our two countries."

President Chutto briefly paused, but heard no further response from President Taylor.

"Well, Mr. President, I wanted to thank you for taking my call. From what I can see, you may have already heard about our situation here in Islamabad. At the academy. Is that correct?"

"Yes, Mr. President, we have. We received a message from Ambassador Jenkins, but he and his staff were short on details. You should also know that Steven Clarke, my Director of National Security, Allen Jefferson, the Director of the CIA, and General Gray, our chairman of the Joint Chiefs of Staff, are also present."

Taylor then continued in a more softened tone.

"I would also like you to know how gratified I am that you called. I was about to call you, sir, to get more details on the situation."

"Thank you, Mr. President, but first," President Chutto said with a gesture at his own advisors who were seated off-screen, "I too have my advisors present. Syid Buledi, my Prime Minister, Director General Pasha of our ISI, and Marshal Khattack, our chairman of the Joint Chiefs of Staff, in addition to Mustaffa Kardar, my Director of Security."

President Taylor nodded at the unseen Pakistani advisors.

"So, sir, what can you tell us of the situation? You must know we are extremely concerned since many of the children are our own American citizens. And, just to let you know, we did see what happened to that little girl," Taylor added, his eyes narrowed with a dark, stony look. "It's also my understanding that she was an American. I have to say, sir, that was one of the most brutal, barbaric acts I have ever seen, and we expect the terrorists to be apprehended and punished. But first, I want to know what steps you are taking to ensure the children's safety, to procure their release. It's also our understanding there may be well over three hundred students in that school."

"Mr. President," Chutto began roughly, wanting nothing more than to lash out at President Taylor's demanding tone, "it is still too early to know *what* is going on. We are working on that. The attack took place just a little over two hours ago. And, sir, I am probably more concerned for the children's safety than you. If you do not know this, my only two sons also attend the school, Vahe and Nasim. They too are hostages of these Taliban scum, and I will do anything to get them released!"

President Chutto felt an urgent tug on his sleeve and leaned toward Syid. In a whisper, Syid urged, "Assif, talk about all of the children! All the children! Don't place too much emphasis on Vahe and Nasim. The Americans have to feel you're as concerned for their children as well as your own. If not, who knows what they will do?"

With a silent nod of agreement, President Chutto looked back at the monitor and met President Taylor's gaze.

"I mention my children, Mr. President, to let you know that I too want their safe release. Along with all of the children," he added.

"Mr. President, I know your children are at the school; Ambassador Jenkins informed us of that fact. I would also like you to know how sorry I am that they are there. I can't imagine how I would feel if I were in your shoes, but I am gratified to hear your determination to free all of the children."

At the conclusion of Taylor's statement, each president paused to think of what those children must be going through. After several seconds of silence, President Taylor broke the interlude.

"But getting back to the school, sir, do you have any idea why the Taliban attacked?"

"Mr. President, we are doing our best to determine their motives. For now we have cordoned off the school with Marshal Khattack's soldiers. We are also keeping the news people away, and have established a no-fly zone that covers a three kilometer radius around the school."

"Have you been in contact with the Taliban? Have you spoken to them?" Taylor asked, trying to draw the Pakistan president out.

"Mr. President, the situation is still too new. Right now we are doing our best to determine the motives of the militants. Once we have further information, we will of course let you know."

"But can we be of any assistance? Troops, surveillance satellites, anything that can help you? As you know, we have a highly-trained counter-terrorist team called Delta who are experts in situations like this." Taylor wanted the United States military included in the loop.

"Mr. President, thank you for your kind offer, but for now we must decline. We have our own drone capability as you well know, and our own Special Forces units. Special Forces units trained in your own United States. Our Special Services Wing troops. But for now we think it best to allow us to determine the motives of the Taliban, to get a better feeling for what they want. Once known you will be the first to know," President Chutto lied straight-faced.

"Very well, Mr. President. I know you must be very busy, so I won't keep you any further. We all know what a trying time this is, and we wish you success in getting both your sons, and all of the children, released. If you need our assistance in any way all you need do is ask." Taylor said, not liking the fact one bit that the United States was going to be shut out by the Pakistanis, but he knew he couldn't push President Chutto any further at this time.

"Thank you, Mr. President, but for now we have everything under control."

All Chutto could feel was relief that President Taylor did not know of the Taliban demand for the PAL codes. As far as he and Director General Pasha's ISI knew, the Americans were still in the dark about the hijacking of the nuclear warheads. There was just no way he could tell the American president about the PAL code demand. If he had, they would know they had lost one of their nuclear warheads to the Taliban, much less two of them. *No,* he thought again. *I need time to think this through.*

"Very well, Mr. President," Taylor replied, bringing the teleconference to a close. "Thank you for your call, sir. And please, keep us advised on the school situation."

"That I will do, Mr. President."

Chapter 42

DAY TWENTY-ONE, 0040 HOURS
THE SITUATION ROOM
THE WHITE HOUSE

AS MONITOR THREE flickered out of existence, President Garrett Taylor tried to absorb what President Chutto had said. He knew no more than what Ambassador Jenkins had already told him, and since the hijacking of the warheads, the Pakistanis had still not uttered a word about their loss.

So, that's another problem hanging out there. And now the situation with the school. But the school had a much higher immediate impact than the nukes, the children now his top priority. But what nagged at the back of his mind was that Chutto had lied. He could tell that he had held back and that pissed him off. He had a sixth sense about these things, and a lot of those kids in that school were American.

No, there's something else out there. Some other problem that's troubling him. And not only that his sons are being held hostage, as if that wasn't enough. So, whatever this other thing was, it had to be bad. Really bad. From nowhere a sudden thought flashed through his mind. *Could the two events be connected? That's not so farfetched, is it? First the nukes are hijacked, and that was just three weeks ago. One would think the Taliban would have lain low at this point, not wanting to draw any attention to themselves. But now they attack a school? And not just any school, but a high-profile school attended by Americans and, more importantly, by President Chutto's own boys? And if the two events are connected, in what way? What's the common denominator here?*

President Taylor absently drummed his fingers on the tabletop, lost in thought as he chewed everything over, his gut instinct telling him that something just wasn't right. Finally, he looked at Director Jefferson.

"Well, Allen? What do you think?"

"Suh, for one thing, we don't know nothin' more than what Ambassador Jenkins just told us. Chutto wouldn't even come right out and tell us if he or one of his folks has talked to the Taliban. He deflected that question, if y'all noticed. Now, given the situation, I'm pretty damned sure they have talked, which means he's lyin'. What I mean by that is, I doubt the Taliban would just throw that little girl out there and then blow her all to hell and gone on TV for no reason a'tall. Why do that and run the risk of the Pakistan Army stormin' the school? No, suh, thinkin' this through, my gut tells me they've talked, and whatever the Taliban asked for, Chutto said no. What happened to that little girl was just their way of showin' they didn't like his answer. To put pressure on him. So that tells me he's hidin' somethin', somethin' he couldn't discuss with you."

Once again Director Jefferson had summarized a complex conundrum into just several sentences.

"General?"

"Mr. President, I agree with Director Jefferson. Something smells in Denmark and it ain't fish. He's hiding something, sir. Bigger than shit!"

With a shake of his head at the general's succinctly blunt answer, he turned to Steven Clarke.

"Steven?"

"Sir, I agree. There's something here that President Chutto doesn't want us to know. But what really bothers me is, given that his boys are in that school, he didn't ask for any help. Zip, zilch, nada. I would've thought he'd have at least asked for satellite surveillance, or drones, or something. What that tells me is they're planning to go this alone. And, as General Gray pointed out, Chutto's primary concern has got to be getting his own kids out of there. Now, that's understandable to a certain degree, but in my book that makes all those other kids expendable."

"Okay, thanks, Steven."

President Taylor plucked his coffee from the table and sat back for several moments, digesting what his advisors had told him.

"All right, gentlemen. Just to let you know, I agree with all of you: number one, I thought he would've asked for help, but he didn't;

and number two, there's gotta be something keeping him from doing that, something he doesn't want us to know. Until we know what that is we're in the dark. Ambassador Jenkins?" he suddenly asked.

"Yes, Mr. President?"

"We need to know what's going on, and we need to find out fast. What's Chutto holding back? I want you to use every resource at your disposal to find out what that is. That's your top priority right now."

"Yes, Mr. President."

"And Allen? Make sure your CIA folks help out the ambassador."

"Yes, Mr. President."

"Mr. President?" General Gray said. "Before we go, sir, there's one other thing we need to determine."

"What's that, General?"

"Sir, I hate to ask this, but what are the rules of engagement for Hearthstone? I know that's one of the first things they're going to ask. And Sir, they're going to need something to cover their ass if this operation ever comes to light. You know as well as I do that as soon as the dust settles on this thing, every do-nothing, know-nothing congressman or senator wanting to make a name for himself will be digging like a mole to find out what happened. So they can play Monday morning quarterback and splash it in the papers to make their political points, and then crucify the guys who actually got the job done."

"Well, General, I'm glad you asked!" President Taylor said, his eyes alight like two incandescent coals. "As they taught me way back when in the Marine Corps, I'm going to tell you exactly where I stand. First, I don't give a shit what any congressman or senator says about this! I'm the one calling the shots, not them! And as far as Hearthstone's ROE is concerned," he continued, his eyes alive with malice, "after what I saw happen to that little girl and her father, and given there are over three hundred kids in there, you can tell Hearthstone there are no rules of engagement! None! Period! You tell 'em to take off the gloves and go in there and clean house! Hunting season is open! Do whatever they need to do! And you can personally tell 'em they have my permission to kill every one of those goddamned terrorist sons-of-bitches they can get their hands on! Those are our rules of engagement, sir! Understood?"

General Gray, his face set as if carved deeply from a piece of New

Hampshire granite, smiled grimly.

"Understood, sir, and thank you."

"All right, everyone!" President Taylor said, standing up. "We know what we need to do! So let's go do it!"

Chapter 43

DAY TWENTY-ONE, 2325 HOURS
TECHNICAL AREA 53
LOS ALAMOS NATIONAL LABORATORY

LIEUTENANT COMMANDER JAKE Stoneman walked up to what he considered to be his humble abode, but before he opened the door he looked up and down both sides of the Baker Hilton's concrete walkway. Even though the lights were out in the other rooms occupied by Hearthstone, he was sure that everyone was present and accounted for. The extra Ford Excursion they had been given was parked next to his own out in the lot.

Jake clicked on the room's light and stepped over to the chest of drawers, digging deep in his trousers for his change, car keys, and wallet, then dumped it all on the top of the dresser. Next he took off his watch and laid it beside the pile, thinking of their team run in the morning. He hoped that Dr. Ross would join them as he had each and every morning so far, much to the annoyance of Hearthstone. He knew the team was pissed that a scrawny civilian—a scientist no less—could run them so easily into the ground, but from his perspective it was one of the best things that could have happened. It had eliminated a lot of the smug complacency that had settled into the team. It also proved that, no matter how good you thought you were, there was always someone out there who could kick the shit out of you, and he would rather have the shit kicked out of Hearthstone on a leisurely morning run than in a firefight with a bunch of jihādist assholes.

Pulling off his shirt, he tossed it on a large pile of dirty laundry at the bottom of his Motel-Six-style closet, then sat on the squeaky, swaybacked bed feeling pretty goddamned tired. But he had to smile when he thought back to earlier in the evening. He had taken Sam out to dinner again to a little Italian restaurant on one of the back streets of downtown Los Alamos. She'd ordered the angel hair pasta while he had tried the baked manicotti, all accompanied by a nice bottle of Chianti as they both enjoyed learning more about one another. He'd loved the way she laughed, but had to be careful when he looked deeply into her turquoise-blue eyes; eyes edged with warmth that twinkled with humor.

He had listened as she spoke of how she had grown up on her family's dairy farm outside Plover, Wisconsin. She had even fessed up to having grown up as a tomboy, given she'd had two older brothers. He had laughed when she'd told him that her survival had depended upon it. Sam also recalled how both of her brothers had attended the University of Wisconsin majoring in Animal Husbandry and, upon graduation, had returned to the family farm to help out their folks. But her calling had been different.

From an early age, she had told him, she'd always been interested in physics and curious as to how computers worked. So, when she had attended the same university as her brothers, she had opted for a double major in Physics and Computer Science. Brilliant in her studies, with her significant talents recognized by her senior professors, upon graduation she had been one of the few nationwide applicants chosen for the combined Masters-Doctorate Program at the Massachusetts Institute of Technology. One thing had led to another, she recalled, and now here she was, head scientist for Project Gabriel.

In return, he had talked more about his humble beginnings in Victor, Montana; his family home having been a double-wide trailer, the Long Branch Saloon, the one and only tiny school in town he had attended, and his days at the University of Montana. She had laughed when he'd told her stories of having to schlump up and down State Highway 93 in the family's old, battered, 1952 pickup truck in the dead of winter to attend his classes. But he had impressed upon her he never would have traded places with anyone, and couldn't have imagined growing up anywhere but in the Big Sky Country of Montana. He'd told her of elk hunts in the fall with his dad; and lazy warm, summer afternoons when he and his friends would float the Bitterroot River in flat-bottomed Mackenzie boats, watching as cut-throat trout swirled about on the lee-side of large boulders, and then rise to pluck swarms of newly-hatched mayflies from the river's surface.

It had been another great evening as far as he was concerned. *Yep, tonight had been another nice night. And she's one hell of a fine lady. Smart, funny, and beautiful.* He had also been surprised that his guilt feelings over the deaths of his wife and son had taken a different turn. Not that he didn't miss his family with all his heart, he always would, but Sam had helped him to better understand what had happened. That it hadn't been his fault a terrorist bomb had been smuggled onboard their flight. He'd finally come to realize that maybe it was okay to have a life, to be happy once again. His time with Sam was just what the doctor had ordered.

Whistling an innocuous tune, he pulled off his trousers and tossed them on the bed, quickly followed by his shirt. Then, thinking he'd better brush his teeth before he hit the rack, he made his way to the bathroom. No sooner had he begun to brush than his cell phone rang unexpectedly in the other room. Spitting out the toothpaste, he quickly rinsed and grabbed a hand towel to wipe his mouth, then headed back into the bedroom. *Who the hell could be calling at this time of night? Sam, maybe?*

Picking up the phone, he was more than surprised to see the call was from the White House.

"Lieutenant Commander Stoneman, sir," he answered with the trace of a question in his voice.

Jake knew it was almost 2330 hours his time, so it had to be o'dark thirty in the morning Washington D.C. time, and that meant something had to be up.

"Good mornin', Jake. Sorry to call so late," Director Jefferson began, "but somethin' important's come up, and I need you and your team to get back to the lab lickety-split. I can't go into the details right now, your phone's not secure, but once you're back at the lab call me on a secure line and I'll brief ya'll in. You got that, Jake?"

"Yes, sir," he said, wondering what the hell was going on, and then it hit him. *By God! They've found the Pakistani nukes!*

"Now, go get a pencil and a piece of paper. I'll give you the number to the Situation Room's Watch Command Center and they'll patch you right through. Let me know when you're ready."

"Yes, sir," Jake said as he snatched a pen and a pad of paper off the end table. "Ready, sir."

"Okay, the number's 202-456-9431. Got it?"

"Yes, sir. 202-456-9431," Jake repeated.

"Good, that's correct, Jake. Now, you and your boys get over to the lab as damned quick as you can."

"Yes, sir, we'll head out soonest. Just give us thirty minutes or so to make it to the lab. But, sir?" he asked, hoping to ask his question before the director hung up. "Does this have something to do with those missing packages we've been concerned about?"

Director Jefferson paused. He couldn't see any problem in at least giving Jake an indication of the importance of his call.

"No, Jake, it doesn't. All I can say is somethin' else has come up that's much more critical, time critical, which'll require your team's expertise, if you get my drift. But again, I'll give you all the details at the lab."

"Yes, sir," Jake said. *What the hell could be more critical than the missing nukes?*

"Thanks, Jake. Call me back as soon as you can. I'll talk to you then." With nothing further to say, Director Jefferson hung up.

Forty minutes later, Jake plucked the secure phone from its cradle in the lab's conference room and dialed the number the director had given him. The remainder of the team feigned nonchalance as they lounged around the table in an effort to overhear the conversation.

As the phone began to ring, Jake looked at his team and shrugged. They knew as much as he did.

"Situation Room Watch Command Center, Major Walton speaking, sir."

"Major, this is Lieutenant Commander Jake Stoneman. I was given this number by Director Jefferson. Can you patch me through, please?"

"Yes, sir! Director Jefferson's expecting your call. Just a moment, sir," Major Walton replied, punching a button that transferred the call to Jefferson who sat at the Situation Room's conference table.

"Allen Jefferson," he heard on the other end of the line.

"Sir, Jake Stoneman here. Just wanted you to know we're all here at the lab."

"Good, Jake, thanks for gettin' over there in such a hurry. Now, go ahead and put me on the speaker phone so all your boys can hear this."

"Yes, sir," Jake said as he flipped on the speaker phone, increased the volume, and motioned for the team to gather round.

"Okay," Jefferson began, unaware he had once again slipped into his deep, southern, Alabama drawl. "Can everybody heah me?"

"Yes, sir," Jake said again, accompanied by a chorus of "Yes, sir's" from the rest of the team.

"Good! Now, just to let you know, I'm in the Situation Room. President Taylor was just here with General Gray and Steven Clarke. They'll be back in a few minutes."

Jefferson then paused to try and think of the best way to bring Hearthstone up-to-speed, to get them to agree to take on the mission, but he knew that wasn't goin' to be the problem. No problem a'tall. The problem, as far as he saw it, was to keep Hearthstone from hijackin' a jet and headin' over there right now once they knew what the problem was.

"Gentlemen, let me fill you in on what's goin' on, and please hold your questions 'till I'm done. When I'm finished talkin' you can ask all the questions you want."

Director Jefferson knew that he had their undivided attention.

"Now, at around eight thirty this mornin' Pakistan time, an unknown number of Taliban terrorists attacked and took over the Islamabad Preparatory Academy. That's a school located in the southeast portion of their capital. Our best guess right now is there had to be at least twenty or thirty of them involved. But that's just a guess; we really don't know. The problem is, the school's primarily American. By that I mean, there's over three hundred students attendin', and from what we can tell, about a third of those kids are American dependents. Children of our diplomats and business folks over there. Compoundin' the problem is that the Pakistan president's two sons also attend the school and are hostages. But the Pakistanis won't let us get anywhere near the school, much less help. President Taylor asked if we could get some of our military folks on the ground over there, but they declined. Seems they want to go it alone. Now, just to show you folks what we're dealin' with, I'm forwardin' to you a video clip of an incident that happened about an hour ago. By now, I guess, you can probably see it on the news, but I'm sendin' you the uncensored version of it. In a nutshell, they've already killed one of our American students, a cute little girl who was only six years old. They strapped her up in one of their goddamned bomb vests, shoved her out the front door into the parkin' lot, and then set it off. Her father, tryin' to rescue her, was also killed. It's not a pretty picture gentlemen," he ended, failing to suppress a catch in his throat.

When the director hesitated, each member of Hearthstone looked at one another, trying their best to get their raging emotions under control, but doing a bad job of it. Their faces hardened into slabs of granite, staring straight ahead with narrowed eyes glowing brightly like cones of molten fire. Hearthstone knew as well as anyone what these Taliban assholes would do to achieve their Islamic objectives; they had seen the results over and over again in Afghanistan and Iraq. They knew the Taliban had no qualms in killing kids; it was just their way of doing business.

"Now," Director Jefferson continued, "President Taylor thinks the Pakistan president may sacrifice the other kids to try and get his own sons back. We also think the Taliban have made demands on the Pakistan government that, at this point, they're unwillin' to do. We don't know what that is right now, but we think that's why they killed the little girl. To make a point. And they'll continue killin' kids, American kids, until their demands are met. The Pakistanis also told us their troops are under orders not to attack, at least for not right now. But if they do, this could end up just like the Beslan massacre that happened to the Russians back in '04 that killed over three hundred of their kids, or the Maalot killings that happened to the Israelis that killed twenty-six of theirs. Of course, given the number of kids being held at that school, our problem's more on the scale of Beslan.

"Gentlemen, this is where y'all come in. Either we sit on the sidelines with our thumbs up our asses hopin' the Pakistanis don't get all of those kids killed, or we do somethin' about it. President Taylor's decided we're gonna do somethin' about it. The plan we came up with was to drop you boys on that school just like we was gonna do with the nukes. Using Gabriel. We've looked at other options but we just don't think they'll work, not with the Pakistanis all fired up to go it alone. And it's probably the only chance those kids got."

Director Jefferson heard nothing but silence on the other end of the line.

"Jake? You still there? Think you boys want'a have a go at this? 'Cause if you do, we gotta lot of plannin' to get out of the way. And we gotta do it quick before they start poppin' other kids, or the Pakistanis attack and get most of 'em killed."

Jake already knew the answer to the director's question; he didn't need to ask Hearthstone. He could tell by their eyes they were all onboard. He knew his men and could tell all they wanted to do was to go in and kill every one of those sadistic, jihādist assholes. As far as Hearthstone was concerned, things were now personal. Very personal. And that made this mission different. You didn't go fucking around with American kids on their watch. He also knew that Director Jefferson was right, that Gabriel was probably the only way to do it.

"Director, I can tell you right now we're all onboard, but we're gonna need some help. Can you dig up some schematics of the school grounds so we can see how everything's laid out? It would also help to have some overhead photos."

"Not to worry, Jake. We'll forward the school's schematics to you ASAP. We've also contacted the NRO and they're gonna park one of their new, thermal imagen' satellites right on top of that goddamned school. Should be in position within the next hour or so. Once that's done, we'll have real-time video imagery before, durin', and after your insert."

"Okay, Director, sounds good to us. Just get us that info as soon as you can. In the meantime, we'll check out our gear to make sure we're good-to-go."

"Sounds good, Jake. As soon as we have the imagery we'll pipe that directly to your monitors at the lab. You'll also have the schematics within the next ten or fifteen minutes. My staff is scannin' them into the computer as we speak. Once downloaded, we'll forward them to you in PDF format. All you gotta do is print 'em out."

"Okay, sir, thanks."

"One last thing. I know that President Taylor and General Gray are gonna want to know the basics of your plan. Once you've got all the data, how long do you think before you can brief us all in?"

Jake paused to think through the logistics. Then the time it would take to identify the Taliban locations to come up with a scheme of maneuver. Then the individual team member assignments to get the job done. Then a communications overlay plan, not only within the team itself, but back to the lab and most likely the Situation Room. He glanced at the wall clock and did some mental arithmetic.

"Director, we can probably come up with a prelim plan in six or seven hours."

"Okay, Jake, understood."

"And, sir? The sooner we get that imagery feed the better."

"You got it, Jake! I'll also let President Taylor know we can expect a briefin' around ten this mornin' your time. That would be around noon our time, just to give you boys a little extra time to put somethin' together."

"Thank you, sir."

"No, thank you, Jake. And thank you, men. Thank you all, and good huntin'," Director Jefferson said, his last comment directed at the team members he knew were listening.

Chapter 44

DAY TWENTY-ONE, 0830 HOURS
TECHNICAL AREA 53
LOS ALAMOS NATIONAL LABORATORY

NEWS OF THE Taliban attack hit the world like a clap of thunder that rumbled unchecked across international borders, surging westward like a tidal wave from the shores of the Arabian Sea that bordered Pakistan to the continental United States. The school hostage situation now front and center on every newspaper, radio, and television station throughout the world. More so in the United States.

Most Americans, ignorant of the unfolding drama, sat around their breakfast tables with coffee cups in hand as they prepared to go to work, stunned to learn of what had happened in Islamabad.

The most prolific networks that covered the situation were American, from Fox News to CBS, NBC, and CNN among others, all of them maintaining 24/7 news coverage of the event. Each news outlet also had their own team of so-called experts that were continually trotted out in front of the cameras. Experts that ranged from psychological profilers who contradicted one another as to the mindset of the Taliban terrorists, to ex-military and civilian pundits who mouthed their own views as to how the situation should best be handled—from placating the terrorists and giving in to whatever their demands may be, to advocating direct military intervention using American forces and to hell with the consequences.

What turned the stomachs of most Americans were the grating platitudes that came from some of their own senators and congressmen. Elected officials who always found fault with their own country. Career politicians that were more interested in a terrorist's nonexistent constitutional rights rather than their own citizens. They saw this as an opportunity to point their fingers at the current administration and bad mouth American policy. How it was America's own fault that the hostage situation existed at all, and not the fault of the kind-hearted, peace-loving radical Muslims. In their view, it was due to the United States not having been more understanding of the jihādists' grievances, not being more sympathetic to radical Islamic regimes. That the Taliban was nothing more than a bunch of poor, uneducated, third world people, and if we had just been nicer to them, the taking of the school would never have happened.

What also came to be known as the "Emily" video had gone viral on the internet, having been posted by an unknown source on You-Tube at around two in the morning Washington, D.C., time. The uncensored version, in just nine hours, had received more than eight hundred thousand hits, its numbers climbing exponentially every minute. And the more it was viewed the angrier and more vengeful the American people became. It was as if a slumbering giant had been finally awakened, stirred to action by the constant nipping of mongrels at its heels. But this latest provocation wasn't a nip at all, but a full-on body blow to the collective consciousness of the United States, just as 9/11 and the chemical attacks on Los Angeles and Atlanta had been. And tens of thousands of angry phone calls and emails inundated the White House.

Frankly, the overwhelming majority of the American people were fed up. Sick and tired of being blamed for the world's ills. Being forced to kowtow to third world cultures and receiving nothing in return. Having to be politically correct. And they weren't going to take it anymore. They were mad as hell and wanted those kids rescued and the terrorists killed, no matter what it took. It was as simple as that.

As rage swept across America's heartland, Lieutenant Commander Jake Stoneman, located in the lab's largest conference room, took a moment to look over the final plan he would pitch to President Taylor. He knew that his televideo conference with Taylor, along with Steven Clarke, Allen Jefferson, and General Gray, was less than an hour away. He visualized in his mind once more the plan of attack, satisfied he had covered all the bases. He felt good about the plan. It would be short, violent, and deadly—at least to the Taliban assholes. From what he could tell it had a very high probability of success.

Jake poured over the reams of printouts sent to them by Director Jefferson to sort out those to be used in the briefing. As he rifled through the various schematics, he heard a muffled "damn it!" to his right. Looking over the paperwork, he couldn't help but smile when he saw Dr. Ted Angstrom at what they now called their Central Command Communications Console busily mopping up some spilt coffee. Sam, standing to Angstrom's left, grinned as she tried to suppress a laugh.

The communications console was located in the centermost portion of the lab and consisted of a large metal desk on which sat an oversized, flat-screened computer monitor and numerous pieces of radio gear. Through that console the lab could talk securely with just about anyone they wanted—from the satellite techies at the NRO, to the president's Situation Room, and finally to each individual Hearthstone team member once they were on-site. All thanks to Dr. Williams who had made some critical adjustments to the team's communications equipment that would now allow direct, encrypted voice transmissions via satellite. This capability, as far as Jake was concerned, having been critical to the mission. Dr. Williams had come through with flying colors.

Jake had called Sam hours before to roust out her scientific team and have them haul-ass back to the lab. Once they'd arrived, he'd briefed them in on the Islamabad Academy and what the mission parameters were going to be. Everyone had also viewed the unedited version of the "Emily" tape that Director Jefferson had forwarded, the tape putting everyone into the proper mindset. As they threw themselves into their work, Sam and her team fully understood how critical their duties would be—to bring Gabriel up-to-speed to save children's lives.

"So, Brett, what do you think?" Jake asked as he groaned a bit standing up from the table, trying to stretch out his back. He, like the rest of the team, was tired. None of them had had a wink of sleep since midnight and figured he was probably on his thirtieth cup of coffee.

"I think we're good-to-go, Skipper," Lieutenant Thompson said, staring at the wall-mounted display monitor that showed a continuous thermal video feed of the academy from the NRO's KH-12S satellite, his responsibility to locate and keep track of each Taliban insurgent on the school grounds. Brett had accomplished this task by using a clear sheet of acetate placed over a grid map of the school, with each bad guy's position now marked in red grease pencil.

The grid map Brett used was very simple. Jake had basically taken a large overhead photo of the school grounds and outlined its brick wall boundaries in red ink, then ticked off twenty meter increments on its vertical and horizontal axis. With the help of a ruler, he had connected the tick marks that effectively cross-hatched the photo into two hundred and fifty-three squares, each of which measured twenty by twenty meters. Jake then labeled the left-hand vertical axis "A" through "K" from top to bottom, and the bottom axis "1" through "23" from left to right; the map now allowing any team member to identify a specific grid coordinate within the boundaries of the school. For example, grid square F1 overlaid the blown-out guard shack at the front entrance to the school.

From having watched the monitor for the last several hours, Brett was sure there were four groups of Taliban that secured the school's perimeter, each group consisting of ten fighters. It had been tough to try and pick out each individual bad guy from the daytime digital photos, but he was pretty confident he had them all identified, especially since he had been able to confirm their locations via the satellite's thermal imaging capability after nightfall in Pakistan. So, for right now, he was pretty damned sure he knew where they were all located.

The first group was roughly congregated around the cafeteria from grid squares C15 south to grid H15, the easternmost boundary of the school closest to the soccer field. A second group was stretched along the northern perimeter wall from grids A6 through A14, with a third group deployed along the southern boundary from grids K6 through K14. The fourth and final group was stationed mostly around the school's western entrance at grid F1, near the blown-out guard shack. As far as he could tell, three fighters manned the interior of the shack with another seven spread out in line formation to each side.

"The positions of the bad guys haven't changed in the last four hours, Skipper," Lieutenant Thompson continued. "From what I can tell, these are the areas they've staked out as their perimeter security. Pretty good deployment on their part, if I say so myself. The only problem is, we don't know how many of them are in the auditorium."

"Yeah, I know," Jake agreed, a frown creasing his brow. "But Jefferson told us they guessed there were only twenty or thirty insurgents involved, but you've already identified forty. So that means their best guess was wrong. Look over here, Brett," he said, pointing at a close-up photo of the faculty parking lot.

Brett looked at what Jake was pointing out. Five large vans were parked parallel to the curb in front of the auditorium with their rear cargo doors gaping wide open.

"Okay," Jake thought out loud. "Let's try some logic. Assume you have a driver and passenger up front, that's two. Now, those van's storage compartments are pretty damned big, and we know they had to use some of that space to store their equipment, like those Stingers they used to bring down the chopper. So, let's assume they could pack another eight men into the back of each van, four per side. Could be less, but let's assume four. That would make it ten fighters per van. Five vans equals fifty fighters."

Jake looked at Brett to see if his logic made sense.

Brett nodded slowly in agreement.

"Yep, I think you're right, Skipper. Probably fifty of the fuckers. The four groups we've identified as perimeter security totals forty, so that means they could easily have ten inside the auditorium. Maybe less, but given the number of kids and teachers crammed in there, ten sure makes a hell of a lot more sense."

"I agree," Jake said, tossing down the pen he had used to point out the vans. "Better to plan on the high side and be safe, rather than assume less and be sorry."

"You betcha, Skipper."

"Okay, let's get everyone in here to go over the final ops plan."

Jake looked over at Sam and Dr. Angstrom who were still busy at the communications console.

"Sam? Could you have your folks join us? I want to go over the final operations plan before we brief President Taylor."

"Of course, Jake," Sam replied, a touch of worry clouding her eyes, and then she headed straight for Dr. Williams and Dr. Ross who were ensconced in the quantum computer room checking its status. When they had first arrived, both scientists noticed an unacceptable temperature variance in the computer's core memory. Although only several degrees, it had been enough to catch their attention and needed to be fixed.

While Sam corralled her team members, Brett stepped over to the chief. He could see that Moczarny was attaching one of their new sound-canceling KAC suppressors to the muzzle of his M4A1 rifle while the rest of the team thumbed cartridges into their magazines.

"Chief? The skipper wants to go over the final ops plan. Could you have the men take a seat at the table?"

"Aye, aye, sir," Moczarny said, laying his weapon aside. "You heard the man. Finish up what you're doing and take a seat in the conference room."

Jake watched as everyone filed into the room. Once they were settled in he began.

"Okay, gentlemen, and lady," he said matter-of-factly with a brief glance at Sam, "time to go over the final operations plan. We've made a couple of changes, so listen up. I know we've gone over this thing several times before, but you know as well as I do that practice makes perfect. If you have any questions I want to hear them now; it'll be too late once we're on-site. If you see a problem, I expect you to speak up."

Jake paused and made eye contact with each person that sat at the table, just to make his point. Hearthstone was all ears. They knew when it came to planning the boss didn't fuck around; all of their lives depended on it.

Sam was more than taken aback by the change in Jake's demeanor. The man she had met and gone to dinner with had been warm, funny, and somewhat shy. More like a big, old, cuddly teddy bear, but not the man who stood before her now. He seemed to be an entirely different person as if a switch had been thrown. He was all business, and through ingrained habit his face—unknown to him—had settled into what looked like a carved piece of arctic ice. Chiseled, angular, and cold. Devoid of any feeling. His jaws clenched together like a bear trap while he spoke in a clipped, no-nonsense monotone voice with eyes hard and brimming with violence.

Sam couldn't help but feel an inadvertent shiver run down her spine. At that moment she finally realized that Jake was a warrior, as was the rest of Hearthstone. Sheltered by academia, she had never really understood what that had meant or had seen that side of life's cruelties, but she had more than an inkling of it now. She realized these men were actually going into battle. To kill people. Real people. *Or be killed themselves,* she thought worriedly, thinking of Jake. She also understood they were not just any warriors, but ones trained to kill their adversaries by any means necessary. Highly-trained killing machines. To kill without mercy as she was sure they had done repeatedly in Iraq and Afghanistan. And Sam knew that SEALs were the epitome of that training, the pointy-end of the spear and a Taliban's worst nightmare.

Sam's scientific colleagues felt the same way. They didn't smile, fidget, or talk, but listened up like school boys on their first day in gym class not wanting to piss off the coach. They listened to every word Jake had to say, each of them feeling like some kind of juicy morsel being appraised by a ravenous praying mantis whenever his gaze slowly passed over them. They once again thanked god that Hearthstone was on their side.

"Gentlemen, you'll find in front of you a grid map of the school along with a printed copy of the Operations Order. Please take a minute to review them. And when I mention grid locations, please refer to the map."

While Jake waited for the men to review the maps and Operations Order, he picked up a wooden pointer and unconsciously slapped it a couple of times against his palm. When he saw that everyone was ready, he stepped over to a three-legged easel that held a hand-printed, oversized, three-by-four-foot white poster board that detailed the Operations Order split into five itemized categories.

Hearthstone instantly recognized the format, the scientists did not. It was called SMEAC, a military acronym that stood for Situation, Mission, Execution, Administration & Logistics, and lastly, Command and Control, the basis of the standard five paragraph Operations Order used by combat units in the Army, Navy, and Marine Corps.

Jake pointed at the heading labeled "Situation".

"The situation, people, is pretty goddamned simple. Fifty Taliban insurgents, our best guess, have assaulted and taken over the Islamabad Preparatory Academy. They're holding over three hundred students and faculty hostage, a lot of them American kids, including the two sons of the Pakistan president. From what we can tell, there are forty insurgents manning the perimeter of the school. In addition, Brett and I are pretty sure there are ten, if not more, inside the auditorium itself guarding the hostages."

Jake stepped up to a second easel that held a larger version of the school grid map that detailed the locations of the Taliban perimeter forces.

"Looking at this overhead aerial, you can see the insurgents manning the school grounds have been divided up into four groups of ten, with each group responsible for a broad section of the perimeter. The easternmost group, here," he said, tapping the area around grid E15 that overlaid the school's main cafeteria, "are covering the approaches from the soccer field. These guys also have, from what we can tell, an M60 set up facing outboard toward the field. Two other groups are located, respectively, along the northern and southern perimeter walls. The northern group here, in the vicinity of grid A10," he said with a slap of the pointer, "are stretched out left to right on each side of the elementary school quad. And a southern group here, at grid K10," he continued, shifting the pointer, "are strung out on both sides of the high school and middle school quads. The last group," he said, pointing at grid F1, "are guarding the western entrance into the school itself. From what we can tell, three bad guys are inside the guard shack with another seven spread out in line formation along these hedgerows here and here," he pointed out. "This is also where we think they have another M60 located. Any questions so far?" he asked, turning back to the group with the pointer clasped behind his back.

Not hearing any, Jake shifted back to the first easel that held the Operations Order.

"Now, satellite photo interpretation and contacts within our embassy indicate the insurgents are armed with AK-47 assault rifles in addition to the M60s we've identified. They also have anti-air capability, most probably Stingers. In addition to the assault rifles, M60s, and Stingers, they have an unknown number of bomb vests, one of which they've already used," he added, obviously referring to Emily. "And, as we all know, we suspect the bomb vests can be remotely detonated. Please keep that in mind. We're also pretty sure they have a number of other kids rigged to blow, okay?"

He paused to let that important fact sink in.

"Now, to the best of our knowledge, the insurgents don't have any night vision capability. We also have to assume that if they think they're being attacked, their most likely course of action will be to kill as many of the kids that they can. Any questions?" After several moments of silence he said, "Okay, let's move on."

Jake tapped the second heading labeled "Mission".

"Our mission, gentlemen, is short and sweet. To kill the insurgents occupying the school. Not to wound them, not to capture them, but to kill them. And to rescue the hostages."

He saw grim smiles appear on Hearthstone's faces, and could tell they'd liked what they'd just heard. It was simple, direct, and pretty goddamned straightforward as far as they were concerned.

Jake next pointed to the third section labeled "Execution".

"As far as our plan of attack is concerned, we'll launch at 0300 hours Pakistan time. That'll be 1700 hours our time or . . . in roughly nine hours. Now, you know as well as I do that's the best time to go in. The bad guys' reflexes that early in the morning should be slower, and hopefully, a lot of them will be asleep. Additionally, as I said before, they don't seem to have NVG capability but we do. We should own the night, gents," Jake said, smiling for the first time. "And it'll make our thermal sights all that more effective."

Hearthstone collectively nodded their heads. They knew the best time to attack was between three and four in the morning, particularly with thermal imaging gear.

Jake pointed at the insert points for the team.

"Gentlemen, please refer to the maps in front of you. Steve and I will be the first to insert, here at grid F6, just behind the auditorium next to this brick enclosure that houses some trash bins. I'll go in first, then Steve. There's also a door at that location that leads into the auditorium's rear hallway. That will be mine and Steve's access point into the main structure. Brett's also determined the insurgents have left this entry port unguarded. Pretty stupid on their part, but we'll take anything they give us. Now, once I'm on the ground and have cleared the area, I'll contact Sam to send in Steve."

Jake looked quickly at Steve and saw him smile and nod in the affirmative. Then he looked at Sam who also gave him a quick nod of understanding.

"Once Steve and I are on the ground, I'll call Sam to send in Brett. He, along with the rest of you, will insert into this next area," he said, indicating grid E11, "next to the northern side of the gym. It's centrally located on the school grounds where you can head out to your assignments. With the insurgents manning the perimeter walls, we don't expect any of them to be in the area."

Jake hesitated and looked at Lieutenant Thompson.

"Brett? When's the last time you saw any of the bad guys in the area of the gym?"

"I've only seen one in the last few hours, Skipper. He headed over to the auditorium, stayed a while, but then he went back to his position on the perimeter. All of the other Taliban movements have been along the perimeter walls, not through any of the central areas."

"Good. I can't guarantee it, but the area oughta be clear when you go in. Once Brett is on the ground, and he's confirmed the gym is clear, it'll be his responsibility to notify Sam to insert the rest of you on-site. At this point I'll just be monitoring transmissions. The order of insertion will be Brett, the chief, Jung-su, and then Squealer. Now, assuming you're able to insert without being spotted, and once everyone's on-site, Brett will let me know. At that point we'll implement Plan Alpha which I'll get into in a second. When I order Plan Alpha, you're to go to your assigned areas of responsibility and begin clearing out the insurgents. Plan Alpha breaks you four men into two combat teams. Brett? You and Jung-su will make up Team One. Chief? You and Squealer will make up Team Two. Now, the plan's pretty damned simple. From the gym area the four of you will make your way east to the main cafeteria here at grid F16," he said, pointing to the location on the larger grid map. "That's pretty much in the center of the easternmost boundary of the school in front of the soccer field. Once you reach the cafeteria, you'll break up into your teams. Brett?"

"Yes, sir?"

"Your team will clear the eastern perimeter from the cafeteria to the southern perimeter wall located at grid K16. From there you'll clear the perimeter west to grid K1, which is the most southwestern corner of the school adjacent to the faculty parking lot. Once you've reached that point hold in place and let me know you're there. Any questions?"

"No, sir," Lieutenant Thompson answered while he and Jung-su traced their index fingers along the path outlined by Jake. They could see they would need to pass the southernmost portions of the middle and high school quads on their way.

"Chief?"

"Yes, sir," Moczarny replied gruffly.

"Your team's area of responsibility is opposite that of Team One. Your team will head due north, skirting the tennis courts and swimming pool, clearing out any insurgents from the cafeteria to the northern wall located at grid A16. From there you're to clear the perimeter due west to grid A1. That will place you in the most northwestern corner of the school grounds adjacent to the bus parking lot and directly opposite from Brett and Jung-su. See that on your map, Chief?"

"Yes, sir."

"Okay, as with Brett and Jung-su, hold in place and let me know when you're there."

"Aye, aye, sir."

Jake stepped over to the edge of the table. He could tell that each team member had a good picture of the scheme of maneuver.

"While the perimeter is being cleared, Steve and I will maintain our position at the rear of the auditorium. The best case scenario is that you'll be able to terminate your targets quietly without raising an alarm. That's the key gentlemen, doing it quietly. Now, assuming that's the case, we'll implement plan Bravo."

Jake picked up another poster board and replaced the one on the first easel. The new poster board, much larger than the grid map, measured five-by-four-feet and was split horizontally across the front. The upper portion showed an aerial close-up of the auditorium that included the guard shack and faculty parking area, with the lower half showing the auditorium's detailed interior building plans, including the building's backstage office areas, small kitchen, stage area, foyer, and audience seating areas.

"Plan Bravo, gentlemen, will be our coordinated assault on the auditorium. You have a smaller version of this board in front of you, so follow along as I outline Bravo."

Jake paused to let the men locate their smaller version of the poster board. When he saw everyone was on the same page he continued.

"If and when I initiate Bravo, your first objective will be to clear out the insurgents manning the front perimeter wall and guard shack. Brett?"

"Yes, sir?"

"You and Jung-su will clear the school's western perimeter from the faculty parking lot north to the guard shack at F1. There you'll wait until joined by the chief and Squealer."

"Yes, sir."

"Chief?"

"Yes, sir?"

"You and Squealer will make your way south toward the main

gate, then join up with Brett and Jung-su."

"Aye, aye, sir."

"Brett, once the chief and Squealer have joined up let me know. Steve and I will be set to go in from the rear. Once you've cleared the shack, I want you and the rest of the team to make it to the auditorium's front doors and set your charges. And be sure to plant enough explosives to blow the shit out of those doors, enough to blow those doors clean across the foyer. If there's any bad guys in there, I want them killed or at least put out of action."

"Yes, sir," Lieutenant Thompson replied.

"Aye, aye, sir," Chief Moczarny parroted.

"And we can't expect the bad guys to have been stupid enough to leave the doors unlocked, but just in case, Brett, go ahead and try the doorknob. Who knows? Maybe they were stupid."

Hearing subdued chuckles from around the table, Jake shook his head in jest, but then continued in a more serious vein.

"But don't count on it. Once your charges are set let me know. When everyone's in place I'll give the order to blow the doors. At that point Steve and I will enter the rear with flash-bangs and go to work. And don't be shy in using your own, the more confusion the better."

The flash-bangs Jake referred to were M84 stun grenades—grenades that looked as if they had been fed a steady diet of steroids given their green-colored, perforated aluminum bodies that measured five inches in length by just under two inches in diameter, with broad brown bands that encircled their tops and bottoms; each canister packed with a mixture of magnesium and ammonium nitrates that, when set off, exploded with more than one million candle power of intense light and one hundred and eighty decibels of mind-numbing sound. Enough to cause flash blindness, deafness, and disorientation to any Taliban fighter within thirty feet of its detonation.

Jake loved the little fuckers as did the rest of the team. As far as they were concerned, it was the best way to enter a room and disable anyone present, especially a room full of jihādist assholes. The only problem was the noise. The flash-bangs were loud, extremely loud. Jake knew that if he and Steve had to enter the auditorium using M84s prior to the perimeter being cleared, the bad guys outside the auditorium—being the clever fellows that they were—would know that something was up and come hauling-ass back to help out their buddies. That's why he and Steve would wait until the main entrance doors had been blown.

"Brett, you and the rest of Hearthstone will clear the entrance foyer here," he continued, pointing at the building plans that showed the front entry area of the auditorium. "Then enter the main hall seating area. That's where we gotta assume they're keeping the kids. Steve and I, at the same time, will enter through the rear and make our way to the stage area, clearing the auditorium's kitchen and office areas to our right. Plan to meet up with us at the stage. At that point, once we're sure all of the insurgents have been introduced to Allah and their seventy virgins, I'll have the Situation Room contact the Pakistanis so they can make their own assault on the school. Of course, assuming everything goes as planned," Jake said, his eyes smiling once again, "all they're gonna find is a bunch of dead Taliban assholes. Once we know the Pakistanis are on their way, I'll call Sam toot sweet and have us extracted. No muss, no fuss!"

"Skipper?" Chief Moczarny asked, looking up from his copy of the school's building plans.

"Yeah, Chief?"

"Two questions, sir. Number one, what about the kids? I mean, just like you said, we gotta assume that more than just the Pakistan president's kids will be strapped into those bomb vests. What do we do about that?"

"Not a thing, Chief," Jake replied evenly. "Our job is to kill the bad guys, nothing more. The Pakistanis can deal with the vests. Remember, we need to get the hell out'a Dodge so we don't compromise Gabriel. They're to have no idea who entered the henhouse and made nice-nice with the Taliban. Next question."

"Yes, sir. Thank you, sir. My second question is, what if the alarm is sounded and all hell suddenly breaks loose? What do we do then?"

"Chief, I'm glad you asked. I was going to cover that in just a second, but I may as well do it now," he said, piercing Chief Moczarny with a grisly look.

Jake crossed his arms and lowered his head, thinking of how best to describe what he called his "Hail Mary Plan". If a firefight broke out between Hearthstone and the insurgents during the clearing of the perimeter, that was the worst case scenario for the kids. All he could envision were the Taliban wading into the children with AK-47 automatic weapons fire and splattering their bodies all over the walls of the auditorium. Those kids wouldn't stand a chance. That was the main reason he had himself and Steve standing by at the rear entrance, not only to coordinate the clearing of the perimeter, but in case the original plan went down the shitter. If that happened, then Hearthstone was expendable as far as he was concerned. Their first duty was to save as many of the kids that they could, and that didn't include zapping back to the lab and safety.

"In a nutshell, Chief, that means we implement what I call the 'Hail Mary Plan'."

Jake stared each team member dead in the eye, his own eyes reflecting the slate-gray color of the Bering Sea in winter.

"If a firefight breaks out before or during the clearing of the perimeter, the original plan is shit-canned. We know the Taliban will start killing the kids pretty damned quick if they realize what's going on. The second Steve and I hear any rifle fire from the perimeter, he and I will storm the rear of the auditorium. Your jobs at that point will be to break contact and haul-ass back. Whoever makes it back first is to secure the rear entrance, to make sure none of our jihādist buddies still guarding the perimeter can enter the building. Anyone else who makes it back is to enter the auditorium to help us out. Gentlemen," Jake said finally, his hands placed firmly on the table, "either we kill these sons-of-bitches and free the kids, or we'll die trying. It's as simple as that, Chief."

Chief Moczarny nodded, his lips set in a grim line.

"Kinda thought that's what the other plan would be, Skipper. Just wanted to check and make sure."

Chapter 45

DAY TWENTY-ONE, 1110 HOURS
THE OVAL OFFICE

"GODDAMNIT TO HELL! I wish I'd known this when I spoke to Chutto!" President Garrett Taylor shouted, pissed as he read the NSA intercept of the call between the head Taliban terrorist and the Pakistan president.

Taylor, now dressed in a dark-gray pin-stripe suit, crisp white linen shirt with button-down collars, muted maroon tie, and highly-polished black wing-tipped shoes, had taken the time several hours before to head back to the presidential quarters to grab a quick shower and a shave, and to change out of his Marine Corps sweatshirt and sweatpants into something more appropriate.

He grabbed his coffee and read the intercept once again.

"Allen? Do we have any idea who this head Taliban guy is talking to Chutto?"

"No, suh, we don't. But the NSA's runnin' a copy of this call through their voice analysis database of Taliban intercepts. If they have this guy on tape they'll make a match. Could take a little time, though."

"Mr. President?" Steven Clarke interrupted. "At least we know what this is all about, why they went after the school and Chutto's kids."

"PAL codes!" General Gray added unbelievably. "Now, to my way of thinking, if these guys want PAL codes, then these gotta be the same gomers that hijacked the nukes."

Gray turned to the president.

"I can tell you this, sir, we're just damned lucky these guys ended up with the newer Pakistani weapons and not any of the older ones."

"And why's that, General?" Taylor asked, confused by General

Gray's statement. *How could he think this was lucky?*

"Wouldn't newer weapons be more destructive? Cause more damage? I would've thought just the opposite."

"No, sir, and here's the good part," General Gray said, hunching forward on the couch. "The most important difference between the newer and older Pakistani weapons are PAL codes. PAL stands for Permissible Action Link, sir. If the Taliban had the older weapons no PAL codes would have been needed, because the fail-safe mechanisms on their older weapons are mechanical, not electronic. Any nuclear tech worth half his salt could have armed the older weapons, and that would have been bad for us. But since these are newer weapons, the fail-safe systems are different. They need an electronic code downloaded to make them operational, PAL codes, just like we do. That's why that warrant officer sits outside your door all day twiddling his thumbs. He's carrying the football with our own nuclear release codes. If you leave, he follows you around just in case you need to release those codes to arm our own weapons. And if the gomers don't have the codes, then the warheads they hijacked are essentially useless to them."

Finished, General Gray leaned back and unbuttoned his uniform coat.

"Please excuse my French, sir, but without those codes, the gomers are just pissin' in the wind."

"Okay, thank you, General. And that explains why they attacked the school; the terrorists' whole intent was to ransom President Chutto's kids for the codes. That also explains why Chutto didn't tell us a damned thing about their demand; they have no idea we know they've lost a couple of their nukes."

"That's correct, Mr. President," Director Jefferson agreed. "From what we can tell, the weapons the terrorists hijacked do indeed require these codes. And since these were some of the newer Pakistani weapons, it was just bad luck on their part. There's just no way they can arm those weapons without their PAL codes, unless they could reconfigure them into dirty bombs or somethin' along those lines. But we doubt they have the degree of sophistication to pull somethin' like that off. So that left them with only two options: either get the codes which only the Pakistan president could give 'em, or go back to square one."

From out of nowhere General Gray began to chuckle.

Everyone looked at the general in bewilderment, wondering what the hell he could find so funny at a time like this.

General Gray was oblivious to their stares. All he could picture was a bunch of ragheaded terrorists, running around like chickens with their heads cut off, when they found out the warheads they'd hijacked were as useless as tits on a boar hog. With a lop-sided grin he caught the president's eye.

"Mr. President, I'm sorry, you'll have to excuse me," he said with a shake of his head. "And please, don't take this the wrong way given what's going on at that school. But, by God! I would'a paid a year's salary to see the looks on those gomers' faces when they found out they needed PAL codes."

General Gray couldn't help but paint the picture as he saw it.

"Can't you just see them standing around in a circle-jerk looking at one another? With really stupid looks on their faces? Asking each other, 'Hey, Muhammad! What the fuck's a PAL code?'"

Everyone sitting there, President Taylor included, didn't respond at first, but when they visualized the picture just painted by the general it hit home and everyone began to laugh. With those few comments, General Gray had done what Director Jefferson had been trying to accomplish all morning: to get the president to loosen up a little and look on the bright side of things. They had Hearthstone to go in there and deal with the Taliban.

"And those ragheads, sir, please excuse my politically incorrect French," he continued as he wiped at his eyes with a napkin, "must'a been shittin' a brick. I'm sorry, Mr. President, but right now all I can picture is that head Taliban asshole, fresh out of shit paper, squatting on some dirt floor out in the Pakistani boondocks making grunting noises."

With that final, succinct embellishment laughter erupted in the Oval Office, bringing some well-deserved levity to a tense situation. Jefferson, bent over at the waist, uncharacteristically slapped his knee a couple of times while Steven Clarke almost squirted a mouthful of hot coffee through his nose. One of the Secret Service agents standing post outside the Oval Office wondered what the hell was so damned funny.

"General, I gotta admit," President Taylor said a lot more brightly, "you do have a gift for putting things into their proper perspective. And for that, sir, I thank you."

"Glad to oblige, Mr. President. Anytime!" General Gray said, tossing the used napkin on the coffee table.

From out of nowhere a new thought bounced around Taylor's head. *If the Taliban are demanding PAL codes, then one or more of those guys has gotta know, or have a pretty damned good idea, where the nukes are hidden.*

"Okay, everyone," he said seriously, "but we could have an opportunity here."

At President Taylor's statement everyone sobered up and waited expectantly.

"Seems to me if these guys are asking for PAL codes, then one or more of them must know where the nukes are hidden."

Taylor's statement lay dormant for several seconds.

"Now, I know this would make Hearthstone's job a lot tougher. But what if they could capture a couple of these guys? And interrogate them to find out the location of the nukes? General, what do you think?"

"Well, sir," General Gray began thoughtfully, "I thought the same thing when I read that intercept. But I also thought about that head gomer telling Chutto he had a remote detonator, with Chutto's boys strapped into those bomb vests. Personally, I think that guy's walking around with his thumb on the button to keep the Pakistan Army from attacking. At least that's what he told Chutto. And remember, that vest on Emily was remotely detonated. The other risk we have to assume is that they got a bunch of other kids wired-up ready to set off."

General Gray sat silent for a couple of moments, tapping a pencil randomly against a writing pad.

"Sir, to be honest, I just don't know what to tell you. I'm sure Hearthstone is just planning on going in there and killing every son-of-a-bitch on-site; that's the safest way for them to do it. But we could let Commander Stoneman know what we know, and if the opportunity presented itself, and if it could be done without endangering the kids, then to go ahead and try to snatch a couple of those guys. But I think we have to leave that call up to Stoneman, sir."

"Thanks, General. Allen?"

"Mr. President, I agree with General Gray. We need to leave that up to Stoneman. He's the one that'll be on-site and it should be his call."

"Steven?"

"Sir, I agree with Allen and General Gray. The primary objective is the kids. If Commander Stoneman can capture a couple of the terrorists, then so much the better. But his primary objective, above all others, has got to be the children."

"So be it," President Taylor concurred, rapping his knuckles on the coffee table. "Looks to be close to noon, gentlemen. Let's go ahead and adjourn to the Situation Room and get Los Alamos on the line."

Chapter 46

DAY TWENTY-ONE, 1145 HOURS
THE SITUATION ROOM
THE WHITE HOUSE

PRESIDENT GARRETT TAYLOR walked slowly down the carpeted West Wing hallway with his crumpled briefing papers in hand, hoping that Hearthstone was up-to-speed. Time was of the essence and the longer the Taliban controlled the school, the higher the risk of losing more kids, particularly given the time frame the Pakistanis had to turn over the codes. He knew that Hearthstone would only have about two hours to get the job done; really less than that. They had to be in and out before the light of dawn, and that would happen around six in the morning Pakistan time.

President Taylor greeted the uniformed Secret Service agent by name that stood post next to the Situation Room, patting him gently on the shoulder.

"Morning, Bill."

"Good morning, Mr. President," the agent said as he quickly opened the door for his commander in chief.

Taylor made his way directly to his black leather chair and shrugged out of his suit coat, then draped it carelessly across the back and grabbed a quick cup of coffee and a doughnut. As everyone took their seats, he took a couple of quick bites of the pastry followed by a swallow of coffee to wash everything down.

While Director Jefferson set up the conference call with Los Alamos, President Taylor smoothed out his briefing papers to go over them one last time. A few minutes later, when the connection was made and the central video monitor came to life, he set the papers aside.

"Good morning, Commander Stoneman. Or can I call you Jake?"

he asked.

President Taylor had picked out the obviously intelligent, confident, well-built SEAL on the monitor before him. He could also tell by Stoneman's weathered face that he'd been around the block more than a few times. Director Jefferson had already briefed him on Hearthstone and told him how much time they had spent in Afghanistan. He was also the type to go with first impressions and was pleased with what he saw, both with Stoneman and the rest of the Gabriel-Hearthstone team arrayed along both sides their conference table.

"Good morning, Mr. President," Lieutenant Commander Jake Stoneman replied easily, "and Jake would be just fine, sir."

Jake and the rest of Hearthstone, dressed in their black-camouflaged BDUs, sat tensely around the table. Jake had never spoken to a president before, and thought he would have been intimidated or nervous. It wasn't every day you briefed in your commander in chief. But to his relief, he felt steady as a rock and he too liked what he saw. President Taylor looked older than he thought he would, but he still had a youthful look coupled with an inquiring face. He also looked to be in shape.

Not wearing a suit coat, Jake could tell that the president had fairly broad shoulders and a good set of biceps given the strain on the sleeves of his white, buttoned-down dress shirt. Taylor also had the sunken, hollowed-out cheeks of a runner. He remembered reading somewhere that the president liked to work out with weights and run. The story was obviously true, but he also noticed the dark shadows under the president's eyes and the tired expression that they held. *This guy's had about as much sleep as we've had, meaning none. But he seems to be holding up and is in a fairly decent mood.*

"Mr. President, if I could, I'd like to introduce the rest of Hearthstone. It's my understanding you've already met Dr. Johnson and the Gabriel team."

"Sure, Jake, no problem. But before we do that, good morning, Samantha!" President Taylor said warmly, spying Sam sitting directly across from Jake. Taylor had a broad smile on his face and was obviously pleased to see the head Gabriel scientist.

"And to you too, gentlemen," he continued, noting the rest of the Gabriel team arrayed to her left.

"Good morning, Mr. President," Sam replied self-consciously, her cheeks slightly blushed, pleased that President Taylor had remembered her name. She'd only met him that one time when she and her team had briefed him on the capabilities of Gabriel.

"Do you remember Dr. Angstrom, Dr. Ross, and Dr. Williams, Mr. President?" she asked.

"As a matter-of-fact I do," Taylor said, his gaze once again sweeping over the three scientists, all three sitting upright in their chairs and looking directly into the monitor. He could tell they were nervous.

"Good morning, gentlemen. And I wanted to thank you for your hard work on Gabriel."

"Thank you, Mr. President," they chimed in, pleased to meet the president again, even if it was over a video monitor.

"Jake, sorry I interrupted. Please go ahead and introduce your team."

"Yes, sir. Thank you, sir," Jake said, pointing out each team member and introducing them in the order they were seated.

President Taylor had a few choice words for each man, thanking them for having accepted the mission to rescue the students. And, as he'd done with Jake, he unconsciously assessed the combat readiness of Hearthstone. From his own experience in the Marine Corps he could tell they were warriors, just by the look of them. They all had that same, hardened, weathered look of their commander, didn't mince words, and looked one directly in the eye. Then he focused on the only black member of the team, remembering what Steven had told him about Tolman's encounter with a camel spider. With a brief smile of recognition, he singled out the big, black, petty officer first class.

"So, Squealer! You think Hearthstone's good-to-go?" he asked, looking Petty Officer First Class George Tolman squarely in the eye.

Taken by surprise, and not knowing the president knew of his trials and tribulations in Afghanistan, Squealer could only stammer out a belated, "Yes, sir!"

"Well, that's good, Squealer," President Taylor said, pleased with the reaction he'd received. "Good to hear it." *And now I bet he spends the next few hours trying to figure out how the hell I knew his nickname.*

"Okay, Jake," the president continued, getting down to business. "You have the floor. Now, how do you plan on getting those kids out of that goddamned school."

For the next ten minutes Jake outlined their plan, at the conclusion of which he saw Taylor nod in agreement.

"Jake? Just a couple of things," Director Jefferson said. "Since y'all will be goin' in at night, would it help if the power was turned off at the school? Just prior to your goin' in? Since y'all got NVGs and the terrorists don't as far as we can tell? We can do that you know, through our folks on the ground over there."

"Sir, that's a good idea, and one I've already thought of, but I think the risk would be too great. Once those lights went out the insurgents would know that something was up, put them on alert. We're just planning on going in there as quietly as we can with most of them, hopefully, asleep. But thanks for the offer just the same."

"Noted," Jefferson said as he scribbled a note on his writing pad. "Scratch lights out at the school. The second thing is, we finally figured out why they attacked the school in the first place. It seems these are the same folks that stole the Pakistani nukes. We found that out through an NSA intercept between the Pakistan president and the head terrorist. Seems the nukes the Taliban stole require PAL codes, Permissible Action Links, to make them operational. So, for right now, those warheads are no better than large paperweights for the Taliban. That's the whole reason for their attack. To grab the Pakistan president's kids to force him into givin' them the codes."

Director Jefferson paused when he saw a puzzled look on Jake's face. "Jake? Do you and your boys know what PAL codes are? What they're used for?"

"To be honest, Director, I've heard of them, but only in general terms. Aren't they some kind of a code that has to be input into a nuke to allow them to explode?"

Jake looked at the rest of his team members. He could tell they too had no idea what Permissible Action Links were.

"Sir, it would help if you could explain that."

Jefferson spent the next minute outlining the importance of PAL codes.

"Well, anyways, Jake, they're usin' the kids, more specifically Chutto's boys, to force him into givin' them those codes. What that means is, it's more than likely one or more of those folks knows where the warheads are hidden."

Jefferson paused to let Jake think that through.

"Now, what we'd like you to do, if given half a chance, is to capture one or more of our jihādist friends, preferably their head honcho or one of his lieutenants. Then interrogate them as to the location of the nukes. But only if it can be done with no risk to the kids. Now, this would only be a secondary objective and strictly your call. If you don't think you can do it once you're on-site, then don't. But again, if you could, it'd be like killin' two birds with one stone, so to speak."

Jake thought through the director's request. As far as he was concerned, trying to capture one or more of the Taliban higher-ups would be tough. Instead of just going in and killing every son-of-a-bitch on-site, now they would have to try and capture a few of these guys. Then take the time to interrogate the bastards to try and get the nuke answers. Then get the hell out of Dodge. *But,* he thought, warming up to the idea, *if we can get the location of the nukes, then so much the better. And if they're asking for PAL codes, then Jefferson's right. The odds of one of them knowing where the warheads are stashed should be pretty damned high. Besides, he was very, very good at interrogating these jihādist rat bastards.*

"No problem, sir," he answered firmly. "If the opportunity presents itself, and if we think we can grab one or two of these guys without endangering the mission, then we'll do it. And if we do get one of them, we'll sure as hell try to find out where those nukes are hidden."

At the end of Jake's statement, President Taylor looked around the Situation Room.

"Any other questions, gentlemen?"

There were none.

"Any questions, Jake?"

"No, sir. No questions."

"Then God speed, Jake. God speed to all of you."

"Thank you, sir," Jake answered for everyone.

President Taylor sat back after the monitor turned dark, his fingers steepled in front of his chin, impressed with the entire Gabriel-Hearthstone team. Scientists and warriors alike. But in particular the SEALs. Here they were, going to use a radically new technology that had its own inherent risks, insert onto the school grounds with greater than eight to one odds against them, and then kill all of the terrorists in an effort to save those kids.

"Well," Steven Clarke said to no one in particular, "if anyone can get those kids out of there, those are the guys to do it."

"Like I said, Steven," General Gray added, "those boys are a Taliban's worst nightmare. If the gomers knew they were coming, it would scare the bejeebers out of 'em."

"Indeed," Allen Jefferson said.

President Taylor hadn't moved a muscle nor said a word. To say he felt better about the whole operation was an understatement. He felt pretty damned confident about Hearthstone—and Gabriel for that matter. If anyone could save those kids it was these guys. Then he smiled when he thought of Hearthstone being like Pitbulls with their dicks tied to a leash. *Well, time for the leash to come off so they can go fuck those terrorist assholes.*

At that moment a poem he hadn't thought of in years popped into his head, prompted by a visual image of unleashing Hearthstone onto the school grounds. A poem he'd memorized years ago in college. It used to be one of his favorites, and he thought it more than apropos for the situation, matching what he hoped Hearthstone was about to do to the Taliban. The poem had been written by William Shakespeare in 1601 for his play entitled *"Julius Caesar"*, and described what happened after Anthony had murdered Caesar, with Anthony regretting his actions that could lead to war.

Just like in this case, President Taylor thought, thinking of the Islamabad Preparatory Academy. As far as he was concerned, the poem described the future actions of Jake and his team more eloquently than he could ever do.

> *Blood and destruction shall be so in use*
> *And dreadful objects so familiar*
> *That mothers shall but smile when they behold*
> *Their infants quarter'd with the hands of war;*
> *All pity choked with custom of fell deeds:*
> *And Caesar's spirit, ranging for revenge,*
> *With Ate by his side come hot from hell,*
> *Shall in these confines with a monarch's voice*
> *Cry 'Havoc', and let slip the dogs of war;*
> *That this foul deed shall smell above the earth*
> *With carrion men, groaning for burial.*

There were two lines he couldn't get out of his head, they kept rolling over and over in his mind like angry ocean surf that crashed against a distant shore. *Cry 'Havoc', and let slip the dogs of war!*

That line applied well to Hearthstone. But the last line was more poignant; it summed up their entire mission. *With carrion men, groaning for burial.* President Taylor's final thought was, *I fervently hope so.*

Chapter 47

DAY TWENTY-ONE, 0249 HOURS
LANDING ZONE ONE
ISLAMABAD PREPARATORY ACADEMY

AKBAR AFRIDI, AN emaciated young man of twenty-two years with greasy-black hair, sunken cheeks sparsely covered by a wispy dark beard, and thin lanky arms, lay huddled on the ground with his back pressed against a red-brick enclosure attached to the rear of the auditorium. His nose wrinkled in distaste at the rotten smells that came from the other side of the wall, all too aware the walled enclosure held the garbage bins for the auditorium's kitchen.

But Akbar was afraid. He expected Mahmood to crash through the door at any minute and shoot him. Not fifteen minutes before he and his friend Yardan had been viciously kicked awake by Nayid Zikari and ordered to go outside to guard the rear entrance. They had been asleep in the backstage area in one of the prop rooms, not to hide from anyone, but to get away from the stink of the infidels.

Forbidden to move all day on fear of punishment, many of the infidels could not control their bowels and had relieved themselves where they sat, teachers and children alike. More than half now sat in their own waste, ashamed and crying with many of the younger ones calling out plaintively for their parents, but too fearful to complain. All to the amusement of their Taliban guards.

Akbar had had no idea why Nayid thought they should have been guarding the door; nobody had told them to do anything. But Nayid had screamed with his face clenched in anger as he repeatedly kicked them about their heads, telling them in no uncertain terms it was a good thing that Mahmood did not know that the rear of the building had been left unguarded all this time.

Terrified and confused, they had stumbled their way over some large plastic bins filled with stage props and folding chairs, skinning and bruising their knees in their haste to escape—looking more like beaten dogs as they scurried to the rear of the building with their AK-47s clutched to their chests. But they knew they had done no wrong.

Breathing heavily, they had stepped into the morning's darkness and made their way toward the trash bins, but Akbar's anger continued to simmer. His honor, he knew, had been besmirched, and he was upset that Nayid would think he would willingly shirk his duty. But that would not matter to Mahmood. Guilty or not, he knew what would happen if Mahmood found out.

Akbar tried to relax as he shivered in the damp air. With his AK-47 propped against the brick wall, he pulled his threadbare jacket close around his shoulders, trying to stave off the chill that was boring its way into his bones. Finally comfortable, he peered into the gloom of early morning but could barely see anything. Mahmood had earlier ordered the circuit breakers switched off for the academy's exterior lights, so the men standing sentry alongside the perimeter walls would not be silhouetted against the school's backlighting. Mahmood knew that darkness would make it much more difficult for his fighters to be observed by the Pakistan military.

To his side he could hear Yardan's heavy, rhythmic breathing as he tried to go to sleep. With a brief look down at his friend, he remembered back to the poor mountain village where they had been raised, and how he and Yardan had been inseparable. He had always taken care of his friend and knew that Yardan did not have all his faculties, and was mentally very slow.

As he lay there, Akbar thought back to today's happenings, proud that he had been chosen for the attack on the school—a school infested with infidel, nonbelieving children who reminded him of cockroaches that infected a pile of garbage. *Cockroaches that now sat in their own shit,* he thought with a smile. He had also basked in the warm glow of praise he had received from both Mahmood and Hammid for having killed one of the guards that manned the front doors to the school.

With that thought in mind, he absently reached into his shirt pocket and pulled out the pair of sunglasses he had taken from the dead guard's body. Although he could not see them all that well in the dark, he savored their touch while he absently stroked their lenses with his thumb and forefinger. He looked forward to wearing them in the morning.

Yardan noisily rolled over, loudly smacking his lips as if he had just finished a large meal. With a brief look down in irritation at his friend, Akbar shifted his position and pulled his knees close to his chest, hugging them tightly to keep warm. With nothing else to do, he gazed skywards and blankly stared at the star-strewn heavens. *If I look hard enough,* he thought, *maybe I'll see one of those shooting stars his Wahhabi from many years ago had told him was Allah's blessing on the truly faithful, for those who were fortunate enough to see one. Not one of the regular shooting stars he had seen many times, but one surrounded by a halo of bluish, orangish-white fire.*

Squinting to see the stars more clearly, he suddenly saw something very strange and frightening. A thin, faint, yellowish-white beam of light had just flashed down from the sky and stopped, just inches above the ground, not six feet from where he sat. Scuttling backwards in fright, he thought his mind must be playing tricks on him.

With a knot of panic exploding in his chest, he anxiously grabbed his AK-47 and drew it across his stomach, then desperately grabbed Yardan painfully by the shoulder and squeezed it hard—roughly shaking him back and forth—whispering, "Yardan! Wake up! Wake up!"

Yardan quickly jerked upright and looked about in confusion.

"What is it, Akbar? Are the Pakistanis attacking?" he asked.

"Look there! Look there!" Akbar said animatedly, stabbing his rifle muzzle at the pulsing column of light; a beam that now writhed and roiled in a subdued ball of light as if alive, quickly becoming thicker and larger as it bulged out in height and width and began to coalesce into the form of a man. *By Allah's will!* he thought frantically as both his and Yardan's faces were bathed in the faint light of the column's throbbing luminescence.

Yardan's eyes widened in fright at the sight of the beam.

"May Allah protect us! What in the name of the prophet is that?"

"I don't know!" Akbar hissed, ready to spray the pulsing light with a stream of automatic weapons fire, but Yardan's question made him hesitate. He really had no idea what it was. As his finger relaxed its pressure on the trigger, he remembered an illustration he had seen many years ago. An illustration that had been burned into his memory when he had been much younger and had attended his madrassa. The picture had been from the book of Jami' al-tawarikh, a book written in 1307AD by Rashid-al-Din Hamadani. It had depicted the winged archangel Gabriel, the Qur'an's most important angel, descending from heaven on a column of light and fire to instruct Muhammad, the one true prophet, in Allah's first revelation. A column of light and fire that looked very much like this one.

What if this shaft of light has been sent by Allah? he quickly questioned himself. *To deliver the archangel Gabriel to assist us in our war against the infidels? It had come from the overhead void! And if it had been sent by Allah, to fire at it would be an unforgivable sin. His soul would be damned for eternity!*

In what seemed to be the flicker of an instant, Lieutenant Commander Jake Stoneman found himself no longer within the tight confines of the Los Alamos Lab's NMR, but in LZ-1 that had been designated as his insert point; a point located at the rear of the auditorium near the garbage bins adjacent to the amphitheatre stage.

Quickly looking to his front through the grainy, dull-green image of his NVGs, it felt as if he had landed in a large fish bowl. To his immediate left and right were two wings of red-bricked classrooms whose walls were fifteen feet that extended outwards to form a forty-five degree angle from where he stood. He knew the left wing belonged to the elementary school quad and the right wing to the high school quad, both wings angling toward his front where they almost met forty meters distant; the wings forming a perfect triangle with the auditorium anchoring its base. But most important was the twenty meter gap that separated the furthest reaches of the quads, for through that gap he could see the northern side of the gym and LZ-2.

In full combat mode, with his back to the enclosure that housed the auditorium's trash bins, it had taken him no more than a second or two to scan the surrounding classrooms. From what he could tell everything was quiet, his brain registering no threats.

Satisfied, he started a slow turn back towards the auditorium, but then froze like a bird dog coming to point, startled to see two Taliban fighters sitting on the ground no more than six feet from where he stood; both staring up at him in astonishment, their eyes glowing brightly with fear. One of the insurgents even fumbled with an AK-47 pointed in the general direction of his chest. The second insurgent—frozen in place like a statue—was either too stupid, or scared, or both to even reach for his weapon. He just sat there immobile with his mouth gaping wide open.

What Jake didn't know was that the Taliban sentries had completely lost their night vision when his insert laser had snapped out of existence. They couldn't see anything as they stared into the blackness of the amphitheatre, much less himself. All they could see were red and yellow splotches that marched across their line of vision with what looked to be the blurred image of the archangel Gabriel standing before them.

Jake instantly entered into what he called his "Automatic Mode". With a slight bend of his knees, he crouched into a modified combat position and raised his sound-suppressed MK23 .45-caliber semi-automatic pistol in one fluid motion, cocking back its hammer with his thumb. Through instinct more than anything else, he aligned its laser on Akbar's forehead and snapped off a quick, silenced round from the hip. As the pistol recoiled, he brought the laser down on his second target and snapped off a second round, the muted click-clack sounds of the pistol's action sounding thunderous to him, but that was just his imagination taking hold. The sounds were so muted that if someone had stood less than ten feet from his position they would have had difficulty hearing the pistol fire, much less the pistol's action as it cycled a third round into the firing chamber.

His first round hit Akbar dead center in the forehead with a subsonic, hollow-point, 185 grain bullet. The second round hit Yardan through his open mouth, slamming through his upper palate into the back of his throat, mushrooming and splitting into several pieces as it carved a path deep into his brain; both fighters' heads snapping backwards from the impact and bursting open as if hit dead-on by a fifty pound sledgehammer.

With the insurgents crumpled in place, Jake stood stock-still and looked over their bodies. He could see where their exploding heads had made splattered, psychedelic tie-dyed patterns of blood and brain tissue on the wall behind them. He didn't move, but stood frozen in place with his pistol still sighted-in on his dead targets. Finally, he relaxed and slowly let out a breath he hadn't known he'd been holding, all the while thinking, *Shit! Murphy is alive and well in Pakistan!*

Not twenty minutes before, both he and the rest of Hearthstone had studied the KH-12S thermal images one final time in the lab; the images showing no bad guys within two hundred feet of this site or the gym, the insurgents' blooming heat signatures standing out in relief much like fireflies on a moonless, midsummer night in the deepest bayous of Louisiana. But between the time he had last looked at the satellite images and entered the NMR, these two guys must have moved into position. *Always be prepared,* he grimly thought, remembering the Boy Scout motto.

Jake lowered himself to his knees while he surveyed the rest of his surroundings, just to make doubly sure that none of the other bad guys had heard the silenced firing of his pistol. *You betcha,* he thought finally, now more relaxed as moisture from the ground soaked into his trousers. *It's always better to be quick than dead. Not like those two assholes lying there.* With the pistol raised to his chest, he slowly stood up and silently made his way around the pools of blood that flowed freely from the insurgents' heads.

Quickly mounting the steps to the amphitheatre, he made his way to the auditorium and pressed his back flush against its red-bricked wall. Then, with easy breaths through his partially opened mouth, he cocked his head and listened for signs of any additional Taliban. All he could hear was silence. Everything was still as death.

Convinced there were no more bad guys within his line of sight, he carefully decocked the pistol and snapped it down in its drop-leg holster, then activated his helmet's communications link, the same link Dr. Williams had modified so it could interface with the voice transmission capabilities of the satellite and still allow intra-team communications. Communications that could be heard not only by Hearthstone, but also by Los Alamos and the Situation Room.

Prior to his insert, Jake had also coordinated with General Gray to provide satellite overwatch coverage for Hearthstone, to give the team an eye in the sky that had constant, real-time video thermal imaging capability that greatly increased their odds of pulling off the mission—particularly if the insurgents moved or changed position. From his birds-eye view of the school, General Gray could effectively see around the corners of school buildings and give warning if needed.

Still breathing through slightly parted lips, he knew it was time to check in with the Situation Room and General Gray—call sign "Big Eye"—to get an updated readout on the Taliban positions, and to let Los Alamos—call sign "Homebase"—know he was safely on the ground.

Jake activated his mic and whispered his first transmission.

"Big Eye, Big Eye, this is Mako Six. Do you copy?"

While he waited for the general to respond, he couldn't help but think back to earlier in the day. Sam had been curious as to how he'd come up with the call sign Mako Six. He had explained that in any combat formation the unit commander was always designated the "Six". That meant he was the Boss, the Head Honcho, at least for that unit. Lieutenant Thompson's call sign, on the other hand, was Mako Five to indicate he was second in command. Chief Petty Officer Moczarny was Mako Four, and so on down the line to Petty Officer Third Class Steve Martinez who was designated Mako One. As for using Mako as the prefix, he'd told her it was a call sign he had used years ago when he'd been a young lieutenant (j.g.) in Afghanistan, back when he had headed up a counter-insurgency team known as Mako 31. It had just seemed appropriate for this mission.

After several seconds of delay, Jake heard General Gray's response, the time lag due to the radio signal having to bounce off two orbiting satellites as well as the physical distance that separated Islamabad from Washington, D.C.

"Mako Six, this is Big Eye. Good to hear from you, boy! We read you five-by-five! What's your status?"

General Gray, obviously relieved, looked at President Taylor who sat to his left, as was Allen Jefferson and Steven Clarke. It was close to 1700 hours D.C. time and the president had cleared his afternoon's schedule. There had been no way in hell he was going to miss watching this operation go down.

"Big Eye, Mako Six, I'm on the ground. Request sitrep on tango locations. Also the status of my position and LZ-2. And just to let you folks know, I had a little surprise when I came in here. If it's all the same to you, we don't need any more of those, over."

General Gray couldn't help but grin at Jake's response. He and everyone else in the Situation Room—President Taylor included—had watched as two Taliban terrorists exited the rear of the auditorium and plunked themselves down smack-dab where Jake was slated to go in. There had been absolutely nothing they could do; Jake was already on his way. With their collective breaths held, they watched as the Los Alamos beam materialized next to the garbage bins, only to be replaced by Jake's thermal image that occupied its space. Nothing seemed to happen for three to five seconds, but then Jake's image moved slowly toward the rear of the auditorium. The two terrorists, however, didn't move, but their thermal images gradually became larger and larger as they slowly spread out along the ground, looking more like hot maple syrup accidentally spilled on a kitchen table.

Sam, who sat at the lab's communication console, had also heard Jake's call. Not able to contain herself, she had jumped straight out of her chair and scared the hell out of her teammates when she screamed, "Jake's made it! Jake's made it! He's on the ground and safe!"

The last several minutes had been agony for Sam, not knowing if Jake was alive or dead since he'd teleported. With her adrenaline now kicked into high gear, she tried to settle down as she listened to General Gray's reply.

"Mako Six, Big Eye," General Gray answered, his eyes riveted on the monitor that showed the satellite's thermal video display of the school grounds. "Yeah, we saw you had company. Sorry about that, but there was nothing we could do. But your immediate area is now clear. LZ-2, from what I can see, is also clear. Gomer positions along the perimeter are unchanged. Do you copy?"

"Copy that, Big Eye, and thanks. But keep your eyes open, I'm gonna take a minute to check things out."

Jake released his mic feeling better about the ground situation, but he knew the satellite couldn't spot any of the bad guys screened by roofs or overhangs. It was time to verify what the general had told him.

He raised his M4A1 rifle to his eye and flicked on the scope's thermal imaging function, his cheek placed flush against the weapon's stock while he scanned the fish bowl to see if any heat signatures had been missed by the satellite, and to make doubly sure that none of the assholes had heard his brief altercation with their buddies. But he knew if any movement on the ground was seen by the general, he would be the first to know.

Jake slowly swung the rifle from left to right to check out a 180 degree arc from his position. To his left he rested the sight on the exterior walls of the elementary school quad. It was clear. Then he edged the scope further to the right to search around the outside corner of the elementary school's computer lab sixty meters to his front. Again "No Joy". Then he scanned the exterior portion of the gym to the right of the lab and the school's library. Again no heat signatures. Then he completed his scan when he reached the exterior walls of the high school quad directly to his right. Satisfied everything was quiet, he stepped sideways to the auditorium rear door and removed his helmet. With the helmet dangling in his hand, he listened to the sounds of darkness.

In the distance, he could hear the muted thump of rotor blades that disturbed the easy stillness of morning. *Two choppers,* he reckoned. *Probably three to four klicks away. One to the north and another to the south.* But other than that there were no other sounds, the campus as silent as a graveyard at midnight on Halloween. No barking dogs or the early morning song of birds. Most importantly, no sounds from the bad guys. Everything was deathly quiet.

Jake pulled his helmet back on and snapped its chin strap in place. With the rifle once again raised to his cheek, he zeroed-in on the heat bloom of the northern chopper's engine exhaust. Once in sight, he confirmed it was about three klicks away and guessed its altitude to be a thousand feet, high enough to view all of the sections within the school. He cranked the rear swivel of the variable scope to its highest setting and watched as the chopper's thermal image filled his sight picture, but he still couldn't make out its type.

With the rifle lowered, he returned the scope's setting to power four, then swung the rifle up and to the right where he quickly acquired the second chopper at roughly the same altitude and distance to the south. Since he couldn't figure out their type, he assumed they were Russian made Mi-171s, the most common type of helicopter in the Pakistan inventory. He also knew they carried forward-looking infrared radar—FLIR packages—located in their nose. *Most likely keeping a close watch on the perimeter of the school,* he thought as he lowered the rifle to his chest. *And probably loaded with troops.*

Jake knew that most airborne FLIR systems could detect body heat out to several miles, and that the Pakistanis would most likely pick up Hearthstone's heat signatures when they hit the ground, but he didn't worry about that. He knew the Pakistanis would think they were Taliban militants, and so far the Pakistan military hadn't made any moves against the insurgents that occupied the school.

Now it was time to go back to work. He knew that LZ-1, his present position, was clear. So he sighted through the gap between the classroom quads out toward LZ-2 where the balance of Hearthstone, with the exception of Steve Martinez, were designated to go in— roughly eighty meters to his front and adjacent to the left side of the gym. After several seconds of scanning, with particular attention paid to areas most likely screened from the satellite, he was satisfied that LZ-2 was also clear. In fact, he couldn't detect any heat signatures at all, the insurgents who manned the defensive perimeter being screened by the intervening classroom quads. He knew it was time to call in Steve.

"Homebase, Mako Six."

Sam sat straight up when she heard her call sign.

"Mako Six, this is Homebase, go ahead."

"Homebase, insert Mako One. I say again, insert Mako One."

"Copy that, Mako Six. Understand insert Mako One. Mako One'll be on his way in just a couple of seconds." Then she couldn't help herself and broke radio procedure. "And Jake? You be careful."

"Copy that Homebase, understand Mako One is on the way," he said, and then responded to Sam's last statement. "And I will," Jake answered softly.

With nothing further to do but wait, Jake flipped up his NVGs in preparation for Steve's arrival. The last thing he needed was to be blinded by the laser. That would tend to fuck up his morning.

Back in the lab, Sam chewed nervously at her lower lip, worried about Jake and the rest of Hearthstone as she nodded at Dr. Angstrom who manned the NMR. With a quick nod back, Dr. Angstrom toggled the switch that began the insert procedure for Petty Officer Third Class Steve Martinez. Since all the men had previously been scanned into the quantum computer, the procedure he initiated digitized one set of Steve's entangled particles stored within the mainframe and fed them through a fibre optic cable to the big laser out at TA-46.

As Jake looked skyward, a faint beam of light flashed downwards into the exact location where he'd greeted his now deceased welcoming party, the beam hovering just inches above the ground as he waited expectantly for his teammate to arrive.

Within seconds, Steve's faintly glowing transport beam snapped out of existence, plunging the fish bowl into pitch blackness. With his NVGs flipped back down, he saw Steve briefly wave as he cautiously skirted the dead Taliban guards.

Steve stepped up to Jake with a questioning look on his face and gave him a light tap on the chest, grinning through his camouflage greasepaint with teeth that gleamed as white as a Cheshire Cat.

"Well? How we doin', Boss?" Martinez whispered with a sidelong glance at the bodies of Akbar and Yardan. "Looks to me like you had a little company when you arrived."

Jake just smiled.

"Yeah, my greeting party," he whispered with an uncaring look at the two dead jihādist assholes. "Too bad for them. Sure hope they liked their one-way ticket to paradise, but right now we gotta get the rest of the team in here." *Business before pleasure*, Jake thought. *The pleasure would come later.*

Chapter 48

DAY TWENTY-ONE, 0305 HOURS
ISLAMABAD PREPARATORY ACADEMY

NAYID ZIKARI GRUMBLED as he stomped his way from the back of the stage to its main floor, still furious at Akbar and Yardan, but angrier at himself for not having checked on them sooner. That had been his fault. Then he stopped and pulled out a rag to cover his nose, the stench in the auditorium smelling more and more like an open sewer from back home. He also made a mental note to check with Zafar Kakazai, the one he had old hours before to make sure that Akbar and Yardan guarded the rear entrance from midnight until six in the morning. But from the surprised looks on their faces when he had kicked them awake, he doubted if Zafar had told them at all. Assuming he could find out the truth, and if that idiot from the Kakazai tribe had not told them, he would be made to pay. *Maybe I should have him clean up the infidel's shit,* he thought as he stared at the teachers slumped across the stage floor. *That would make him understand my orders are to be obeyed.*

But his smile disappeared. It had been his responsibility, and if Mahmood—Allah forbid—had checked the rear entrance, it would have been his head on the chopping block, not those two goatherds from the Peshawar Province or that shit-for-brains Zafar. He knew he had dodged a bullet.

Still thinking of how close he had come to infuriating Mahmood, Nayid caught the attention of one of his fighters that guarded the teachers.

"I'm going to check the main gate. If Mahmood wakes up tell him where I went, and that I will be back in twenty or thirty minutes."

The guard nodded.

"Yes, Nayid."

"And keep an eye on our friends here. I think today will be a big day for them."

The guard smiled.

"I will, and hopefully we'll be out of this infidel shithole by tonight, Allah willing."

"Yes, Allah willing."

Nayid made his way to the edge of the stage, adjusting the AK-47 on his shoulder as he walked down the stairs to the main auditorium floor, and then made his way slowly up the inclined, left-hand aisle between the rows of sleeping students headed for the foyer. Halfway up he stopped and pulled out a crinkled pack of smokes. *Anything to get rid of this smell,* he thought as he lit a cigarette with his cheap butane lighter.

From the corner of his eye, he couldn't help but notice a young female student—one of the few who happened to be awake—staring up at him not three seats away, her dark-green eyes filled with fear. He liked seeing her fear, and guessed that she was only thirteen years old or so. She had dark-brown hair, high-sculpted cheekbones, and full rich lips—obviously an American—and very beautiful. To her left sat a boy who looked to be a couple of years older, hunched over on his side with his wrists zip-cuffed tightly behind his back. He looked from the girl to the boy, but saw only hate in the boy's eyes.

Dismissing the boy as irrelevant, Nayid looked back at the girl and took a long drag of his cigarette—letting the smoke slowly trickle through his nostrils—unable to take his eyes off the infidel bitch while he smiled a knowing smile. With a slow wink, he pursed his thick lips in a silent kiss. *At least this one has not shit herself, and look at the size of her tits for one so young!* he thought, feeling his manhood surge within his trousers.

On impulse, he reached down and groped himself in front of the young girl, wanting to see how she would react. Her eyes flicked down at his bulging groin, and then back up with a look of pure horror on her face. *By Allah! This infidel could be fun for one of the faithful, and she has to be a virgin.* He also knew of several offices up front where they could have some privacy, and there was duct tape to seal her mouth in case she screamed. But he would only use that as a last resort; there were many things he would enjoy doing with her mouth. *Maybe when I get back from checking the main gate. It has been a long time since I've bedded a woman, and this one looks ripe for the taking. And after I'm done, the rest of the men can take turns having their pleasure in her as reward for a job well done.*

With a parting smile, he continued up the aisle in a much happier mood, looking forward to completing his security tour so that he could come back and have his way with the American infidel.

Nayid closed the auditorium door, making sure it didn't bang shut, and listened as his fighters locked and bolted it securely behind him. Satisfied, he paused to survey the darkened parking lot that lay before him, then plucked the still burning cigarette from his lips and flicked it into the parking lot. In the darkness, he watched as it splashed in a small shower of sparks when it hit the asphalt pavement.

With graphic thoughts of what he was going to do to the American girl, he reached into his pocket and pulled out another smoke. He could care less if the Pakistanis saw the flare of his lighter; he knew they could do nothing at this point. With the smoke pulled deep within his lungs, he took a moment to relax and enjoy the cool morning air, thinking through the rest of the coming day. With a glance towards the east, he could tell that sunrise was only a couple of hours away; the faintest shades of dark-blue just beginning to highlight the eastern horizon.

Turning back to his front, he looked pointedly at the main gate on the far side of the faculty parking lot, then lifted his gaze and stared at the darkened silhouettes of the Pakistan Army trucks and news vans in the distance, each vehicle standing out starkly against a still blacker background.

When his eyes regained their full night vision, he could just make out the outlines of the news van's antenna dishes. He couldn't see any of the army troops or reporters, but he knew they were there, the Pakistanis probably busy with their night vision devices and watching his every move. But for right now he felt invulnerable, just as Allah's one true prophet, Muhammad, must have felt when he blazed the sword of Islam across the ancient world, slaughtering the unbelievers who lay in his path. He knew the Pakistanis could do nothing to him or their Taliban fighters, not while they held President Chutto's boys as hostages. And the sight of that little infidel bitch exploding into a ball of flame had to be fresh in their memories, especially the Pakistan president's memory. He was sure that Chutto could think of nothing but his own sons being blown up into small stringers of charred meat.

Nayid grinned and scratched his filthy beard. The Pakistanis had no idea how far they would go to secure the codes. It had been ordered by Qudos, and so it would be done. Mahmood had also told him what would happen if the codes were not given to them by eight o'clock this morning. More examples would be made, with an American child killed every hour beginning at nine until the codes were released. All in bomb vests in the middle of the parking lot. All within sight of the media cameras so their deaths could be broadcast to the world. Infidel children to be sacrificed for Allah's greater glory, and to show the Pakistanis and Americans the Taliban's displeasure for every hour their demands were not met.

With an inward sigh, he almost wished the Pakistanis would not give them the codes. He could picture himself wading into the infidels with his AK-47 set on full automatic, just so the world could see what happened to those who did not follow the teachings of Muhammad.

Nayid jammed his hands into his trousers and walked down the steps to the parking lot, his head bent as he stepped by the black gash where the little girl had been killed. He could see where the asphalt had been streaked with long black stains and torn up into fist-sized chunks by the blast. *By Allah*, he thought wistfully, reliving the scene with a deep sense of gratification. *I just wish I could have seen their faces when the vest exploded.*

As he continued toward the guard shack he chuckled softly under his breath. Nothing felt more powerful than having these children's lives in their hands, being able to dispose of them in any way they saw fit. As far as he was concerned, they should be killed out of hand once their mission was completed. He knew they would only grow up to breed like so many rats, to become the enemies of the jihād and Islam. He knew it was better to kill them off while they were still too young to fight back.

Chapter 49

DAY TWENTY-ONE, 0322 HOURS
LANDING ZONE ONE
ISLAMABAD PREPARATORY ACADEMY

LIEUTENANT COMMANDER JAKE Stoneman and Petty Officer Third Class Steve Martinez crouched motionless in the dark, hunkered down on their knees on each side of the rear auditorium door; their backs pressed lightly against its wall with their NVGs flipped up and out of the way as they watched the last, and barely discernible beam flash down beside the gym.

"Well, sir," General Gray said with a quick look at President Taylor, "they're all in."

General Gray was relieved that the insert had gone off without a hitch. It had been a long time since he'd found himself in such a stressful situation, the last time he'd commanded troops in combat having been well over ten years ago, back when he'd been the regimental commander of the Fourth Marines during the second Iraqi war. Although he didn't command Hearthstone directly, his function of being their eyes and de facto intelligence officer was nerve-wracking enough. But he liked what he was doing; it sure beat the hell out of just being a paper shuffler with no more use to anyone than a wart on a pig's ass. He relished doing something concrete, something that could help Hearthstone. And besides, he couldn't wait until the team went into action. *God forgive me*, he thought apologetically, *but I've got the best goddamned seat in the house. I can't wait to see those gomers get their asses kicked big time by Hearthstone.*

General Gray smiled and turned to President Taylor.

"As you can see, sir," he began, picking up a laser pointer, clicking it on, and placing its red dot on the monitor where the thermal images of Jake and Steve were unmoving. "Jake and Martinez are still at the rear of the auditorium."

Then he highlighted the four red blobs that stood motionless beside the gym.

"The rest of the team is adjacent to the gym, here. Any minute now, Jake will confirm everyone's in place and release them to their assignments."

President Taylor felt pretty damned useless just sitting there as he watched the mission unfold, wishing deep within his psyche that he was on the ground with Hearthstone to say "howdy" and deliver justice American style, but that had been a different time and a different place. All he could do now was hope that Hearthstone was successful in taking out the terrorists and saving the children.

He also felt drained. He had spent most of his day fielding calls from senators and congressmen alike who demanded to know what the hell was going on, most of them career chairwarmers that had never spent a day in uniform and had no clue as to what was going on. The networks had also had a field day as they got in their below the belt licks.

At three o'clock that very afternoon, during a press conference, the mainstream media had gleefully trounced him every which way they could, even referring to him as the "gutless wonder". That he cared more for wanting to maintain good relations with what they considered to be a corrupt Pakistan government, rather than trying to rescue the children. But in order for Hearthstone to be successful, he knew he couldn't say a thing, much less that Hearthstone and Gabriel were going to make things right. All he could do was try to reassure everyone that he was doing all within his power to secure the release of the students, but beyond that, he could give no further details.

Back at Los Alamos, Sam and her team monitored the Situation Room's and Hearthstone's communications. Though their jobs were done for the moment, they had to be aware of everything that was going on, ready to do an emergency extraction should Hearthstone need it. Sam, who still manned the communications console—her lower lip now chewed to shreds—could see the KH-12S satellite feed as could Drs. Angstrom, Ross, and Williams, each scientist having installed a monitor next to their work stations prior to the mission. All of them had watched as the balance of Hearthstone silently announced their presence on the school grounds.

General Gray pulled his headset back into place and listened as Lieutenant Thompson called to Jake from the gym.

"Mako Six, Five. All team members are in place. I say again, all team members are in place with no sign of tangos," he whispered.

"Roger that, Five. Understand everyone's in place with no sign of tangos," Jake answered curtly, hearing the first sounds of morning come to life on the campus.

In just the last few minutes, both he and Steve had heard birds beginning to rustle about the trees as they darted from limb to limb, shortly followed by their intermittent chirps as they called out to one another. In the far-off distance they could also hear the muffled crow of roosters and barking dogs, everyone getting ready for the new day.

"Mako Five, Six, standby. Time to check in with Big Eye," Jake said.

"Roger that, Six."

"Big Eye, Mako Six. "

General Gray had heard Jake's transmission and was ready for his inquiry, having a pretty good idea what he was going to ask. He'd only seen one gomer moving around the school grounds, one that had exited the auditorium just a few minutes before, and then made his way toward the main gate. As he watched, the gomer had moved slowly from heat signature to heat signature down the line of terrorists arrayed on each side of the burnt-out guard shack. *Gotta be one of their lieutenants*, he had thought. *Making the rounds. Checking their frontal security.*

"Mako Six, Big Eye. Go ahead."

"Big Eye, request sitrep on tango locations."

"Mako Six, right now the gomers' rear and side perimeter security is unchanged. Haven't seen any movement at all except for one. Be advised one gomer exited the front of the auditorium. Looks like he's walking the line to check out their security around the guard shack. No threat at this time."

"Roger that, Big Eye. Understand one tango is checking the front perimeter."

Jake paused to digest that bit of information, but agreed the insurgent making the rounds wasn't a factor. Then he looked at Steve who, like all of the team members on the comm net, had heard what the general had to say. Steve looked back and shrugged, then flashed him a brilliant white smile through his greasy-black camo paint.

"Looks like we're good-to-go, Big Eye. Break!, Break! Mako Five, Six!"

"Six, Five," Lieutenant Thompson immediately replied.

"Did you copy Big Eye's last?"

"Roger that, Six."

Brett was ready for this, more than eager to go to work as he looked at Chief Moczarny, then Petty Officer First Class Jung-su Pak, and lastly Squealer who had all taken a knee. By their stern expressions he could tell they were ready to go. At that moment Squealer echoed everyone's sentiment when he growled in a low voice, "Time to go get some people." Unknown to him, everyone in the Situation Room and Los Alamos nodded in agreement.

"All right, execute Plan Alpha! I say again, execute Plan Alpha!" Jake ordered firmly.

"Six, Five, roger that! And good luck, Skipper."

"Good luck, Five."

Chapter 50

DAY TWENTY-ONE, 0325 HOURS
ISLAMABAD PREPARATORY ACADEMY
LANDING ZONE TWO

LIEUTENANT (J.G.) BRETT Thompson unslung his rifle and rested it on his thigh, peering into the darkness that surrounded the gym. Not hearing any sounds from the insurgents that manned the perimeter wall, he looked at the team.

"Okay, everyone knows their assignments. Make sure your thermal sights are on. We'll start out single file and keep close to the gym. Once past the gym assume a standard fireteam formation. Jung-su? You're point. I'll go second and take right security. Squealer? You'll be third and take left security. Chief, you're rear-end charley. Once we hit the cafeteria we break up into our teams. Any questions?"

Brett didn't hear any, just saw the men nod silently in agreement.

"Okay, you heard the Skipper. Let's move on out."

The men stood up and stepped off in single file with their weapons facing outboard, careful to keep a thirty foot interval between each man.

"Six, Five. We're heading out now."

"Copy that, Five," Jake answered, silently wishing them good luck.

When they reached the corner of the gym, Jung-su raised a clenched fist for everyone to stop, get down, and freeze. With everyone crouched into position—their rifle muzzles pointed outboard—he scanned the middle school quad to his right and the tennis courts to his front left. Even though Big Eye watched their every step, he knew it was better to be safe than sorry. He didn't want to end up dead like some dumbshit rookie if he'd just walked nonchalantly into the open.

Satisfied there weren't any targets to his front, Jung-su stood up and raised an open palm to indicate the area was clear. With his rifle once again raised to his cheek, he pulled the buttstock firmly into his shoulder, stepped out, and sighted through its thermal imaging scope to his front, scanning their ten to two o'clock position. When he was roughly thirty feet from the corner, Squealer and Brett stepped out with their rifles raised. Then Squealer shifted twenty feet diagonally to the left while Brett moved twenty to the right, both intent on their assigned areas of responsibility. Squealer's sector was their seven to ten o'clock position with Brett responsible for their two to five. When they cleared the gym, Chief Moczarny assumed his spot as rear-end charley, walking mostly backwards while he checked out their five to seven position.

General Gray flicked on the mute button and turned to Director Jefferson.

"Allen, get a hold of the satellite techs. See if they can tighten up the picture on the cafeteria area, but not so tight as to where we lose sight of the perimeter walls, okay?"

With no response, Jefferson picked up the direct line to the NRO and spoke softly, then nodded at what he heard over the landline.

"General, they'll bring it down to a resolution radius of three hundred feet, centered with the cafeteria buildin' to the right."

Everyone sitting at the Situation Room conference table watched, then leaned toward the monitor as the view of the school zoomed-in to a six- by five-hundred-foot rectangular image of the campus, the cafeteria building now centered on the right most portion of the screen with the northern and southern perimeter walls anchored at the top and bottom. To the left of the screen was the rear portion of the auditorium that included the steady thermal images of Jake and Steve.

"Mako Five, Big Eye," General Gray called out.

"Big Eye, Five," Lieutenant Thompson responded.

"Five, roughly eighty feet to your front right, on the field side of the cafeteria, I can see two gomers. Looks to be an M60 position. And about forty feet to their right, just south of the M60, are three more."

General Gray paused and looked closely at the monitor.

"There's five more gomers clumped together in a gaggle at the eastern tip of the changing room, to your direct left. I guess maybe seventy yards or so north of the M60."

Brett hunkered down in the open just feet from where the teams were to split-up, the four SEALs silent as tombs as they listened and breathed slowly. Then they caught the unmistakable smell of tobacco that wafted towards them on the morning breeze, the smell seeming to come from the far side of the cafeteria directly to their front.

"Copy that, Big Eye, and thanks."

Having acknowledged General Gray's report, Brett turned to Moczarny.

"Chief, Jung-su and I are going forward to take out the M60 and the second group to the south. You and Squealer break north and take care of the other five, then continue as planned."

"Aye, aye, sir," Chief Moczarny whispered, bending forward to stand up.

"Everyone know what to do?" Lieutenant Thompson asked.

They all nodded.

"Okay. Chief? Squealer? See you at the guard shack. Jung-su, take point. I'll cover the rear. Head straight down the middle between the changing room and cafeteria and we'll go to work."

"You got it, Boss."

General Gray keyed his radio when he saw the four men break up into their teams.

"Mako Six, Big Eye. Be advised the teams have split-up at the rear of the cafeteria. Team Two is turning north for the changing room, and Team One is heading further east toward the soccer field, going for the M60."

"Roger that, Big Eye. Please continue surveillance."

"Six, will do, out."

Jung-su and Brett approached the furthest corner of the cafeteria as the smell of tobacco became stronger. *What a dumbshit,* Jung-su thought scornfully. *Out here guarding the perimeter and smoking a goddamned cigarette. May as well shoot off a fucking flare! Son-of-a-bitch is just lucky the Pakistanis aren't allowed to shoot. One of their choppers with a FLIR could hit that asshole with a 30mm round from over a klick away.*

Several feet from the end of the building, Jung-su knelt down and lay prone on the deck with his body stretched out full, his rifle tucked into the crook of his arms as he inched slowly forward using his forearms and elbows. At the end of the building he stopped and silently lowered his NVGs into place. With his head no more than four inches off the ground, he edged his eyes around the corner of the building.

Immediately to his front, no more than thirty feet away, were two insurgents spread out on the ground. One obviously asleep with his raggedy-assed hat pulled low over his eyes while the other lay on his side, propped up on his elbow and smoking a cigarette. Between them rested a 7.62mm M60 machine gun with its barrel held off the ground by its bipod, its linked belt of copper-jacketed rounds inserted into its left-side feedway. As far as Jung-su could tell, it looked ready to rock'n roll. Further to his right, no more than forty feet away, were three more targets lying next to one another, their backs pressed up against the cafeteria wall with their legs stretched out full across the concrete walk, obviously asleep with their heads drooping toward their chests; all armed with AK-47s that rested lightly across their thighs.

Jung-su scrunched back from the corner and looked at Brett with two fingers raised to signify two targets, then pointed at himself to let his lieutenant know he would take care of those two. Then he raised three fingers, pointed at Brett, and made a right-handed curving motion to let his partner know he was to take out the three to the right. Being this close to their targets, he sure as hell didn't want to chance even a whisper to his lieutenant.

Both moved stealthily back from the building's corner, making sure their sound-canceling KAC suppressors were firmly attached to their rifles' muzzles. With their selector switches now set to "Semi", they raised the buttstocks to their shoulders, flipped on their laser aiming modules, and took a deep, calm breath. Each knew it was time to say "Rise and Shine" to the bad guys to help them greet the new day.

Brett patted Jung-su lightly on the shoulder. With no hesitation they deliberately stepped forward, Jung-su in the lead followed closely by his lieutenant as they turned right at the corner.

Asshole Number One was lying on the ground smoking a cigarette, all in an effort to try and keep awake. Except for the helicopter attack yesterday morning nothing much had happened, the Pakistanis content to maintain their positions behind the hedgerows on the far side of the soccer field. But he had enjoyed yesterday's attack, and had even shot several of the SSW jackals as they exited the chopper. He remembered screaming with delight when his rounds had kicked up puffs of dirt on their uniforms.

But now he was wet, uncomfortable, and bored. Occasionally he looked at the shattered remains of the helicopter where he could just make out some of the lump-like forms of dead soldiers that littered the field, and given the light breeze from the east, the stink of their bloated bodies—bodies that were covered with buzzing, overfed flies—sometimes made it to his position. It was enough to make one puke, but for now it was bearable. By Allah's grace, with morning coming soon, he hoped they would have a better idea when they could leave this godforsaken place.

The cigarette began to burn his lips, so he reached up and plucked it from his mouth, spitting out a couple of stray tobacco strands that had stuck to his tongue. As he did this he noticed some movement to his left, the hairs on the back of his neck beginning to bristle and rise.

Straining to see into the gloom, his skin crawled when he spotted two large, ghostly apparitions that had moved silently around the corner of the building, both headed his way. To him they looked like huge erect insects bearing down on him. Frozen in fear, unable to scream, the last thing he remembered was a grazing red beam of light that seared the insides of his eyes.

Jung-su held his laser steady and squeezed the trigger, sending one suppressed, 5.56mm four-gram hollow-point round straight into the fighter's left eye. When the round hit it yawed sideways, splitting into several pieces that whipped around one another like a high-speed mixer; a mixer that instantly turned the soft tissues of the fighter's brain into a mass of scrambled eggs.

Jung-su edged his rifle slightly to the right and zeroed-in on Asshole Number Two who was still asleep next to the M60, then pulled the trigger.

Brett treaded silently forward, making a beeline toward the three remaining targets, his sight lined up on the nearest bad guy. The insurgent, however, must have sensed that something was wrong and jerked awake in confusion, grabbing for his AK. But Brett was a tad faster as he calmly pulled the trigger three times.

His first round hit the insurgent fumbling with the AK-47 just below the bridge of his nose, shattering his upper jaw as the round plowed its way through his head and lodged in the base of his skull. His second target was hit in the upper side of his neck, the round ripping through his throat and larynx. His third target was hit squarely between the eyes, the 5.56mm round drilling a small neat entry hole—half the diameter of a dime—dead center in the middle of the fighter's forehead that passed on through his skull, blowing off a baseball-sized chunk of bone from the back of the jihādist's head.

Two hundred feet to their left, Chief Moczarny and Squealer quickly dispatched their own targets. In less than five minutes, ten bad guys were down with only forty more to go.

"Mako Six, Five," Lieutenant Thompson whispered softly over the dead Taliban fighters. "Five tangos down. Now proceeding to the southern perimeter wall."

"Five, Six. Understood, out."

Not ten seconds later, Jake received a second call.

"Mako Six, Four," Chief Moczarny grumbled.

"Four, go ahead."

"Ditto, five tangos down. Now heading for the northern wall."

"Roger that, Four. Good luck."

Jake looked at his watch and knew that his men had made good time, and had been lucky so far. *Real lucky!* None of the Taliban knew they were on the school grounds and he just hoped to god it stayed that way. He didn't like the idea of him and Steve having to pull a "John Wayne" on the auditorium. Too much risk for the kids and teachers, much less to themselves. So Steve and Jake continued their lonely vigil, chafing at the bit. All they could do was wait until the teams had cleared the perimeter.

Chapter 51

DAY TWENTY-ONE, 1740 HOURS
THE SITUATION ROOM
THE WHITE HOUSE

"MAKO FOUR, STAND fast and freeze! Stand fast and freeze now!" General Marion Gray shouted.

For the last twenty minutes General Gray, President Taylor, Allen Jefferson, and Steven Clarke had watched with gruesome fascination as each team made their way relentlessly down the opposite perimeter walls, watching as they paused roughly every forty to fifty feet—sometimes further and sometimes shorter—as their thermal images merged with those of the terrorists. Then, after just a few brief seconds, the teams moved on, silent as nighthawks as they glided effortlessly through the morning's dark air toward the western perimeter of the school.

The men who sat in the Situation Room knew all too well the terrorists would never again move, having just been terminated with extreme prejudice compliments of Uncle Sam. But as General Gray watched Team Two approach the northern corner of the elementary school quad, he was surprised to see a new image suddenly appear out of nowhere. An image that had moved out from the quad's northern wing of classrooms, and it wasn't the gomer completing his rounds at the front of the school. *Son-of-a-bitch must have been asleep! Or doing something in one of those goddamned classrooms!* he thought angrily.

"Mako Four, Big Eye! And don't respond back!" Gray continued in a strained voice. "I've got a new gomer making his way toward the northwest corner of the elementary quad. Son-of-a-bitch just came out of nowhere. He's less than sixty feet from the corner and should approach your position in the next ten to fifteen seconds."

Chief Petty Officer Walter Moczarny and Petty Officer First Class George Tolman immediately dropped to the ground, not daring to move a muscle.

When told the direction of the threat, they turned toward the quad while the chief keyed his transmitter in silent acknowledgment. Even though the distance was short, less than forty or fifty feet, the chief didn't want to take any chances. He tapped Squealer on the chest and pointed at himself with a raised finger, then pointed at Squealer with two fingers to indicate he was to take the second shot.

The chief hastily looped the rifle sling around his left forearm and settled into a modified sitting position, his sight picture steadied up on the front corner of the building. Taking a deep breath, he slowly let it out and held it. Not three seconds later, through the grainy-green image of his scope, he saw a leg, immediately followed by a body, as it stepped around the quad's corner.

The insurgent, short and thin, stood no more than five-foot-five and had a dense black beard that almost obscured his face. The fighter, dressed in a billowing, long-sleeved shirt sloppily tucked into baggy trousers, had an AK-47 gripped loosely in his hand.

The chief slowly squeezed the trigger. A split second later his rifle fired with a barely noticeable coughing sound, the butt of the rifle smacking softly into his shoulder. Not half a second later he heard the muted thump of Squealer's rifle just above his head.

The chief's shot caught the insurgent several inches below and to the right of his collarbone, the round drilling its way through the asshole's upper chest and exploding out his back. Squealer's shot took the target in the left temple just above the ear and exited the right side of the fighter's skull. Even though Squealer had aimed at the insurgent's forehead, the impact of the chief's shot had caused their target to spin wildly to the right, his temple exposed for a perfect deflection shot.

Thrown violently backward by the impact of the rounds, the fighter's lifeless arm inadvertently flung his AK-47 high into the air where it came down and banged noisily on the dirt.

The chief and Squealer kept their sights on their target and followed him to the ground, just in case they needed to administer a coup de gras, but no additional shots were needed. After a couple of seconds, they both breathed a sigh of relief. The AK must have been set on safe. If not, they were sure it would have fired when it hit the ground.

With a final look for any signs of life, Squealer smiled. *Damned nice shot if I say so myself. Straight through the fucker's x-ring.*

With their target down, they stood upright beside the perimeter wall, their backs pressed gratefully against its cool surface as they paused to listen, waiting to see if any of the dead fighter's buddies had heard the AK-47 hit the ground. Ten seconds later, satisfied they were in the clear, they continued their journey that would take them to the most northwestern point of the campus.

"Big Eye, Mako Four," Moczarny whispered after he had taken a couple of steps.

"Mako Four, Big Eye."

"Thanks for the heads-up, and scratch one more tango by the way. Guess we owe you a cold one when we get back."

General Gray smiled.

"Make that a six pack, Four. Samuel Smith's to be exact, and we'll call it even."

"You got it, sir," Chief Moczarny replied, smiling as he signaled for Squealer to take point.

At the rear of the auditorium, Jake and Steve had also monitored the transmissions between Mako Four and Big Eye. When they'd heard an unknown bad guy was headed for Team Two's position, they both assumed the worst was about to happen.

Without a word said, each had dug deep into their cargo pockets and extracted two M84 flash-bangs, ready to perform a breach operation into the rear of the auditorium should all hell suddenly break loose. With one of the grenades gripped tightly in his hand, Jake took the other and slipped it in the top pocket of his ballistic vest. Then he had a sudden thought and reached for the door, gently twisting its knob. To his complete surprise the door was unlocked, the knob turning easily in his hand. He pulled the door open no more than an inch or two to make sure it wasn't shackled, and then quietly closed it. After the door latch reengaged, he felt like slapping himself for stupidity. *Figures! This just gets better and better. Stupid fucking ragheads must feel pretty secure in there. Should have tried the damned thing earlier!* If he had, they wouldn't have had to spend the time rigging the door with explosives. When Jake heard the bad guy was down and that Team Two was back on track, he relaxed into the wall and shrugged at Steve. Steve just grinned, but didn't say a thing.

President Taylor sat motionless staring at the monitor, his elbows planted on the conference table with his chin cupped in his hands, not having moved since the operation had begun; his coffee cold and forgotten. He could also feel a pressure building deep within his chest as if he'd been thrust straight down into the deepest recesses of the ocean. He knew that the most dangerous part of the operation was just minutes away, the actual storming of the school and, hopefully, the rescue of the children and teachers. *Goddamn this is draining,* he thought as he mouthed a silent prayer for Hearthstone.

Not five minutes before, he had heard General Gray ask Jefferson to once again contact the NRO, to have them shift the satellite visuals from the eastern half of the campus to the western half. When the adjustment had been made, the main entrance to the auditorium and bombed-out security shack were now centered on the screen's image, with the top and bottom portions still anchored by the northern and southern perimeter walls. General Gray had requested the adjustment since both teams had moved so far west they were in danger of dropping off the monitor.

With its new positioning, the Situation Room watched as each team made their assigned turns at the northwestern and southwestern corners of the school, both teams stealthily making their way along the western perimeter wall towards the guard shack. In their wake the academy's northern, southern, and eastern perimeters were now devoid of human life, littered with the bodies of thirty dead Taliban terrorists.

"Mako's Six, Five, and Four, listen up," General Gray announced. "Be advised the gomer who was checking out the front perimeter is heading back to the auditorium. It also looks like he stirred things up a bit, so be careful. These guys look to be awake."

In acknowledgment, the overhead speaker crackled to life.

"Six."

"Five."

"Four."

Chapter 52

DAY TWENTY-ONE, 0355 HOURS
THE GUARD SHACK
ISLAMABAD PREPARATORY ACADEMY

NAYID ZIKARI CURSED as he stumbled his way across tree roots along the western perimeter wall, but was pleased that most of the men were awake when he crouched down beside them, their positions given away when he could hear them speaking in low tones or by the glowing ends of their cigarettes. When he asked them what they had seen of the Pakistanis, he had received the same answer. Nothing. Everything was quiet.

Those few he found asleep he had kicked roughly in the backs of their heads, watching as they scurried out of his way like ground crabs with their arms raised like claws. He told them if he ever found them asleep on sentry duty again, he would personally have their heads spitted on wooden stakes as a lesson to the other men.

But overall he was pleased, and Hammid had done everything he could have wished. Hammid had two men, plus himself, stationed inside the destroyed shack with the balance of his fighters placed at strategic positions along the broad expanse of the western perimeter. Just before he had left, he heard Hammid order the two fighters inside the shack to relieve the guards stationed at the northwestern end of the school.

At the end of his tour, Nayid made his way back to the auditorium. He knew he needed to check the other perimeter walls, in particular the M60 machine gun position on the far side of the cafeteria. Mahmood had told him this was where he expected the main thrust of any future Pakistan attack to occur, probably by another airborne assault with helicopters coordinated with an attack on the front gate.

He also made a mental note to double-check on Akbar and Yardan, to make sure those two idiots were still at their post and awake. But before he did that, he couldn't think of a better time to get acquainted with the young American girl. He knew that once everyone was up and about his chances of taking the girl would be slim. With that thought in mind he massaged his groin, smiling in anticipation of what was to come.

Nayid walked through the foyer and entered the main auditorium where the sewer-like smells hit him like a brick wall. With a disdainful look at the rows of sleeping, unclean infidel children, he saw that his fighters were still at their posts. He knew they had been up for close to twenty hours, but they seemed to be alert and awake. One sat on a metal folding chair at the rear of the stage in front of the curtain, tilted back with his AK-47 slung across his lap as he stared sleepily at the teachers sprawled at his feet. Three more guards stood sentry in the main hall itself. Two in the aisle to his left and one to his right up near the stage, each trying to keep their eyes open as they trudged silently up and down the carpeted aisles with their rifles carried indifferently in their arms.

The students, for the most part, were asleep; slumped over at weird angles with the older children's wrists still zip-cuffed behind their backs. Some had even lowered the seats of adjacent chairs in an effort to lie down.

Chapter 53

DAY TWENTY-ONE, 0400 HOURS
ISLAMABAD PREPARATORY ACADEMY

AT THE MOST northwestern corner of the school, Chief Petty Officer Walter Moczarny and Petty Officer First Class George Tolman moved soundlessly into some thick hedgerows that grew parallel to the wall. They had seen two thermal images lying quietly on the ground suddenly roll over and stand up no more than sixty feet to their front. As the Taliban fighters jabbered away in low voices, they began to walk toward their position. After several paces, the one to their right stopped and lit a cigarette, the flame of his lighter briefly illuminating a rugged, bearded face. Now each time the son-of-a-bitch took a drag off his cigarette, the bad guy's thermal image bloomed brightly within their scopes.

"Mako Four, Big Eye!" General Gray announced abruptly. "I've got two gomers headed your way!"

"Big Eye! We got 'em spotted, out!" Chief Moczarny whispered. "Squealer, go to NVGs."

In unison they snapped down their goggles and turned off the thermal imaging function of their scopes.

"Let 'em come to us," Moczarny said. "I'll take the one on the left, you take the one to the right."

Squealer didn't reply; he just pulled his rifle up and sighted down the length of its barrel.

"Once they're down we'll need to move quicker down this line. With the assholes up and walking around, our best bet is to just wade into them. They'll probably think we're one of them anyway. When we reach the front gate we'll dig in and wait for the LT."

"Got it, Chief."

Thirty seconds later, they stepped carefully onto the pathway and made their way around the two lifeless bodies, ignoring the dark mass of blood that pumped freely from their heads. When Squealer passed by the target he'd taken out he paused, then crushed out the fighter's cigarette with the toe of his boot. *Guess nobody ever told this shithead that smoking was bad for your health,* he thought, his face devoid of any emotion.

"Mako Six, Four. Two tangos down. Now heading for the guard shack. We oughta be there in just a few minutes," Moczarny whispered as he made his way slowly down the front perimeter wall, his rifle raised while he methodically scanned the area to his front.

"Roger that," Jake answered. "Mako Five, you copy Four's last?"

Brett and Jung-su had just made their own turn at the southwest corner of the school adjacent to the faculty parking lot. Brett thought the three insurgents they'd almost tripped over were probably in the middle of introducing themselves to Allah, asking where the hell their seventy virgins were. They had seen the fighters sleeping in a copse of trees and the bad guys never knew what hit them. They had just pumped a couple of rounds into their heads as they glided on past. When Brett heard Jake's call, he kneeled in position while Jung-su posted himself as security.

"Six, Five. Affirmative. Three more tangos down. We're roughly sixty feet south of the main gate."

"Okay, Five, understood. Time to check in with Big Eye, out.

"Big Eye, Mako Six. We need a sitrep on the remaining tangos."

General Gray had waited for this call. He'd watched as both teams had taken out another five gomers on their way to flank the security shack, the teams now within striking distance of the front gate itself. *Only five more to go before they can assault the auditorium,* he reckoned.

"Mako Six, Big Eye. From what I can see, there's three gomers inside the security shack with two outside. Maybe ten, twenty feet to the north standing near the entry gate. They haven't moved in the last minute or so. I recommend Team Two take out the gomers by the gate, and Team One take out the ones inside the shack. Looks to me like One can approach from the south and slip around the corner, over."

"Big Eye, copy that."

Jake paused to think through the general's recommendation, visualizing the layout of the school that was now more familiar than the back of his hand. He had to agree with Gray's recommendation.

"Big Eye, Six. I concur. Mako's Five and Four, listen up! Go with the general's plan. Five, you'll be lead. Do you copy?"

"Six, Five. I heard that, out."

"Four, this is Five. When you hear two clicks take out the tangos in the driveway. Once they're down make your way to the auditorium and secure the front. We'll clear the shack and meet up with you there. Just give us a minute to get into position."

"Five, Four, understood."

Squealer and the chief settled in quietly and got good sight pictures on their targets, waiting for the lieutenant's signal.

Not eighty feet from Team Two's position, Brett peered through his NVGs at the single-storied hut less than forty feet to their front. Then he flipped up his NVGs and looked to the right—a frown momentarily creasing his face—surprised to see the first hint of dawn beginning to lighten the eastern sky. *No more than an hour, hour and half 'till sunrise.* He knew the longer it took to clear the main gate, the more likelihood their being spotted by the bad guys, or by the Pakistani troops he was sure had the school under surveillance with their own night vision gear. *So, time to get a move on lieutenant.*

Still situated next to the western wall, surrounded by low hedges and a stand of scraggly trees, Brett turned to Jung-su.

"Okay, we'll make our way up to the right corner. I'll take point. Once we're in position I'll signal the chief to take out their targets. When they're down, we go in and take care of business. Got it?"

"Got it," Jung-su said.

"Once done, we haul-ass to the auditorium. Okay?"

"You betcha, Boss."

Brett and Jung-su made their way toward the rear corner of the guard shack, bent over as their boots made no more than low squelching sounds on the damp earth, then skirted a large eucalyptus tree where they carefully pushed aside several of its low-hanging branches. When they made it to the rear of the building, they pressed their bodies flush against its southern wall and slid silently to their knees.

"Auto," Thompson whispered.

Without comment, both men flicked their rifle selector switches from "Semi" to "Auto". Now, as long as the trigger was pulled, the rifle would spit out a continuous stream of rounds.

Brett and Jung-su sat silent as they listened to muffled voices that came from within the hut, accompanied by the rattling around sounds of what seemed to be some pots and pans. Without warning, something big and metallic suddenly crashed to the deck, shattering the stillness of morning. Banging around as if kicked.

Scared shitless and taken by surprise, Jung-su and Brett felt their hearts lurch within their chests, wondering what the hell was going on. Then they heard some muffled laughter answered by what they recognized to be angry Pashtu curse words. All Brett could think was, *Jesus Christ! What the hell was that!* As his heartbeat finally calmed down to no more than two thousand beats per minute, he thought again, *One of those assholes must have dropped a big fucking pot or something! Probably trying to make tea! Clumsy goddamned bastards!*

While the insurgents babbled away, Brett poked his head around the building and looked down its front. Just four feet from where he kneeled was a large shattered window, followed a little further down by the jagged edges of a blown-out door. Moving his eyes to the right, he could see the other two fighters standing casually by the security pole, both insurgents looking curiously at the shack as they said something to one another and laughed.

Brett slowly pulled back and caught Jung-su's eye, then pointed at himself with a raised single digit to let his partner know he would take point. With a deep breath, he silently keyed his mic.

Within seconds, a couple of muted coughs came from their right. As Brett watched, the two fighters standing next to the security pole suddenly pitched over and fell hard to the tarmac, their weapons clattering noisily on the black asphalt driveway. Brett and Jung-su—primed and ready to go—edged their way around the building's corner, then walked rapidly down to the blown-out entrance door and stepped inside.

With their targets down, Chief Moczarny and Squealer immediately pulled out of position and hauled-ass to their left, dodging between the parked cars as they made a beeline for the main entrance to the auditorium. Not five seconds later Brett and Jung-su also hauled-ass, less than thirty meters to their rear.

"Six, Five!" Lieutenant Thompson said breathlessly, his boots pounding a rhythmic cadence on the hard surface of the parking lot. "Be advised the perimeter is secure! Both teams now heading for the front entrance to set our charges!"

Jake, having monitored the teams' communications, was well aware of what was going on.

"Five, Six, copy that! Let me know when the charges are set!"

"Will do, Six!" Lieutenant Thompson answered as he bounded up the auditorium steps and slid in next to the chief.

"How goes it, Chief?" he whispered, his chest heaving from the mad dash across the lot, then he felt something like sticky-thick sludge soaking through his trousers. With a brief look down, he saw what appeared to be a huge pool of congealed blood that covered the concrete entryway. Then the smell hit him. An overpowering sickly-sweet, rotten smell that kicked in his gag reflex.

"Jesus Christ, Chief!" You smell that shit? Where's it coming from?"

The chief looked at his lieutenant with an inward sigh.

"Well, sir, to answer your first question, just peachy-keen. Couldn't be better. And the answer to your second question is lyin' right over there," he added with a quick jerk of his head to the side.

Four bloated corpses, stacked on top of one another like railroad ties, were lying not twenty feet from where they kneeled. The bodies dressed in black suits riddled with bullet holes and covered with rivulets of dried blood. Their arms and legs splayed out stiffly to their sides, looking more like dead bloated cattle that had sat out too long in a West Texas summer sun.

Through a thick swarm of huge, blue-green bottle flies that feasted on their rotting flesh, Brett could see the stomachs of the bodies had split wide open, their intestines spilled onto the concrete walk.

"Reckon those guys were security guards or somethin, LT," Moczarny said matter-of-factly. "Probably here to protect the Pakistan president's kids. Not too pretty to look at when they sit out in the sun all day. Get kinda ripe, if you know what I mean."

The chief smiled broadly, his teeth standing out like miniature ivory piano keys in his black, grease-stained face when his lieutenant continued to gag.

"Aw, c'mon, sir. Don't let those boys bother you none. You just gotta learn to lighten up a little and smell the roses, so to speak. I haven't had this much fun since Kandahar. This is just like strolling through Central Park poppin' these fuckers. And you gotta admit, it sure was nice of 'em to get all bunched up in this here place.

Surrounded by these walls so we could get at 'em better."

Brett lowered his head, still aware of the noxious smells, but he couldn't help but smile. *Leave it up to the chief to find the one silver lining in this operation.*

"Okay, Chief. But right now we gotta rig this door!"

"You got it, sir!" Moczarny said, and then he turned and pointed at Squealer. "Right security." Then he pointed at Jung-su. "Left security. Me and the LT will set the demos."

With nothing further said, Squealer moved fifteen feet to his left and took up a kneeling position behind one of the pockmarked planters, doing his best to keep upwind of the dead presidential guards. Jung-su moved the same distance to the right and scrunched up behind a second planter.

With their security in place, Brett and the chief pulled their demolition rucksacks over their heads and began to set out the small, conical-shaped demolition charges.

Chapter 54

DAY TWENTY-ONE, 0420 HOURS
MAIN AUDITORIUM HALL
ISLAMABAD PREPARATORY ACADEMY

NAYID ZIKARI SILENTLY made his way down the aisle and stopped next to the exhausted American girl. He could tell that she was asleep. Her dark eyelashes were closed and her head rested against the back of the chair with her mouth slightly parted. *Yes,* he thought again, *she is very beautiful.* He couldn't help but feel his manhood swell again in anticipation of what was to come. All he could picture was this young, nubile girl nude and subservient beneath him with her creamy thighs spread wide to receive him.

Nayid reached over and gently began to stroke the girl's long dark hair, but after just a couple of strokes, her eyes popped open and she let out a blood-curdling scream, a scream that shattered the calm of the auditorium. Shocked by her outburst, he jerked back as the infidel continued to scream at the top of her lungs, her face screwed up into a stark picture of revulsion.

Angry that he had tried to show compassion to the infidel bitch, Nayid slapped her hard across the face, choking off her screams as her head snapped violently to the side. Now quiet, the girl continued to lie there, curled up into a tight ball with her knees pulled to her chest, whimpering and snuffling as a small streak of blood slowly dripped from the corner of her mouth. At that moment he lost whatever remaining control he had. *How dare this infidel resist me! I will teach her the ways of Islam and how a woman should please a man!*

With his hand raised to strike her again, a hard small body suddenly slammed into his side, knocking him into the opposite row of chairs. Taken by surprise, and grunting from the impact, he lost his grip on his AK-47 that fell noisily to the floor. With a look of astonishment, he realized the young boy who sat next to the girl had flung himself bodily into him. Scrambling to his feet—nursing a throbbing pain in his side—he saw the infidel was sprawled lengthwise across the girl's lap, squirming from side to side as he tried to stand up.

With a roar of anger, Nayid roughly grabbed the boy's hair and dragged him into the aisle. When the boy flopped to the floor, he slammed the infidel's head hard against the floor again, and again, and again, all the while screaming out Pashtu curses.

Exhausted, he finally stood upright and kicked the boy squarely in the mouth with his steel-toed boot, breaking the infidel's jaw with a distinctive snap and littering the floor with several of the boy's teeth. As the semiconscious boy groaned and bled from his mangled mouth, Nayid looked at the girl with a maniacal grin splashed across his face.

"This is what we do to nonbelievers," he said hoarsely. "For those who resist our will and laws."

Reaching behind his back, he slowly pulled out a large razor-sharp knife, its bluish-steel blade hissing like a snake as it rasped against its worn leather sheath. He enjoyed watching the girl's terrified eyes as they focused on the blade, the blade reflecting shards of light from the muted overhead lighting.

As the girl watched in disbelief, Nayid dropped to the floor and planted his knees roughly in the boy's back, then grasped the infidel's head and pulled it up and back with his blade pressed hard against the boy's throat. With one deft stroke he slowly drew it across the exposed flesh, slicing open the infidel's throat from ear to ear as one would do a sacrificial goat. Nayid drew back as dark fountains of arterial blood splurted across the aisle.

When the blood flow had lessened, he pressed the boy's head firmly to the floor and waited for him to drown in his own blood—grinning as the infidel's body bucked beneath him like a wild horse in its death throes. When the boy no longer moved, he cleaned his bloody knife on the infidel's shirt and sheathed his blade.

Horrified by what she had seen, the girl lunged out of her chair and tried to run further down the seat row, but Nayid was quicker when his hand shot out and grabbed her long hair—twisting it around his fist into a tight knot—and jerked her back. As the girl squealed in pain, now surrounded by the screams of all of the other children within the great hall, he pulled her into the aisle and began to drag her up toward one of the offices. Not thirty feet from the foyer he heard his name called out from below.

"Nayid! What in the name of Allah is going on?" Mahmood shouted, standing at the lip of the stage with his hands cupped around his mouth, wearing his camouflage jacket in preparation to check the perimeter walls.

Nayid snapped the girl's head sharply to the side.

"Nothing, Mahmood! I'm just going to teach this infidel whore the proper way to show respect for her betters!"

Mahmood lowered his hands and smiled. He knew exactly what his lieutenant had in mind and saw nothing wrong with it. Infidels had been placed on this earth to do the bidding of Allah's faithful, and to pleasure them with their bodies when need be.

"Do not take too long teaching her *respect*," Mahmood yelled with a laugh deep in his throat. "We need to check our fighters. When you are done, give her to the guards. So they too can show her how to be respectful."

Nayid looked at the sniveling girl and cruelly tugged her head back up.

"That I had already planned to do! But this should not take too long! I think twenty minutes should do it!"

"More like three I would think!" Mahmood shouted with another laugh, motioning for him to carry on.

"Well, you heard my commander, little one," he said as his rotten breath washed over her. "Time for me to teach you how to respect the faithful. And when I am done, you can show the same respect to the rest of our fighters."

Nayid yanked her back to the front and resumed his walk up the aisle.

The guards tasked with watching the students looked expectantly at one another, smiling in anticipation. They had heard Mahmood and Nayid talk, and now looked forward to their own turn with the young, infidel American whore.

Chapter 55

DAY TWENTY-ONE, 0427 HOURS
THE AUDITORIUM ENTRANCE
ISLAMABAD PREPARATORY ACADEMY

"MAKO FIVE, THIS is Six!" Lieutenant Commander Jake Stoneman almost shouted, wondering what the hell was going on. Just seconds ago it sounded like everything had gone to shit-in-a-handbasket. All he could now hear were the muffled shouts and screams of what seemed to be every kid inside the school pounding through the door.

Up until now everything had been going to plan, better than he could have hoped. Almost too good. He'd just keyed his mic to have Brett blow the main doors when all hell seemed to break loose. Now, with all this shit going on, he knew their job had just become a hell of lot harder. *Jesus Christ! Every asshole in that place has gotta be awake!* With a questioning look at Steve, Steve just looked back with a blank stare, shaking his head as if to say, "Beats the hell out of me, Boss". *Well, goddamnit to hell, something bad is going on in there.*

"Six, this is Five!" Lieutenant Thompson answered, also wondering what the hell was going on, nervous with the distant screams that reverberated through the auditorium doors. Not two minutes before they had finished setting their complement of charges and had expected Jake's order to blow the doors. All four team members psyched up and ready to enter the building, aligned on both sides of the entrance doors in their breach positions, flush against the building's walls with their NVGs flipped up and out of the way with their rifles raised in the assault position.

"Five! I don't know what the hell is going on! But blow the doors in ten seconds! I say again, blow the goddamned doors in ten seconds!"

"Six, Five! Roger that! Blow the doors in ten seconds!"

"Copy is correct, Five!"

"Okay, Chief, you heard the man!"

"Got it, sir!"

Moczarny let go of his rifle, letting it hang muzzle down across his chest, and quickly double-checked two electrical wires connected to a small detonator he held in his hands, a detonator that looked like a pair of oversized pliers. He knew when he squeezed the handles an electrical charge would shoot down the bundled wires and set off the charges.

At the rear of the building Jake and Steve were ready to go, standing motionless with their backs pressed against the wall waiting for the seconds to count down. Steve had already pulled out two M84s with the pin pulled on the one in his right hand that held its safety spoon firmly in place. The second flash-bang he held in reserve in his left, just waiting for Jake to pull open the door.

Jake could feel that familiar icy calm flow throughout his body, just as if he were on some knoll sighted-in on a bad guy with his Mark-107—the screams of the children no longer a part of his consciousness. Right now he was totally focused on the mission and wouldn't let any distractions blunt the killer instinct that surged within his chest.

"Fire in the hole!" he heard shouted through his earpiece.

As far as the chief was concerned, there wasn't any need to be quiet anymore. When the assholes heard the charges go off, they would know that something bad was in the compound. Something bad that was coming to get them. He squeezed down hard on the handles.

A millisecond later the charges exploded, shooting three-foot-long tongues of yellowish-red flames out towards the parking lot, the building shaking as if it were caught in a small earthquake. The charges, designed to bore pencil-thin streams of superheated gasses through the thick steel door frames, sprayed the interior of the building with molten cores of liquefied metal, followed immediately by the doors as they slammed their way across the foyer.

Squealer and the chief, engulfed by swirling clouds of whitish-gray smoke, quickly bulled their way through the jagged, blown-out opening and searched for targets. Jung-su and Brett quickly surged from behind, peeling off to the left and right in search of their own.

When Jake heard "Fire in the hole" he jerked open the door. As soon as the door opened, Steve popped the safety spoon on the first grenade and, hearing the snap of the igniter, slid the M84 hard down the linoleum-tiled hallway. As the grenade skittered its way down the long passageway, its path marked by a smoky-white trail, a distant rumble shook the building. *Doors blown!* Jake thought.

Without thinking, Steve shifted the second M84 from his left to his right hand, pulled the pin, popped the spoon, and chucked it after the first. When he pulled away from the doorway he hesitated. He had seen a raggedy-assed bad guy wearing a dark camouflage jacket stumble out of an office at the end of the corridor.

Mahmood, braced against the opposite wall with his arms outstretched, looked down in disbelief at the grenade that sizzled at his feet, and then dully spied a second one quickly coming his way. As if in a daze, he looked further down the hall and saw a soldier's body framed in the rear doorway, his mind trying to comprehend the ghostly countenance of the black, grease-stained face that stared back at him.

Steve knew the son-of-a-bitch would take the brunt of the first grenade. *Hope it blows your balls off,* he thought briefly. Then, not able to stop himself, and knowing he had a few more seconds before the first grenade exploded, he pursed his lips and blew the ragheaded piece-of-shit a quick kiss. With his head pulled hastily back, Jake slammed shut the door.

Mahmood stood frozen like a chunk of petrified wood, staring dumbfounded at the grenade that lay at his feet, his numbed brain barely having time to register that this was not a normal grenade, at least not one he had seen before. Instead of round and bulbous and painted dull-green, this one looked more like a short piece of pipe with brown bands that encircled its top and bottom. As his bowels voided in fear, soaking his trousers with runny waste, the first grenade exploded, his thoughts confused as to why his fighters who manned the perimeter had not sounded the alarm.

A brilliant flash of bright-white light instantly filled the corridor, a burst of light that exceeded over one million candle power of illumination. With his eyes painfully seared shut as if his head had been thrust into a thick bolt of lightning, Mahmood felt his eardrums shatter caused by the mind-numbing explosion of well over two hundred decibels of sound that accompanied the flash, a sound many times louder than if one were standing next to the most powerful clap of thunder or having a .44-caliber magnum pistol fired next to one's ear. The effects more than doubled within the tight confines of the hallway.

Lifted up bodily by the concussion, Mahmood was blown backwards through the plate glass office door as blood spilled from his mangled ear canals. He never heard the second grenade explode.

When Jake heard the second grenade go off, he jerked open the door. As Steve hauled-ass through he followed closely behind, their boots crunching on shattered glass that now littered the hallway. When they reached the area where Steve had seen the fighter, Jake glanced briefly to his right and registered a brief snapshot of a grungy, bearded terrorist lying prostrate on his back. The fighter unconscious and covered with shards of broken glass while a small pool of blood gathered around his head. *One less shithead to worry about,* he thought as they continued to jog slowly down the corridor.

With the stage less than eight feet to their front, Jake knew they needed to clear the area as quickly as possible, to take down the bad guys before they had a chance to spray down the kids. Their best offense was speed, to catch the insurgents with their dicks in their hands and to pump as many rounds as possible into their raggedy-assed bodies.

He also worried about the Pakistanis. He knew they had to be going apeshit by the explosions that had wracked the school, desperate to know what was going on with Chutto's sons. He also knew, if he were in their shoes, he'd sure as hell be preparing to go over there and find out. *All we need now*, he thought, *is to have a combat platoon of Pakistan infantry poking their noses into our business.* So speed was paramount, but he didn't think the Pakistanis could get their shit together for at least another thirty minutes, and most likely needed President Chutto's authorization to go in. So maybe they had an hour. But Hearthstone needed to move fast. He knew they couldn't take that kind of a chance.

In the foyer, Chief Moczarny saw three targets through the haze of smoke, two of them blown backwards against the far wall that separated the foyer from the main auditorium—their bodies jumbled about at odd angles, either dead from the blast or knocked unconscious—and a third bad guy that lay crumpled up in the corner; but this guy was very much alive as he numbly brought his weapon to bear.

With an instinctive lurch to the side, the chief tried to bring his own rifle around, but before he could fire he saw the insurgent's head snap back hard against the wall, his forehead drilled with a neat red hole. Two more quick impacts blew off the entire left side of the fighter's skull, his mutilated head jerked around like a puppet on a string. With lifeless fingers, the bad guy dropped his AK-47 to the floor and slumped sideways against the wall, his journey marked by a smeared trail of blood behind his head.

The chief quickly recovered and looked over his shoulder. Lieutenant Brett Thompson stood no more than six feet to his right and calmly pumped a final round into the dead fighter's head. With a grim nod of approval, he ran up to Brett and slapped him on the back.

"Thanks, LT! But now we gotta haul-ass!"

Without a word said, both teams ran across the shattered foyer to their assigned entry doors that led into the main hall: Brett and Jung-su flush against the wall next to the left-side entry door with Chief Moczarny and Squealer taking up opposite positions to the right. When both teams were in place, they turned and faced inwards, slapped fresh magazines into their rifles, and charged their weapons. All in preparation to storm the main auditorium.

Jake stretched an arm across Steve's chest, bringing them both to a halt just short of the hallway's corner that spilled onto the stage. Now flattened against the corridor's left wall, he edged his eyes around the corner—ignoring the bodies and pleading eyes of the teachers that lay on the stage—totally focused on locating targets while he scanned the immediate area to his front. Then he shifted his gaze further into the main hall over a sea of students hunkered down behind their chairs. He immediately spotted two insurgents in the right-hand aisle just a little up from the stage, both armed with AK-47s as they desperately tried to find cover.

Jake couldn't help but smile. Both of these guys looked stunned and scared shitless as they swiveled their heads to stare at the blackish-white smoke that gushed through the upper foyer doors, and then back at the stage area where the M84s had gone off. He could tell they were all fucked-up and had no clue what they were supposed to do.

He spotted two more targets to his left, one standing up like a dipshit in the left-hand aisle up close to the stage, and another one way the hell up the aisle not fifteen feet from the foyer. But this guy stood motionless with his arm wrapped tightly around the throat of a young girl, trying to use her body as a shield for whatever was going to come his way through the foyer doors. All he could see of the girl was long dark hair and that she was wearing a dress while she screamed and jerked her body from side to side in a futile attempt to get loose, clawing at the insurgent's head with her nails.

When Jake pulled back from the corner, a slight movement to his left caused him to freeze. Another bad guy was on the stage not twenty feet from where he stood. He had completely missed the son-of-a-bitch! At first he could only see the heels of boots, but then he watched as the fighter partially rose up, rolled over, and flopped behind a teacher who was lying parallel to the stage; the bad guy resting his AK-47's barrel across the teacher's stomach that effectively created a living, breathing, sandbagged position courtesy of the hostage. *Only problem this fucker has is now I can see his whole side.*

Jake looked at Steve.

"Okay, Steve, here's the picture. We've got five targets out there. One on the stage using a teacher as a sandbag. I'll take him out. There's another one in the left-hand aisle up close to the stage. You take him out. There's two more in the right aisle, but I don't think we can get at 'em from here. Too many kids in the way where they're crouched down. We'll wait on them until the rest of the team comes in. There's one last target further up the left-hand aisle near the foyer holding a girl hostage. Again, we wait on that one. Don't want a round going through his back and hurting the girl. When the rest of the team comes in we go to work. Got it?"

"Got it, Boss," Martinez said, his face a blank mask.

Not half a second later, Jake and Steve heard the stuttering, crackling bark of AK-47 automatic weapons fire fill the auditorium. With a quick look around the corner, Jake watched as Jung-su and Brett made their assault into the main hall, emerging from the drifting smoke that clogged the right-hand foyer door.

With the bad guys' attention riveted on Jung-su and Brett, Jake skooched quickly around the corner and brought his weapon to bear on the sandbagged fighter, his shot lined up as the red laser dot wavered on the bad guy's temple. At the same time Steve stepped to his right, sighted-in on the fighter standing in the left-hand aisle up closest to the stage.

Jake's target, seeing some movement to his right, looked over and stared—his eyes wide with shock—then opened his mouth to shout a warning.

Jake gently squeezed the trigger, his round striking the son-of-a-bitch in the right side of his forehead. Above him Steve took his own shots, catching his target just after the fighter began to fire wildly across the seat rows at Jung-su and Brett. With a quick glance up, Jake saw Steve's target crumple to the floor, obviously deader than shit.

Back up near the foyer doors, Jung-su and Brett were greeted by a wild fusillade of AK-47 automatic weapons fire when they stormed into the hall, four rounds snap-cracking past their heads and plowing into the masonry wall behind them. With nerves of steel, they both continued their relentless march toward the stage, concentrating on the two bad guys at the far end of the aisle, each Taliban fighter trying their damnedest to hide behind a row of chairs. With his rifle sighted-in thirty meters to his front, Jung-su blanketed out the screams of the kids when he saw one of the insurgents fumbling desperately with his rifle, looking as if he were trying to clear a blockage. He could tell these guys were scared shitless when they stupidly stood up and looked wildly about, probably hoping for help from some of their buddies they thought still guarded the perimeter walls; fighters they didn't know were already dead. As far as these two knew, they were firing at what they thought to be demons from hell, demons that had emerged like silent death from the smoke-filled foyer.

With his sight steadied up on the target closest to him, Jung-su double tapped his trigger and sent two rounds streaking down the aisle. One round ripped through the center of the bad guy's chest and punched a gaping hole through his back. The second round plowed into his throat. With a shocked look of disbelief, the fighter was smashed back hard against the stage wall. Jung-su saw his second target had cleared the blockage to his AK, but before the insurgent could fire, he again double tapped his trigger, striking his target dead center with two shots to the chest.

Brett, still to the rear of Jung-su, heard the distinctive bark of AK-47 fire erupt from their right front. With a quick turn to his right, he scanned the rows of chairs before him. All he could see were kids screaming and yelling for their lives, most of them flat on the floor using their chairs as shields. *Good! Keeps 'em out of the way.*

Looking further over the expanse of chairs, he spotted a lone fighter in front of the extreme right-hand portion of the stage, wildly firing his weapon over the rows of kids. He laid his sights on the insurgent, but before he could pull the trigger his target was blown sideways to the right, hit by at least three rounds that smashed him to the floor. Wondering where the good guy fire had come from, he looked toward the stage and saw Steve raise the smoking muzzle of his rifle toward the ceiling.

With a brief wave of acknowledgement, Brett looked to his front but couldn't see any more targets, and then he wondered where the hell Squealer and the chief had gone off to. Turning to his right, he blanched when he saw them standing in the upper left-hand aisle confronting a lone insurgent just a few feet from the foyer doors, a fighter who was using one of the female students as a shield.

When Squealer and Moczarny had burst into the auditorium, they were abruptly brought up short by a bad guy who stood firmly before them with a young girl draped across his front. They also saw his AK-47 lying on the floor behind him, too far out for him to go after it. They also saw they couldn't kill the fighter without possibly hitting the girl that squirmed within his grasp. Stopped dead in their tracks, they withheld their fire to assess the situation.

Nayid, with his forearm locked tightly around the girl's throat, quickly pulled out a wicked looking knife—the same knife he had used to slit the throat of the infidel boy—and pressed it hard against her throat, its edge puncturing her skin and causing a thin-red-line of blood to well up across her neck. The girl immediately stopped her struggles, her eyes alight with panic.

"Come any closer you black, infidel, piece of camel shit and I kill the girl!" Nayid blurted in Pashtu, staring in horror at the gigantic black man that stood before him. "And you!" he shouted at the chief who had tried to move over to get a better angle of fire. "Stay where you are! Come any closer and the girl dies!"

Squealer took a couple of steps back and ignored the firing in the hall. Both he and the chief knew the other team members could take care of the bad guys they'd seen. With a cold smile on his face, Squealer locked his dark-black eyes on those of the Taliban fighter.

"You kill the girl, asshole," he said agreeably in Pashtu, "then you're dead meat."

Nayid arched his brows, surprised that the infidel black knew their language.

A few seconds later, from his lower periphery vision, Squealer saw the opening he needed. The girl, in her struggles to free herself, had managed to slide her body off to the side that exposed the lower portion of the insurgent's body. He knew the old shithead standing there had no idea he was now in a world of hurt.

Squealer slowly lowered his rifle as if in defeat, maintaining eye contact with his target while he let the muzzle of his rifle casually point down, its laser aiming dot pointed at where he thought the son-of-a-bitch's balls ought to be. With a smile that crinkled his lips, and still looking his target dead in the eye, he pulled the trigger—the M4A1 rifle spitting out one 5.56mm round that blew straight through the jihādist's right testicle and passed on through his nut sack.

Nayid's eyeballs almost burst from their sockets. With a shrill scream, his mouth flecked by red spittle that bubbled down his chin, his fingers opened and dropped the knife to the floor. Then he pushed the girl to the side and desperately clutched at his shredded groin, slumping backwards onto his ass as blood gushed between his fingertips.

Squealer and the chief stood stock-still and looked indifferently at one another—their eyebrows raised questioningly—and then back down at the Taliban asshole, hoping the son-of-a-bitch bled out. Then they allowed themselves a brief smile at the fighter's antics as he rocked back and forth on the blood-soaked floor.

At that moment they both check-fired, deciding not to place a round through the fucker's head. They knew the skipper would just love to have a little heart-to-heart chat with this guy.

Chapter 56

DAY TWENTY-ONE, 0427 HOURS
THE SITUATION ROOM
PRESIDENTIAL PALACE

PRESIDENT ASSIF CHUTTO sat slumped like a slab of beef over the conference table, still wearing the same old sweat-stained suit he had put on the previous morning, his face stubbled with short dark whiskers while he rested his head wearily on his forearms, having finally succumbed to the stress of the last twenty hours.

Bluish-gray wisps of cigarette smoke lingered in the Situation Room's air, and the table on which he rested his head was strewn with overflowing ashtrays, half eaten plates of food, discarded plastic water bottles, and stained diagrams of the Islamabad Academy. Not an hour before kitchen stewards had tried to clear the mess from the table, but Chutto, irritated by their intrusions, had angrily ordered them from the room.

Along the far wall a monitor glowed dimly with the front entrance of the auditorium centered on its screen, but only shadowy dark shapes could be seen of the school grounds, the result of the Taliban having blacked out every external light on the campus the previous evening.

Prime Minister Syid Buledi—his stomach clutched in protest—poured what had to be his twentieth cup of bitter tea, stirring in some cream and sugar while he made his way back to the conference table. He saw Mustaffa Kardar, the president's Director of Security, sitting several chairs to the right, trying to sleep with his chin tucked into his chest.

Syid had chosen to stay by the side of his president during these stressful hours, his brow creased with concern as he looked at his friend. Late last night he had tried to get Assif to return to the presidential quarters to get some rest, telling him that his constant presence in the Situation Room was not needed. But Assif had flatly refused, insisting he needed to be close to the communications equipment so that he could keep up-to-date on what was happening at the school. Syid knew better than to argue; he would have felt just the same if it had been his own sons being held hostage; he couldn't have left and gone to bed either. He also knew that his president had less than four hours to respond to the Taliban demand for the release of the PAL codes.

If the codes were not released, then the leader of the militants would kill more students, with more bomb vests and useless deaths for the news media to broadcast around the world. Maybe even the deaths of Chutto's own sons. But he was the only member of the Security Council who knew that President Chutto had earlier decided to release the codes, having convinced himself that Director General Pasha, along with the ISI, could locate the warheads before they could be used. He did not believe this for a second, but he knew his objections would be futile.

With the cup poised in front of his lips, he flinched when a burst of white light flashed across the conference room's monitor, immediately followed by what sounded like the distant rumble of thunder. Unsure of what had just happened he stood transfixed, wondering what in Allah's name he was seeing. When the picture slowly settled down and returned to normal, he could see the auditorium doors had been blown wide open, with dirty-gray smoke billowing onto the parking lot through a jagged opening where the doors had once been. What his eyes couldn't believe was what appeared to be a small squad of armed soldiers storming through the opening, briefly illuminated by the muted internal lighting of the auditorium as they vanished into the interior.

"Assif! Assif!" he shouted, his forgotten tea dropped to the floor, shaking President Chutto roughly by the shoulder. "Wake up! Wake up!" he yelled, his eyes rigidly locked on the scene before him. "Something is happening at the school!"

Chutto jerked up in confusion and looked at Syid, at first not remembering where he was. When the cobwebs cleared from his mind, he followed Syid's outstretched arm that pointed at the monitor. He could see the entrance to the auditorium was swathed in curling wisps of dirty-whitish smoke accompanied by the sharp crack of automatic weapons fire. Finally grasping what had occurred, he gripped the edge of the table and pushed himself erect, muttering, "Allah, no! Allah, no! Please! Please! May the prophet protect my sons!"

President Chutto turned on Syid and Mustaffa, the deep furrowed lines of his face stretched taut with anger.

"What damned idiot authorized an attack on the school? Who could have done this? Those orders were to come only from me!"

At the end of the conference table the military communications phone suddenly came to life, warbling a soft tone accompanied by a flashing red light that identified the active line. A line directly linked to Colonel Solangi's headquarters.

President Chutto stared dumbly at the instrument until he realized the call had to be coming from the colonel. Frantically, he reached for the phone, but fumbled with the receiver and dropped it to the floor. Swearing out loud, he grabbed the damned thing by its coiled cord and pulled it back up to the table.

"Colonel Solangi! Colonel Solangi! Is that you?" he screeched.

"Yes, Mr. President!" the colonel barely choked out before he was abruptly cut off.

"Why are you attacking the school? Who in Allah's name gave you the authorization to do this?"

"Mr. President!" Colonel Solangi shouted back. "I did not authorize an attack on the school! We don't know who has done this! You have to believe me in this, Mr. President!"

Solangi was scared. He knew that his career, and maybe even his own life, was now fully at stake. Thinking quickly, he grasped at the first straw that came to mind.

"Sir, maybe it was the Americans! Maybe they found a way to enter the school without us knowing! Maybe they parachuted in!"

"I don't give a camel's fart in hell what you think, Colonel!" President Chutto screamed into the receiver. "It was your job to make sure the perimeter was sealed! No one in and no one out! Remember? So you better find out what's going on and protect my sons!" Then he continued in a more chilling, softly cadenced tone, a tone that sent shivers down the colonel's spine. "Or it will be your ass, Colonel! Do you understand my meaning?"

"Yes, Mr. President! I understand!" Colonel Solangi stammered, feeling as if he had to throw up. "Sir, I have a platoon of special forces getting ready to head over to the school! I will lead them personally! I've also alerted another company to mount up in trucks should they be needed!"

"You do that, Colonel! But if one fucking hair of my sons is hurt you will pay, sir! Personally! Do you understand?" President Chutto shouted, ending the call by throwing the phone across the room.

Chapter 57

DAY TWENTY-ONE, 0437 HOURS
ISLAMABAD PREPARATORY ACADEMY
THE AUDITORIUM MAIN HALL

THE SILENCE WAS deafening. The last echoes of AK-47 weapons fire smothered in the dim recesses of the hall. Wisps of gunsmoke drifted slowly toward the ceiling while the acrid smell of cordite blanketed the air like leaden clouds.

Lieutenant Commander Jake Stoneman casually slung his rifle and stared grimly at the three hundred terrified students spread out before him, students who had been confined to their seat rows for the last twenty hours. He watched as many of the children tentatively raised their heads to see what was going on, and then popped them instantly back down in fear, looking more like startled African Meerkats who sensed danger and sought safety within their burrows. Then they cautiously raised their heads again to look about with anxious eyes, not wanting to focus any attention upon themselves, but curious and bewildered. Most of the other students cringed backwards whenever a Hearthstone team member walked nearby, not knowing if these strange, fearsome-looking creatures were friend or foe.

Jake grimaced when he saw two young Pakistani boys sitting on the floor below the stage, their arms bound tightly behind their backs as they recoiled from his gaze, each strapped into a bomb vest primed and ready to go, the same kind of vest that had been worn by Emily. *Well, those two gotta be the Pakistan president's boys,* he thought, trying to rein in his raging emotions. Then he shook his head in frustration, not able to understand how the Taliban—who believed the Qur'an to be the one true word of God—could twist their religion into such a perverse caricature of itself that it allowed for the killing of innocents, especially young kids. All in the name of jihād. But deep down inside he knew what it all boiled down to; he had seen it played out over and over again—the assholes just couldn't tolerate other religions or less-strict interpretations of the Qur'an, and would do everything in their power to enforce their beliefs on others. He also knew they didn't give a shit as to how they did it.

Jake tore his gaze from the boys and looked at the trussed bodies that littered the stage. He could almost taste the outpouring of relief from the thirty-odd teachers lying there as silent tears flowed unchecked down their cheeks. Many more were still in shock, fearful of his presence, not wanting to meet his eyes, not daring to believe their worst nightmare may have come to an end. And lying near to them in congealed pools of rust-colored blood were the grim reminders of the insurgent attack, the four members of the Pakistan president's Secret Service detail who had been lined up and ruthlessly executed.

With a quick look up from the teachers, Jake saw Brett and Jung-su stooped over the Taliban fighters shot down in the right-hand aisle, busily going through their pockets to look for anything of intelligence value. Shifting his gaze to the left, he saw Squealer squatting on his knees in the left-hand aisle speaking quietly to the sobbing girl he and the chief had rescued, patting her gently on the shoulder. Then he watched as Squealer slung his rifle and gently scooped her up in his massive arms as if she were no more than a feather. The girl instantly wrapped her arms tightly around his neck, hanging on for dear life, not wanting to let go, her face buried deep within his broad chest as he began to walk slowly down the aisle. Even at this distance he could see the moisture that glistened on Squealer's cheeks.

Hearing screams from further up the aisle, he looked toward the foyer doors. With a quick smile, he saw Chief Moczarny riding herd on the slobbering little shit Squealer had shot in the nuts. *All right, time for our final chore,* Jake thought, amazed that Murphy hadn't fucked-up the operation. *Then we can get the hell out of Dodge.* But he still had a major concern regarding the Pakistanis, and knew how they were going to react to the explosions and automatic weapons fire that had rocked the school. They would send troops over as soon as they could. So Hearthstone had to move fast and interrogate any of these jihādist rat bastards still lucky enough to be alive. With a final look around the great hall, he slowly raised a hand to his mic. The last thing he wanted to do was shout out loud and scare the hell out of the kids.

"Chief? Any idea where we can interrogate any of these guys still lucky enough to be alive?"

"Sir," Moczarny said, his brow furrowed in thought, "we've got three down in the foyer. One's dead, but the other two are just knocked out, I think. Plus this sumbitch I'm standing over. Instead of hauling these guys down there to the stage, I think we oughta have our little chat up here in the foyer. That way we can keep a lookout for the Pakistanis."

"Okay, Chief, you got it. Haul that dickless piece-of-trash back up to the front. We've got another one, I think their head honcho, down in one of the offices back here. If he's still alive, I'll have Steve and Jung-su haul him up to where you are."

"You got it, sir," Moczarny replied, grabbing the still blubbering Nayid roughly by his shirt collar and dragging his sorry, bloody ass up the aisle.

"Jung-su!"

"Yes, Boss!"

"I want you and Steve to check out this guy in back. If he's still alive, haul him up to the foyer."

"You got it, Boss."

Jung-su made his way down the aisle and bounded onto the stage, headed for the back office.

"Steve, make sure you guys check out that back office real good. That's the guy that probably had the remote detonator. See if you can find it. We don't need any accidents right now, but make it quick. I've got a bad feeling we're starting to run out of time."

"Will do, Boss," Steve said, turning to catch up with Jung-su, his boots crunching noisily on the shards of glass that covered the floor of the hallway.

"Brett, you go with the chief. I'll meet up with you in a few minutes."

"I heard that, Skipper," Lieutenant Thompson said, standing up from the dead fighters. "And just to let you know, these guys didn't have dick squat on them. No ID, no papers, no nothing."

"Okay, understood. Now get moving, I'll see you in a couple of minutes."

"Squealer?" Jake asked, looking down the left front row of seats where he was gently setting down the girl. "Do me a favor. When you're done with the girl, we've got the Pakistan president's kids over here strapped up into bomb vests. Get 'em out of those vests and then shitcan the vests. Okay?"

"Aye, aye, sir," Squealer said, looking down the row of chairs and spotting the two young boys sitting on the deck.

"When you're done with that meet us up front."

"Yes, sir."

As he headed toward the boys, Squealer looked at the teachers tied up on the stage floor.

"What about all those folks, Skipper?"

Jake could see the concern on Squealer's face, the original plan to let the Pakistanis free the hostages. But when he looked around the hall, he could see that some of the older kids—their hands still zip-tied behind their backs—were already up and about, moving warily from their seat rows and standing around the bodies of the dead insurgents.

"Well, I think we're gonna to have to free some of these people after all, so they can take care of the kids and keep 'em here in the auditorium. Go ahead and take care of Chutto's boys; get 'em out of those goddamned vests. I'll try to find out who's in charge up here."

Squealer had also seen the children beginning to mill around.

"I think you're right, Skipper. I'll get those vests off the kids and head up front."

Jake nodded, then shifted his rifle to the side and kneeled by a teacher that lay at his feet.

"How ya doing, partner?" he asked with a couple of pats to the teacher's shoulder.

The teacher, he could see, was having a hard time of it. His eyes were wide and bright, and he was breathing heavily through nostrils caked thick with crusty sheets of dried mucus. The little guy had even flinched when he patted his shoulder, acting more like a beaten dog.

"It's okay, partner," Jake continued in a soft voice. "I'm not gonna hurt you, but what I am gonna do is remove that duct tape from your mouth. Now, that's gonna hurt a little bit, but once that's done I'll cut those zip-ties off your wrists, deal?"

Ned Thumel, the small, balding assistant superintendent of the school, could barely nod his head, relief filling his eyes when he realized he was going to live. He didn't have the slightest clue as to who these guys were, but he could pretty much tell they were Americans. They also looked like God's gift from hell dressed in their black-camouflaged BDUs with weapons and grenades draped all over their bodies, their faces smeared with zigzagging lines of dark and light greasepaint. He had also seen how good they were at killing, how quickly they had killed the terrorists in the auditorium. He just thanked god they were on his side.

Jake grabbed a corner of the tape that sealed the teacher's mouth shut, and then jerked his hand to the left, ripping it free. On the underside of the tape, looking as if it had been sprinkled with flecks of dark pepper, were some of the teacher's whiskers that had grown out since yesterday morning.

"Sorry about that," Jake said as the teacher grimaced in pain, "but that's the best way to get it off. Quick and clean. Now, roll over and I'll cut those zip-ties off your wrists."

"Okay," Thumel managed to croak, trying to flex his jaws and dry, cracked lips as he rolled over and held out his wrists.

Jake pulled out his combat knife and deftly slipped the blade behind the little guy's hands, quickly slicing through the nylon bindings.

"There you go," he said gently.

Then seeing the teacher was having a problem standing, he pulled the diminutive man up to his feet.

"My, God! I don't know how to thank you!" Thumel exclaimed excitedly, his legs wobbly as he tried to massage his wrists. But before Jake could cut him off, the little guy spiritedly began to describe what he and his fellow faculty members had gone through.

"These terrorists attacked us yesterday morning—"

Jake raised a hand and cut off the teacher in midexplanation.

"Sir," he began impatiently. "I'm sorry. I don't have the time to go through all of that right now. What I need to know is if you're the one in charge of the school."

"Oh! Oh, no! No, I'm not!" Thumel answered, flustered as he unconsciously picked at his stained and misshapen necktie. "I'm Ned Thumel. I'm just the assistant superintendent. Pamela Raynor is the superintendent," he said, pointing at another bound hostage near the edge of the stage. "There, that's Pamela over there."

"Okay, thanks. Now stay here and don't move. Got it?

"Oh, my! Yes! Yes! Stay here! I understand!" Thumel repeated quickly. "Don't move!"

Jake walked quickly over to Pamela Raynor and knelt by her side, going through the same routine to free her as he had with Thumel. As soon as he helped her to her feet, she threw herself into his arms, sobbing and crying. He felt as if he was clutched in a death grip when she wrapped both arms tightly around his waist and buried her face deep within his chest, saying over and over again, "Thank you! Thank you! Oh, God! Thank you!"

"Ma'am, we don't have a lot of time," Jake said, more than a little embarrassed as he reached behind his back and gently pulled her arms to his front. With her wrists still firmly held, he looked into her tear-streaked face smeared with mascara and makeup.

"Ma'am? Are you Pamela Raynor? The superintendent of the school?" he asked quickly, needing to get going with what needed to be done.

"Yes, I'm Pamela Raynor. I'm the superintendent of the school," she said, looking up at her rescuer, her hand raised to her mouth as she began to cry softly. "Yesterday was our first full assembly," she continued between sniffles. "I'm new here. Then these animals, these beasts, took over the school! They killed Bruce McAllister and all of the school guards! And . . . Oh, my God! They killed that little girl Emily!" she wailed as tears streamed down her cheeks like a broken dam, her chin lowered toward her chest as her shoulders heaved back and forth.

"Yes, ma'am, I know," Jake softly said with a quick, gentle squeeze to her shoulder. "But for now you gotta be strong, for your students and teachers. And just to let you know, all of the terrorists are dead, even those outside. Except for the ones we have up front. What I really need you to do," he continued, gently tilting her chin up and looking into her eyes, "is for you and Mr. Thumel to free the others, and to watch over the kids. Don't let them out. As I said before, we don't have a lot of time and the Pakistanis should be here pretty quick. They'll take care of you."

Then, knowing she needed something to free the others, he placed his combat knife in her hands. "Here, take this, to cut their bindings. But whatever you do, don't let anyone into the foyer. Keep everyone down here by the stage. Can you do that for me?"

"Yes, yes I can do that," Pamela said gratefully as she blankly stared at the large knife he had placed in her hands, and then back up at the tall—and she was sure—American Special Forces soldier who stood before her.

"But, please! Please, excuse me!" she said, regaining some of her lost composure. "How did you get into the building? Who are you? And—"

"Ma'am," Jake interrupted with a raised hand, "we don't have a lot of time. So, please, just do as I asked. Can you do that for me?" he asked, giving her a smile of assurance.

"Yes. Yes, of course! And thank you! But you just don't know what we've been through," she said, her voice trailing off into a whisper.

"No, ma'am, I think I do," he answered solemnly. "But I gotta go. So just take care of your kids and staff."

As he moved to make his way off the stage, Jake slowed and looked back. He could see that Pamela was still rooted to her spot, but now her shoulders were back with a glint of determination in her eyes.

"Ma'am, like I said, all of the other terrorists are dead. They can't hurt anyone now, and the Pakistanis should be here pretty soon. So just take care of your kids and sit tight. Okay?"

"Okay," Pamela murmured.

Jake took the stage stairs two at a time down to the auditorium floor and began to jog up the aisle toward the foyer. It was time to contact General Gray to see what was going on with the Pakistanis. As he continued up the aisle he keyed his mic, struggling to ignore the futile questions and frightened looks of some of the older kids.

"Big Eye, this is Mako Six."

At the sound of Jake's staticky transmission, four heads jerked up in unison around the Situation Room conference table, relief written on their faces as President Taylor, still sitting to General Gray's right, leaned forward with his fingers steepled in front of his lips; his eyes totally focused on the monitor before him. For the last fifteen minutes he had tried with all his might to see through the walls of the auditorium, to get an inkling of what was going on.

General Gray, who had nervously ripped at his fingernails since the assault had begun, eagerly bent over to respond, more relieved than he knew to finally be back in contact with Hearthstone. None of them had known how the attack had gone, only catching bits and snatches of the team's garbled communications.

"Mako Six, this is Big Eye."

"Big Eye, Mako Six. Be advised that all tangos are down with four captured. With no casualties to students, teachers, or the team during our assault. I say again, with no casualties. The auditorium is secure and we'll begin our interrogations in the next couple of minutes."

It had been less than fifteen minutes since Hearthstone had blown the doors, but to General Gray and the others it seemed as if hours had gone by. All they could do during the attack was sit mute like bumps on a log, wondering what the hell was going on. And until Jake's call, they didn't know if the students and faculty had been freed or hosed down by the terrorists. But with that one static-laced transmission, the pressure that had built within the Situation Room had been immediately released. All was now right with the world as far as they were concerned. To his right, General Gray saw President Taylor slump tiredly in his chair, murmuring "Thank God" several times to no one in particular. Alan Jefferson and Steven Clarke sported broad smiles of "Mission Accomplished" that split their faces.

"Mako Six, Big Eye. Understand that all remaining hostages and the team are okay."

"Affirmative, Big Eye. But right now we need to know what's going on with the Pakistanis. Any movement on their part?"

"Mako Six, right now it looks like they're firing up a few trucks, with what looks to be a company of troops assembling around the vehicles. But there's another group, maybe platoon-sized, that looks about ready to head out across those fields directly in front of the main gate."

With the light of dawn quickly overtaking the school, General Gray could make out the finer details on the ground, especially those of the Pakistani troops. To him they looked to be well-armed and loaded for bear.

"I suggest you do whatever you gotta do and then get the hell out. From what I can see, that platoon will be headed your way at any moment."

"Copy that, Big Eye, out," Jake ended with a silent curse.

Now he knew they didn't have as much time as he thought they had. *Time to get this whole show over with. Sooner rather than later,* he thought, steeling himself mentally for the unpleasant task he needed to do.

"Homebase, Mako Six."

"Mako Six, Homebase here," Sam instantly replied, dizzy with relief that Jake was okay.

Unbeknownst to Jake, Sam's last fifteen minutes had been pure hell, the worst fifteen minutes of her life. Not knowing if he was alive, or dead, or lying wounded on the ground somewhere within the school. She was also a little ashamed of herself, caring and thinking more of Jake than the hostages or other team members.

"Homebase, Mako Six. Just a little heads-up. You may want to crank up that NMR and have it ready to go. When we call to have you pull us out of here, there won't be a lot of time. You'll need to be ready to go fast."

"Understood, Mako Six," Sam replied as she turned and caught the eyes of Dr. Ross, Dr. Angstrom, and Dr. Williams, but she didn't need to say a thing. The Gabriel team had been ready to extract Hearthstone on an emergency basis ever since the operation had begun. She could see that her colleagues were busy with their equipment, making sure the computer was at a hundred percent. But more importantly, the electron measurement scanner that would trigger the reversal of the quantum entanglement process.

"We're all set to go here, Mako Six."

"Copy that, Homebase. See ya soon," Jake ended softly.

"See ya soon, Mako Six."

Chapter 58

DAY TWENTY-ONE, 0450 HOURS
ISLAMABAD PREPARATORY ACADEMY

LIEUTENANT COMMANDER JAKE Stoneman stepped quietly into the debris-strewn foyer and slammed shut the door. He didn't want the children or teachers to get an inkling of what was about to happen. With a quick look around the space, he saw that Chief Moczarny had forced the insurgents to sit in a line with their backs flush against the far right wall, their wrists and ankles zip-cuffed tightly together.

The chief stood to the left of the scumbags, his face dark with malice with his rifle cradled nonchalantly across his chest, the weapon looking like a toy stick in his thick arms. Brett stood to the right of the group with his weapon trained inboard, just in case their guests decided to do something stupid. Squealer leaned casually against the east wall that separated the foyer from the auditorium, his legs crossed absently at the ankles, just hoping the skipper would let him go up and kick that wannabe rapist son-of-a-bitch dead center in the crotch, wounded or not. He just couldn't tolerate what that shithead had planned to do with that cute little girl. He knew if it hadn't been for him and Hearthstone, that girl would have had a very long and horrendous night of it, and then had her throat slit when they were done with her. Jung-su and Steve were stationed outside in overwatch positions, prone behind the concrete planters on the lookout for the Pakistani platoon General Gray had warned them about.

Jake turned toward Squealer.

"Squealer, lock the doors. Make sure no one comes in from the auditorium."

"You got it, Skipper," Squealer said, pushing off the wall to secure the foyer doors that led into the auditorium. Once the doors were locked, he took a quick look through one of their glass windows just to make sure the students and teachers were still down by the stage.

Jake turned to the line of jihādist fighters and saw that Dickless, the name he'd given the insurgent that Squealer had shot in the nuts, was plunked down furthest to the left. The asshole grimacing in pain as he morbidly watched his lifeblood seep slowly between his fingers to form dark pools of blood on the floor.

Nayid was more afraid than he had ever been in his life. He didn't know who these infidel pigs were, but he was afraid. Deathly afraid. They were not like the other soldiers he had fought, soldiers that were naïve and stupid. Soldiers who had helped his fallen comrades with medical aid, food, and shelter, and who played at war with stupid rules like the Geneva Convention. These men were not like that at all, these men were more like the Taliban—ruthless, vicious, and totally without mercy. He could see it in their eyes. These were the men who now held his life in their hands.

Next in line were the two insurgents that had been caught up in the foyer blast, sitting side by side to the right of Dickless. These two appeared groggy and disoriented as they leaned over on their sides like drunks, but Jake could tell they were still cognizant when they furtively turned their heads and looked up at him from beneath their scraggly, bushy eyebrows. Their eyes almost swollen shut that had turned a deep, black, yellowish-purple color. Their faces criss-crossed with slashes, cuts, and dried streaks of blood from the lacerations they had received when the front doors had been blown.

And last but not least, the son-of-a-bitch he thought of as Honcho who sat to the right of these two. The one he was pretty goddamned sure had strapped that bomb vest on Emily and then blown her all to hell and gone. He was convinced that Honcho was the leader of this fanatical bunch of jihādist killers, given that Steve and Jung-su had found the remote detonator in this guy's office back stage. He could also see that Honcho now seemed to be fully conscious as the Taliban leader glared around the room, leaning over with a defiant, crooked smile on his face; his blood-shot eyes smoldering with hate.

Seeing these four big, tough baby killers sitting there, still alive and breathing, really pissed Jake off. But he knew he had to get a handle on his emotions. So he took a couple of deep breaths, shoved his feelings to the side, and looked over the line of Taliban jihādists.

He immediately discounted the two fighters who sat in the middle.

Those two guys are just low level troops, he thought, but Honcho and Dickless were a different matter. The fact that Dickless had had the balls to try and rape one of the female students marked him as one of their higher-ups, possibly a lieutenant or team leader. If anyone knew where the nukes were hidden it had to be Honcho, or Dickless, or maybe even both.

The way he decided he was going to play this was to start in on the two guys in the middle, the fighters who had been caught up in the foyer blast. They probably didn't know too much of anything anyway, so that made them expendable. Nothing more than training aids for Dickless and Honcho. But Jake knew he couldn't fuck around. He had to be as quick and hard and ruthless as these bastards were, and knowing what they had done he didn't have a problem with that. He'd do whatever it took to discover where their buddies had stashed the nukes. He just hoped when he was done with the two in the middle, that Dickless and Honcho would become a hell of a lot more talkative. *And who knows? Maybe I'll get lucky. Maybe one of these guys in the middle can tell me where the nukes are hidden.*

Jake stepped across the foyer and took up a position directly in front of their Taliban guests, looking down until he had their full and undivided attention.

"Now, gentlemen," he said in fluent Pashtu, the four bad guys' eyebrows lifting in surprise that the infidel knew their language, "we do not have a lot of time. My friends and I have just one question to ask. If you answer truthfully, and if we believe you, you will live. If you do not answer truthfully you will die. It's as simple as that. I'll just put a bullet through your head and move on to the next," he explained, shrugging as if he didn't give a shit.

Mahmood Tahqi, a.k.a. Honcho, hocked up a huge glob of reddish-green phlegm and spit it at Jake, hitting him on the upper right side of his ballistic vest. As the glob of spit ran down Jake's front, Mahmood strained forward and shouted at the top of his lungs, "Do not listen to this infidel pig! He will do nothing! He is bluffing! Say nothing to him or you will answer to Qudos! Allahu akbar! Allahu akbar! Allahu—"

But before Mahmood could yell "Allahu akbar" a third time, Brett slammed him full in the mouth with the butt of his rifle, knocking out his front teeth. As the Taliban leader pitched downward toward the floor, Brett grabbed him by the hair and jerked his head upright, then slammed it hard against the wall.

"Do that again you piece of pig shit," Brett hissed quietly in Pashtu, "and I'll knock the rest of your goddamned teeth out. Got that?" Then, with a disdainful flick of his wrist, he released Mahmood's hair and stepped back.

Mahmood's head slumped forward toward his chest, his jaw throbbing with blinding pain as Jake stepped in front of the first foyer guard seated to the right of Dickless. With a grim smile all for the benefit of Honcho, who now looked bleakly at him with pain-filled eyes, he clicked off the safety to his M4A1 rifle, pressed its KAC sound suppressor into the center of the fighter's forehead, and pushed his head firmly against the wall.

"Okay," Jake said. "We know your buddies stole a couple of Pakistani nuclear warheads a few weeks ago. The question to you is, where are they hidden?"

The Taliban underling looked at Jake with panic-laced eyes, then clicked his eyeballs to the left and right, trying to seek guidance from Nayid or Mahmood. When he couldn't make eye contact with either of them, he returned his swollen eyes back to his captor. Eyes that filled with tears as his lower lip began to quiver.

"Saaqhib," he stammered, lurching his shoulders forward to try and make obeisance to this infidel foreign devil that stood before him like a wrathful God. "Please! Please!" he blubbered as whitish-yellowish snot coursed from his nose and dripped onto his upper lip. "Yes! Okay! Okay! It is true! I have heard that such things were taken from the Pakistanis! Everyone has heard this! But as Allah is my witness, you have to believe me! I know nothing about them! I cannot tell you what I do not know!"

Jake pulled the trigger, his rifle coughing out one suppressed 5.56mm round—a round that punched squarely into the center of the fighter's forehead and exited the rear of his skull, the wall behind him splashed with bright, red-streaked sunbursts of blood.

As the Taliban's lifeless body crumpled to the floor, Jake softly said, "Sorry, asshole. Wrong answer."

With his lips drawn tightly into a thin white line, Jake felt absolutely no remorse for having killed the jihādist piece-of-shit. Then he shifted his stance to the right and took up a position in front of the second foyer guard.

"Okay, Tonto. Same question I asked your friend. Where are the warheads hidden?"

The second fighter didn't utter a sound, but just looked at Jake with eyes as large as baseballs. His body mute and frozen while his jaws silently worked backwards and forwards, looking more like a deer caught in the headlights of an eighteen-wheeler roaring un-checked down a country road toward him.

Jake had no pity for this shitty excuse for a human being, and had to mentally restrain himself from just lashing out and killing the bastard outright. This guy, he was sure, had absolutely no remorse for what he and his buddies had done to the school, the people and children they had killed. And, given half a chance, would've gladly strapped up more kids into those goddamned bomb vests and will-ingly set them off. Again, all in the name of jihād. But instead, he smiled cruelly into the fighter's face.

"Tell you what I'm gonna do, Tonto. I'm gonna count to three," he said, pressing the rifle's suppressor into the guard's sliced-up fore-head. "And if you haven't told me what I want to know you'll be dead, just like your buddy lying there. With your brains splattered all over that wall behind you. Do you understand?"

The fighter glanced frantically down at his dead companion. All he could see was a dark, pulpy-red-mush of what used to be the back of his friend's head. Then he looked feverishly at Jake, but he only saw death and damnation staring back at him. It was as if he had just looked into the cold, dead, unfeeling eyes of a pit viper ready to strike.

"Sir," Lieutenant Thompson interrupted in Pashtu, getting the bad guys' attention. "This sorry piece-of-trash doesn't know any-thing. Just kill him so we can talk to the other two. It would save us a lot of time."

"No! No, Saaqhib!" the fighter screamed as he glanced fearfully at Brett, then Chief Moczarny, then Squealer, and finally back at Jake, but he could see no mercy in their eyes. Just a strong, hateful resolve. "I will tell you what I know! I swear by Allah I will tell you everything!" he shouted, twisting and jerking his head about in a futile attempt to dislodge the suppressor that was pressed painfully into his forehead. "I have heard, Saaqhib! I have heard that what you seek are in the mountains near Wana!"

"One," Jake said evenly. "Which mountains near Wana?"

"Shut your mouth!" Mahmood yelled through his mangled mouth, desperate to get the attention of his fighter. "Do not tell them anything!"

Brett immediately reacted to Mahmood's shout and slammed him once again in the mouth with the butt of his rifle, shattering the remainder of the Taliban leader's teeth as he fell heavily to the floor, bleeding even more fiercely from his crushed mouth.

"Saaqhib!" the fighter screamed. He could care less about Mahmood right now as he fought for his life, his eyes totally focused on Jake's index finger, watching with mounting horror as it caressed and tightened on the rifle's trigger. "I am not sure of the mountain's name! But I think they are the Shinkai Mountains! The bombs hidden in a valley to the north of one of our training camps! But I cannot tell you the camp's name, Saaqhib! I have never been there! You have to believe me! I swear on my ancestor's graves if I knew I would tell you!" he shrieked.

"Two," Jake said, his gut telling him this guy was telling the truth.

"Oh, Allah! Allah! Help me! Help me! Please help me!" the fighter moaned, swaying from side to side as if spellbound by the music of an Indian snake charmer, his voice now hoarse and raspy, slobbering and crying as he desperately looked around in final terror. He knew he was going to die at the hands of this cursed, infidel foreign devil. Then, in an act of final desperation, he threw himself to the floor, grunting with effort as he tried to use his knees and shoulders in a vain attempt to burrow under his stunned leader's body.

Jake was surprised by the fighter's sudden move. *Damnit! I've wasted too much time on this guy!* he thought, maneuvering his rifle over Mahmood's inert body, then pressed its muzzle hard against the asshole's temple just as he turned and looked up at him.

"Three," Jake said, pulling the trigger.

Jake raised the rifle muzzle to the ceiling, his face set in a rigid, stony mask, and then he glanced at Squealer. Squealer, still standing nonchalantly by the left foyer door, just nodded in grisly approval. As far as he was concerned, the execution of those two shitheads had just been too clean and quick. They should've been made to pay a hell of a lot more. Personally, he would have strapped 'em up into their own bomb vests and told 'em to run for it.

Jake caught Brett's eye and saw him also nod. Then Brett grabbed

Honcho by the hair and jerked him off the dead fighter's body.

"Skipper," Chief Moczarny stated flatly with an indifferent look down at Dickless who cringed at his feet, "both those sumbitch's should've just told you what you wanted to know. Too bad they couldn't answer the question, but maybe dickhead here can," he said, nudging Nayid's thigh with the toe of his boot. "Betcha this guy can't wait to talk to you."

"Betcha you're right," Jake said, moving next to the chief, his attention now directed at Dickless.

"Squealer? Isn't this the guy that slit that kid's throat in the aisle? And was all set to rape the girl?"

"Yes, sir, Skipper. That's the one," Squealer responded amicably, looking down at Dickless as if he were a bug to be stepped on, wanting nothing more than to ram his rifle up this guy's ass and pull the trigger ten or twenty times. "If you want, I'd be more than happy to ask him a few questions, sir."

"No . . . no thanks. Just askin'," Jake said while he watched Dickless slowly bleed out on the floor.

"Okay, partner," he said with a tap to Dickless' forehead. "Listen up. Same question I asked your other two buddies. Where are the warheads hidden?"

Nayid, his teeth clenched tight to try and suppress the waves of pain that wracked his body, stared silently at Jake, his fuzzy brain trying to think of a way to save his life. He had just watched this infidel blow the brains out of his fellow Taliban fighters as if they were no more than vermin. But the last fighter had already told him the general location of the warheads, and he could tell that this man had believed what he had been told. *What harm would it do now to tell him the name of the camp? And the gap between the two mountains where the bombs are hidden?* he thought desperately, trying to rationalize any answer he could give this man. *And if I tell him what I know, there would still be time to move the bombs, if I can stay alive long enough to warn Qudos. Yes! Yes! That is my duty to Allah! To stay alive! And to warn Qudos about these men!*

"If I tell you what I know," Nayid spit out cautiously as he glared into the hideous blue eyes of what had to be an American standing before him, "how do I know you won't kill me anyway?"

"Well, partner, you don't. You're just gonna have to have a little faith in Allah, is all. But if you *don't* tell me what you know, your next few minutes are gonna be a real bitch. That I can guarantee."

At the end of that final statement, Jake jammed the rifle's suppressor hard into the center of Nayid's bloodied crotch, right where Squealer's round had gone through his testicle and groin. Then he shoved the suppressor a couple of inches further into the open wound, just to make the point he didn't have the time to hear any bullshit.

Nayid's lower body exploded with rippling waves of excruciating pain, his eyes wide with shock as he kicked wildly against the blood-slicked floor, all in a vain attempt to lunge away from the blinding pain being inflicted upon him by this cursed, infidel devil. But being plastered up against the wall, there was no place for him to go.

When the infidel finally withdrew the rifle from his groin, Nayid slumped gratefully onto his side, breathing heavily as waves of nausea choked his throat, his teeth having bitten through his lower lip. When he hit the floor, Chief Moczarny grabbed him roughly by the hair and pulled him back up, then planted his boot squarely in the middle of Nayid's chest and pushed him upright against the wall.

"Mako Six, Big Eye!" Jake suddenly heard through his headset, as did every other member of Hearthstone. "That Pakistani platoon is moving out now, across those fields to the west. Maybe four hundred meters from the main gate."

With a quick look down at Dickless, who was busily heaving out his guts, Jake couldn't help but chuckle when he saw a sour look plastered on the chief's face; the chief's ripstop nylon boot, still firmly planted in Dickless' chest, now thoroughly soaked with Taliban puke.

"Copy that, Big Eye. Understand the Pakistanis are on the move. Thanks for the heads-up. Break! Break! Jung-su? What do you and Steve got to your front? Got the Pakistanis spotted?"

"Boss?" Jung-su whispered. "We just picked 'em up. Coming at us in what looks to be three squads. Call it forty troops total from what we can see. Walking low and slow. Being real careful, Boss. I reckon we got less than fifteen minutes before they'll be here."

"Okay, Jung-su, standby," Jake said, glancing around the foyer at Brett, then Squealer, and then Chief Moczarny. "All right, it's time to start pulling out of here. Jung-su? Steve?"

"Yes, sir," they responded immediately.

"I'm going to pull Steve out of here first. I only want one of you left to bring out. Understood?"

"Yes, sir," they responded again.

"Brett? Squealer? You two'll be next. First Squealer, then you Brett. Jung-su? The chief and I are going to stay here a few minutes longer. I want you to cover the front and be our eyes while we try to pin down the location of the nukes."

When Nayid heard the infidels speak he was hopeful, it seemed as if they had forgotten about him for now. He didn't know what they were saying, but as long as they didn't ask any more questions he knew he would live a few moments longer.

"Then it will be Jung-su, the chief, and then myself. Understood?"

"Yes, sir," they all said.

Nayid watched the blue-eyed devil closely as he pressed something on his shoulder and spoke out loud.

"Homebase, Mako Six!"

"Mako Six, Homebase!" Sam replied immediately.

"Time to start pulling us out of here! Order of extraction will be Steve, Squealer, and then Brett. Jung-su and the chief and I are going to stay here a bit longer. We'll call when we're ready to go. Copy that, Homebase?"

"Copy that, Mako Six!" Sam replied, waving an arm frantically over her head to get Dr. Angstrom's attention. "Did you get all of that, Ted?"

"Got it, Sam. Starting the extraction sequence as we speak."

Dr. Angstrom, Dr. Williams, and Dr. Ross turned to their work. Thirty seconds later, Dr. Angstrom toggled a switch on the electron scanner to initiate the recall sequence.

"Mako Six, Homebase. Starting extractions for Steve, Squealer, and Brett. Will advise upon completion of each extraction."

"Okay, Homebase. Mako Six, out," Jake finished with a confident look at his team. No more than five seconds later Homebase reinitiated contact.

"Mako Six, Homebase. May as well keep this line open. Steve is back and we're now extracting Squealer," Sam said.

Jake, the chief, and Brett looked expectantly at Squealer, all of them anxious to see the disappearing act.

Nayid, now faint from the loss of blood, was curious as to why the infidels had turned to look so intently at the huge black man, so he too watched. Then, before his astonished eyes, the black man abruptly disappeared as if he had been nothing more than a wisp of smoke!

With a scream stifled deep within his throat, paralyzed by fear, Nayid feverishly began to mutter a Nafl salat—voluntary prayer—to Allah for the deliverance of one's soul from evil. *He had been wrong! These were not American soldiers! They could not be!* his blood-starved brain told him. He could think of nothing else other than these men were not of this earth, convinced they were not made of flesh and blood, but had to be the Shay-tan's Jinn. The *Al-'Adiyat.* The plunderers of one's soul dressed in the uniforms of his ene-my. The devil's unholy warriors the one true prophet Muhammad had cautioned were cast up from the depths of hell to persecute the faithful. Soldiers created by Shay-tan from smokeless fire and clay according to the holy teachings of the Qur'an: the true enemies of Allah.

His fevered brain now believed this with all his heart and soul. There was nothing else that could explain how these six vicious ap-paritions could have entered the compound and silently killed al-most fifty armed members of Allah's faithful, and then disappear in a cloud of smoke as if they had never existed.

Nayid moaned as he slowly rocked back and forth, continuing his fervent supplications for Allah's protection, his eyes tightly closed as he tried to ignore the pain that pulsed through his groin. He knew these fearful *Al-'Adiyat* warriors would drag his screaming soul down to hell where he would dwell forever out of the light of Allah.

"Mako Six, Homebase, Squealer's back! Now starting on Brett."

Jake nodded at Brett in appreciation. "Happy trails, Lieutenant."

Brett smiled, but before he could utter a word he too blinked out of existence.

"Boss?" Jung-su whispered. "You best hurry, sir. Those Paki-stani troops are about a hundred meters from the school. Looks like they've stopped and gone to ground to check things out, but I expect they'll be coming on pretty damned quick."

Chapter 59

DAY TWENTY-ONE, 0505 HOURS
ISLAMABAD PREPARATORY ACADEMY

AS HE LED the platoon's center-most squad toward the school, Colonel Solangi was surprised they had not encountered any enemy fire. Intelligence and overhead recon photos had shown close to forty Taliban militants manning the school's perimeter, including ten positioned on the western wall, all armed with AK-47s and possibly one M60 machine gun. He had also ordered his men to retreat if they received any fire from the militants, not to press home any kind of an attack. He did not want to be the one to place President Chutto's sons in jeopardy.

He raised a clenched fist to bring the platoon to a halt, each soldier immediately squatting down on their haunches, trying to use the low-growing bracken for cover while they kept a wary eye out to their front. Solangi feared an ambush and was uncomfortable with the silence that surrounded the academy. With his FN F2000 rifle laid across his thighs, he unsnapped the cover of his light-sensitive binoculars and a took a few brief seconds to scan the front perimeter; his gaze moving slowly from left to right, but he couldn't see any movement along the wall.

With his attention now focused on the main gate, he couldn't be sure, but in the lessening darkness of early dawn, it looked as if two bodies were lying face down on the asphalt, just behind the metal pole that blocked the entrance into the faculty parking lot. Lowering the binoculars, he briefly rubbed his eyes to wipe away some sweat that had gathered in their sockets. Even though the morning was cool, he was sweating.

With the binoculars once again raised, he concentrated on the inert bodies. *Look to be Taliban militants,* he thought. But not seeing any movement he assumed they were dead. *Who the hell could have done this?* he asked for the thousandth time. *Who the hell could have attacked the school? And why aren't the other militants guarding the perimeter trying to retake the auditorium? Why is there no rifle fire?*

Unable to answer those questions, he swung the binoculars to his right and focused more clearly on the blown-out entrance doors of the auditorium.

Chapter 60

DAY TWENTY-ONE, 0510 HOURS
ISLAMABAD PREPARATORY ACADEMY

"MAKO SIX, HOMEBASE! Brett's back with no problems!" Dr. Samantha Johnson shouted, relieved that Hearthstone was finally pulling out of the academy. "Let us know when you want the other extractions!"

"Homebase, Mako Six, will do."

Lieutenant Commander Jake Stoneman watched as Dickless prayed to his god, then tapped him on the head with the muzzle of his rifle.

"Okay, partner, we're about out of time here. One last time. I want to know the exact location of the warheads. Where in the Shinkai Mountains are the weapons hidden. Which valley?"

Nayid looked up from his prayers when he heard the leader of the *Al-'Adiyat* warriors speak, but was fearful to gaze upon the evil entity that stood before him. With visible effort, he mustered what little courage he had left, deathly afraid of what would happen to him in the afterlife.

"Oh, mighty, *Al-'Adiyat* warrior!" he croaked out loudly, trying to mask his fear. "Please do not take my soul! I beg of you! Have mercy! I wish to dwell in Allah's house forever! If I tell you what you want to know, you must promise me that I will ascend to paradise and not down into hell!"

Jake stepped back puzzled. *What the hell's an Al-'Adiyat warrior?* But if it would get him the location of the nukes, then so much the better. He would gladly send this son-of-a-bitch off to paradise. He just had to play along with this guy's fears for the moment.

"I promise you, as an *Al-'Adiyat* warrior," Jake said, thinking to use the name Dickless had called him, "if you give me the exact location of the warheads, I will send you to dwell in Allah's house forever. That I do swear."

He hoped these words of promise would do the trick with this bastard. *And besides, I was going to send this asshole off to see Allah anyway.*

Nayid could think of nothing but that he had to believe what the evil Jinn had said.

"What you seek, Al-'Adiyat, is located at the northern point where the Tipakai and Shinkai Mountains meet. There is a small cleft high up between the mountains. Very hard to see from above, but with many tunnels. What you seek are kept in the most northeastern tunnel, four kilometers north of a training camp we call Gengi Kel where our leader of the Tehrik-e-taliban, Qudos Mehsud, now trains Allah's faithful."

Nayid lowered his head, his eyes clenched shut.

"Will you now keep your promise? To send me to paradise and not to hell?"

"By all means," Jake said as he stepped back a foot, lowered the rifle's muzzle, and pulled the trigger. With a raised brow he looked at the chief.

"Beats the fuck out of me, Skipper! Damnedest thing I ever saw, though," Chief Moczarny said as he removed his helmet and scratched the top of his almost hairless head, as confused as Jake by the rantings of the Taliban lieutenant. "First time I ever heard one of those sumbitch's begging to be sent off to see Allah, but if it worked for him, it sure as hell worked for me," he finished, smiling as he pulled his helmet back on and snapped its chin strap back in place.

"Boss?" Jung-su called out. "The Pakistanis are just across the road from the guard shack. They've stopped again, no more than fifty meters to our front. Between you, me, and the fencepost, sir, I think it's time we got the hell out of here!"

"Okay, Jung-su. See you back in Alamos."

"You got it, Boss!"

"Homebase, Mako Six!"

"Mako Six, Homebase!"

"Extract Jung-su, and without further orders the chief."

"Will do, Mako Six. Extractions beginning now. We're also ready for you whenever you say the word," Sam said, wanting him to get the hell out of there as soon as possible.

"Understood, Homebase. Just one more thing to do and then I'm out'a here."

Jake slapped Moczarny hard on the chest.

"Well, Chief? I never thought we'd get the location of those nukes."

"To be honest, Skipper, neither did I."

Not two seconds later Chief Moczarny disappeared.

Jake turned from where the chief had been standing and made his way to where Honcho sat, the Taliban leader still groggy and almost unconscious. He had a couple of chores to do and only a minute or so to get them done.

"Big Eye, Mako Six!"

"Mako Six, Big Eye, go ahead!" General Gray replied.

"Got a pretty good location on the nukes. Near Wana, Pakistan. The Tipakai and Shinkai mountains. There's a small cleft where the mountains meet, riddled with tunnels. But the tunnel hiding the nukes is the most northeastern one. I say again, the most northeastern tunnel. For reference, there's a Taliban training camp four kilometers south called Gengi Kel. Recommend we get a satellite on that location."

"Mako Six, Big Eye, we copied all of that! We also think it's time for you to get the hell out of there!"

"Will do, Big Eye! I'll be gone in just a minute!"

Jake lowered his hand from the mic and looked at Honcho.

"Well, partner," he said with a look of pure contempt at the militant, jihādist killer that sat before him, "today just wasn't your day, was it."

Jake leveled his M4A1 rifle, clicked off its safety, and blew the bastard's head clean off. With his weapon clicked back on "Safe", he knew he was pushing his time envelope. It was time to get the hell out of Dodge.

"Homebase, Mako Six! Ready for extraction! Initiate at any time!"

"Mako Six, Homebase! See you in a few moments!" Sam said, completely relieved, feeling as if three tons of deadweight had been lifted from her shoulders with Jake on his way back home.

Chapter 61

DAY TWENTY-ONE, 0515 HOURS
ISLAMABAD PREPARATORY ACADEMY

COLONEL SOLANGI CREPT cautiously up the concrete steps to the blown-out auditorium doors, making sure to keep his silhouette low to the ground as he slid his way up to the left-hand side of the jagged opening. Two other Pakistani soldiers, with FN F2000 5.56mm rifles in hand, took up positions opposite from their colonel.

When they had earlier made their way past the main gate, Solangi had confirmed that the two bodies lying on the tarmac were indeed Taliban militants, both shot in the head and still slowly bleeding out. As he and his squad advanced across the parking lot, the other two squads—one to the north and the other to the south—had told him of dead Taliban fighters scattered along the entire length of the perimeter wall. To them, the school grounds looked as if a vengeful grain harvester had come through and cut down the militants like stalks of ripe wheat.

By Allah, he thought again, his nerves jittery as hell. *Who the hell can be in this building? Or, better yet, what is in this building?*

As he crept further up to the opening, he slid the barrel of his rifle fully around the corner and quickly looked inside, then froze like a chunk of stone. What had to be a foreign soldier stood silently near the far right wall less than five meters to his front, the soldier ignorant of his presence with his back turned toward the auditorium doors.

The soldier was tall, and dressed in black-camouflaged utilities, a ballistic vest, and wore a helmet with some kind of night vision device attached to its front. He also carried a short stubby rifle that looked to be a cut-down version of an M16 with a big fat silencer attached to its muzzle. Solangi also saw the soldier's index finger raised to his shoulder and pushing down on something. *A communications device?* he thought. Then he heard the soldier speak out loud in English, but couldn't make out what was being said. *Probably talking to his men.*

"Uh, Homebase? Mako Six. Just to let you know, I'm still here. What the hell's going on?"

Lieutenant Commander Jake Stoneman had a sick feeling in the pit of his stomach, and hoped that now was not the time for Murphy to fuck things up. *Shit! I knew everything was going too good!*

"Mako Six, this is Homebase! We know! We know!" Sam choked, frantic with worry. "Something's gone wrong with the scanner! Richard is tearing it apart now! He hopes it's just a burned-out board! It should take just a minute to fix, Jake!"

"Okay, Sam, understood. But I'm kinda swingin' in the breeze here, if y'all know what I mean!"

Immediately to the soldier's front Colonel Solangi saw four Taliban militants crumpled up on the blood-soaked floor, neatly aligned in front of a wall covered with bright streaks of blood sprays. Obviously dead with their ankles and wrists tightly bound.

"Freeze!" he shouted in accented English, his rifle trained on the soldier to his front, his finger gripping the trigger. "Don't move or I'll fire! And get rid of the weapon! Put it on the floor! Now!"

Jake stiffened when he heard the shout to his rear. Then, ever so carefully, as if in slow motion and not wanting to twitch a muscle, he leaned over and placed his rifle on the deck. Once back upright, he slowly raised his hands and cupped them behind his neck. When he turned partially towards the opening, he could see a Pakistani officer, a full colonel by his collar tabs, crouched down on one knee with his rifle unwaveringly sighted-in on his chest.

Well, hell! he thought quickly. *You better play this real cool, Jake! Least till that scanner's fixed! That colonel looks like one pissed-off camper!*

"Who are you? What are you doing here?" Colonel Solangi shouted. "And keep your hands up where I can see them!"

Jake turned fully towards the blown-out doors.

As he did so, Colonel Solangi saw a pair of bright-blue eyes surrounded by a face smeared with light and dark camouflage greasepaint. *This man has got to be an American! And that makes sense. This school has a lot of American students. But how the hell did he and his men get onto the school grounds? No way they could have parachuted in! Our soldiers would have seen their chutes! As would the Taliban guards!*

"Sir, with respect," Jake answered levelly as two additional Pakistani soldiers, both armed with FN F2000 rifles, entered the foyer and took up positions opposite from their colonel, "I can't tell you who I am, but I think we both had the same mission. To free these kids and the teachers. They're now free, and all of the militants are dead."

Colonel Solangi pondered this man's answer, his rifle still centered on the soldier's chest. It was true, the militants at the front of the school were dead, and none of the other Taliban who manned the school's perimeter had come to assist them. Finally, he stood fully erect, careful to keep the muzzle of his weapon pointed directly at what he had now determined to be an American commando. With a quick glance at his two soldiers, he nodded toward the foyer doors.

"Check out the main auditorium! Find President Chutto's sons! But be careful! And keep your eyes open for more commandos!"

"Yes, sir!" they said as they hustled their way into the main auditorium.

Solangi returned his attention to the American.

"Where are your men? There is no way you did this by yourself!"

Jake knew he had to buy more time for Gabriel to fix the scanner, so he lied.

"Colonel, if you would allow me, you are correct. I do have more men. Scattered in hidden positions throughout the school. All armed with automatic weapons. If you would let me contact them," he asked as he slowly lowered his arm and pointed at his mic, "I will try to call them in. But first you must give me your word as to their safety."

"Mako Six?" he heard through his earpiece. "The scanner'll be fixed in a few more seconds, so just hang in there. We'll have you out of there lickety-split!"

Colonel Solangi thought through the commando's answer. The last thing he wanted was to get into a firefight with this man and his soldiers who had wreaked such havoc among the Taliban, much less having to root them out of the school grounds.

"All right!" he said with a nod of approval. "Go ahead! Contact your men! Tell them they will be treated fairly and will not be harmed! But tell them to be very careful and no weapons. With their hands locked behind their heads. And, sir, if this is some kind of a trick, you will be the first to die. Do you understand?"

"Yes, sir, I understand," Jake replied as contritely as he could. Then he keyed his mic and spoke in a low, mumbled voice the colonel couldn't overhear.

"Yo, Sam! If that damned gizmo's fixed, now would be a good time to get me the hell out of here!"

"Jake, just hold on!" Sam replied anxiously.

Dr. Ross finally inserted a new board into the guts of the scanner, smiling as he gave her a thumbs up.

"You're on your way!" she shouted.

"Well? Are your men coming in? Answer me!" Colonel Solangi demanded. *Could this be some kind of a trick?* he suddenly thought.

The American commando didn't respond. All he did was give him a tired, wistful smile, twiddled his fingers in a small wave, and then abruptly vanished into thin air, as did his rifle and all of the spent shell casings scattered about the floor.

Pamela Raynor, still busy cutting zip-ties off the few remaining bound hostages, looked down at her hand in disbelief. The combat knife given to her by the Special Forces soldier had suddenly disappeared into nothingness.

Chapter 62

DAY TWENTY-ONE, 0615 HOURS
GENGI KEL TRAINING CAMP
SOUTH WAZIRISTAN PROVINCE

QUDOS MEHSUD LOOKED irritably at the satellite phone as it continued to ring on his desk. He had not expected to be called until just after eight, the time agreed for Mahmood to give him an update on the school, and whether the Pakistanis had agreed to release the PAL codes.

He stepped away from a small kerosene stove where he had been making some tea and saw the number displayed on the phone's screen. It was not from the Islamabad Academy, but for a satellite phone that belonged to one of his Pakistani military informants; an Air Force captain who was on the personal staff of Marshal Khattack, the chairman of the Joint Chiefs of Staff. Now worried, he quickly snatched the phone from the table.

"Qudos here!"

"Hakim! Captain Jarza! If you do not remember me, I am on the staff of Marshal Khattack!"

"Yes! Yes! I remember you, Jarza! But why are you calling me on a satellite phone? You know the military and Americans can intercept these calls!"

"Hakim! Yes, I know that! But I needed to call you quickly! I thought you should know that some unknown force stormed the school early this morning and freed the hostages! And killed all of your fighters! The Army and SSW, as we speak, are occupying the school grounds!"

Qudos stood riveted to the floor, trying to comprehend what Jarza had just told him, then slumped heavily into his chair. It felt as if someone had just kicked him in the stomach, his plan to secure the

PAL codes now crumbling to dust in his hands.

"When did this happen? Who took over the school?"

"I am not sure, Hakim! Even the military does not know! All I know it was not the Army, or SSW, or ISI. Most think it must have been the Americans, but there was no way they could have entered the school without being seen. All we have is a video showing the front doors to the auditorium being blasted open with four or five soldiers entering the building, and then the sound of rifle fire for several minutes. After that there was only silence. When the army finally entered the school they found all of your fighters killed!"

Qudos took several deep breaths and slammed his fist against the desk.

"What of President Chutto's sons? And the hostages? Were my fighters able to kill them?"

He wanted the president to suffer, as he now suffered with the loss of his men and the ability to obtain the PAL codes.

"Hakim, the boys live and are now back at the palace, closely guarded by the Secret Service. The rest of the hostages also live and have been freed."

"But what of Mahmood? My second in command?"

"Hakim, he too is dead! From what I've heard, Mahmood, along with Nayid and two other fighters, were found with their arms and ankles bound. Each with a single bullet hole in their heads. It looks like whoever took over the school had the time to interrogate them."

Qudos jerked erect and looked around his empty, sparse head-quarters; both Mahmood and Nayid knew the location of the tunnel complex and where the nuclear warheads were hidden. At that moment he knew he had to move the bombs as quickly as possible, the only problem was that he could not move them that day. He did not have the mules or trucks to transport them. It would take at least a day, if not more, to have trucks or mules travel to the camp. He also had to think of a new place where they could be hidden. But once the bombs were safe, he was sure that he and the pilot Zalmay MahMund could come up with another plan to obtain the PAL codes.

"Okay, Jarza, I understand! You have done well! If you learn of anything else call me immediately! Allahu akbar!"

Chapter 63

DAY TWENTY-ONE, 0710 HOURS
THE SITUATION ROOM
PRESIDENTIAL PALACE

"COLONEL SOLANGI! PLEASE! Please, come in and have a seat!" President Assif Chutto exclaimed, a forced smile on his face as he greeted the colonel. Prime Minister Buledi, Marshal Khattack, Director General Pasha, and Mustaffa Kardar eyed the colonel critically as the president shook his hand.

Prime Minister Syid Buledi thanked Allah with all his might that Assif's children, and all of the remaining hostages, had been rescued unharmed. The nightmare of the academy finally resolved. But many questions remained not only in his own mind but in that of President Chutto's as well, eager to learn more of what had happened. But most importantly, who had defied the president's order and made an assault on the school?

Less than an hour before, an Mi-171 helicopter had ferried the president's sons back to the palace, accompanied by an overzealous contingent of ten armed Secret Service agents who had surrounded the boys like a protective pack of wolves. The boys, greeted not only by their father, President Chutto, but also by their hysterical mother, were whisked immediately to the presidential palace infirmary for complete checkups. Once the president had been assured that his sons were uninjured, he had left them in the care of their mother and returned to the Situation Room, expectantly awaiting the colonel's arrival.

Colonel Solangi followed President Chutto to the conference table and sat down in the chair indicated by the president. While Chutto took a seat next to his own, the colonel looked at the other persons present in the room, uncomfortable by the grilling he knew he was about to receive. He knew he could not tell them of the American commando he had confronted in the school's foyer, or how the commando had simply disappeared like a ghost into thin air, as did all the evidence of the commando's men who had killed the Taliban militants. They would think he was crazy and not believe a word he said. That he was just trying to cover his own ass for having allowed an assault on the school. Even he found it difficult to believe what he had seen with his own eyes, questioning his own memory of the event.

Immediately after the commando disappeared, he made sure that President Chutto's boys were taken as quickly as possible to the soccer field and choppered back to the palace. At the same time, he had another contingent of troops free the remaining hostages while the balance of his soldiers scoured the school grounds for evidence that could identify the nationality of the commandos. Commandos that had silently killed fifty heavily-armed Taliban militants.

Solangi was sure they had been Americans, but he needed proof to back up his claim. He knew that would be the first question asked of him by the president and his advisors. But the only thing his men had discovered were dead Taliban fighters scattered along the perimeter walls of the school, most with a single bullet hole in their heads. The majority of shell casings found were from the militants' 7.62mm AK-47 assault rifles and M60 machine gun, all of these located in the area of the school's cafeteria on the eastern border of the school, the vehicular entrance gates, the parking lot, and within the auditorium itself. The only other shell casings found had been 9mm in caliber, most probably from the presidential guards' Uzi submachine guns.

He had even thought that forensics could possibly identify the caliber and make of rounds found in the dead Taliban bodies, to at least confirm they had been manufactured in the United States. He clearly remembered the cut-down version of the M16 he had briefly seen on the foyer's floor. So he had ordered his medics to perform field autopsies on several of the militants who had been shot in the chest. But after digging through numerous entry wounds, no bullets had been found. It was as if the rounds had never existed. The Taliban fighters seemingly killed by phantom projectiles that had carved deep and bloody paths into their bodies.

"So, Colonel!" President Chutto began with a slap to the table.

"Tell us what happened! Who was it that defied my order and attacked the school, and put the lives of my sons in jeopardy?"

Colonel Solangi looked bleakly at his president, not knowing how to answer, but answer he must.

"Sir, I am sorry. We have no idea who freed your boys or the hostages. In speaking with your sons and the school staff, including the superintendent of the school, it seems a force of five or six commandos, nationality unknown at this point, gained entry into the auditorium after killing the militants who manned the perimeter walls. A force that totaled forty insurgents, sir. Then they killed the remaining ten militants who guarded the hostages. How they did this, sir, we have no idea. There was no way they could have penetrated our cordon around the school. All I can think of, Mr. President, is that they somehow parachuted onto the school grounds, escaping detection not only by our own soldiers, but by the Taliban as well," he ended weakly.

President Chutto looked skeptically at the colonel, his eyebrows raised questioningly. Even he knew the possibility of soldiers parachuting undetected onto the school grounds was impossible, as impossible as just five or six commandos killing fifty armed Taliban fighters.

"Then how the hell did they get out, Colonel? Did they just vanish into thin air like ghosts?" he asked sarcastically, his temper beginning to boil. He knew if commandos could enter a compound surrounded by close to a thousand troops, and then disappear without a trace, they could easily penetrate the palace and possibly assassinate himself and his family.

"Mr. President, I can't answer that question at this time," Solangi replied, unable to tell the president he was closer to the truth than he knew.

"Then find out, Colonel! I want to know how anyone could have gained access to that school, much less leave undetected! Do you understand?" President Chutto demanded, slamming his fist once again on the table. "I want answers! And I want them now!

"Yes, sir! I will, sir!" Colonel Solangi answered, knowing he was boxed into a corner with no way out.

Epilogue

DAY TWENTY-TWO, 0322 HOURS
GENGI KEL TRAINING CAMP
SOUTH WAZIRISTAN PROVINCE

CROUCHED SILENTLY IN the dark, listening hard—beneath a cloudless sky ablaze with stars framed by a quarter moon forty degrees off the horizon—Lieutenant Commander Jake Stoneman dared not move a muscle as he squatted on a filthy, debris-strewn dirt path between two cinder-blocked structures. Structures that shielded his body from eighteen similar dwellings within the confines of Gengi Kel.

Hearthstone, when they had studied the KH-12S satellite imagery, had determined these were the barracks that housed the fighter recruits and training cadre within the camp itself, with the centermost structure on his side of the road being what they thought to be the Taliban headquarters. North of the compound, less than one hundred meters distant, was a relatively flat, rock-strewn piece of land with a raised wooden platform in its center, probably used for early morning physical conditioning they had thought; and adjacent to this plot of dirt was what looked to be an obstacle course with logs set at waist height with climbing ropes and other obstructions used for training. Further north still was an entanglement course with eight corridors strewn with barbed wire and fire-blackened pits.

Five hundred meters to the south was a primitive shooting range, and roughly sixty meters to the east were three additional cinder-blocked structures surrounded by a chain-link fence topped with coiled razor wire. The only thing their high resolution photos had shown at any given time was up to twelve children who occasionally played outside the buildings. Most appeared to be very young, ranging in age from only seven to twelve years old, the children overseen by armed Taliban fighters.

At first, Hearthstone had thought this smaller compound was used to house the families of the militants assigned to the camp. But after careful review of subsequent photos, taken at different times and angles during the day, no women were ever to be seen; only the children who played in the dirt yard of the enclosure.

Chief Moczarny had told Jake that it looked exactly like a suicide bomber training compound he'd seen in Khowst, Afghanistan, up near the northwestern Pakistan frontier.

"Those little assholes are worse than the older assholes," he had stated bluntly. "Once they're all brainwashed up with that jihādist shit, they can mostly waltz into any army compound and set themselves off. May not be their fault," the chief had reasoned, "but when you're dead, you're dead. No two ways about it, sir."

Sixty feet directly to Jake's front, invisible if he hadn't been wearing his NVGs, was Steve and Squealer set up in overwatch positions at the end of the barracks; both down on one knee as they scoped out a building ninety feet to their right they thought to be the Taliban headquarters, then confirmed several seconds later when they saw four armed fighters grouped around its front door.

Two of the guards stood in the road with their AK-47s slung casually over their shoulders, smoking and talking in muffled tones, their images blooming within their M4A1 thermal scopes whenever one of the bad guys took a drag off his cigarette. The other two guards were plunked down on a wooden bench by the front door, their legs stretched out full with their heads lowered toward their chests, most likely asleep they imagined.

"Skipper," Squealer whispered, "we've got four tangos outside their headquarters. Maybe thirty meters to our right. Two awake, two asleep. No threat at this time."

Having noted the location of the Taliban guards, Squealer and Steve continued to search for additional threats as they peered intently up and down the dirt paths between the buildings to their front, left, and right. All three team members dressed in their black-camouflaged BDUs with camo greasepaint smeared over their exposed body parts, wearing the same equipment and carrying the same weapons they had used for their assault on the Islamabad Preparatory Academy.

"Mako Six, Big Eye," General Gray called out.

"Big Eye, Six, go ahead," Jake whispered.

"Ghost Rider Flight is now on station circling one hundred and fifty miles due north at forty thousand feet."

"Roger that, Big Eye. Be advised, no hits on our detectors in the camp."

Each Hearthstone team member carried an ultrasensitive, compact radiation detector that could sniff the slightest readings of shielded radioactivity out to six hundred feet, but so far Jake and his team had scored no hits. For the last forty-five minutes they had scoured the confines of the camp trying their best to find any latent readings from the nuclear warheads, but none had been found.

"Acknowledged," Gray answered.

General Gray, ensconced in the Situation Room with President Taylor, Steven Clarke, and Director Jefferson, was the liaison between Hearthstone and Ghost Rider Flight. Even though Los Alamos, Hearthstone, and the Situation Room were on the same comm net, communications with Ghost Rider Flight was different. It required a high-frequency radio and there had been no way to jury-rig Hearthstone's commo gear to allow them to speak directly with the aircraft. General Gray performed that function with a separate radio link patched into the Situation Room from the Watch Command Center.

Ghost Rider Flight—two B2-A stealth bombers that had gone wheels up out of Anderson Air Force Base, Territory of Guam, eleven hours earlier—had traveled over six thousand nautical miles nonstop at a cruise speed of five hundred and sixty knots with one en route midair refueling just east of the Maldives, an island group located in the northern Indian Ocean. Ghost Rider Flight having arrived on station in just the last five minutes.

Ghost Rider One, the lead bomber, was commanded by Colonel Bill Evans, call sign "Papa Bill". Colonel Evans, a tall, slim, wiry-built individual of fifty-five years with short wispy gray hair, intelligent blue eyes, and sporting a pencil-thin gray mustache, had more combat missions under his belt than he cared to remember. A Texan, born and raised in Uvalde, Texas, he was the overall mission commander for both aircraft. The pilot of Ghost Rider One, Major John Konogeris, was a veteran of numerous missions in Iraq and Afghanistan back when he'd flown F-16s as a first lieutenant. He sat in the left seat.

In the belly of Ghost Rider One was one GBU-57 A/B bunker-buster bomb called a "Massive Ordnance Penetrator" or MOP, but was more affectionately known in the Air Force as the "The Big Bad Green Fucker". The GBU-57, recently developed by Northrop Grumman and Lockheed Martin, was new to the United States Air Force inventory and had never before been used in combat. Today was to be its debutante coming out party, to be put on display for the entire world to see.

The GBU-57 weighed-in at over fifteen metric tons, just eight thousand pounds shy of the B-2's forty thousand pound payload capacity, and dwarfed the largest bunker-buster bomb currently in the United States inventory—the older five thousand pound GBU-28.

The GBU-57, painted olive-drab, had an overall length of twenty-one and a half feet with a diameter of just under thirty-two inches, and was packed with a 2.4 metric ton warhead that could penetrate up to two hundred feet of steel-reinforced concrete, or one hundred and thirty feet of hard rock—all via a high-velocity jet of molten steel just like the one huge, big-assed shaped charge which it essentially was—and could deliver well over one hundred and ten million foot-pounds of energy to the target area in less than ten milliseconds upon impact. Coupled with an extremely accurate GPS guidance system, the "Circle Error of Probability" of the weapon striking its intended target was less than five meters. It was perfect for today's mission—to take out and collapse the tunnel complex where the Pakistani nukes were thought to be hidden.

All things considered, Papa Bill thought, *the last place on earth I want to be is where that GBU-57 hits. Those folks on the ground are gonna be real unhappy after this morning.*

Papa Bill gently gripped the control stick as the massive bomber continued its lazy three hundred and sixty degree standard rate turn to the right. Papa Bill liked to fly, hands-on flying, not using the autopilot; and had also disregarded Major Konogeris' objections who had been designated the mission pilot for Ghost Rider One. All things considered, he couldn't keep his hands off the controls; it just felt too good. Besides, he was a full-bull colonel and a brigadier-general-designate to boot, whereas Konogeris was just a lowly major. The major could wait his turn he'd reasoned. Rank did have its privileges.

Ghost Rider Two, commanded by Lieutenant Colonel Benjamin

Soriano and piloted by Captain Jim Parker, carried thirty-four CBU-103s—Cluster Bomb Units—jammed into its bomb bay. The CBUs destined for the main terrorist camp at Gengi Kel, all thanks to Hearthstone.

When the mission parameters were being drawn up, Hearthstone had vehemently pressed General Gray and President Taylor to authorize the bombers to also take out Gengi Kel. The one GBU-57, they had argued, would be more than enough to take out the nukes, but the ability to take out the Taliban terrorist training camp was just too good to pass up. As far as Hearthstone was concerned, taking out the camp was analogous to a twelve-year-old kid unwrapping his first shotgun on Christmas morning. It was a gift you just couldn't refuse. And besides, Hearthstone wanted to make sure they killed as many of the jihādist assholes that they could. The argument that finally won the day was: if they didn't take out that camp, those jihādist terrorists would just end up across the border in Afghanistan doing their damnedest to kill American troops.

The thirty-four CBU-103s carried in Ghost Rider Two's bomb bay were nothing more than CBU-97s fitted with a newly developed "Wind Corrected Munitions Dispenser"—WCMD for short—also engineered by Lockheed Martin, in effect turning the "Dumb" bombs into "Smart" bombs. With the WCMD attached, the weapons could now adjust their flight path with winged stabilizers utilizing GPS targeting data.

Each CBU was packed with two hundred and two bomblets, each of which weighed around six pounds, with each CBU capable of dispersing its load over a variable area dependent on when the canisters were programmed to open. Today's mission called for each individual CBU to cover a target area that measured three hundred and sixty yards in length by three hundred and sixty yards in width—an area that totalled just over one hundred and twenty-nine thousand square yards. With thirty-four CBU-103s onboard, six thousand, eight hundred and sixty-eight sub-munitions would be strewn across the camp, with every seventy-five- by seventy-five foot-patch-of-dirt theoretically set to receive at least one bomblet. The CBUs had also been programmed to deploy their munitions in an oval pattern whose path of destruction would stretch more than two miles in length and just under three-quarters of a mile wide, more than enough firepower to scrape the camp off the face of the earth.

"Big Eye, Mako Six. Time to call in Team Two."

"Copy that, Six. Out," General Gray responded.

"Homebase, Mako Six."

"Mako Six, Homebase," Sam answered, seated at the same communications console she had used for the school operation while Dr. Angstrom, Dr. Williams, and Dr. Ross busily oversaw the quantum computer.

"Insert Team Two. I say again, insert Team Two."

Team Two, already scanned into the quantum computer's core memory, was made up of Lieutenant (j.g.) Brett Thompson, Chief Petty Officer Walter Moczarny, and Petty Officer First Class Jung-su Pak. The team just waiting for Sam and the Gabriel scientists to begin their insert procedure, each man equipped with the same radiation detectors as Jake and his team.

"Copy that, Mako Six. Team Two is on its way."

Sam looked at Dr. Angstrom and gave him a thumbs up to begin the insert.

General Gray, hunched over the Situation Room's conference table, kept a close watch on the KH-12S satellite feed; his job to scan the mountain ridgelines that overshadowed the tunnel complex—to make doubly sure the gomers they had identified as sentries hadn't moved and to keep track of their yellowish-red blobs that glowed in the night. The general also kept a close watch on Team Two's insert point. The team's insert point centered on a well-screened ledge of rock that measured thirty by forty meters where the two mountain peaks almost came together, positioned less than fifty meters above and to the north of the tunnel opening Dickless had told Jake was where the nukes were supposedly hidden.

Jake slowly moved a few feet to his rear, squatting in the dirt with his rifle laid across his thighs. He could barely make out the distant mountains to the north through his NVGs, his attention focused on where the two mountain peaks almost came together. Not two seconds later he saw the faint outline of a laser slash downwards from above, its endpoint lost to sight behind some craggy ridgelines. Then a second beam flashed down closely followed by a third.

Jake almost shit when he heard the rippling, booming crack of distant AK-47 automatic weapons fire that echoed down from the mountains, with more firing joining the first, quickly building in intensity. *Holy fucking Christ!* he thought as he unconsciously stood up and looked worriedly at Team Two's insert point. *Sounds like a huge goddamned firefight is going on!*

General Gray could only wince when he saw a gomer come out from beneath a stony ledge, a sentry he'd never seen who was only twenty feet from where Jung-su had just inserted. *Jesus H. Christ!* he thought as the entire mountain came alive with moving globs of heat, the ridgeline looking as if an ant hill had been kicked over, crawling with gomers this way and that as they came up and out of their positions and converged rapidly towards the firing and Team Two's insert point.

"Six, this is Five! Six, this is Five!" Jake heard blaring through his earpiece. "Jung-su's hit and down!" Lieutenant Thompson shouted. "I say again, Jung-su's hit and down! Some asshole in the rocks just cut him in half with AK-47! He looks pretty fucked-up, Skipper! Don't think he's gonna make it! We need to get him the hell out of here!"

"Roger that, Five!" Jake answered, his stomach twisted into a knot, hoping that Jung-su would make it, but he also had a mission to complete.

"Homebase! Homebase! Mako Six!"

"Mako Six, Homebase!" Sam answered, feeling nauseous, having monitored Brett's transmission.

"Extract Jung-su! I say again, extract Jung-su! And make sure the medical team's standing by!"

Prior to the mission, Hearthstone and Gabriel had already planned for this eventuality, by having a military medical team on standby in the main floor medical facility should any of the team members need their attention.

"Understood, Mako Six! Extracting Jung-su now!"

Sam turned and desperately signaled for Dr. Williams to bring Mako Two back to the barn.

"Five, did you copy my last?" Jake hurriedly asked.

"Affirmative, Six!" Lieutenant Thompson shouted. "Understand Jung-su's on his way back!"

"You got it, Five! Now, we don't have a lot of time! What are the readings on your detectors!"

"Six, Five! We've got positive readings all over the goddamned place! The needles are almost pegged to the stops! Those nukes are here and these assholes are getting a hell of a lot closer!"

"Okay, Five, got it! Homebase, this is Six! Extract Team Two! I say again, extract Team Two now!"

"Six, this is Homebase! Extractions beginning now! I say again, extractions beginning now!" Sam shouted as she bit her lower lip, then turned and looked worriedly inside the NMR, fearfully awaiting Jung-su's return.

Dr. Angstrom, having flipped the final recall switch for Chief Moczarny and Lieutenant Thompson, ran over to the NMR also awaiting Jung-su's return.

Both he and Sam feared the worst, expecting to see a tangled, ripped-up bloody corpse lying on the floor of the scanner. But when Jung-su appeared, they both stared at the intrepid warrior in disbelief.

Jung-su stepped unsteadily from the NMR with his M4A1 rifle clutched to his chest—his face white and colorless—and then slumped tiredly into a sitting position, his back to the NMR as he looked dreamily about the lab.

Sam was shocked. She couldn't see any wounds, blood, or any other signs of trauma. Jung-su looked exactly the same as when he had first been scanned into the computer.

Dr. Angstrom leaned over and helped Jung-su to his feet.

"How you feelin', Jung-su?" he asked as he critically looked the stoic SEAL over. He too couldn't see any signs of wounds or blood.

"I guess okay, Doc," Jung-su said, confused. "But what the hell's going on? The last thing I remember was getting hit and blown backwards. Hurt like hell, like getting the crap beat out of me with a shitload of baseball bats. Then nothing. Guess I blacked out at that point."

"Well, we kinda hoped this would happen, at least at the theoretical level. I can't really explain it right now," Dr. Angstrom said, patting Jung-su's shoulder, "but in some way your duplicate set of particles in the computer overrode what happened to you out in the field. Just like what happened when you and your team was extracted from the academy. I mean, when all of your ammunition, grenades, and other equipment used at the school came back intact."

Dr. Angstrom turned to Sam.

"Sam, I'm gonna take Jung-su up to the medical team. Just to make sure he's okay. Think you, Richard, and Ken can handle the extractions until I get back?"

"Can do, Ted. Go ahead," she replied as she swivelled back toward the NMR, waiting for Brett and Chief Moczarny to appear, totally relieved that Jung-su seemed okay.

As Team Two was being extracted, Squealer and Martinez saw movement on the road that bisected the camp, the two fighters that had been asleep in front of the headquarters building now up and on their feet, fingering their AK-47s as they looked nervously toward the mountains where the distant crack of automatic weapons fire could still be heard. The other two guards had dropped their cigarette butts to the ground and unslung their rifles.

The front door of the headquarters' building unexpectedly slammed open, and a pudgy fat terrorist ran outside closely followed by two others. One who looked to be dressed in a soiled khaki flight suit, and a much shorter thin man wearing thick eyeglasses and carrying a bulky red toolbox. The fat terrorist suddenly stopped and waved violently at the guards standing in the street, shouting for them to follow.

When the militants ran up the road directly to their front, Steve and Squealer zeroed-in on the bad guys, wanting nothing more than to blow the bastards away for what had happened to Jung-su, but through an unspoken command they withheld their fire. They didn't want to give away their position. The shit was hitting the fan and they didn't want to get splattered. Besides, there was what was called valor and then stupidity. They knew they were in a camp surrounded by close to two hundred fanatic, Islamic jihādists, and getting themselves killed sure as hell wouldn't help out Jung-su all that much.

"Big Eye, Mako Six!" Jake blurted. "Team Two's confirmed the nukes are still in the area of the northern tunnel! Recommend you call in Ghost Rider Flight! I say again, call in Ghost Rider Flight before they can pull those nukes out of there!"

"Mako Six, roger that! Contacting Ghost Rider Flight!"

General Gray hastily switched comms.

"Ghost Rider One, this is Big Eye!"

"Big Eye, Ghost Rider One. I hear you five-by-five," Papa Bill answered in his slow, easy, west Texas drawl while he scanned the readouts of his heads-up display, still wondering about, but not objecting to, the chairman of the Joints Chiefs of Staff being his controller.

"Commence your attack runs! I say again, commence your attack runs now!"

"Copy that, Big Eye! Commencing attack runs!" Papa Bill acknowledged. Then, with a quick glance and a smile at Major Konogeris, he racked the B-2 into a forty-five degree bank to port and leveled the massive bomber out on a heading of 175 degrees; the crosshairs of his heads-up electronic aiming module centered on the opening in the mountains one hundred and fifty nautical miles to their front.

"Two, this is One. Y'all set to go, pardner?" Papa Bill asked while Major Konogeris armed up their GBU-57.

Ghost Rider Two, following in trail, had heard his boss' transmission as he slid his bomber to the right of Ghost Rider One.

"All set, One," Lieutenant Colonel Soriano responded. The pilot, Captain Jim Parker, lined their bomber up on the GPS coordinates of the Taliban training camp while Soriano busily armed up their CBU-103s. Five minutes later the colonel announced in the clear, "Bomb bay doors coming open, One."

"Copy that, Two," Papa Bill acknowledged as Major Konogeris toggled open their own bomb bay doors, both B-2s knowing this was the most ticklish part of their mission.

Ever since they had gone feet dry near Karachi on the Arabian Sea, they had been constantly painted by the Pakistan Air Force's new AN/TPS-77 Air Surveillance radars—high-tech radars delivered and installed courtesy of the United States that could see out to two hundred and fifty nautical miles and up to one hundred thousand feet in altitude, a part of the United States ongoing military aid program to the Pakistan military. Although well below detection thresholds throughout the mission, with their bomb bay doors now open and flapping in the breeze, Ghost Rider Flight's radar cross-section had just been multiplied fifty times over as if they'd just painted a big red bulls-eye on their back.

Papa Bill saw their threat receiver flickering on and off, an indication that the Pakistan Air Force radars were now able to paint intermittent returns off their aircraft.

"Big Eye, Ghost Rider One!"

"Ghost Rider One, Big Eye! Go ahead!"

"We're now on our bomb run. Ten minutes out from our initial release point. If you got any good guys on the ground down there, now would be the time to pull 'em out."

"Copy that Ghost Rider, and good luck!"

"Affirmative, out!" Papa Bill replied.

"Mako Six, Big Eye!"

"Big Eye, Mako Six!"

"Be advised the B-2s are on their bomb runs. Weapons release in ten minutes. Suggest you boys call it a day and come on home."

"I heard that, General! Homebase, Mako Six!" Jake called.

"Mako Six, Homebase!" Sam replied, still rooted to her spot at the communications console.

"Team Two all back?"

"Affirmative, Jake. Team Two's back. And you won't believe this, but Jung-su's okay! He doesn't have a scratch on him! Looks to be good as new! Dr. Angstrom just took him up to the medics to make sure, but everything seems okay. Ted'll be bringing him back down in just a couple of minutes."

"Good to hear that, Sam! Don't understand that right now, but go ahead and initiate extractions. Steve, Squealer, and then myself."

"Okay, Mako Six. Extractions beginning now!"

Qudos Mehsud—winded and nursing a painful stitch in his side—continued to run up the dirt road toward the tunnel complex with Zalmay MahMund, Abdul Farooqi, and his four bodyguards bringing up the rear, panicked by the continuous firing of AK-47s that echoed down from the nearby cliffs. *By Allah!* was all he could think as his stomach flipped over. He just knew that the Pakistan ISI, or military, or the unknown force that had stormed the school had discovered their hiding place and was now attacking the tunnels.

To his rear, the Taliban trainees and instructors had boiled out of their sleeping barracks and gathered in the middle of the road, confused as they looked frantically about and jabbered at one another about the gunfire they could hear to the north. Most were only partially dressed, but they all carried their AK-47s. Then they spotted their commander in the not too far distance, running awkwardly up the dirt road toward the sound of rifle fire with what looked to be six fighters following closely behind. With a cry of "Allahu akbar" on their tongues, they all turned as one to try and catch up with their leader, the bedraggled group looking more like a huge gaggle of geese as they surged forwards in the darkness.

Jake stepped out of the NMR and was almost knocked over when Sam flung herself into his arms.

"Whoa, Sam!" he shouted, taken by surprise as he lifted his rifle clear and placed it on a table next to the NMR, then he reached around her waist and hugged her close to his chest.

"Everything's okay, Sam," Jake said tenderly, not knowing how to respond to the sobs that wracked her body.

Sam moaned, unable to release her death grip with her head buried deep within his chest, gripping Jake tightly to her breast.

"When I heard Jung-su had been hit, I realized that could've been you! And I don't know what I would've done if you had been killed!"

"Well, everything's okay now. We're all back safe and sound, so nothing for you to worry about. And you did say Jung-su's okay?"

"Yeah, Jake," Sam said, wiping away the tears that streaked her cheeks. "Dr. Angstrom just called. Jung-su's fine. The chief's already gone up there to help Ted bring him back down to the lab."

"You're sure?" he asked again, still not understanding how Jung-su could be okay.

"Yeah, Jake, I'm sure," she said again, finally getting her emotions under control. "They oughta be back here in just a minute."

"Okay, then," Jake said as he looked deeply into her eyes, then tilted her chin up and drew her lips up to his own.

"I've been looking forward to do doing that for a long time," he said gruffly, pulling his head away from hers. Then he smiled and chuckled. All he had managed to do was smear her mouth with his camouflage greasepaint. "Sorry about that, Sam. Got you all messed up with my camo paint. Here, let me get that stuff off you."

"Don't bother, Jake."

Sam cupped her hands behind his neck and pulled his lips down to her own. To return the favor.

"So," Jake said gently as Sam pulled her head down and once again rested it on his chest. "How about us joining the rest of the folks and watch the big show?"

"Okay, Jake. Whatever you say."

With a hand placed in the small of Sam's back, he guided the both of them toward the larger conference room where the balance of the Hearthstone team and Gabriel scientists were congregated, the men standing elbow to elbow as they stared at the monitor that showed the KH-12S satellite feed of the Gengi Kel area.

The lab doors hissed silently open, revealing Dr. Angstrom, Chief Moczarny, and Jung-su as they stepped into the lab. Jake quickly released Sam and ran across the lab. He could see that Jung-su was pale and shaken, but seemed to be okay.

"How ya doing, Jung-su?" he asked with a quick look at Dr. Angstrom and the chief.

"Boss, I'm doing just fine. But I gotta admit, it sure felt like getting hit by a twenty-ton brick. Knocked me dead on my ass!" he joked, his face drawn but sturdy as a rock. "But, believe it or not, I don't have a scratch on me. Don't know how that happened, but after all this shit I couldn't miss seeing those B-2s taking out those nukes."

"Good man!" Jake answered with a slap to Jung-su's chest. "You're just in time. The show's gonna start in just a couple of minutes."

Carefully they maneuvered Jung-su into the conference room and pulled out a chair for him to sit down, the team curious as to how he could still be in one piece, smiling as they patted him on the head. Jung-su grinned at the jokes thrown his way by Hearthstone, most of them having to do with remembering to duck next time. When all the pleasantries were over, Jake edged his way back over to Sam and slipped an arm around her waist, then turned back to the KH-12S satellite feed and waited for the show to begin.

"Big Eye, this is Ghost Rider One," everyone heard over the monitor's speaker. "Weapons release! I say again, weapons release!"

When the GBU-57 left the B-2's bomb bay, Ghost Rider One surged upwards as if thankful to be shed of its thirty-two thousand pound payload. In trail to Ghost Rider One, Ghost Rider Two toggled off all thirty-four of its CBU-103s. As the GBU-57 honed in on the tunnel complex, the CBUs spread rapidly across the sky to hit their assigned targets in the training camp, the weapons arcing through the blackness of early morning on their ballistic trajectories.

"Trick or treat, assholes," Jake muttered as the monitor's scene pulled back to encompass both the terrorist training camp and tunnel complex to the north, an area that covered a four-square-mile patch of ground, including the gaggle of more than two hundred Taliban militants running towards the tunnel complex; their thermal images grouped together in a surging mass that bobbed up and down in stark relief against the much cooler ground. Everyone could see the jihādists were more than three kilometers from the mountain complex and less than a kilometer north of the training camp, well within the lethal kill sack of the CBU-103s pointed their way.

The GBU-57 struck the earth in the relatively flat area that separated the entrances to the various tunnels. In the blink of an eye, its massive shaped charge exploded in a blinding flash of light as if a billion strobes had been triggered off at once, the darkness of early morning turned into the searing brilliance of a blazing sun; its fireball clawing skywards more than nine hundred meters. Within milliseconds upon impact, the weapon's molten core of steel bored its way straight through the dense layers of mountain rock into the bowels of the earth—unimpeded as if someone had picked up a sharp knife and sliced through a warmed stick of butter—and then spent itself when it reached a depth of one hundred and forty-two feet.

Massive rings of shock waves rocketed outwards from the epicenter of the blast, the rings clearly outlined by the thin, gauzy clouds of moisture compressed before them out of the morning's cool air. As the shock waves hammered everything before them with their enormous overpressures, a gut-wrenching, earsplitting crack of thunder that rivaled the eruption of Mount St. Helens followed closely behind.

With disbelieving eyes, everyone silently watched as the mountain shuddered along its entire length, shifting sideways and upwards as if hit by a twelve magnitude earthquake—an earthquake that triggered a massive avalanche of millions of tons of rock that flowed over the tunnel openings as if pushed from behind by the mother of all tsunamis.

The tunnels themselves, buried deep within the hard granite, snapped and collapsed inwards upon themselves when the ceiling of rock settled downwards, the mountain looking as if it was just plain tired and wanted to sit down and rest for a while. The Taliban guards who manned the tunnels never knew what hit them, not having time to shout or even scream as they were instantly crushed flat into smears of oblivion.

When the clouds of billowing dust parted, the flat area from which the tunnels had been cut was no more, but filled with massive chunks of rock as if a cement truck had just poured out a huge parking lot.

Qudos crashed to a stop on the dirt road, flinching when he saw the first flash of the explosion, his head turned from the blinding, hellish scene before him. Then he was hit by the shockwave that slammed him fully in the chest as if kicked by a mule, a force so powerful that it physically picked him up and threw him more than three meters from where he had been standing. As he rolled over in the dirt to try and recover from the blow, he stared at the mountain in shocked disbelief.

The rest of his fighters, also slammed to the earth, shakily picked themselves up and made their way to where their commander lay, worried that he had been injured. But Qudos ignored the fighters who now surrounded him, unable to tear his eyes from the mountain that swayed to his front. He could also feel the wrath of Allah as it rumbled its way through the earth, for only Allah could do such a thing, to make a mountain tremble and shake with fear.

Pulling himself abruptly to his knees, he raised his arms to the star-filled heavens with his eyes clenched shut, beseeching the black void as to how something like this could have happened, but was suddenly startled into silence when he heard what sounded like hundreds of firecrackers going off far above his head. Quickly opening his eyes, he strained to see into the darkness, curious as to what had caused those sounds. But what he saw only made him cringe in fear as a shiver of panic slashed down his spine, confirming that he had been abandoned by Allah and the one true prophet, Muhammad. He knew he was a dead man as he watched the tiny flashes spread far across the darkened sky. His covenant with Allah, he finally realized, had only been a dream.

"What are all those little flashes, Jake?" Sam asked curiously, pointing at the monitor. "Covering the sky over the camp and the terrorists?"

"Well, Sam, those gotta be the fuse charges going off that pop open the CBU canisters. Each cluster bomb has eight of those that need to fire, four per side. They're kinda like a clamshell. Once the canisters open up and separate, each CBU will scatter over two hundred bomblets on the camp, hopefully taking out the bad guys."

"Oh! Okay, Jake. I got it. Thanks."

Sam continued to stare at the monitor with rapt attention, wanting to avert her eyes from what she knew was going to be a horrendous scene, but unable to do so. Curious as the others as to what was going to happen.

Abruptly, thousands of brilliant, eye-numbing balls of explosions rippled their way across the distant horizon like overgrown hand grenades, throwing out thirty-meter-circles of jagged, white-hot shrapnel as they surged from north to south like a giant, crested, pyrotechnic tidal wave—a wave that fully engulfed and swept over the mass of Taliban fighters who stood in its path.

As the bomblets continued their relentless journey toward Gengi Kel, the ground was churned as if dug up by an enormous rototiller charged with high explosives. When the wave of airborne munitions impacted the main camp, each bomblet—when it struck a roof or hard surface—instantly converted itself into a shaped charge, blowing streams of superheated molten steel into the structures.

All Sam could picture was the painting titled *"Dante's Inferno"*, a painting from hell as the two-mile-long swath of earth was instantly converted into a ghastly scene of explosions, death, and destruction. After the final bomblets had done their job, Gengi Kel lay ripped and sundered, draped in a dark, silent shroud of coiling black smoke, burned-out structures, and the shredded, unrecognizable bodies of dead Taliban terrorists.

The satellite feed from the KH-12S suddenly flicked off and was replaced by the grim countenance of President Garret Taylor.

"Jake," the president began solemnly, taking in the lab scene with Hearthstone still carrying their weapons, dressed in their black-camouflaged BDUs and flanked by the Gabriel scientists, "we just wanted to thank all of you for what you people did tonight. Myself, General Gray, Director Jefferson, and Steven Clarke. It was a nasty operation, but I can't think of how many lives you may have saved, getting those nukes out of the hands of that madman, Qudos. And," he continued with a mirthless smile, "given what I saw, I don't think he or his men will be giving us any more trouble. But again, that was one hell of an operation you folks pulled off, just like you did at the academy."

President Taylor then spotted Jung-su. With a broad grin on his face, he singled out the young petty officer first class.

"Jung-su? How you feeling, son? Everything okay? You sure had us going there for a minute or two."

Jung-su sat up as straight as he could and smiled back. "Couldn't be better, sir. Just wanted you to know I'm good-to-go."

"Good man!" Taylor said with a laugh, slapping the top of the Situation Room's table. "And again, thank you all for removing the threat of those nukes."

Briefly interrupted, President Taylor listened to something whispered in his ear by Director Jefferson. With a quick nod of agreement, he directed his gaze back at Jake.

"The director just asked me, Jake, if you would be kind enough to call him in the next day or so. Seems we have a new situation brewing, and he thinks that Hearthstone and Gabriel may be just what the doctor ordered."

"No problem, sir," Jake answered as he paused and glanced at Sam with a gleam in his eye, and then at all of his team members gathered about the room—Hearthstone and Gabriel alike.

"But, sir? If it's all the same to you, could you ask the director if I could make that call in six to ten days? We have a few things needing to be done," he said, tightening his grip around Sam's waist.

"Jake, I think that should be just fine. No problem at all," President Taylor answered with a tired smile.

www.ingramcontent.com/pod-product-compliance
Lightning Source LLC
Chambersburg PA
CBHW060341260626
47160CB00006B/2165